Praise for Lori Roy

Lake County

"Roy keeps things taut and tense throughout, springing surprises and making all her characters count."

—*Kirkus Reviews*

"Roy is as adept as ever at bringing the South's beauty and soft-edged dangers to life. In this complex tale, fierce family love is pitted against ambition, obsession, and contested power."

—*Booklist*

"*Lake County* is a unique and imaginative page-turner that examines the difference between power and strength. In this thriller that races toward the end, Lori Roy's voice is so entrancing you can almost smell the orange blossoms and blood. I loved it."

—Michael Connelly, #1 *New York Times* bestselling author

"A deftly crafted and simply riveting read from start to finish, *Lake County* by Lori Roy is a compulsive page-turner of a read."

—*Midwest Book Review*

"*Lake County* is an irresistible slice of Florida noir fashioned of great American mythmaking. James M. Cain meets Harper Lee. The story excels as both an exciting crime novel and a fine example of Southern literature."

—Ace Atkins, *New York Times* bestselling author of *Don't Let the Devil Ride*

"Suspenseful, atmospheric, and surprising, *Lake County* pulls you and slowly ups the tension until you're holding your breath. Another remarkable crime novel from Lori Roy."

—Meg Gardiner, #1 *New York Times* bestselling author

"*Lake County* is the best book yet in Lori Roy's remarkable career, a beautifully written blend of suspense and heartache, where Hollywood longings intersect with Florida crime syndicates in an ever-intensifying squeeze. An atmospheric, haunting read."

—Michael Koryta, *New York Times* bestselling author of *An Honest Man*

Gone Too Long

"Gripping, gut-wrenching thriller."

—*Publishers Weekly*

"A riveting mystery, brilliantly crafted and weighted with real-world resonance . . . A timely thriller that will stay with the reader long after the last page has been turned."

—*Kirkus Reviews* (starred review)

"This compelling, issue-oriented story by Edgar Award–winning author Roy is a creepy, eerie account of a young girl and a community held hostage by the Klan."

—*Library Journal* (starred review)

"Filled with a creeping, entangling sense of danger. It's the kind of writing you would expect from the Edgar-winning author, but it's made even more powerful here, filled with the purpose of exposing a hateful legacy and issuing a timely warning of its historical ebb and flow."

—*Booklist* (starred review)

"This electrifying novel . . . [is] a gripping mystery with a timely, unnerving message—you won't be able to look away."
—*People* (Book of the Week)

"A book so good you can't look away."
—*O, The Oprah Magazine* (Best Books of Summer)

"Ms. Roy excels at depicting scenes of consummate tension involving a heroine whose courage has long lain dormant."
—*Wall Street Journal*

"Florida writer Lori Roy brings a powerful literary voice to the crime genre with this dark, corrosive tale . . . *Gone Too Long* is a hauntingly detailed story of survival."
—*Chicago Tribune*

"Quietly unnerving . . . a niche for lyrical prose in a noir story."
—*Sun Sentinel*

"[Roy] has always been deft at creating suspense, but she hits a new level with this finely crafted thriller . . . Roy crafts the book's triple plots with skillful misdirection and sure timing . . . *Gone Too Long* is a compelling thriller, and it's also a story of how hatred and violence toward the other create a legacy that follows those who hate home."
—*Tampa Bay Times*

"This darkly addictive tale is ultimately an engrossing portrait of survival and perseverance."
—*BookPage*

"*Gone Too Long* is Lori Roy's fifth novel—and her best, which is saying something... People often disappear in Roy's Southern settings, which become characters in their own right. Dusty dirt roads, swampy lakes, towering oaks dripping with moss: in Roy's world, nature never smiles. The acorns feel dangerous."

—St. Pete Catalyst

"Every Lori Roy novel promises to be a reckoning, but this one should satisfy on a number of levels."

—CrimeReads (Most Anticipated Crime Books of Summer)

The Disappearing

"Lori Roy is one of the most elegant and enchanting writers to cross my path in a long, long time. I was transfixed by *The Disappearing*. A story of buried secrets rising to the light, it unfolds with a hypnotic grip that won't let go until the last secrets are revealed on the final page. This is a deep, dark, and wonderful book."

— Michael Connelly, #1 *New York Times* bestselling author

"Roy's new novel is impossible to put down or forget, a masterful show of suspense."

—CrimeReads (Most Anticipated Summer Reads)

"Gripping... [Roy is a] rising star."

—*O, The Oprah Magazine*

"As atmospheric as a summer's night."

—*Family Circle* (Summer's Best Books Reading List)

"An irresistibly propulsive mystery wrapped in the haunted atmosphere of Southern Gothic and inspired by real Florida crimes... her best book yet."

—*Tampa Bay Times*

"Lori Roy . . . is a remarkable writer, especially when she is tracking with a strange elegance a family steeped in death. What makes her prose lyrically different from most mysteries is her capacity to build her plot from shreds of horror."
—*Washington Times*

"[An] exceptional novel. Lori Roy's writing oozes atmosphere."
—*Star Tribune* (Summer Reading List)

"Beautifully written and expertly plotted, *The Disappearing* is a twisty, haunting, and utterly riveting thriller. Lori Roy just gets better and better."
—Alafair Burke, *New York Times* bestselling author

"Lori Roy has been on my must-read list since her debut. There's a reason she's already won two Edgar Awards—exemplary plotting, clever twists, and compelling characters—but for me it is her voice that holds the most power. She writes with an ingenious, whispering menace and a masterful understanding of the way the past works on the present, and on the human heart. *The Disappearing* is her finest work to date."
— Michael Koryta, *New York Times* bestselling author of *An Honest Man*

"As dark and atmospheric as a Northern Florida summer night, *The Disappearing* is Lori Roy at the top of her game. Her simmering tale is, at the heart, a compelling mystery. But it's also a deep meditation on family and the secrets and lies that can twist through our lives like a strangler fig. The powerful sense of place and a haunting cast of characters linger long after the book is closed. If you haven't read Lori Roy, now is the time."
—Lisa Unger, *New York Times* bestselling author

"Lori Roy is an impeccable writer—original, fearless, and insightful. *The Disappearing*, with its dark secrets and damaged souls, is another triumph of Roy's skill: it's insidiously sinister, seamlessly plotted, and relentlessly haunting."

—Hank Phillippi Ryan, *USA Today* bestselling author

"This contemporary slow burner oozes with atmosphere, and Roy effortlessly weaves numerous plot threads together without sacrificing her characters, who are very flawed and all too human. Secrets and lies abound, and Lane's struggle to be a good mother while fighting her own considerable demons will resonate with readers, as will the chilling finale. A twisted Southern Gothic winner."

—*Kirkus Reviews*

"Roy has created a town with a frightening past that just keeps getting worse. You get the chills just reading her hypnotic tale, which makes this four in a row when it comes to fantastic books written by Lori Roy."

—*Suspense Magazine*

"Roy . . . delivers another creepily atmospheric, cunningly plotted suspense tale . . . excruciating tension throughout."

—*Booklist*

Let Me Die in His Footsteps

2016 Recipient of the Edgar Award for Best Novel

"This Depression-era story is a sad one, written in every shade of Gothic black. But its true colors emerge in the rich textures of the narrative, and in the music of that voice, as hypnotic as the scent coming off a field of lavender."

—*New York Times Book Review*

"Roy excels in depicting the menace lurking in the natural world."
—*Washington Post*

"As the mystery deepens, so, too, does the suspense and affection for each Kentuckian who pulls up a chair at the kitchen table."
—Associated Press

"Roy does wonderful work weaving her complementary narratives into a naturally cohesive novel, and the central mystery . . . unravels in a way that is simultaneously elegant and unexpected . . . Though this mystery provides its engine, the novel demonstrates an undeniable literary bent."
—*Los Angeles Times*

"[A] richly detailed, highly suspenseful Gothic novel filled with indelible imagery."
—*Huffington Post*

"[*Let Me Die in His Footsteps*] has elements of crime fiction but moves into a new genre for Roy: Southern Gothic. It teems with family feuds, forbidden love, second sight, and wronged innocents, all held together by Roy's taut style and gift for suspense."
—*Tampa Bay Times*

"*Let Me Die in His Footsteps* gracefully moves toward a stunning finale as Roy unfurls insightful character studies . . . [It] is a story about what links families and drives them apart."
—*Sun Sentinel*

"Reading Lori Roy is a sinuous, near-physical experience, her stories so rich and well told they twine into the reader in a manner both gentle and profoundly deep. I consider her writing a love sonnet to American letters. Simply lovely."

—John Hart, *New York Times* bestselling author

"Something to tide you over until Harper Lee's book release: This is an addictive Southern Gothic thriller . . ."

—*Elle Canada*

"This is a beautifully observed story whose details of time, place, and character are stunning little jewels sure to dazzle the eye on every page. Quite simply put, I loved this book."

—William Kent Krueger, *New York Times* bestselling author

"There are echoes of Flannery O'Connor here: poverty, violence, malevolence, and grace. Roy's writing is spell-like, using a simplicity of language, deft characterization, an understanding of the dark side of human nature, and relentless plotting in order to pull together every aspect of the conjuring necessary to create a masterpiece of Southern Noir."

—Historical Novel Society

"The scents of Lavender and regret are heavy in this suspenseful coming-of-age novel . . . This powerful story . . . should transfix readers right up to its stunning final twist."

—*Publishers Weekly* (starred review)

"Edgar-winner Roy's third novel is an atmospheric, vividly drawn tale that twists her trademark theme of family secrets with the crackling spark of the 'know-how' for a suspenseful, ghost-story feel."

—*Booklist* (starred review)

"Young love, Southern folklore, family feuds, and crimes of passion . . . Roy describes life on a lavender farm in rural Kentucky in vivid detail, and the mystery of what happened years ago will keep readers engaged until the end."

—*Library Journal*

"Roy (*Bent Road*, 2011, etc.) draws a Faulknerian tale of sex and violence from the Kentucky hills . . . [Her] characters live whole on the page, especially Annie, all gawky girl stumbling her way to womanhood through prejudice and inhibition."

—*Kirkus Reviews*

Until She Comes Home

2014 Edgar Award Finalist for Best Novel

"That's the simple, heartbreaking truth Lori Roy delivers, sotto voce, in *Until She Comes Home*, a quietly shocking account of the tiny tremors in the life of a city that warn of cataclysms to come."

—*New York Times Book Review*

"Roy adroitly captures the atmosphere of the time, when racial tensions were bubbling over and fear of integration was prevalent. The author slowly draws the reader in, as violence flares and dark secrets emerge; this is a superb, tense suspense tale that's one of the year's best crime novels."

—*Lansing State Journal*

"Roy's language pulses . . . Days after finishing [*Until She Comes Home*], the lives of these women still haunted me."

—*Milwaukee Journal Sentinel*

"Lori Roy mixes lyrical prose, a noir approach, and gothic undertones for an urban story set in 1958 about a community pulled apart by racism, fear, and image..."

—*Sun Sentinel*

"Beach Reads you won't want to put down... In this thriller set in 1950s Detroit, a group of seemingly genteel women grapple with racial tension, gender violence, and two murders that throw their tidy suburban neighborhood into a tailspin."

—*Ladies' Home Journal*

"Extraordinary. Compelling. And beautifully, quietly disturbing... These gorgeously drawn characters and their mysteries will haunt you long after you turn the last page. Lori Roy is an incredible talent."

—Hank Phillippi Ryan, *USA Today* bestselling author

"A suspenseful, atmospheric work of crime fiction as well as a clear-eyed look at relationships between the sexes and races in mid-twentieth-century America."

—*Tampa Bay Times*

"A beautifully written, at times lyrical, study of a disintegrating community. Roy, author of the Edgar Award–winning mystery *Bent Road*, tackles similar themes here with equally successful results."

—*Kirkus Reviews* (starred review)

"What seems to begin in the glowing warmth of a homey kitchen transforms into a probing emotional drama that speaks powerfully to women about family, prejudice, power... and secrets."

—*Booklist* (starred review)

"Rich . . . lyrical . . . Roy delivers a timeless story that gives shape to those secrets and tragedies from which some people never recover."
—McClatchy-Tribune News Service

"Lori Roy has entered the arena of great American authors shared by Williams, Faulkner, and Lee."
—Bookreporter

"A tour de force of mood and suspense."
—*BookPage*

Bent Road

2012 Recipient of the Edgar Award for Best First Novel

"Writing with a delicate touch but great strength of purpose, Roy creates stark studies of the prairie landscape and subtle portraits . . ."
—*New York Times*

"A remarkably assured debut novel. Rich and evocative, Lori Roy's voice is a welcome addition to American fiction."
—Dennis Lehane, *New York Times* bestselling author

"Dropping us in a world of seeming simplicity, in a time of seeming calm, Lori Roy transforms 1960s small-town Kansas into a haunting memory-scape. Bringing to mind the family horrors of Jane Smiley's *A Thousand Acres* and the dark emotional terrain of Tana French's *In the Woods*, *Bent Road* manages to be both psychologically acute and breathtakingly suspenseful, burrowing into your brain with a feverish power all its own."
—Megan Abbott, Edgar Award–winning novelist

"In her promising debut novel *Bent Road*, Lori Roy proves that dark secrets hide even in the most wide-open places. Set in the beautifully rendered Kansas plains, *Bent Road* is a family story with a suspenseful gothic core, one which shows that the past always has a price, whether you're running from it or back toward it. Crisp, evocative prose, full-blooded characters, and a haunting setting make this debut stand out."
— Michael Koryta, *New York Times* bestselling author of *An Honest Man*

"Don't be fooled by the novel's apparent simplicity: what emerges from the surface is a tale of extraordinary emotional power, one of long-standing pain set against the pulsating drumbeat of social change."
—NPR

"Roy . . . proves herself to be a new talent to watch in the mystery genre. *Bent Road* is one of the best debuts of 2011."
—*Sun Sentinel*

"Roy's outstanding debut melds strong characters and an engrossing plot with an evocative sense of place . . . Roy couples a vivid view of the isolation and harshness of farm life with a perceptive look at the emotions that can rage beneath the surface. This Midwestern noir with gothic undertones is sure to make several 2011 must-read lists."
—*Publishers Weekly* (starred review)

"This tautly written, chilling piece of heartland noir is . . . an impressive debut. Roy takes a bucolic setting—rural Kansas—and makes it an effective stage for a suspenseful tale of tragedy and dread . . . *Bent Road* is rich in sensory details . . . that anchor the story in its place and time. Roy populates that world with a believable cast of characters, deftly marrying a story of domestic violence and familial love with a gothic mystery that is compelling at each turn of the page."
—*Tampa Bay Times*

"Even the simplest scenes crackle with suspense."

—*People*

"Roy's exceptional debut novel is full of tension, complex characters, and deftly gothic overtones. Readers of Tana French's *In the Woods* will find this dark and satisfying story a great read. Highly recommended."

—*Library Journal* (starred review)

"Roy's suspenseful debut novel presents readers with a rich mix of troubled characters planted against the backdrop of a small Kansas farming town and the mysterious deaths of two young girls . . . This odd, dark, and often creepy tale of a dysfunctional community and a family that fits right in will keep readers wondering right until the last page."

—*Kirkus Reviews* (starred review)

THE FINAL EPISODE

ALSO BY LORI ROY

Bent Road

Let Me Die in His Footsteps

Until She Comes Home

The Disappearing

Gone Too Long

Lake County

THE FINAL EPISODE

A Thriller

LORI ROY

THOMAS & MERCER

This is a work of fiction. Names, characters, organizations, places, events, and incidents are either products of the author's imagination or are used fictitiously. Otherwise, any resemblance to actual persons, living or dead, is purely coincidental.

Text copyright © 2025 by Lori Roy
All rights reserved.

No part of this book may be reproduced, or stored in a retrieval system, or transmitted in any form or by any means, electronic, mechanical, photocopying, recording, or otherwise, without express written permission of the publisher.

Published by Thomas & Mercer, Seattle

www.apub.com

Amazon, the Amazon logo, and Thomas & Mercer are trademarks of Amazon.com, Inc., or its affiliates.

EU product safety contact:
Amazon Media EU S. à r.l.
38, avenue John F. Kennedy, L-1855 Luxembourg
amazonpublishing-gpsr@amazon.com

ISBN-13: 9781662526916 (hardcover)
ISBN-13: 9781662526923 (paperback)
ISBN-13: 9781662519956 (digital)

Cover design by Jarrod Taylor
Cover image: © Maresa Pryor-Luzier / DanitaDelimont

Printed in the United States of America
First edition

*For all the ones
who will bend history
or who already have*

EPISODE 1

INT. FARROW HOUSE – PREDAWN

Beverley Farrow folds the quilt back and eases her legs over the edge of the mattress, but her movement still wakes her husband. Robert stretches an arm over his head like he always does first thing in the morning, except it isn't quite morning.

"I got it," Beverley says, resting a hand on that outstretched arm.

She doesn't want to leave her spot next to Robert. These early hours, when she teeters between being awake and asleep, are the only quiet moments in her day. The bed is warm, too, while the house is cold and dry. They keep it that way for Francie. Just thinking about her feet hitting the cold floor makes Beverley shiver.

Settling back on the warm sheets, hoping it was a dream that woke her, she glances at her doorway again.

Yes, one of the girls is standing there. She has to get up.

Once on her feet, she takes a moment to steady herself. Blood races to her head, followed by a dizzy rush that quickly fades. She points and flexes each foot. It takes a bit longer to get going these days.

"I'm coming, sweetheart," she whispers to the figure in her doorway.

The feeling of being watched most likely woke Beverley. When Francie was little, she'd creep to Beverley's bedside. Eventually, Beverley would wake, never knowing how long Francie had been watching her, and throw back the covers, and little Francie would crawl in. That's a favorite memory. Beverley smiles and lets out a long sigh, her way of cutting loose the sadness that those little-girl years are gone.

Minding her step by trailing a hand along the footboard, Beverley smiles at the memory and then at Nora, because it's Nora standing in the doorway. Not Francie. Beverley can see that now.

Nora is good for Francie. She's outgoing and always pleasant and well mannered when she spends the night. Maybe she enjoys spending time in a stable home, though it isn't Beverley's place to judge. It's really just a hunch anyway.

"Are you okay, sweetheart?" she says.

Nora stares straight ahead as if she's woken from a bad dream and isn't sure where she is.

"Nora, sweetheart, are you okay?"

Nora and Francie both have long blond hair, the type that still shimmers like new, but Nora's a head taller. She's two years older too. Francie still has wiry arms and legs and knobby shoulders. But Nora . . . in the past year, Nora's taken a giant step toward becoming a young woman.

Drawing closer, Beverley understands why she confused the two girls. Nora has wrapped herself up in her arms. Her shoulders are drawn in and rounded forward, making her look narrow and frail, and her head droops. She looks like a little girl again.

"Bad dream?" Beverley says, resting a hand on Nora's warm cheek.

No fever. That's good. Beverley prides herself on being the mother who doesn't panic over every little predicament. She has Francie's real health issues to contend with, doesn't have to manufacture concerns. She's older than the other mothers too. They have more energy, but Beverley is more settled. She doesn't mind that the younger mothers are better at getting woken in the middle of the night and still being bright eyed come morning. She's counting on showing up strong for the long game.

The Final Episode

Two doors down, Francie's doorway is dark, but at the other end of the hallway, a soft orange glow spills through the window. The sun is just beginning to rise.

"How about we get you back to bed?" Beverley says.

Nora lifts her chin to look up at Beverley. The shine coming off the hallway's single night-light catches in her blue eyes. They glisten with the beginnings of tears. Her chin quivers.

"What's wrong, sweetheart?" Beverley kneels and draws Nora into her arms.

Nora smells of soap and deodorant. Francie hasn't started wearing deodorant yet. It's good to know that when she does, she'll still wobble back to being a little girl occasionally. Just like Nora is now. Beverley holds her and strokes her long hair.

"Francie's gone," Nora whispers into Beverley's neck.

Nora's warm breath makes Beverley shiver. She continues to stroke Nora's silky hair. She continues to smile. And then the words that tickled her neck sink in.

"What did you say, sweetheart?" Beverley says.

"Everything okay?" It's Robert's voice, drifting out of Beverley's warm bed.

"We're fine," Beverley says. And then to Nora. "I think you're having a bad dream. Let's get you back to bed."

Beverley guides Nora down the hall, but when they reach Francie's doorway, Nora stops and shakes her head.

"Oh, baby," Beverley says, sinking to the floor again and saying and doing the things she hopes another mother would say and do for her Francie if she woke during a sleepover and was afraid in a strange house. "Bad dreams can't hurt you."

Nora pulls away, refusing to go into Francie's room.

When they redecorated Francie's bedroom a few years ago, they put in two twin beds. They'd hoped that setting up the room for sleepovers would make for more friendships. Francie has to be so much more careful than the other kids. Careful about what she eats, when she goes outside, how long she stays out. No pets. No cigarette smoke. And for sure, no peanuts. She's that kid.

Leaving Nora in the doorway, Beverley takes a step into the quiet, dark room. It's somehow different, emptier, and yet she can't see how or why.

The bed on the right is for guests. But Nora has been the only friend to sleep over, so it's become known as Nora's bed. Though Beverley would never tell Francie, Nora stays because her mother, Lily Banks, helps Beverley with the cleaning. It's a daily job. Vacuuming. Dusting. Bleaching. And endless laundry. It isn't that Beverley uses Lily's paycheck as leverage. It's always a polite invitation with promises of Nora's favorite foods and later-than-usual bedtimes. And Lily appreciates the chance for a date night. The arrangement suits them both.

The bed on the left is Francie's. Its pink quilt and top sheet have been thrown back as if Francie just popped out of bed. The oak floors glisten in the soft orange light coming through the room's only window. They took out all the carpet the year Francie was born and put in wood, hoping she might breathe easier during the night.

Beverley steps up to Francie's bed and rests a hand on the mattress, expecting warm sheets and Francie's smell on them. Francie always takes a bath just before bed to wash the pollen from her hair and skin. But the sheets are cool and smell of nothing.

Beverley switches on a lamp, as if in the dark, she might have missed Francie in the jumble of bedding. The sudden brightness makes her squint. Still no Francie.

Moving in a slow circle and seeing nothing out of place in a room that is dusted and vacuumed daily, she stops when she faces Nora again. She's backed into the hallway and still cradles herself with her arms.

"I kept my eyes closed, pretended I was asleep. But I think he knew I wasn't."

As Beverley walks from Francie's room, her chest grows heavy. Her throat, tight. The floor wobbles. The walls buckle.

The Final Episode

"Who are you talking about?" Beverley rests her hands on Nora's shoulders.

"The man who came into Francie's room."

"A man?" Beverley says, her throat clamping down on the words. "What man?"

"He said not to wake you," Nora says, dipping her chin to her chest. "Or else."

Beverley sweeps Nora close with an arm around her shoulders and crosses down the hall, Nora stumbling to keep up.

"Robert, get up," Beverley shouts into her bedroom as she rushes past.

In the bathroom, with Nora still pressed to her side, Beverley switches on the light. The white tile floor glistens. The smell of the bleach she uses to kill mold and mildew stings her nose. She turns at the sound of Robert stepping into the hallway. He looks both ways, squinting, already seeing that Francie is missing from the picture.

"Nora says a man told her not to wake us." Beverley repeats the words exactly as Nora said them. They feel awkward on her tongue, like words from a foreign language.

Robert stares at Beverley. As the news lands, he takes one backward step and then another and then swings around. His footsteps fade as he runs down the stairs and calls out Francie's name.

"I need you to answer me very carefully," Beverley says, kneeling again and taking Nora gently by both shoulders. "What man told you not to wake us?"

Nora uncrosses her arms and with one hand points at Francie's room, the light from the bedside lamp still spilling into the dark hallway.

"He told Francie, 'get up.'"

Beverley's hands tighten as she draws Nora to her. Nora flinches and pulls away.

"I'm sorry," Beverley says, loosening her grip.

Downstairs, Robert's voice rattles the house as he runs from room to room, calling out Francie's name. Beverley pushes against the urge to jump up and help him look. She's always the one to find what's missing.

"Please, sweetie," Beverley says instead, her voice barely breaking through. "Look at me. I'm sorry. What happened then?"

"Francie asked where they were going," Nora whispers.

"And?" Beverley says, the word leaking out on a trickle of air.

"He said the swamp is always a good place."

It's nowhere near lunchtime when Jenny Jones and her daddy, Paul, pull up to their vacation house on the edge of the Big Cypress Swamp. The simple two-story where they spend summers sits alongside Halfway Creek, the dividing line between a living, breathing world on one side and the soggy, dark swamp on the other.

Throwing the car in park, Daddy switches off the engine. The radio switches off too. That means no more reporters going on about the little girl from Fort Myers who got snatched out of her own bed. Jenny does her best to tuck away the bad feeling that one little girl disappearing means any little girl could disappear.

Not wanting to disturb the sudden quiet, she holds her breath. This is her favorite moment at the swamp. The just-before moment when the whole summer is ahead of them.

She's already smiling when Daddy turns to face her. Daddy is smiling too. She covers her mouth so a giggle won't slip out and ruin the stillness. Daddy's eyes flick side to side, his way of saying . . . hear that? And then his mouth drops open like he can't believe it. What they're hearing is nothing. Sweet silence. Finally.

For the next ten weeks, no one will shout hurry up, we're going to be late. Summers at the swamp are an escape from schedules and routines, and a chance to make memories. There's no being late at the swamp.

Like they've done every summer, Jenny and Daddy loaded up their suitcases on Memorial Day and drove forty-five minutes from the house in Naples, Florida, to the house at the swamp. But this summer

The Final Episode

is unlike any other. This summer, come June 2, at exactly midnight, Jenny will turn eleven years old. For the women of her family who came down her mama's and Grandma Dehlia's line, turning eleven is the most important birthday. Usually, Jenny wants the summer to pass slowly, but this summer, she wants time to race past, leaving nothing behind but a blur.

June 2, one week from today, can't hurry up and get here fast enough.

"Old place fared well," Daddy says, looking in the rearview mirror to see Jenny in the back seat. His blue eyes shine against his tanned skin. His white teeth shimmer.

Jenny drapes her arms over the back of the front seat and nods like she thinks the old place fared well too.

Daddy is handsome, make-people-stop-and-look handsome. Jenny is old enough to know grown women think the same. Especially the ones who know Jenny doesn't have a mama. As Jenny was busy being born, Mama was busy dying.

Jenny's also old enough to know Daddy has no time for those women. And she's glad about that.

Hearing something outside the car, Daddy crosses his arms over the steering wheel, leans forward, and tips his squared-off chin toward the sky. Dark hair clings to his forehead, stuck there by sweat. Jenny hears it too. It's the sputter of blades as a helicopter crosses over their house and continues toward the swamp. It happens every summer. Usually, they're looking for a hiker or hunter.

As the sound of the helicopter fades, silence settles back in but so does the bad feeling Jenny tried to stuff down deep. Today, the helicopter might be looking for the little girl.

"Think they're looking for Francie Farrow?" Jenny asks.

"How do you know about her?" Daddy's eyes are wide. He's not angry, but he is surprised.

"Heard it on the way here," Jenny says, nodding at the radio. "And on the TV this morning."

Daddy lets out a long breath, relieved Jenny has a reason for knowing about the missing girl. He gets scared when he thinks she's showing signs of having second sight, of knowing things she shouldn't know. He doesn't believe in it, but that doesn't stop him from worrying about it. So maybe he does believe, a little.

Grandma Dehlia, just Dehlia to Jenny, has second sight. Jenny's mama had it too. All the daughters of Margaret Scott, Jenny's great-grandma many times over, have it. Jenny's second sight will come with her eleventh birthday, though it's been simmering since the day she was born. Already, the kids at school call her a wetland witch for having it. "Just like your grandma, Dehlia," they say. They call Jenny evil too. "Don't let her touch you. Jenny Jones is so evil, she killed her own mama." But no matter all that, Jenny can't wait to get second sight so she can be like Dehlia and Mama. Being like someone must be better than being like no one. Because being like no one is lonely.

Besides, Jenny's not a witch. That's for sure. Neither is Dehlia. Neither was Great-Grandma Margaret Scott, though she was hanged for being one.

But the part about Jenny killing her own mama, that's true.

"Suppose the news is everywhere by now," Daddy says, resting his chin on the seat back. "But no, I don't think they're looking for that little girl, sweetheart. Fort Myers is over an hour away. You're kind to be thinking of her, though."

They sit quiet a bit longer, making sure they don't hear another set of blades. Daddy is wrong. A helicopter appearing today and not on another day means something. All kinds of things that need to disappear get dumped in the swamp. Every year, her class picks up garbage on Loop Road. One year, they found a refrigerator dumped in among the mangroves where the swamp had almost swallowed it whole. That helicopter sputtering by means the swamp might be getting ready to swallow Francie Farrow next.

The Final Episode

Sitting at her kitchen table, Beverley holds a cup with both hands. The coffee inside has gone cold. Still, she takes a sip as she stares at the kitchen windows and the back door. The police think one of the windows was the man's way in and the door his way out. They're wrong. Somehow, Beverley knows it, but she can't settle on why.

She startles when the cup moves. It's Lily Banks, coming to top off her coffee.

"Let me heat that up for you," Lily says, leaning in so Beverley will hear.

Most days, they have to talk over the sound of trucks rumbling down makeshift construction roads east of the neighborhood. The whole city of Fort Myers is growing, and the noise has become a staple. It's true for all South Florida. But not this morning.

This morning, the house is oddly quiet. Oddly empty.

Another difference this morning . . . the way Lily looks. Every other morning, when she comes to help Beverley with chores around the house, she wears shiny pink gloss on her lips, and brown liner highlights her pale-blue eyes. But this morning, she came straight out of bed. Her short dark hair, nipping in at her neck like it does, and her freshly washed face make her look like a child herself.

"Will you eat a little something?" she says, and sets buttered toast in front of Beverley. "You need to be at your best."

That's the problem. Beverley isn't at her best. If she had been, a strange man wouldn't have walked into her house and back out again with her daughter.

It's been four hours since Robert dialed 911. That was at 5:58 a.m. exactly. Lily Banks, Nora's mother, was the next call. She and her husband, Levi, almost beat the police to the house. Sitting next to Beverley as she wailed into a pillow, Lily held her and talked quietly so Beverley wouldn't slip away. Like one soldier to another . . . hold on, don't let go. Someone tried to give Beverley a pill. She didn't take it. Exhaustion and Lily holding tight to her were the reasons she finally stopped crying. And now, hunched over her coffee cup and sitting at the kitchen table, she's so weak she can barely sit up.

"You should be with Nora," Beverley says, pushing the toast away.

Lily is the age of all the other mothers. Taut, smooth skin. Slender arms. Sharp jawline. Boundless energy. She probably doesn't sleep as heavily as Beverley. She'd have heard a stranger walking through her house.

"Nora's fine," Lily says, gathering Beverley's hands. "She and Levi, they're with the police."

Beverley clings to Lily. From off to the left, that window and door are tugging at her again. They mean something, and she can't figure out what.

Beverley was the first one to see the missing screen in the kitchen window. It had been torn out, leaving jagged edges hanging from the frame, and the window's latch was open. She noticed the door to the backyard too. It was also unlocked.

The front door slams, startling Beverley. She clings to her chair and closes her eyes. Like a reflex, her body braces for bad news.

"Traffic's still getting through." Robert bursts into the kitchen and is met by a man wearing a blue uniform. "Goddamn it. I'm outside watching it from my own driveway."

Beverley hadn't noticed the officer, but he must have been there all along.

"We've blocked off the adjacent neighborhoods," the man says, easing back as Robert quiets down. "Shut down construction. Checking cars and going house to house."

Robert drops into a chair. It barely creaks. No matter what Beverley feeds him or how much, all the calories get sucked up by his height.

"We need more people," he says. "And flyers. Missing person flyers."

"Flyers have been made," Lily says, setting a cup of coffee in front of Robert. "Volunteers are passing them out. Others are posting them at the trailheads."

"We're going to find her," Robert says, lifting his eyes to meet Beverley's. After all their years together, Beverley knows it's hard for him to meet her gaze. He's afraid he'll see disappointment looking back. "I have clients with ties to the FBI office in Tampa. I've called them all."

While Beverley was crying into a pillow, Robert was doing something. Other people too. But not Beverley. She had wasted so much time, but she couldn't stop. The tears poured like blood gushing from an open wound.

"Thank you, Robert," she says.

Anyone who meets Robert likes him. Beverley can be a bit bristly, not as easy to like. And people trust Robert. He manages their money, helps them plan their retirement. Beverley wishes she could say more to comfort him, because he deserves it. But she's empty, and she isn't as strong as him.

Taking Beverley's hand, Robert kisses it and stands. He hugs Lily, gives the officer a pat on the shoulder, and is gone again, off to do more while Beverley sits doing nothing.

As Lily floats around the kitchen, rummaging in a few drawers as if looking for something, the morning light that spills through the windows makes the countertops and cabinets shimmer. They're white, crisp and clean. The stainless steel sparkles. The floors shine. But there are things Beverley can't see. Powdery yellow pollen. The random dog hair. Specks of mold growing behind the drywall. All morning, people have been traipsing through the house. No telling what they've tracked in.

"We should get to work," Beverley says. This is what she can do to help. "Francie can't come home to a house like this. We can do the laundry, and we should vacuum."

"I don't think we can do that," Lily says, sitting at the table and handing Beverley paper and a pen. "The police, they said not to touch anything. But they do want a list."

"A list?"

"Of places Francie likes to go," Lily says. "A friend's house, maybe? A relative's?"

"They think Francie went to a friend's house?"

"I'm not sure, Beverley," Lily says. "I think this is just what they do."

Lily speaks in a soft voice, because she knows what Beverley knows. Francie has no favorite places. She rarely goes anywhere. Robert has been saying that needs to change. She's stronger now. They need to do ordinary things with her, let her grow up.

Beverley buries her head in her hands. The police think Francie left the house on her own. They don't understand, and probably they're not looking for her at all. Probably, they're just waiting for her to come back on her own.

When Beverley opens her eyes, she's staring at the floor.

"Who made those smudges?" she says, pointing and dropping to her knees. "And there. That's sand."

Two oblong smudges are visible on the oak floors just inside the back door, and a few grains of sand shimmer in the sunlight.

When no one answers, Beverley stands, looks over her shoulder, and points.

"You," she says to the officer, who is still in the kitchen. "Was it you?"

The officer takes a few steps so he can get a closer look.

"I don't think it's a footprint," he says, and leans and squints at the speckles of sand.

"That's not what I mean," Beverley says, jabbing a finger at the floor. "There is not a smudge anywhere in this house. Not a stain or a speck of dirt."

"Ma'am?" the officer says, not understanding Beverley's point.

"That smudge, that sand was not there last night," Beverley says. A tightness works its way down her arms and into her hands. "It was not there when I went to bed. It was not there when I kissed my little girl good night."

Beverley's mouth and throat are dry. A sharp pain throbs between her eyes. She's been working all morning on what the torn screen and the unlocked back door mean, turning it over and over, looking at it every which way.

"They'll look into it," Lily says, guiding Beverley back to a chair. "I'll make sure."

The Final Episode

Lowering herself into a seat at the kitchen table, Beverley wraps her hands around a warmed-up cup of coffee.

"Show him our chart," Beverley says.

Confused but doing as Beverley asks, Lily grabs the laminated cleaning schedule they follow every day and hands it to the officer.

"You see on there that I clean these floors seven days a week," Beverley says. "It's right there. The 'PM' means I do it after Francie goes to bed."

The officer still doesn't understand. None of them do.

Snatching the chart from the officer, Beverley explains again.

The chart is a map to keeping the house safe for Francie. It's why there are no smudges or specks of sand on the floors. There is no dog hair, mold, or pollen in this house. The chart proves that the windows are never opened. Never. Because the asthma is that bad. It proves that the back door wasn't accidentally left unlocked. No one goes in the backyard. They don't do barbecues. Francie doesn't play in the grass or on the swing set. Ever. Because the asthma is that bad.

The chart is how they can be sure the window and door weren't left unlocked. Whoever came into the house didn't get in through that door or that window. They got in some other way. The police are looking in the wrong place.

This house is not like other houses.

When Daddy throws open his car door, Jenny figures it's safe to be happy again, even if it isn't the same kind of happy now that a helicopter has crossed into the swamp. She gives Daddy a kiss on his scratchy cheek and takes his keys, then runs for the house.

"I'll be late getting home," Daddy calls out after her. "Mind Mrs. Norwood and make yourself useful."

Daddy doesn't get summer break and still makes the trip into Naples most days to show houses or write up contracts. That means

Jenny spends most of her time across the road at the Norwoods' house, where Mrs. Norwood keeps an eye on her.

Tiptoeing over the wobbly pavers outside the front door, Jenny gives Daddy a wave and is glad he can't get an up-close look at her and see that she's up to no good. Daddy promised to take her into the swamp tomorrow, but she can't wait. Not this year. She has to go today, even if it means going alone. Even if it means going when the helicopter makes her afraid of what she'll find out in the swamp. Or what might find her.

In exactly one week, Jenny will turn eleven and fulfill a destiny that's been coursing through her veins since the day she was born. It's a destiny shared by every daughter of Margaret Scott. At midnight on Jenny's birthday, Margaret will appear and guide Jenny toward doing something so amazing that it will bend history. Because that's what Margaret Scott did. Moments before she was hanged for being a witch, she bent history in a whole new direction.

And today is the day Jenny starts preparing for that moment. She has until her birthday to find a real ghost orchid in the swamp. When she does, the orchid will be a promise from Margaret Scott herself, a calling card, that she's coming for Jenny.

Unleashing hot inside air when she throws open the door to their summer house, Jenny leaves it ajar for Dehlia, who just pulled up. Dehlia always comes in a separate car, and cleansing the house is the first thing she does. This year, with thoughts of Francie Farrow racing around inside her, Jenny wants a little cleansing for herself.

Hurrying up because Dehlia isn't far behind, Jenny runs upstairs and, at the end of the hall, unlocks the owner's room with Daddy's keys. This is where Daddy stores the things he doesn't want the renters getting into—the good fishing poles, his shotguns and liquor, his gator-hunting equipment.

Jenny grabs what she came for, a white plastic tub filled with everything for making silk ghost orchids. Another part of her turning eleven is making as many orchids as she can. Hauling the tub to her

The Final Episode

bedroom, she sets it down and readies herself for what comes next. She doesn't usually stick around for Dehlia's cleansings, but today she figures she needs to. Even though she has the best summer ever ahead of her, she can't stop thinking about Francie Farrow. She's the same age as Jenny, practically lives in the same town, and Jenny can't shake the feeling that Francie getting snatched is only the beginning.

A minty, smoky scent seeps into the room first. Carrying a bundle of smoldering sage, Dehlia comes next. A long brown braid hangs over her right shoulder, she is barefoot, and she wears a tan, flowing skirt that nicks the ground. She looks nothing like most grandmas and has always insisted Jenny call her Dehlia. Her being called grandma would lump her in with a sea of grandmas, and Dehlia wants no part of that.

Whispering to herself as she steps up to Jenny, Dehlia waves her glowing bundle of sage. Jenny's skin tingles as the minty smoke chases the bad spirits out the tips of her fingers. She feels the littlest bit better, like Francie will be okay. When Dehlia floats to the next room, Jenny runs downstairs, throws open the front door, and leaps from the wobbly pavers to the prickly grass. She spins in a slow circle, looking for more helicopters, but the sky is empty. Yes, better.

"Don't forget you're having supper at the Norwoods'," Daddy shouts from the car, where he's still unloading the trunk. "Likely won't see you until morning."

Across the road, Tia appears at her front door. Holding it open, she makes a hurry up motion, no doubt waiting for her sister, Mandy. Much as she might want to, Tia never yells at Mandy to hurry up. Tia and Mandy spend summers at the swamp, too, and like Jenny, live in Naples the rest of the year. They're identical twins with long blond hair that's slippery straight, but Jenny can always tell one from the other.

When Mandy finally steps outside, Tia lets the door slap closed, runs down the driveway and into the road, and wraps Jenny up in a hug that nearly knocks her over. This feeling, the feeling of having a best friend who's happy to see her, sinks in like butter on hot toast and warms Jenny's insides.

"Mom is making grilled cheese for lunch," Tia says, whispering so Mandy doesn't hear. "It okay if we go looking for orchids after we eat? Should be hot enough by then."

Tia has a whole plan ready to go. Her remembering that Jenny has to find a ghost orchid this summer is why she's the best friend, only friend really, Jenny's ever had.

"After lunch is good," Jenny says, because even though the swamp feels especially scary now that Francie might be lost in it, Jenny will never bend history if a bad feeling is enough to scare her off.

Giving a nod, Tia takes off running toward her house, and Jenny follows. At the front door, Tia walks on inside, already talking Mandy into going orchid hunting, but Jenny stops. She hears them first and then sees them. Two helicopters buzz past, both following the path of the one she saw with Daddy. Before the bad feeling can find her again, she ducks inside.

When the show they've been watching ends, Mandy doesn't jump to her feet, but Tia and Jenny do. It's lunchtime, and the two of them run into the kitchen where Mother has grilled cheese and lemonade already waiting.

Digging in the cushions for the remote control, Mandy wishes she'd thought it over more before promising to go orchid hunting. When she first agreed, the sun was far from its highest point, and she knew they wouldn't leave for a few hours. She liked pretending she wasn't scared, if only for a short time. But now, the sun is high, it's almost time to go, and she wants to claw it all back.

All morning, while they were lying on the living room floor, Tia and Jenny were biding time until the day got good and hot. As soon as the sun beats down and waves of heat shimmer like steam in the air, the gator that likes to sleep in the grassy patch at the end of their road will slide into the creek and into the shadowy culvert that runs underground. That's where the coolest, blackest water flows. They call him the Old Man, and Jenny's dad says he's as old as the swamp. Sometimes Mandy dreams about him slipping in through her bedroom window and dragging her into the swamp, which is almost exactly what happened to the little girl from Fort Myers.

Jenny and Tia think when the Old Man heads for the cool water, it'll be safe to cross Halfway Creek and go into the swamp. Mandy thinks they're wrong.

Finding the remote, she points it at the television but stops when Tia bursts into the room. She's always bursting into rooms and sending Mandy stumbling backward.

"Don't turn it off," Tia says, hissing in a voice Mother won't hear. She pokes at a button on the TV, turning down the volume.

Jenny is right behind Tia, and the two of them press close to the television where Francie Farrow's picture fills the screen.

Not looking at the TV, Mandy hands the remote to Tia. She doesn't want to hear any more about Francie Farrow. Francie is the same age as Mandy and has the same hair and probably likes the same things, and that makes Mandy afraid someone will take her next. Like just being a girl is enough to put her in danger. It's wrong to be thinking of herself, but she can't help it. Mandy is scared most of the time, and she doesn't know why.

In the kitchen, she eats her grilled cheese and drinks her icy cold lemonade, the two swirling together in her stomach and making her queasy. But queasy is good. She'll tell Mother she has a stomachache. Mother will tell her to lie down, and Mandy won't have to go orchid hunting in the swamp. That's a good plan. A plan she can pull off.

Out in the living room, the TV switches off. Jenny and Tia walk into the kitchen, whispering to each other. Taking the last bite of her grilled cheese and choking on her lemonade, Mandy doubles over, hoping to make it look real.

"You okay hunting orchids tomorrow?" Tia asks. "When Jenny's dad can go?"

Mandy lets go of her stomach and shrugs as if she doesn't care when, really, she's relieved. She likes pretending she isn't afraid again.

But then another thought occurs to her, and her stomach is back to feeling not so good.

Jenny and Tia saw something about Francie Farrow on the TV, and whatever it was, it scared them away from orchid hunting until Jenny's dad could go too. Whatever it was, it scared them bad.

Beverley clings to Robert as they walk into the dark night, leaving behind a brightly lit house full of people, ringing phones, and squawking radios. Even at this hour, the soggy air chokes her.

When they reach her driveway, she lifts her eyes. Up and down the street, a light shines on every porch. But something isn't right. The porches are brightly lit, but the rest of each house is dark. All the blinds and drapes have been drawn shut. No one wants whoever got into Beverley and Robert's house to get into theirs. It's as if they're saying . . . nothing to see here.

As they walk beyond the glow of their own porch light, shadows in the shape of people appear across the street. They're gathered in an empty lot, and if not for the candles they hold, she might not have seen them. They stand in silence, barely moving. She nudges Robert. He sees it too. They both stop, afraid to disturb the silence.

Over a hundred people must be gathered, all of them having come for Francie, because Francie is gone. Because this is really happening.

The silence makes Beverley want to clamp her hands over her ears.

Someone comes up behind them. It's Elizabeth, the woman who's been helping them all day. She's young but stern, and tall like Beverley. Her cropped, shoulder-length dark hair might come off as harsh if not for the lavender jacket she wears.

When they first met, Elizabeth introduced herself as a volunteer family liaison. She would guide them through the coming days, sure to be the hardest of their lives. She'd answer their questions, tell them what to expect, and put Francie's story in every living room in the country.

The Final Episode

"This way," Elizabeth whispers, like she doesn't want to trample the silence either.

Beverley and Robert drift in the direction Elizabeth's nudge sends them. At the end of the drive, another nudge sends them right. Up ahead, at the end of the block, the local news has set up lights behind police barricades.

When Elizabeth first told Beverley and Robert about the opportunity to speak on the news, she suggested they appear on camera together and put on a united front.

"It's no front," Robert said. "We are united."

Elizabeth looked to Beverley as if wondering whether Beverley felt the same way, because the husband is always a suspect.

"We are united," Beverley said.

Elizabeth also suggested Beverley wear pink. It would make her seem approachable, which meant she'd been deemed unapproachable. Pink would make her soft, womanly, agreeable. Those traits would make people stop changing channels and listen.

"You're pretty too," Elizabeth said. "Not everyone has that going for them. Don't hesitate to use it. Exploit the shit out of it. Now isn't the time to take a stand."

Up until that moment, Beverley hadn't fully trusted Elizabeth. But that was an honest comment. It was crass. It was sad. But it was true. So she brushed her long hair and put on a pale pink shirt before walking with Robert from the house. Anything to get people on their side, because everyone knew it was usually a parent. They had to deal with that reality first so the police and the viewers would move on to other suspects.

As they pass the silent crowd, Beverley only glances in their direction. So many times, she's seen vigils like this, in a movie, on the news. And now it's for her daughter. She can hardly breathe to be near all these people.

"You should say something to them," Elizabeth whispers.

"Say something?" Beverley says, fear making the words stick in her throat.

Elizabeth answers with a you-got-this squeeze to Beverley's shoulder and turns Beverley to face the crowd. As Robert slides up alongside her, she takes his hand.

"I want so badly to say the right thing to all of you," Beverley says.

"Louder," Elizabeth whispers.

"I'm not good with words," Beverley says, lifting her chin and her voice.

Wearing pink isn't enough. By nature, Beverley is too direct for many people's liking. She needs to be vulnerable, and right now, she can hardly speak. That has to make her vulnerable. Other than the moment she realized Francie was gone, the silence pouring out of this candlelit crowd is the most frightening thing she's faced so far.

"Robert and I," she says, her voice cracking as she tries to speak up. "We thank you all for being here for Francie. You're generous and kind."

This is true. This is genuine. She feels stronger, more stable on her feet.

She looks across the crowd, and as her eyes adjust to the dim light, the mass separates into its parts. People stand in small groups. Some are families. Others are clusters of young girls, clinging to each other as they cry. And straight ahead, at the front of the crowd, Nora Banks stands with her parents, Lily and Levi.

Nora's hair hangs loose, hiding her face, making her look small. When she sees Beverley looking at her, she wobbles. Lily tightens her arm around Nora's shoulders and bends to check that she's all right. Levi stands behind the two of them, a hand clamped on Lily's neck. He reels her back in when she's done checking on Nora.

"We thank you for your prayers," Beverley continues, her eyes fixed on Levi.

Levi Banks is a large man. He's tall and broad, with hands like mitts. Beverley has never liked the way he towers over Lily or the way he is always at the house at precisely the moment Lily's hours with Beverley are through. They never have time for a glass of wine at the day's end or a little small talk. Levi Banks isn't just large in a literal way. He is large in Lily's life, crowding out everything that isn't him.

The Final Episode

"We're truly overwhelmed," Beverley says, tripping over the words as if she choked on them, when it's really the sight of Levi Banks that tripped her up.

Images of his large frame disappearing into Francie's bedroom make her waver.

Next to her, Robert squeezes her arm as if he feels her fading. She nods, letting him know she's all right, and looks to Elizabeth for approval. She can't be more than twenty-five, but she's already become a lifeline.

"That was perfect," Elizabeth whispers, this time just to Beverley. "Do the same for the cameras, and we'll go national by morning. They'll want to know if Robert has taken a polygraph. Are you confident he'll agree to take one?"

"I am confident," Beverley says, knowing Elizabeth is probing her for any lingering doubts about Robert. "Is anyone else going to take one?"

She just wants to know about one person. Levi Banks.

"Not my department," Elizabeth says, guiding them toward the cameras.

As Beverley drifts toward the lights that await her at the end of the block, the image of Levi disappearing into Francie's room still plays in her head.

FADE OUT:

CHAPTER 1

Twenty-two years later...

The distant rumble of an engine made me sit up in bed. I held my breath and listened. I was already awake, because it's in my blood to wake at just the right time. It's in my blood to know when trouble is coming.

When the hum of the engine continued to grow louder, and I was certain a car was headed this way, I paused what was playing on my phone. Same as I'd been doing for the past six weeks when I couldn't sleep, I was watching the first episode of *Inspired by True Events*.

This season, the show is recreating the case of Francie Farrow. It's telling our story. I'm not sure if you know that. Probably, you do. It's odd, watching versions of all of us on the screen, saying and doing the things we said and did that last summer on Halfway Creek.

A week from today, the final episode will air. That's the one that has me worried. And that's why I'm writing to you again. It's been a while, not that you'd know that. I suspect you never read these letters. But I need to write now, because once the show ends, I think I might never want to again.

Closing my eyes, I pressed my lips into a hard line and willed the car to drive past my house. It didn't. I knew it wouldn't. Instead, the tires slowed. Gravel stopped raining down. An engine rattled and went silent.

The sound of a car approaching deep in the night was like a familiar voice, a warning I'd been hearing since you went away twenty-plus years ago.

That's what Dehlia and I call it. You went away. We don't say you went to prison.

Slipping out of bed, I smoothed my sheet and comforter and tidied the corners. I'd say I like order. Others would say I'm compulsive. When I was a kid, Dehlia sent me to several doctors. They all said my need for neatness was a way of bringing order to a life that had been dumped upside down. She'll outgrow it, they said. I didn't.

After scooting Belle, my three-year-old lab, into her kennel, I tiptoed toward the living room. Once there, I pressed against the wall next to the picture window and peeked outside.

It was Beverley Farrow in that car, and I'd been expecting her. Not that I knew for certain she'd come tonight and yet, I did.

But I don't have second sight. I promise, I don't. I wouldn't call it that.

I knew it was Mrs. Farrow because every time in the past twenty years when a car pulled up late in the night, it was always her.

Episode seven brought her. It didn't deliver the big reveal everyone was waiting for. If this season is like the last, that will come in the eighth episode, the final episode. But anyone who watched the show tonight is now certain you were the one-and-only villain that summer. No doubt about it. They believe that two decades ago, you took Francie Farrow and almost certainly killed her. To be fair, most people have always believed that, and you being in prison for what you did to Nora Banks isn't enough for them.

To Mrs. Farrow especially, episode seven is proof of what she's always thought. And if you took Francie Farrow, that must mean I know more than I've been telling her.

Under a trickle of foggy moonlight, I saw nothing outside my window that didn't belong. At the far edge of my mostly gravel yard, a stand of ragged pines blocked my view of the road running past my

The Final Episode

house. Knowing I wouldn't be able to see her, Mrs. Farrow always parked behind those pines.

A car door slammed. Holding my breath, I listened. What came next was important.

I closed my eyes even, reasoning I'd hear better that way, but they popped open again. The moonlight on my face made me realize my mistake. I'd forgotten to draw the drapes. Now Mrs. Farrow could cup her hands around her eyes, press them to the wide-open window, and see inside. Maybe see me.

Mrs. Farrow's late-night visits started in the months after my eleventh birthday. You had gone away by then, and Dehlia and I still lived together at the house in Naples, the one we all shared. Everything in my life either started or ended with that birthday. With that summer. You could say the same, I suppose.

Not having time to pull the drapes closed, I scanned the living room to make sure I wasn't casting a shadow. Mrs. Farrow getting a glimpse of me, even the shadow of me, was like water on a grease fire. Those nights always erupted into something bad.

When a second car door closed, I exhaled. That was what I'd been hoping for. Relief made my fingers tingle as the blood started flowing again. Two doors closing meant Robert Farrow was with his wife. Robert Farrow meant less chance of trouble.

From behind the pines, Mrs. Farrow appeared and began walking toward the house. She was only a shifting shadow, but with every step, her lines sharpened. She wore a thin nightgown, was barefoot, and carried something as she marched across my ragged lawn. Under the moonlight, her gown shimmered, and as she gathered speed, it fluttered in the breeze. She drew closer.

Yes, she cradled something in her arms.

Still hugging the wall, I fixed my eyes on the pines. Even though there had been a second slamming car door, no second shadow appeared. No sign of Mr. Farrow. And no one else would come to help me. Being this far outside of town, the lots are large and the pines are thick. No one was going to hear. No one was going to call the police.

Mrs. Farrow had almost reached the porch. Her long hair, faded from blond to white after all these years, hung loose. It fluttered in waves that brushed her shoulders and the sides of her face. You'll remember her, I'm sure. She's still beautiful. Still tall and straight. And still strong, because in her arms, she carried a cinder block.

The second door that slammed hadn't been Mr. Farrow. It had been Mrs. Farrow opening and closing it when she took the cinder block from the back seat.

"I know you're in there, Jenny Jones," she shouted.

I didn't dare look out from my hiding place, but from the sound of her voice, she'd stopped at the stairs leading onto the porch.

"If you have a decent bone in your body, you'll come out here right now and tell me the truth."

A wooden tread creaked—Mrs. Farrow stepping on the first stair leading to my porch.

"Why won't you tell me?" she said, her voice strong. "You still hoping they'll let him out? They won't. They'll never let him out."

Another tread creaked and then another. As she stepped onto the porch, the soft floorboards absorbed her weight. She made no more sound. But as she came closer, she blocked the moonlight, throwing a shadow through the window.

First, only the shape of her head and shoulders fell across my floor, but as she walked closer, the whole shape of her crawled into the living room.

"I know you're in there," she said, her voice now little more than a whisper.

The shadow that fell across the floor began to move. It shifted and morphed as Mrs. Farrow struggled to readjust the cement block.

Leaning just enough, I peeked out the window. Like a batter stepping up to the plate, Mrs. Farrow shuffled her feet to get a better angle. Her long white hair hung in her face, and her cotton nightgown drooped off one shoulder. Her chest lifted and lowered. Her mouth hung open. Her eyes were wide.

Seeing what was coming, I stumbled away from the window and beyond the reach of her shadow. From there, I stared out at the real Mrs. Farrow, her on one side of the window, me on the other. With her eyes pinned on me, she shifted her weight, sending her hips backward and letting momentum carry her arms forward. She repeated the motion, building speed.

"Don't, Mrs. Farrow," I shouted, waving both hands as if waving off a throw.

A snapshot of what was coming slid through the dim, cloudy space behind my eyes. I swayed, nearly fell.

"Please, don't. I'm here," I said as her momentum continued to mount.

One last time, she threw her arms back, took a step toward the window, and as she drove her shoulders forward, her arms followed.

"Tell me where my daughter is," she screamed as she let go and the cinder block sailed toward the window. "Tell me what your father did to my little girl."

CHAPTER 2

The window shattered, and shards of glass blew into my house like a driving rain. The concrete block skidded across the floor. I stumbled backward, shielding my face with my arms.

When I looked up, the block had come to rest near my feet. The house was quiet, and Beverley Farrow was gone.

I didn't move until the rumble of Mrs. Farrow's engine faded into silence. As a funnel of warm, damp nighttime air rushed in through the hole she'd left in my window, a hot spot erupted in my chest. It widened and spread up my neck. Sweat bubbled on my top lip, but still I shivered. I steadied myself with a hand on the back of the sofa. My legs felt numb; my spine, like a strip of wet rope.

Next came the trembling. It started in my hands and traveled up my arms. Turning one palm up and staring at it, I realized the trembling came from my phone. I lifted it to my ear and pressed the button to connect the call.

"Jenny? Are you there?"

It was Mr. Farrow, but I already knew that.

"Jenny, it's Robert. Sweetheart, I think Beverley's headed your . . ."

"Already come and gone," I said as I studied the room, looking for something familiar. I felt I'd been sucked under and spit back out in a new place.

"Did she hurt you? Are you hurt?"

"I'm fine."

"She's in such a bad way," he said, his voice strained. "It's the show. Seeing it all come to life again, it's so hard."

"She's on her way back home," I said, forcing a casual tone to ward off Mr. Farrow's fussing. "Everything's fine here. No need to worry. Thank you for calling."

I hung up before Mr. Farrow could ask any more questions and because his kind words were harder to hear than that cinder block flying through my window.

Once I was certain he wasn't going to call back, I switched on a lamp and took in the mess. Mrs. Farrow had caused damage a few other times. When she threw red paint on my sidewalk, I used a wire brush and soapy water to scrub it clean. When she hung pictures of Francie from nearly every pine outside my house, I used a staple remover to take them down. But a broken window, I didn't think I could tackle that on my own. And I didn't think it could wait to be fixed until tomorrow.

Staring at my phone's dark screen, I found myself hoping Arlen had heard the breaking glass. But living two houses down from me, he surely hadn't. If he had heard the commotion and texted me first, that would have been easier. But my screen stayed dark.

Arlen Danielson is the man in my life and has been for a few years. Taking his help is hard enough when he offers. I try never to ask. I've always wanted him to believe I'm no more trouble than any other girlfriend. I don't want him to one day decide I'm not worth it.

It took me two tries to pull up his name on my phone, because my hands were shaking so badly. I hated that he'd know Mrs. Farrow did this. He already had his theories about her, and a cinder block was only going to reinforce them.

If you're up, can you come over?

Hitting send, I stared at the phone and waited for the three dots that would tell me he was responding. When they appeared, I smiled. If you're up . . . of course, he wasn't up. And yet, I knew he'd text back.

His message read . . . coming now.

I felt steadier knowing Arlen was on his way, but the mess in my living room looked worse. The hole in the window was bigger; the spray of broken glass, wider. A potted plant lay on its side, broken, dirt spilled out on my rug. A side table was tipped over, one of its legs snapped in two.

If Arlen saw the damage at its worst, he'd have plenty to say about Mrs. Farrow. It would make him worry about me, too, and same as I didn't want him thinking I was too much trouble, I didn't want him worrying about me. Having to worry about someone all the time is exhausting.

When I got old enough to understand what being in prison meant, I worried about you. All the time. I worried you wouldn't like the food and that you'd be lonely without Dehlia and me. And the older I got, the more worries I had. I worried about someone hurting you in prison. Someone killing you. Older still, I worried because I still loved the man you were before and didn't know what to do with the man you were after.

All my worries wore me out to the point that I began plucking my eyebrows bald and chewing my nails until they bled. Dehlia took me to half a dozen doctors, the same ones who had said I'd outgrow my need for order. I didn't outgrow either. I just got better at hiding them.

I didn't want to wear Arlen out with worry. I never talked about all the clients I'd lost since the series began. I never mentioned the bills I couldn't pay or the tires on my car I couldn't afford to replace. Arlen worrying about me was one more reason he might decide I wasn't worth the trouble.

"Doesn't look so bad." It was Arlen.

He looked in on me through the hole in the window, his chest pumping from him having run from his house to mine.

I smiled, not only because I was happy to see him, but because I was always happy when something surprised me.

The Final Episode

Those surprising moments offset the times I see something happen before it happens. All these years, Dehlia has kept on telling me I have second sight. Every time I'm surprised, it's proof positive I don't. I find that a comfort.

Stepping carefully through the glass, I opened the dead bolt on the front door, and Arlen walked in.

"How you doing?" he said, taking both my hands.

"Sorry to bother you," I said.

"Any dizziness? You steady on your feet?"

I brushed him off and smiled, though I was dizzy and I wasn't steady.

"Well then," Arlen said. He took me by the hand, swept me up in his playful way, dipped me, and kissed me hard. "I seen worse. We'll have this cleaned up in no time."

CHAPTER 3

The solution was easy. Arlen pulled out one of the sheets of plywood my landlord stored in the garage to secure the windows during a hurricane. The holes were already drilled and each piece was numbered to show which window it fit.

By the time he finished hanging the plywood, I had swept up all the glass, rescued my plant, and run the vacuum. I resisted vacuuming the baseboards. Arlen knew I liked to keep things just so, knew I made a living off my talent for decluttering, sorting, and organizing, but he didn't know it went far beyond me liking a tidy house.

"I should have thought of that," I said, nodding at the boarded-up window. "Shouldn't have woken you."

"Woulda, shoulda, coulda," he said, giving a wink so I'd know he was playing with me. "I have an easy day tomorrow. No need for a full night's sleep."

He wrapped his arms around me again. His dark hair and skin were damp from working in the soggy morning air, because it was morning now. Early morning, but close enough to getting-up time it made no sense to go back to bed. I leaned into him, my head resting on his chest. As he eased the vacuum cleaner from my hand, I let go, even though it felt like letting go of a lifeline.

Arlen is a good head taller than me and twice as wide. I like that, him being taller, broader, stronger. I feel safe up against him, but not just because of his size. He's steady. He never flails. He never loses his temper. He laughs more than he grumbles. He cares about things bigger than himself. And he's a hard worker.

You'd like him. I'm sure of it.

"So," he said. "You going to tell me what happened?"

"It was tonight's episode," I said, already making excuses for Mrs. Farrow. "It had to be hard on her, seeing it. It would be hard on anyone in her situation."

"You know what I'm going to say," he said, his arms still wrapped around me.

I knew.

"At least until the show ends," he said. "Seven days, and it'll be over. Not asking to move in permanently. But I worry about you here all alone. I worry all the time."

And there it was. He worried about me all the time, and eventually, that would wear him out.

"How about I promise to call next time," I said, easing away so I could see his face and know if he was worried about me or tired of me. "If there even is a next time."

Arlen's jaw was clenched, sharpening the angles of his face. He wasn't worried or tired. He was angry.

"There will always be a next time," he said. "You know that. I know that. Only question is how bad will next time be?"

"Nothing will happen," I said, stroking the sides of his face to ease the sharp angles.

"Christ, she broke your window," he said, closing his eyes and leaning into my touch. "I don't get it. You're so careful with everything else, everybody else. But not her. This is getting dangerous, Jenn. No, strike that. It's already dangerous."

He opened his eyes and took a backward step, putting more distance between us. Without him pressed against me, I was suddenly chilled, a taste of how I'd feel if I lost him.

"Did you at least call the police?" he asked, rubbing his head because he already knew the answer. His anger had eased, but exhaustion had set in.

"I didn't," I said quietly, wanting to draw him back to me, but he was already drifting toward the door. "If my landlord does, there's nothing I can do. But the call won't come from me. I can't do that to her. I won't."

Standing at the front door, his hand on the knob, Arlen took the deep breath of a man who has had enough.

"Have you thought about what'll happen if the show finds Francie Farrow?" I said, wanting to stop him from leaving. "If the last episode delivers her body?"

He nodded but said nothing. He knew what I knew. Most people think the final episode will solve the case of Francie Farrow because that's what the show is known for. In its first season, it upended a long-settled case, sent a serial killer to prison, and set an innocent man free. This year, everyone believes the final episode will deliver the location of Francie Farrow's body along with evidence that proves it was you all along.

That you took her. That you killed her.

For two decades, I've been wedged between believing you couldn't have done any of it—not what happened to Nora, not what happened to Francie—and worrying you did it all. I've felt ashamed for feeling that way, for not being able to let go of the man I thought you were. I feel ashamed even now.

Dehlia has never doubted you. Not once. She's already planning for the day you're released. But I'm afraid the final episode will rip your homecoming away from her. If you did it, if you took Francie Farrow and you killed her, your twenty-five-year sentence for what you did to Nora will become a death sentence. That will destroy Dehlia, and I'll be certain that you've been a figment of my imagination this whole time.

"If that happens, if they find Francie," I said, "my life here, Dehlia's and my life here, will be over. We'll have to leave. People will think we knew all along, that we kept it a secret."

"You're assuming the evidence will point to your dad," Arlen said. "And maybe it will."

I started to speak, but he quieted me with a lifted hand.

"But what if it points to Beverley Farrow?" he said. "It's not normal, what she's doing. You think she's the person you see on the show, but she isn't. She threw a cinder block at you. She's desperate, Jenn, and dangerous."

We'd had the argument before. He thought Mrs. Farrow's behavior wasn't normal, not even for a woman who had lost her daughter. He thought guilt might account for all her late-night visits and desperation. I couldn't let myself believe that.

As hard as it is for me to consider you might have done it, it's equally hard to consider Mrs. Farrow might have. Things that grotesque, they have a hard time sinking in. Maybe that's what keeps me wedged between acceptance and denial. It's all too grotesque to sink in.

"I'll come by after work," Arlen said when I didn't answer him. He looked sad and tired. "Got a light day. I'll see about getting the glass replaced."

"You've mentioned that a few times," I said. "That you have a light day."

He turned away and rubbed his brow, both things so he didn't have to look me in the eye. He'd realized his mistake.

"But Wednesday's your busiest day," I said, knowing the ebb and flow of his schedule as well as I knew my own.

"Can be," he said.

Arlen runs a landscaping business. Like me, he built his business from nothing. He went from a single truck and two guys to five trucks and twenty guys.

"You lost a client," I said. "Because of me. Because of the show. How many others?"

I knew all about losing business. In the past six weeks, the amount of time the series had been running, I'd lost every client but one, and my bank account had enough left in it to cover Dehlia for a month and me for about two weeks.

"Thank you for coming over," I said. My words were stiff, like Arlen and I were strangers. "Please, don't worry about the broken glass. I'll see to getting it fixed."

"This it, then?" he said, his body so close to mine that I felt the heat of his skin. "You're ending things. Just like that? Because of one client."

"Just like that," I said, straining against the urge to touch him.

I'd told him before that I wouldn't let our relationship hurt him. My name had already ruined my business. I wouldn't let it ruin his.

I opened the front door and stood clear of Arlen's path.

"I'm moving back to Halfway Creek," I said, surprising myself as much as I probably surprised Arlen. "At least for a while. I should have the day the first episode aired. As many times as Dehlia's said she's fine, I know she isn't. She shouldn't be alone right now. And I'm broke. I either move out or get kicked out."

"You don't have to move, Jenn," he said, trailing his fingers down my forearm and taking my hand. "I'll back off. But stay. Have Dehlia come here. I can help out with money."

"You know Dehlia'll never leave that house," I said, my cheeks burning at his offer to pay my bills. "And no, I don't want your money."

"Will you at least let me help you move?" he said, raising a hand in apology. "You'll need my truck for the big stuff."

I nodded, though I couldn't look him in the eye. I'd been doing a good job of hiding from the feeling that I was a failure, but his offer of money put an end to that. I didn't feel like a failure. I was a failure. Eight years of work gone in six weeks.

"Just consider this," Arlen said, giving my hand a quick squeeze. "Beverley Farrow is a danger to you, whether you admit it or not. And the second you move into Dehlia's house, she's a danger to Dehlia too. I'm worried about what comes next, Jenn. I hope you are too."

EPISODE 2

INT. RENTAL HOUSE – COMMAND CENTRAL – DAY (31 hours missing)

Beverley sits in a rental that's next door to her house. From a chair at the kitchen table, she has a clear view into her own kitchen and backyard just yards away. She pinches her eyes every time someone new traipses through her house. No telling what they've tracked across her floors.

"How many acres of swamp do you think are within an hour of here?" Beverley says when the FBI agent who moved them into this house walks into the kitchen.

His name is William Watson, and he's been upstairs all this time with Robert, asking him questions, while Beverley has been here, waiting her turn.

"Pardon?" he says.

"Hundreds of thousands," Beverley says. "Don't you think?"

She hasn't been able to stop trying to calculate how many thousands of acres of swamp are within a short drive of here. She has no idea, but she is certain no one sends a search party into a swamp. It wouldn't be safe. If the man did take Francie to a swamp, that's why he did it. He did it because no one would follow him.

"We search them by air," the agent says. "Already doing it."

"Everything you're going to ask me," Beverley says, looking at the agent for the first time, "I've already answered a half dozen times."

"Understood. But humor me. I'd rather not rely on someone else's notes."

Beverley hadn't wanted to leave her house, but when Agent Watson arrived from Tampa, he told everyone to get out. He called her house a crime scene. Not to her face. But when he walked in her front door, that's what he said. This is a crime scene. We're setting everyone up next door.

Those two words made it real. Crime. Scene. Those two words grabbed Beverley and shook her until she felt it deep down where her panic lived. Those two words made it so she couldn't bear the sound of a door opening, a car driving up, voices growing louder, because every one of these things might bring the news that Francie was gone for good.

"You understand the dangers of Francie coming home to a house like that?" she asks. "With all those people coming and going?"

She leans to get a better view of the people next door who are walking through her kitchen and in and out her back door.

"Won't insult you by saying I do," the agent says. "But we have medical personnel on standby, and your friend, Lily, she gave us the contact information for Francie's physicians."

"Do you understand now that she wouldn't leave the house on her own?" Beverley says. "That when I tell you that, it isn't like another parent saying it?"

"I believe I do."

Ten years ago, when Beverley and Robert moved into their home, it was the first built on the street, and they thought it was special. They'd loved the Mediterranean flair of the arched entry, the red barrel-tiled roof and the wide-open floor plan. And then, every home that followed looked exactly the same. Only the colors varied. Muted gray, pink, or white. What they loved hadn't been authentic, and it hadn't been unique. Instead, it was duplicated up and down every street in the subdivision.

Now, sitting in a house just like hers and yet entirely different, she wonders . . . why them? Why her Francie? If every house looks exactly the same, why not someone else's?

"And do you know about the sprinklers?" Beverley says, staring next door at her perfectly trimmed lawn.

An officer who came to photograph the house in the first hours after Beverley and Robert called 911 was angry no one had turned off the sprinklers.

"Before we get started," the agent says, nodding because he knows about all the evidence that might have been destroyed, "I want you to know we've been canvasing the neighborhood since yesterday. Going back a second time today. We also have roadblocks in place, are searching all construction sites, and to the extent we get permission, we're searching all cars and trunks."

"You think he'd give permission?" Beverley asks, continuing to keep watch over her kitchen next door. "If you were to happen upon the man who took Francie, you think he'd let you look in his trunk?"

"No telling what will turn up where," the agent says.

"I understand you have to start with us, with Robert and me," Beverley says, lifting tall in her chair so the agent will know she's ready. "But please, do what you have to do so we can move on."

All morning Jenny's been at Tia and Mandy's, but Daddy is home. Finally. Leading the way, Jenny runs across the road toward her house. Tia and Mandy follow.

Already Jenny is sweaty and sticky. But sweaty and sticky is good. That means the Old Man will be feeling the same, and he'll have slithered into the culvert where they won't have to worry about him. It's safe to cross Halfway Creek.

When they reach Jenny's yard, Tia and Mandy wait by the road, huddling together in the shade of a cabbage palm. At the front door, Jenny turns to tell them she'll just be a minute, and that's when she sees it. A white pickup truck is parked at the house down the road. All the years Jenny's been coming here, she's never seen anyone staying in that house.

She points at the truck so Tia and Mandy will look. They shrug because they don't know anything about it either.

Jenny and Tia decided not to sneak across the creek yesterday after watching a news report about Francie Farrow. The reporter said another little girl had been in the room when Francie was kidnapped. She heard the man who took Francie say he was taking her to the swamp because the swamp is always a good place. The man saying that meant he'd taken other little girls to the swamp too. It meant maybe Francie wasn't his first and maybe she wouldn't be his last.

When the report ended, Tia and Jenny looked at each other and shivered as if that bad news had turned the air icy cold. They agreed that Jenny had plenty more days before her birthday to find a ghost orchid and that waiting for Daddy to take them wasn't such a bad thing.

Inside her house, Jenny runs straight upstairs. During the nine months of the year that aren't part of summer break, Daddy rents the house to fishermen and gator hunters. Its cinder-block construction and terrazzo floors make it darn near indestructible. And with only three houses on the road, it's plenty private. But the summers, those are for Jenny and Daddy. Dehlia left yesterday after cleansing the house and unloading groceries. All year, the three of them live together, but Dehlia says she needs her break, too, which means getting a few months to herself. Except for Jenny's birthday. Dehlia always comes back to the swamp for Jenny's birthday.

Before Jenny can knock on Daddy's bedroom door, it flies open. He's already changed out of his work clothes and pulled on his swamp boots.

The Final Episode

Even though Francie Farrow still hasn't been found, and twice today Jenny's seen helicopters, she isn't afraid to go into the swamp now that Daddy is going too.

"You see new people moved in?" Jenny asks as Daddy sweeps her up and slings her over his shoulder.

"That's an old friend of mine and her family," Daddy says. "They have a little girl, about your age. We'll go say our hellos after they've settled in."

Hanging upside down, Jenny laughs as Daddy lugs her downstairs. When they reach the entryway, Daddy throws open the front door and marches outside.

"Who's going orchid hunting today?" he calls out. "Anyone? Anyone?"

Shielding his eyes with his hand, he scans the yard as if no one is there. Tia and Mandy jump and wave their arms so Daddy will see them.

"Here we are," they both squeal.

"Well, I'll be," Daddy says, as if just now seeing Tia and Mandy. "Where you been? Been waiting all day. You two seen Jennifer? We got orchids to wrangle. Where'd that girl get off to?"

There's more squealing and jumping as Tia and Mandy point and shout that Jenny's right there. Right there on your back. Daddy turns left and right, looking over each shoulder and pretending he doesn't see Jenny.

"I'm here, Daddy," she says, pounding his back with her fists. "Right here."

"What's this?" Daddy says, as if just now noticing Jenny's feet tucked under his forearm. "How'd you get yourself stuck up there?"

Letting Jenny slide to the ground, he exhales a loud groan and pretends she gave him an awful kink in his back.

As much as Jenny likes to laugh with Daddy and likes the way she feels when he slings her over his shoulder, she likes seeing her friends like him even more. That's only fair because sometimes back home in

Naples, Daddy asks if Jenny would like to have a friend over and looks sad when she says she doesn't have any. Seeing him worry about her not having friends is harder than not having them.

"Who's next on these shoulders?" Daddy calls out.

Like Jenny did, he takes a quick glance toward the house that's always empty. It's still quiet, and the white truck is still parked in the driveway. Tia and Mandy don't look because Tia is busy shoving Mandy toward Daddy, and Mandy is busy jumping and waving her hands in the air so Daddy will see her. That's how much they love Daddy.

Besides having the same slippery blond hair, Tia and Mandy smile the same, are the same height, and wear the same size shoes. They even sweat the same, tiny beads that glisten on their cheeks and top lip. But that's where the sameness ends. Mandy's clothes are smooth and sharp. Tia's are rumpled and faded. Mandy's hair is always pulled back. Tia's is a mess of tangles. In short, Mandy is pressed. Tia is line dried. Jenny figures she falls somewhere in between. They're all three a perfect fit.

Across the road, Mrs. Norwood stands at the end of the drive with her camcorder. Every day that they're together, she'll do the same. For one whole summer when Jenny was six, she dreamed about Mrs. Norwood becoming her mama. She had long red hair that was as wild as Jenny's dark brown hair, and she was always hugging Jenny and always had her favorite foods in the house. But then Jenny heard Mrs. Norwood tell Daddy she was altogether worn out with the twins, and that meant she didn't have room for taking on another daughter.

"Wave to the press, ladies," Daddy says as he swoops up Mandy, which is always the way it goes.

They all wave and throw kisses to Mrs. Norwood. Tia and Jenny go strutting down the road like they're girls who are all dressed up, and from up on Daddy's shoulders, Mandy waves and blows more kisses to the camera.

Jenny likes being busy with friends, so busy they sometimes have to run from one thing to the next. She doesn't get that during the rest of the year, and she tries not to mind too much. Dehlia says Jenny will grow to love being the odd duck and other people will grow to love her for it. She says to be patient, as if eventually plenty of people will want to be Jenny's friend as much as Tia and Mandy do, but being patient is hard.

Riding high on the shoulders of Jenny's dad is about Mandy's favorite place to be. She can see most everything and nothing can reach her. It's the one time, the only time, she feels safe. She especially likes it today because before he swept her up onto his shoulders, Jenny's dad promised they wouldn't stay in the swamp for long.

Besides being up high, Mandy loves that when she's riding on these shoulders, she doesn't have to worry about falling behind. Jenny's dad does all the keeping up.

Every day, Mandy struggles to keep up with all kinds of things, but mostly with Tia. She gets tired of pretending she has as many friends as Tia. She gets tired of trying to be brave enough to do all the things Tia does, smiling as much as Tia smiles, laughing as loud as Tia laughs. School and any kind of learning that comes from a book are the only parts of life that are easier for Mandy. The rest, every other single thing, is easier for Tia.

"Before we head out," Jenny's dad says, squeezing Mandy's ankles to prove he has a tight hold. "Rules of the swamp. Let's hear it."

"Sunscreen," Mandy says, shouting an answer first and liking how that feels almost as much as being up high. "And bug spray. Every day."

"No digging holes more than elbow deep," Jenny says, snapping to attention, her hands pressed to her sides, and standing straight and tall.

"And if we dig," Tia says, falling in line next to Jenny, "fill it in because we don't want twisted ankles. And nothing goes in your mouth unless you're sitting in a kitchen."

Every year, a kid from Indiana or Minnesota or somewhere else cold digs a hole and breaks an ankle in it or gets buried when it caves in on them. Or they eat a rosary pea or a castor bean and end up in the hospital. Sometimes they end up dead.

"And," Jenny's daddy says, his voice deep and serious, "no pestering the Old Man and no crossing Halfway Creek on your own. Agreed?"

All three girls together . . . "Agreed."

Reaching the end of the road where it dead-ends into a thick scrub of pines and a wooden marquee marks a trailhead, Jenny's dad stops in a shady spot. Jenny and Tia creep on ahead. People park their cars here in the cooler months so they can hike the trail that'll take them to panther territory going one way, and across Halfway Creek and into the swamp going the other.

At the creek, Jenny and Tia tip forward until they can see enough to make sure the Old Man isn't sunning himself on the cool, muddy bank below.

When Jenny gives the thumbs up, meaning the Old Man is nowhere in sight, her daddy glances at Mandy. This is where she gives the okay sign, meaning yes, she's ready to go into the swamp. But today, she's not quite sure. Even though she likes being up high and even though they won't be staying long in the swamp, she can't stop thinking about Francie Farrow. Over and over that name chimes, going on so long it's turned into a song that won't stop playing. Francie Farrow. So much sorrow. Hope she comes back home tomorrow.

Pinching her eyes closed and shaking that song about the missing girl out of her head, Mandy gives Jenny's daddy the okay.

They always cross the creek at the same spot. It's the narrowest stretch where thick mangroves don't block their way. There's also a set of flat stones, perfect for stepping on, that peek above the surface so long as the water isn't too high.

Sliding down the steep bank first, Jenny steps lightly on the first stone, spreads her arms wide for balance, and hops to the next stone and the next. Tia follows. Jenny's dad and Mandy go last. He goes slow because this is the first scary part. Mandy keeps an eye out for the Old Man, always does, even though no one ever asks her to.

The Final Episode

"Where to, commander?" Jenny's dad says once they reach the other side.

"Dead ahead," Mandy says, her voice rattling the silence. She clamps her mouth shut, worried about what might have heard her, but she still smiles. This is her favorite moment, the moment when she gets to say which way because she knows the orchids best.

The only reason Jenny and Tia invite Mandy is because of everything she knows about one special orchid that dangles in the trees growing in the darkest, dampest parts of the swamp. Her knowing about orchids and every other thing that lives in the swamp comes from books. Some think the delicate white orchid that Jenny is desperate to find looks like a ghost. Others claim it looks like a frog. But to Mandy, the tender bloom is a tiny stick angel with slender green wings and a long, white, silky gown that swirls around her tiny feet. Even though she's never found one, Mandy likes knowing they're out there, deep in the swamp. She imagines all those tiny angels are watching over her and keeping her safe.

Same as always, Jenny and Tia lead the way, walking in the direction Mandy pointed. It's the same way she always points. She picks the main trail every time because it's highest and driest. It's safest.

At first, slivers of sunlight filter through the cypress trees and throw yellow speckles on the mushy swamp floor. As the four of them work their way deeper into the swamp, Mandy tells about strangler figs and tree frogs, and slowly the speckles disappear, soaked up by the tangle of branches that grow tighter and hang lower. Their footsteps stop crackling and turn silent as the trail turns soft and muddy. The farther they walk, the heavier, thicker, and darker the air grows, and Mandy starts thinking it's time to turn around. Closing her eyes, she draws a deep breath in through her nose, trying to smell the soapy scent of a blooming ghost orchid. But she only smells wet mulch and rot.

At a fork in the trail, Jenny takes the wider path. She doesn't ask Mandy which way to go because Mandy always picks the wider path.

That's probably why they never find a ghost orchid. They keep looking in the same place.

After a few steps, Tia stops and grabs Jenny's arm, stopping her too. Jenny's dad slows but continues until he reaches the two of them. Mandy clamps her legs tight and holds on. She already knows something is wrong. Tia pulls Jenny close and, with her free hand, points at something. Mandy scans the branches overhead. If Tia were pointing at a ghost orchid, the white petals would shine in the dark branches, but she sees nothing.

"We should turn around," Tia says in a whisper meant only for Jenny, but Mandy hears, too, and she sees what they're looking at.

A sheet of paper hangs from a strangler fig well on its way to strangling a cabbage palm. The face of a little girl looks out from it. Her blue eyes shine where a sliver of sunlight hits the flyer. Her blond hair is long and straight, just like Tia's and Mandy's. And she's smiling like she still has something to be happy about. It's one of the flyers the reporters have been talking about on TV.

"Probably one out at the trailhead too," Jenny's dad says, and he looks up at Mandy. He's smiling like it isn't a bad thing that they're seeing that flyer. "Must have missed it when we passed by."

"Is that Francie Farrow?" Mandy says, squirming to get down. Way up here in the air, anything and anyone could see her. "Did that man bring her here?"

"This is a good thing," Jenny's dad says, lifting Mandy up and off his shoulders. He keeps hold of her hands until he's sure she's okay letting her feet touch the mushy swamp floor. "These flyers, they're going up in lots of places. Seeing one here, that doesn't mean Francie is here. You girls are safe. You all understand?"

Because Tia and Jenny nod, Mandy nods, but she doesn't understand. The man who took Francie Farrow said the swamp was a good place for taking little girls. That's what scared Tia and Jenny away from coming to the swamp yesterday. That flyer being right here means

The Final Episode

maybe the man picked this swamp. Maybe Francie is here, somewhere close. Maybe one of them will be next.

For as long as Jenny can remember, she has been staring up into the highest branches that tangle themselves over the swamp, hoping to see a ghost orchid dangling by a web of thin roots. Seeing one would prove that Margaret Scott is really out there, and that would feel like proof Mama is out there too. Margaret Scott and all her daughters are connected in life and in death, that's what Dehlia says. All that together means Jenny seeing a ghost orchid would give her hope that when Margaret Scott comes on her birthday, Mama will come too. She's afraid to ask Dehlia if that might happen. She's afraid the answer will be no.

But now, she's seen something that might be better than seeing a ghost orchid.

"I think it's time to get back home," Daddy says, turning them all around with wide-stretched arms that block them from seeing the flyer.

Jenny goes first, wanting to get home, where she can think things over. Tia follows, and Mandy and Daddy come last.

"You still have plenty of time before your birthday," Tia says when they reach the fork that dumps them onto the main trail. "You still have time to find a ghost orchid."

"I think I saw something better," Jenny whispers, making sure Daddy doesn't hear. "I think I saw another kind of sign."

The swamp's hot, sticky air makes her itch, and the more she wants to scratch, the faster she walks.

"What sign?" Tia says, forgetting to whisper.

Jenny pinches her brows, a reminder for Tia to keep it down. As they continue walking, their footsteps rustling when they hit a patch of pine needles, Jenny cups her mouth again.

"That flyer," Jenny says. "It's from Margaret Scott. It has to be. I think it's her way of telling me what my one great thing will be. She's not waiting for my birthday to guide me. She's doing it now."

The flyer wasn't at the trailhead where just anyone could see it. It was on Jenny's trail. The same trail they take every time they go orchid hunting, every time since she was five years old.

"I think she's telling me I'm going to find Francie Farrow," Jenny says. "I think that's how I'm going to bend history."

In 1692, Margaret Scott had been a penniless, starving widow. When two wealthy families grew tired of seeing her beg for food and weary of the guilt they felt for having never helped her, they called her a witch.

A trial came next and then a guilty verdict. And as Margaret stood waiting to die, a rope wrapped around her neck and her only sin making the wrong people uncomfortable, she shouted a warning to the crowd that had gathered to watch.

"The governor's own wife is a witch," she cried out. "Before you hang another soul, hang that beast. That mutant. That demon. She'll be the death of you if you don't."

The next day, terrified his own wife would be the next woman arrested and hanged as a witch, the governor declared an end to the Salem witch trials.

Even as she faced death, Margaret Scott outfoxed them all. She bludgeoned them with their own hatred, and there's no telling how many lives she saved. Now all the Scott women in all the world, Jenny included, must bend history in their own way.

Jenny's way is going to be finding Francie Farrow. That's what the flyer means, but by the time they've crossed the creek and reached the road home, she wonders if she can be as brave and clever as Margaret Scott. She wonders if she can be as strong. Because if she's supposed to find Francie Farrow, she will for sure have to be stronger than she is scared.

The Final Episode

The FBI agent pulls a tape recorder from the bag at his feet and sets it between himself and Beverley. Beverley grabs the edge of the table and clings to it as if clinging to the side of a boat.

"Care for a glass of water?" Agent Watson asks, pointing at Beverley as he stands. "My wife is always on me to drink more water. The heat, you know?"

He's posturing himself as her caregiver, so she'll trust him. She'll focus on the nuts and bolts of his strategy. That'll be familiar territory. That'll give her room to breathe. Her grip on the table loosens. Soon, he'll try to relate to her, find common ground. He must know she's a psychiatrist. He must know she'll see the mechanics of what he's doing.

"Thank you," Beverley says, and realizes Lily is no longer with her.

The offer of a glass of water brought Lily to mind. If she were here, she would have already offered them both a drink. She's thoughtful like that. She must be with Nora, another thought that makes breathing easier.

Agent Watson sets a glass in front of Beverley along with a coaster. "Figured you for a coaster person," he says.

Beverley takes a drink, letting him know she'll play along, and counts the people she can see in her kitchen next door. Seven. That's so many. It makes her feel things aren't going well.

"Wife's always right," the agent says as he wipes his mouth with the back of his hand. "But isn't that always the case? Is it that way for you and Robert?"

He's moved on to establishing common ground.

"Do I ask Robert to drink more water?" Beverley asks.

"I was talking more generally," Agent Watson says, waving off the question. "As you pointed out, you've probably already answered the questions I'm going to ask, but I believe this is a worthwhile exercise."

He pauses, likely waiting for Beverley to nod, and she does. His shirt has already pulled loose. His collar is flipped up in the back. He's that kind of man. Always rumpled. Somehow, that makes her trust him more, as if he's so committed to his work, he doesn't have time to tuck in his shirt.

"Tell me," he says. "Has Francie ever turned up missing before?"

"Never."

"Never?"

"She has never gone off on her own, she was not angry with her father or me, no fluctuations in the family dynamic, no money problems, no recent changes to anyone's health or employment. She went to bed as usual. Her pink pajamas are missing, and we have accounted for all her inhalers except one, meaning wherever she is, she may have one or maybe not."

The agent nods as he makes some notes. "You're very thorough."

"I have to be," Beverley says.

The agent slides Beverley's laminated cleaning chart across the table. It's been placed in a plastic bag.

"Speaking of thorough, this must keep you busy," he says. "I never really knew it could be like this. So severe, I mean."

"Can we move this along?" Beverley says.

The agent is picking around the edges of what he wants to know, and she wants to dive right in. She wants him to ask what he must and move on, because until he does, he won't find Francie.

"It must have been a big change for you," the agent says, nodding. Again. Nodding to keep her happy. Nodding to keep her talking. "Don't guess you and Robert get away much anymore."

"Get away?" she asks.

The agent slides a few more things across the table. They're pictures of the walls in her living room where she's hung photos. Some are from a trip she and Robert took to Tuscany. They went there for their first anniversary. There are pictures from Athens, Yellowstone, and Paris. The photos from Botswana are her best. Before they had Francie, their travels were what they loved most.

"You've traveled about everywhere it seems," the agent says.

The Final Episode

"No, we don't get away anymore," Beverley says, scooting her chair as the glare on the kitchen windows shifts. "Not since we had Francie. And no, we don't miss it."

She knows where the agent is going, so she helps him get there quicker.

"Must be stressful," he says, glancing at the chart again. "Am I correct that you follow this every day? You do all these things every day."

"With the help of Lily Banks," Beverley says, counting the people in her kitchen again. She can count only four now. She hopes less people means they're closer to finding Francie.

"And now that Francie's in school, the stress must weigh on you even more," the agent says, looking where Beverley is looking as if wondering what she sees over there. "Can't control school, I'm guessing. Must be frightening. Exhausting even."

"Yes. It would exhaust any parent. We're hopeful she'll outgrow the worst of it. But she doesn't go to school. I teach her here at home. For now, at least. That's why Lily is such a help. It's difficult to manage it all."

The agent nods, leans back in his seat, and lets the silence sit. He wants Beverley to fill it. He wants her to say the stress has become overwhelming, that she drops into bed every night exhausted, not so much from the work but from the worry. That she worries because Francie has no friends. That she worries because Francie can't play soccer or go to birthday parties. And Beverley lives in constant fear, but she's been afraid of the wrong thing. She was afraid asthma would take Francie. A dozen emergency room visits clarified how high the stakes were. Yes, life has become overwhelming. Some days. But it'll never be too much. Never.

"You're actually Dr. Farrow?" the agent says, glancing at a small tablet he pulled from a shirt pocket. "A psychiatrist?"

"That's correct," Beverley says, and then continuing to hurry this along, she gives him the rest. "I don't practice or teach anymore. Haven't since we discovered the extent of Francie's asthma and allergies. We started working with Lily in hopes I'd carve out the space to return someday."

Robert says Beverley does too much, has been saying it for the last few years. He says it so often now, they sometimes argue about it. Francie is good at keeping her inhaler handy, she is better at knowing what foods to avoid, when to come in from outside. She can do more, but not if Beverley keeps doing too much.

For a short time, Beverley tried it Robert's way. She cleaned less, managed less, did less. But then Francie had an episode while sitting in front of the television. She got to coughing so hard that she almost vomited. Robert said Francie handled it. She had her inhaler close at hand. She calmed herself. But Beverley still went back to doing everything and more.

The compromise, though Robert still made his opinions known, was for Beverley to hire Lily Banks. With her help cleaning and managing the house, Beverley planned to eventually return to her practice. She sometimes missed seeing patients. She was good at it, helping people. Even as a child, the brain fascinated her. Two years later, her return is still their goal, though Beverley doesn't think about it much anymore. So maybe it's Robert's goal.

"That's admirable," the agent says. "Giving up your career. Can't have been easy."

"Easiest decision I've ever made," she says. "And no, it's not admirable. It's what I wanted. How is that admirable? I'm lucky I had the choice."

The agent is trying to ease a confession out of her, and the saddest part of that . . . he's doing it because it's so often the case. He has to play the odds. He has to check her off his list. She understands, but dear God, she wishes he would hurry up.

"You had Francie later in life," the agent says. "Is that fair to say?"

He's suggesting Beverley didn't want a child, maybe wondering if Francie was a mistake. Beverley tamps down the reflex to spit back an answer. It's his job. It's what he has to do.

The Final Episode

"Because Robert and I married later in life," Beverley says as she pushes away from the table and stands at the window where she can look directly into her kitchen. "And yes, our lives changed in innumerable ways. For me, that's been the best part."

"Your house smells strongly of bleach," the agent says, his voice dropping back to a flat, all-business tone. He's done picking around the edges.

Beverley nods at the laminated chart tucked in a plastic bag.

"You'll find the answer to why that is on the chart," she says, the volume of her voice creeping louder. "I'm extremely careful when and how I use it. Good ventilation, always diluted. But it's the best at controlling the issues we have."

"The upstairs bathroom in particular smells of bleach," he says, again pushing his theory. "And there are virtually no fingerprints anywhere."

He's asking if he smells bleach because Beverley used it to clean up her daughter's blood.

"The bathroom smells of bleach," she says, "because this is Florida and mold is everywhere, all the time. All. The. Time."

She tries to choke down the image of Francie's blood and focus instead on the end of the conversation, which is finally drawing near. But just by asking his question, even in his roundabout way, the agent has seared an image into her brain. Francie's blood seeping across the floor, splattered on a ceiling, smeared down a wall. The image grows stronger, brighter, more gruesome. She can feel it sticky on her fingers, smell the metallic tinge of the blood, see it thicken where it pools. She worries that just by imagining it, she'll make it so.

"The chart will tell you I spray the shower with diluted bleach every evening after Francie bathes."

She takes a step toward him, and her voice grows louder.

The agent tries to calm her with outstretched arms, but he brought this on.

"And every surface is scrubbed at least once a week. This time of year, when pollen drips from the trees, more often. The ragweed can make her cough so badly that she cracks a rib, cough so badly she can barely manage her inhaler."

She's screaming now, and Agent Watson is on his feet, reaching for her, trying to stuff her back in the bottle.

"I didn't kill my daughter and use bleach to clean up the blood. I didn't wipe fingerprints away to save myself. Ask me the fucking question."

"Mrs. Farrow," the agent says, lowering himself back into his seat. He keeps his eyes on Beverley's as if dragging her along with him. Once she has settled in her seat, too, he leans back in his chair. "Did you harm your daughter?"

Beverley shakes her head.

"No," she says, not knowing tired could feel like this. Not knowing fear could be so exhausting. Her head pounds. Her chest is so heavy she can barely inhale.

"Do you have cause to think your husband harmed your daughter?"

"No."

"I understand this is difficult," the agent says.

"No, you don't."

"Just a few more questions," he says, nodding because Beverley is right. "I need the names of all Francie's friends and their contact information."

"You really don't understand," she says, placing her hands flat on the table because she's starting to feel dizzy. "Francie doesn't have friends. None. I have no names for you."

"Nora is a friend," the agent says, his voice softer because he doesn't want to inflame her again.

"Nora is my maid's daughter," Beverley says. "She spends the night because I pay her mother."

The moment Beverley says it, she wants to grab those words and drag them back.

"That sounded hateful," she says. "I didn't mean it that way. Lily is so much more than a maid. She isn't a maid at all. And yes, Nora is a friend, a family friend."

"Last question," the agent says. "Have you had any visitors here at the house, regular or sporadic?"

"The occasional delivery," she says. "It's hard to have people over. Perfumes, things they track in."

"What about a handyman maybe? Landscapers? Any sorts of repairs?"

She starts to say that Robert does the mowing. It's his exercise. And they try to handle everything else themselves too. It's easier. Other people in the house is complicated, risky. But she doesn't say those things because Lily drifts into Beverley's kitchen next door. Accompanied by an officer, she grabs a stack of flyers from the table.

"Levi," Beverley says when Lily floats out of view again.

Levi who never lets Lily out from under his thumb and never lets her linger for a minute.

"Levi Banks often drops Lily at the house and picks her up. Not always. I think their second car isn't so dependable. And he's done some work for us. Yes, Levi Banks has been to our house often."

"And Mr. Banks," the agent said. "Would he have a key to your home?"

Beverley stares so long that the agent touches her hand.

"No," she says. "But Lily Banks does."

Mandy sits on her living room floor and, with one hand, props open a single slat on the blinds. Flipping through a book about the Everglades, she pretends to use the extra sunlight to study a certain picture, but really, she's hoping to get a glimpse of the new girl who moved in next door. Two cars are parked there now, meaning both parents are finally home.

Behind Mandy, Jenny and Tia sit cross-legged on the couch. A spring creaks as the two of them unwind their legs, creep up to the front windows, and peek outside. They've been doing it ever since coming home from the swamp. They're not watching for the new girl like Mandy. They're watching the end of the road for any sign of a strange man or little girl with blond hair, because they think Jenny's one great thing is going to be finding Francie Farrow.

After they got back from trekking through the swamp, Jenny's dad sat them down in the shade and explained again about the flyers going up all over South Florida. He told them there was nothing to be afraid of but also reminded them not to cross Halfway Creek without him. Ever. Then he told them all about the new girl who was moving in and promised to call Mother as soon as they could all go down to meet her.

"Met her myself several times, and every time, she's nicer than the last," he said. "Quiet, sweet, polite. In fact, she's a lot like you Mandy. Likes to read, I know that. But she's also almost thirteen. You all know there's a world of difference between almost thirteen and you all's ages."

He paused then, dipped his head and cocked his brow until all three of them nodded that they understood almost thirteen was different from almost eleven.

"But the most important thing for you three to understand," Jenny's father said, "Nora and her family have been through a troubling time. Are still going through a troubling time. It's up to you all to be good friends and mind yourselves. Don't go being nosy about things that aren't your business."

To Mandy, hearing the new girl was going through troubling times meant she'd need a friend for sure. A best friend. If Jenny's dad was right, and Mandy and the new girl like the same things, the new girl will probably be fine staying inside with Mandy. That'll be good because Mandy is never going anywhere near the swamp again, and almost the whole outside is the swamp.

When the telephone rings, Mandy jumps to her feet. From the kitchen, she hears sounds of Mother talking to someone.

The Final Episode

"You girls, come help me carry," Mother says after she hangs up. "Time to go meet our new neighbors."

Carrying the pitcher Mother handed her like a trophy, Mandy runs toward the front door. Jenny carries a tray of cheesy grit fritters, and Tia holds a jar of hot pepper jelly in each hand. They all tumble down the stairs, and Mother, wearing a strappy yellow sundress and teetering on a pair of platform sandals, follows.

"Girls, check yourselves," she says, her way of telling the girls to slow down. "This isn't a party. It's just us taking a little something to make them feel welcome."

Mandy is the first one outside, maybe for the only time ever. Being first feels good. Already, she's one of a pair instead of the third of three.

Jenny hangs back with Tia, while Mandy runs ahead. The two of them walk backward so they can watch the end of the road for any sign of a car, a man, a little girl. When Mrs. Norwood hollers at them to quit goofing off, they turn around and walk the right way.

Daddy is already standing in the new people's driveway, helping to pull luggage from the back of a white pickup truck. Another man works alongside him.

"Hot as hell here," the other man says, yanking a large bag from the truck and dropping it on the ground. "Just like Lily to say nothing about it being this goddamned miserable."

The man has a booming voice. It washes over Jenny like a blast of hot air, making her stop short of the driveway. Tia, Mandy, and Mrs. Norwood stop short too. The man is a few inches taller than Daddy and wider through the chest and neck. Straightaway, Jenny doesn't like him.

"Levi," Daddy says, nodding at the three girls so he'll know not to curse anymore. "These are our girls. That one there is mine. Jennifer. We call her Jenny. That's Tia and Mandy. Girls, this is Mr. Banks."

"Bet I can guess which one is the troublemaker," Mr. Banks says, tipping his head as he looks the girls over. Then he winks at Jenny. "It's you. Am I right?"

"Nice to meet you, sir," Jenny says, and looks Mr. Banks in the eye and shakes his hand.

"And this is Mary Grace Norwood," Daddy says.

"The girls and I brought a few things," she says. "Moving day is always so exhausting."

Mr. Banks runs his eyes up and down Mrs. Norwood and gives Daddy a wink.

"Lord, look at that hair," he says. "You know what they say about redheads."

"That we mind our manners and have little patience," Mrs. Norwood says, smiling with her mouth while the rest of her is saying she doesn't much like Mr. Banks either. "Pardon us. We'll just take these things to the kitchen."

As Mr. Banks goes back to unloading the truck, Daddy starts in about some gutters he'd be happy to help Mr. Banks clean and gives Mrs. Norwood an I'm-sorry look.

Shaking her head and mumbling to herself, Mrs. Norwood gestures for the girls to follow. Jenny glances back every few steps, feeling like Mr. Banks is the kind of thing that'll slither after her if she doesn't keep an eye on him.

Before they reach the front door, it opens. A woman walks out. She has short dark hair that makes her neck look long and lean, and she has slender arms and bony knobs on the top of each shoulder.

"Look at you three beautiful girls," the woman says. "So nice of you all to come greet us like this. I bet we're taking you away from things that are far more entertaining."

As she walks toward them, the woman smiles, but her eyelids are heavy, like she's sad—probably about the troubling times Daddy said they've been through.

The Final Episode

Daddy introduces the woman as Lily Banks, Mrs. Banks to the girls. She's the friend he's had since childhood. She grew up spending all her summers in the house that's always empty.

"Lily," Mrs. Banks says. "Please, call me Lily."

Mrs. Norwood is pretty in a big, splashy way, even though she's not very tall. She can do a backbend and a cartwheel, and her long red hair slaps you in the face the moment you see her. But Lily is pretty in a delicate, breakable sort of way.

"I'm so thrilled to meet you," Lily says, zeroing in on Jenny first.

She cups Jenny's shoulders and pulls her into a hug, taking care not to crush the tray of fritters.

Lily smells like she's been baking, like butter and sugar, and her hug lasts a long time. Long enough for Jenny to close her eyes, stop feeling shy, and start feeling sad, though she doesn't know why.

"My goodness," Lily says, pulling back to look Jenny over. "You're the spitting image of your mama. Your hair, your beautiful hair, just like hers."

Jenny's seen plenty of pictures of her parents from before she was born, and Mama did have beautiful hair. It was wild, full and dark, and it tumbled over her shoulders. But she never thought of her hair being pretty like Mama's. Lily Banks is the first person, other than Daddy and Dehlia, to tell Jenny she's the spitting image of anyone, and she likes knowing she looks like her mother. She touches her hair, and it's almost like touching Mama's.

As Jenny stares at Lily, questions begin popping into her head. She wants to know everything Lily knows about Mama, but she can't settle on what to ask first, so nothing comes out. Lily rests a hand on Jenny's face and smiles at her like she's letting Jenny know there will be time for all those questions later, making Jenny wonder if Lily has a little of the second sight too.

"Why don't you girls come on inside?" Lily says, standing back and leaving a cold spot behind where Jenny's body had been pressed up against hers. "I'll introduce you to Nora."

After setting the food and drinks on the kitchen table, the three girls follow Lily down a hallway. This part of the house is dimly lit, the sunlight from the front room not following them this far. At the first door on the left, Lily taps lightly and turns the knob.

Same as Levi Banks's booming voice, the sweet perfume that spills out of Nora Banks's bedroom makes Jenny stop short.

"Let's keep the visit short, girls," Lily says. "Nora's had a long few days. Okay, Nora?"

The girl sitting on the bed doesn't much look like a girl at all. She's sitting cross-legged, a newspaper spread out over her lap, but even all bent up, she looks at least as tall as her mama, if not taller. She's definitely rounder than her mama. Lily Banks is all arms, legs, knobs, and knees, which is what Dehlia says about Jenny, but Nora is all curves. Her hair is nothing like her mama's either. It's long and blond like Tia's and Mandy's.

"Yes, Mom," Nora says, not quite looking at her mama as she says it. "We'll keep it short."

When the door closes, Nora exhales as if she'd been waiting days for her mama to leave, folds over the newspaper, and looks up from it. She squints like the light hurts her eyes, even though the drapes are drawn closed, and the only light comes from a single lamp next to her bed.

Jenny has never read the newspaper and is certain Tia and Mandy haven't either. But Mandy is looking at Nora with wide eyes like she can't wait to be just like her, so Jenny guesses Mandy'll be reading the paper from now on.

"I've been seeing you three outside," Nora says, flashing a thin smile and folding the newspaper again as if hiding something in it. "I'm not much for going out."

Her lips shine with a fresh coat of gloss, and a thin black liner makes her pale-blue eyes shimmer even in the dim lighting.

"We can stay inside," Mandy says. "I mean, I like staying in too. Tia and Jenny, they're the ones who like to be outside. You just wait, they'll be going into the swamp every day now."

Jenny gives Mandy a look like she better not tell about Margaret Scott and Francie Farrow and Jenny bending history. Mandy shouldn't have said anything, not even something in a roundabout way. Jenny knows enough to know someone new like Nora will laugh at her. Mandy knows that, too, but she said it anyway.

"We won't be going in the swamp every day," Tia says. "We don't even go outside all that much."

Jenny wants to say that's not true, because how can she and Tia go looking for Francie Farrow if they don't go outside anymore. Ever since they got home from orchid hunting, Jenny and Tia have been planning when to go back into the swamp to find the next sign pointing Jenny toward finding Francie. Since Margaret Scott left one sign, she'll surely leave another and then another. But just like Mandy, Tia is already staring at Nora like she can't believe Nora is real.

"You three girls, you are so amazing to come over here and welcome me," Nora says, covering her mouth like she might cry.

"We brought lemonade made with real lemons," Tia says.

Mandy frowns, probably because she doesn't like Tia trying to slip in front to make friends with Nora first.

"I love your hair," Mandy says, topping Tia's lemonade. "I wish mine would grow so long."

"We could be sisters, us three," Tia says, meaning she, Mandy, and Nora could be sisters.

But not Jenny.

Nora tips her head off to the side and smiles like Tia saying they could be sisters is the sweetest thing she's ever heard.

"We had to move here," she says. "I'm not supposed to say why, but that wouldn't make us very good friends, me keeping a secret."

"It's okay if you don't want to tell," Jenny says, hoping to keep her spot somewhere right between Tia and Mandy. "My daddy said we shouldn't ask questions. We should let you have your privacy because you're having a troubling time."

"You don't have a mother, do you?" Nora asks, rubbing her shimmery lips together.

The question cuts like one of the harpoons Daddy keeps from when he used to hunt alligators. It rams Jenny in the gut, leaves a narrow path of pain, and then is gone. Jenny nods because she can't pull any words together.

Nora uncrosses her long, grown-up legs and swings them over the edge of the bed. Once there, she rests her hands in her lap and picks at her nails.

"And you two," she says to Tia and Mandy, "your mom and dad are divorced?"

They nod. They never talk about their daddy, who they don't see anymore, or the new wife he has now.

"I think you'll understand," Nora says, studying each of them and then smiling as if she likes what she sees. "Even being young as you are."

They nod again.

"We moved because of my mom," Nora says. "She had an affair."

Nora looks up right on the tail of saying what she said, looking from one to the other of them. Looking to see if they understand. Looking to see if they think that's really bad or just a little bit bad. Jenny thinks it's pretty bad.

"An affair?" Mandy says, doing the exact right thing by taking Nora's hand. "We know about that. Our father did that."

Two summers ago, Tia told Jenny all about her daddy moving out. He packed three suitcases, and as he was leaving, he told Tia and Mandy he didn't get to pick who he loved. I didn't go looking for an affair, he said. It just happened. Daddy explained it all to Jenny and said he was sorry she had to learn about something so grown up when she was so far from being a grown-up.

"My mom loves my dad and me," Nora says, nodding like she isn't surprised to hear Mandy and Tia already know all about affairs. "So she came clean. Says it's the worst thing she's ever done. Swears she's sorry and that it's over."

The Final Episode

"Who was it with?" Tia says. "Did your mom tell? Our dad wouldn't, but he got married again, so I think his affair was with her."

"She didn't say," Nora says, nodding that Tia's probably right about her dad. "But I know who it was with. So does my dad."

"Did your dad catch her?" Mandy says, and she says it like she knows all about affairs and married men. "Our mom caught our dad."

"We just know," Nora says. "But it's over now. We moved here for a fresh start, and so the police didn't find out."

"You can't get arrested for that," Jenny says, her words louder than she wanted them to be.

Plenty of kids at Jenny's school have parents who are divorced, and mostly, no one cares. She sure doesn't think the police ever cared.

"My dad says if the police find out, everyone will find out," Nora says, and she stares at Jenny so hard it's like she's pressed a hand over Jenny's mouth. "He says him and me don't deserve that."

"Sure," Mandy says, shooting Jenny a dirty look for making Nora angry. "It's nobody's business."

"My dad says that's the one thing that will damn sure not happen," Nora says, still staring at Jenny, already not liking Jenny. "He says our business is nobody else's business. So maybe you're right. Maybe you better not ask me any more questions."

FADE OUT:

CHAPTER 4

I didn't bother going back to bed after I sent Arlen home, even though I wanted to. The moment I closed the door on him, the empty spot he left behind took seed. I'd felt it before, back when you first left me. It was a chill that moved like a shadow through the house, trailing me everywhere I went as I got to work packing. Hard work has always been my way of staying ahead of loneliness.

When it was almost time to leave for my one appointment of the day, I called Dehlia to tell her I was moving back to Halfway Creek. By sharing my plans with her, I was giving myself no room to change my mind.

"Your sheets are in the washer," Dehlia said, as if she already knew I was coming.

The drive from my place to my appointment took thirty minutes. You wouldn't recognize Naples. Money has poured in over the past twenty years. Gated neighborhoods and carefully coordinated shopping centers have taken over, turning the small town into a spit-shined city where people like me can't afford to live. We have to live on the dirt roads outside of town. Our reception is bad, and our power is the last to come back when the storms roll through, but we have room to breathe.

As I drove down Immokalee, I kept watch for Mrs. Farrow. It was a habit that first started when the series began. That was when she took to following me during the day as if I might lead her to Francie. I looked for her at the gas station where she sometimes waited for me and at every red light. Each time I didn't see her, I relaxed, only to brace myself again at the next red light.

I didn't stop looking until I pulled into Eva Oakley's neighborhood—a manicured, freshly mulched community of waterfront houses. I watched the street in my rearview mirror as the gated entry closed behind me. Traffic raced past, going both ways, no one slowing to turn in behind me. Easing my foot off the brake, I took one last look, and a dark-blue sedan just like Beverley Farrow's appeared. It rolled slowly past the entrance but didn't turn in. And then it was gone.

In Eva's drive, I threw my car in park and swung around in my seat. I looked down the street for any sign of Mrs. Farrow. She had never shown up at a client's house, but she'd also never thrown a cinder block through my window. When my phone chimed, I kept my eyes on the street and tapped the notification on my screen.

A view of my backyard appeared. Only glancing at my phone and keeping watch for Mrs. Farrow, I made a clicking sound. My voice carried through to the motion-detection camera that had caught Belle walking outside through the dog door and into the backyard. It let me keep an eye on her when I wasn't home. Panning the camera with the app on my phone, I waited. When Belle came into frame, I told her she was a good girl. She cocked her head in that way dogs do, and then she was gone.

Feeling good that at least Belle was happy, I wondered how long it would take Mrs. Farrow to find Eva's house on foot. The gate at the entry would keep her car out, but nothing would stop her from coming. I'd already accepted that I'd be waiting tables or tending bar within a few weeks, but I had hoped to keep this one last client. She was one of my longest standing, almost five years. If I was ever going to resurrect my business, my life, after the series ended, having at least one client to build on would be a start.

Up on the porch, the front door flew open, and Eva's latest assistant appeared. Glancing in the rearview mirror one last time and thankfully seeing an empty street, I grabbed my backpack and got out of the car.

Like all the assistants who had come before her, the girl wore a pale-blue shirt embroidered with the Verifiably Vintage logo. Her name was Tanya, and as she crossed the front porch, leaving the door open, she yanked a ponytail holder from her long blond hair and threw it back inside.

Another quick way to get fired would be to get mixed up in whatever was going on. Tanya and I had been friendly in the weeks she'd been working for Eva, but I always kept a safe distance from the other hired hands because of drama just like this.

"She fucking fired me," the girl said, screaming at the open front door as she slapped her front pockets and pulled out her keys.

Taking a wide arc to stay clear of her, I kept my eyes on the empty street and backed toward the house. I wanted to tell her to keep her voice down. If Beverley Farrow was wandering the neighborhood, the shouting was going to guide her right to me.

"Fired you?" I said, still edging toward the door. I should have said more. If I'd been a real friend, I would have, but we weren't friends, and I had bills to pay.

Tanya stared at me, her head rolling off to the side as if she were thinking I should have said something more, too, and dropped into her car.

Eva's assistants, usually straight out of college, came and went so quickly I barely had time to learn their names. This latest one was the first who was about my age, and if she had lasted, we might have become friends. She had a freewheeling way about her, and I could have used a little more freewheeling in my life.

Then again, the last time I had a real friend, I was ten years old, getting ready to turn eleven.

Starting her car, the latest assistant in a long line of assistants rolled down her window, shook her head at me for being a kiss ass, peeled off her Verifiably Vintage polo, and threw it at me as she drove away.

Watching the street until she was gone, I picked up the shirt and tucked it in my backpack. It was a gift. Just like that, there was an opening for a job I was perfect for.

I'd spent the last six weeks living in the past. Watching episode after episode, I kept hoping for a different outcome. I was like the people who obsess over hurricane models, hoping the latest storm takes a turn for the better. I kept hoping the show would lead to an outcome that was better, one where you weren't looking at a death sentence and I wasn't looking at an empty bank account and a life alone. But there was no other outcome. The only thing I should have been thinking about all this time was how to pay next month's bills.

I needed a job, and I needed to stop pretending the bottom hadn't already fallen out of my life.

Before I could think too much about what I was doing, I headed inside, knocked on my very last client's office door, and eased it open.

Eva Oakley gave me a wait-just-a-moment finger as I sidestepped tubs and boxes overflowing with the vintage clothes she sold in her online shop.

Like usual, Eva wore cutoff jean shorts, a simple T-shirt, and her red hair hung loose. Eva was likely older than she looked, though money could do that for a person, and she had plenty of money.

Clasping my hands so I wouldn't be tempted to start organizing, I sat and scanned the cluttered office for something to compliment. I did the same with all my clients, started off with a compliment. I settled on a black-and-white photo. It was a picture of a woman standing on the beach, the sun setting behind her. It might have been Eva, though I couldn't be sure. With her arms stretched overhead and her chin tipped toward the sky, the woman created a long, elegant curve with her body. It was the largest picture in the room and likely a favorite of hers.

"Okay," Eva said, pushing back from her desk. "I'm all yours."

"Nice photo," I said, leaning in to study it as if particularly impressed by the picture. "It you?"

"Depends what you think of it," Eva said.

I smiled, not wanting to risk an answer. I usually did all my communicating through Eva's assistants, so I didn't know her well enough to know if she was teasing me or challenging me.

"I ran into Tanya," I said instead, getting right to the point and hoping a cinder block didn't come sailing through a window as I tried to sell myself.

"I take it you're not surprised?" she said, still looking at the picture as if it brought back good memories.

"I wonder if you might consider me for her position. I know the work, and I know I could do a good job for you."

Eva's eyes slid over to me, and she gave a slight nod as if she hadn't thought of it, but it wasn't a bad idea.

"I tell you what," Eva said, scanning her cluttered office. When she looked back at me, she'd manufactured a smile. "Shoot me a copy of your résumé, but I'll warn you, I've already started interviewing. Next week, when you're here again, we'll discuss it some more. If the job's still open."

"Sounds good," I said, trying not to assume she was putting off the decision until after the final episode, but she was. The manufactured smile gave her away.

Everyone, me included, was waiting to see what the final episode held, so I couldn't blame her. Still, I had a chance at a steady paycheck, and I knew about hard work. Despite all the mistakes I've made in the years since you went away—not always being patient with Dehlia, waffling on how I felt about you—I've always worked hard.

Going forward, I couldn't change your outcome. I couldn't give Francie back to her parents. I couldn't stop my name from ruining Arlen's business. And I couldn't save mine. But I could get a regular job with a regular paycheck and do what needed doing.

CHAPTER 5

Clouds were rolling in from the Everglades, turning the light a dusty purple by the time I finished up at Eva's and headed home. I kept a close eye on my rearview mirror, but Mrs. Farrow never showed up, and as I made my last turn, the spot where she always parked outside my house was empty too. But my driveway wasn't.

Mr. Farrow's car was parked there, and he stood on my porch, a broom in hand. I should have known. He was always the one to clean up after Mrs. Farrow's visits.

"I hope you don't mind," Mr. Farrow said, sweeping a pile of glass into a dustpan. "I had a repairman meet me here. He'll come tomorrow to do the work. We're paying, of course."

"I appreciate it," I said, taking the porch steps two at a time. "But I'd rather you let me handle it."

I grabbed a garbage bag Mr. Farrow must have brought and held it open for him. He nodded his thanks, tipped the dustpan in the bag, and went back to sweeping.

We're an odd pairing, me and Robert Farrow, and have been for twenty years. I'm a poor substitute for the daughter he lost, and he's a poor substitute for you. We didn't go looking for this. We're both uncomfortable with it, go out of our way to keep at a safe distance from one another. But we can't stop it from being true.

"I've already paid him, the repairman," Mr. Farrow said, sweeping where he'd already swept. "He won't need to get inside to do the work. He won't bother you."

"That's fine," I said, reaching for the broom. "I think you got it all."

"I can't imagine how frightened you were," Mr. Farrow said, nodding that yes, he'd gotten it all. His deep-set eyes stayed closed for long stretches when they blinked shut. "Beverley only recently gave up her practice. Helping others, it helped her. But now with the show and all this extra time, she's struggling. She's struggling like she did in the beginning."

Mr. Farrow was thinner than the last time I saw him. His shirt bagged and his pants pooled on his shoes.

Grief, twenty years of it, has drained Mr. Farrow, but it's kept Mrs. Farrow young and strong, likely because it hasn't let her sit down even once. Every time I've seen her, she's walked at a frantic pace, like she isn't leaving this world until, one way or another, her daughter comes home. Or as Arlen would suggest . . . she walks at a frantic pace because she's trying to outrun the truth of what she did twenty years ago. But Mr. Farrow, he's tired.

"There's no need to explain," I said. "But I do worry about Mrs. Farrow. I've never seen her like she was last night, and then she got in a car and drove. Maybe you should take her keys away before something happens. And she follows me sometimes, during the day, when I'm working."

I wanted to tell him I had a chance at a regular job with a steady paycheck, and I couldn't afford to lose it because of something Mrs. Farrow might do. I needed money. I needed to take care of Dehlia, buy groceries, and keep the lights on. But I couldn't say those things while Mr. and Mrs. Farrow were still searching for their daughter after twenty years.

"I worry she'll get arrested," I said instead and because it was true. "Or worse, that she'll get hurt."

He nodded slowly.

"I will try," he said.

The Final Episode

"You'll take her keys?"

Again, he nodded.

"Can I ask one last thing of you?" he said.

"Anything," I said, relieved for Mrs. Farrow and relieved for me.

"Have you kept up with Nora Banks?" he said.

"I haven't seen her since . . ." I trailed off because the last time I saw Nora was the day you were arrested.

"We think of her often," Mr. Farrow said. "She was Francie's friend, the last to see her. We've hated that we've lost track of her."

"She was in California last I knew. That's where she and her parents went . . . after. Her mother had a sister out there, I think."

"Yes, that's right, but she's not there anymore," Mr. Farrow said, gathering the garbage bag and his broom. "Not since she was twenty-two. Twenty-three maybe. After that, she appears to be nowhere."

"Nowhere? How do you know that?"

As a child, I hated Nora. I thought it was her fault you were gone. As an adult, I knew she didn't deserve that. Her being nowhere felt like a bad thing, like something terrible had happened to her, and I didn't want that. I promise I didn't.

"The police told us," Mr. Farrow said. "The show won't tell us anything. Even now that we're at the end. They said whatever they found, they'd share with the police. It's up to them, the police, what to tell us. And they tell us very little."

"Why are they looking for her?" I said. "Did they tell you that?"

"Only said they wanted to ask her questions," he said, wiping his brow with a kerchief. "They told us she got herself in trouble out in California for stealing. From a boyfriend or fiancé, I think. And then nothing. Not another sign of her in the ten years since. They asked if we'd heard from her."

"I'm sorry I can't help," I said, wishing I didn't want him to leave so badly.

Every time I see Mr. Farrow, I feel a rush of happiness to see him and a rush of wanting him to leave. His kindness is always too painful.

"Have they told you anything?" Mr. Farrow said, letting out a long sigh. "The police? The people from the show?"

"Nothing," I said.

"But you talked to them," he said. "The people from the show. Gave them interviews. That's why so much of the series is your story. They got it all from you."

"I was just a few years out of college when I gave those interviews," I said. "They paid me, and I needed money. But they used police reports, too, and court records and newspaper articles. Not just me."

"It's painful, isn't it?" he said, another shallow smile trying to break. "Watching ourselves go through it all over again."

"What about your story, the parts of the show that are about you and Mrs. Farrow?"

"Beverley talked to them," he said. "She wanted the show to be made. She thought they would finally give us answers. I don't think she realized how difficult it would be, the waiting."

I wanted to ask more, but I smiled instead and nodded.

"And you wonder how much of our story is true," Mr. Farrow said. "You wonder if that's how our part really happened. Same as we wonder about your part."

"I suppose I do," I said.

"Our story, it's all true, painfully true," he said, but then he paused as if he had to think about it. "At least, as far as I know, it's all true."

I lifted my eyes at hearing the last of what he said.

When the most recent episode ended and everyone saw you as the only villain again, all the suspicions that swirled around Robert and Beverley Farrow disappeared. Now, hearing what he said . . . as far as I know . . . I wondered if he still had suspicions of his own about Mrs. Farrow.

"Our hope, it's wafer thin," he said. "But all these years, we've had it. We always thought knowing would be best. Now, we're afraid. We're afraid that once we know what happened to our Francie, our hope ends."

Yes. Wafer-thin hope.

The Final Episode

As a little girl, I held out hope for you, too, Daddy. I hoped it was all a mistake and that you would come home. I hoped you were the man I thought you were. I didn't understand how I could be so wrong about you. I didn't understand how I saw no sign of the anger and hatred that must live inside someone who could do the things you did. But I'm afraid when the final episode airs, my wafer-thin hope will be lost too.

CHAPTER 6

I waited on the front porch until Mr. Farrow drove away. By the time I got inside, Belle had stopped barking. I turned my phone off, not wanting to risk a call from Arlen, sent a current résumé to Eva, and spent the rest of the evening packing. I felt hopeful but cautious, thinking I might have a steady job ahead of me, and the packing left me tired, the exact thing I was aiming for. Tired in a can-hardly-lift-my-arms sort of way. Being that tired didn't leave room for thinking or for feeling alone.

I walked Belle once the sun was down, keeping clear of Arlen's house, showered, and before climbing into bed, I double-checked that the doors and windows were locked. I always checked them when rain was threatening.

Since that last summer we spent together at the swamp, I've come to hate the rain. You'd been gone a year when a photographer took the picture of Dehlia that's been making the rounds in newspapers and online ever since. Dehlia had been kneeling in the backyard in the middle of a driving rain. She did it often, knelt outside during a storm and screamed into the rain pouring down on her. She must have seen the photographer when she stood to go inside, because the picture captures her pointing at him, her mouth gaping as she yells at him to leave us be. It's the picture that most convinces people she and I are witches.

The Final Episode

Every time it rains, I worry she's out in it, somewhere, screaming into a dark sky. I guess I double-check my locks as if they'll somehow keep her inside.

Once I was in bed, Belle curled up next to me in the spot left empty by Arlen, I draped an arm over her and opened the MoreFlix app on my phone. I tapped the number one show of the week and hit play on episode one. I fast-forwarded through the scene where Mrs. Farrow discovered Francie was gone, and as a wide shot of the Big Cypress Swamp filled my screen, I slid down in bed to watch.

The shot narrowed and fell on a small road that ran parallel to a creek. Closer still, and three houses came into view. And then the Hollywood version of you came on screen, and I ached like I ache every time I watch it. The actor tilted his head, same as you always did. His voice had the same slow, gravelly way about it. It was you from before.

"The old place fared well," the Hollywood version of you said, and I swallowed hard because the hurt, like always, stuck in my throat.

Closing my eyes, I listened. I felt sweetness and pain all at once, and it burned like ice. The music came next, a gritty, meandering melody. It was the beginnings of swamp blues playing on an old-fashioned record player, and it filled me with more sweetness and pain. But as much as it burned, I couldn't turn it . . .

The phone chimed. My eyes popped open. I must have dozed off.

It was another notification from my camera in the backyard. I patted the bed, and when I felt Belle next to me, I knew she hadn't been the one to set it off. But, of course, it wasn't Belle. It couldn't have been because I always close the dog door before going to bed.

Stretching my eyes wide, I tried to wake myself up. Episode one was still playing on my phone. I knew because ten-year-old me was standing alongside ten-year-old Tia in her recreated living room, pressing our ears to her TV as we listened to a reporter tell us the man who kidnapped Francie Farrow took her to the swamp. I *had* dozed off but not for long.

Once in a while, a cat wandered through the backyard. My six-foot fence did little to stop them. They didn't concern me, but I was always on the lookout for coyotes. I tapped the notification, and a live view of my yard appeared on the screen. It was dark except for the streetlight that reached around the side of the house and the moon that filtered through the orange birds of paradise growing along the fence. The two together threw a broken glow across the wooden deck right outside my bedroom. I panned the camera left and right using the arrow icons on my phone. I saw nothing. I tapped the menu to bring up the saved clip that would show what set off the notification.

It was my backyard again, but this time, a shadow the shape of a body spilled across the decking, moving slowly and steadily toward the French doors that led directly to my bedroom. The shot panned right when the camera detected the motion of whatever or whoever was throwing the shadow. The shadow stopped. A hand came into the shot and closed over the lens. The screen went black. The clip ended.

Kicking off the sheets, I scrambled out of bed and stumbled over Belle, who was darting between my feet. Excited by the sudden commotion, she jumped on me and began to bark. Fumbling with my phone, I poked at the screen until a live view of my yard and deck returned.

At my bedroom door, I closed and locked it before Belle could run into the hallway. Then I leaned against the door as if I could keep it closed with my weight and squinted down at my phone. The hand that had covered the screen was gone and so was the shadow. I made the camera pan left and right and strained to see anything hovering on the edges of its reach. Right outside the French doors, a deck board creaked. The sound rolled like a wave and crashed at my feet.

I stared at the white sheers hanging over my French doors and stumbled again when Belle pushed past me. She slid under the sheers and jumped on the glass, barking and clawing to get out.

I backed farther away. The phone was like a brick in my hand. I stared down at it. Shaking out my fingers, trying to shake life into them, I sent Arlen a text.

Someone in my backyard. Think they're trying to get in.

Three dots rolled across my screen. Rolling. Rolling.
He responded.

OMW call 911.

EPISODE 3

INT. RENTAL HOUSE - COMMAND CENTRAL - DAY (51 hours missing)

Beverley sits in the kitchen chair that has already become hers in the short time they've been in this rental. The police know it's her chair, the FBI agents, Robert, Lily, everyone. Her world has been whittled down to this one chair in this one house.

Taking the last sip of her second cup of coffee, she clings to it as if it can somehow comfort her. A cup of coffee is the one thing that reminds her of what normal feels like.

Robert sits across from her. Leaning on the table with both elbows, he rests his head in his hands. His breathing has turned deep and steady, but soon enough, he'll jerk and wake himself up. And then he'll let out a long sigh because he'll remember. That's why they've barely slept. Because if they sleep, they have to wake, and the pain hits them new.

Not wanting to disturb Robert and be the one to put him in that pain, Beverley slips her legs from under the table and slowly pushes to her feet as she goes for another cup of coffee.

"Get me one too?"

It's Robert's husky voice. Without glancing back at him, she pours a second cup. She can't bear to watch the moment when it hits him.

"That agent is back," she says. "Got here a few minutes ago."

The Final Episode

She warns him so he'll have time to prepare too. They've been through this so many times already, bracing for news that will take Francie from them. Every time the front door opens, a phone rings, a radio crackles, they hold on to something, widen their stance, clench their fists, take one last deep breath, only to be asked more questions or told that the news is no news. It takes longer to find the strength every time.

She's afraid that when the news does finally land, they won't be ready.

Beverley sets Robert's cup in front of him, steadies herself against the counter to wait for the agent, and stares out the rental's back windows. This house has the same view onto its backyard as hers. When they first moved in, there was only scrub out this far, but the city keeps creeping east. Off in the distance, houses have started to spring up. She counts them as far as she can see. It's something to occupy her mind.

"Speaking of," Robert says at the sound of footsteps coming down the hall.

He lowers his head, his way of preparing.

Agent Watson appears, rumpled though it's not yet nine o'clock in the morning. Nodding to each of them, he crosses to the table and sits. He takes his time pulling out a pad of paper and a pen. He fiddles with the pen, clicking it open, clicking it closed. He's contemplating what he should tell them first.

Beverley and Robert exchange a quick glance. Good news would spill out. It isn't good news.

"We haven't received a ransom call," the agent says. "And given the extreme heat we've had since Francie disappeared, dogs aren't having much luck catching a scent either."

"Why do you mention a ransom call?" Robert says.

"There are a number of reasons a child can be targeted," the agent says, letting out another sigh, one that sounds as if he's said this too many times and still finds it difficult. "Ransom is one of those reasons."

"But you don't see that being the case here?" Beverley asks, planting both hands on the table.

"It's unlikely in any disappearance," the agent says. "But it's still a possibility. We could still receive a call, a letter."

"And the other reasons?" Robert says, dipping his head again as he readies himself for the answer.

"We're bringing someone down from Tampa with equipment," the agent says, looking to Robert.

"For the polygraph?" Beverley says.

They explored the overwhelmed-mother reason on day one, and maybe they still were. The polygraph is part of the perverted-father reason. They've already taken Robert's computer, not only the one from the house, but also the one from his office. They've pulled all Beverley's and Robert's financial records, phone records, credit card statements, and tax returns, as if financial trouble or phone calls would somehow lead to Robert harming his daughter. They've searched their bedroom closet, the attic, under all the mattresses, all the places a pervert must try to hide proof of his perversions.

"It will be quicker and likely more effective to bring the equipment here to Fort Myers instead of having Mr. Farrow travel to Tampa," the agent says. "We can bring in an experienced investigator too."

"And the other reasons?" Beverley says. "Are you considering those as well? Are you looking at anyone else?"

"We are," the agent says. "We have also set up a PO box where people can send tips or information."

"A PO box?" Beverley says.

"A letter gives greater anonymity," the agent says. "If people feel safer, they're more likely to help."

"But ransom is our best hope, isn't it?" Robert says. "Because that would mean she's alive. Or trafficking. That would mean she's alive too. Because that's another possibility, right?"

Beverley cups a hand over her mouth. Trying to take in a breath, she chokes. She wants Robert to take it back and never say it again, but it's too late.

The Final Episode

He's put it out there and made it a possibility. And until Francie comes home, Beverley will live with that possibility, maybe for the rest of her life. She'll live with the thought of Francie out there, alone, struggling to hold on, wondering why Beverley doesn't come for her. Trafficking. My God, why did he have to say it out loud?

The agent doesn't answer Robert's question. Not yes. Not no.

"We're exploring all possibilities," he says.

People keep telling Beverley not to give up hope, as if doing so might doom Francie. But hope isn't the key. Hope is easy. The key is not giving into fear. The key is being strong enough to wade through whatever nightmare lies between her and her daughter and not giving up, no matter how unfathomable it gets or long it takes.

For the first time, Beverley considers that she might live the rest of her life not knowing what happened to Francie. That might take the most strength of all.

Running out her front door to meet Tia and Mandy on the road, Jenny is smiling. With a towel draped over her shoulder, she's already wearing her swimsuit under her clothes. Today at Nora's won't be so bad. Nora doesn't like to go outside, and a whole summer of being stuck inside sounded boring to Jenny. But if they have to stay at Nora's house all day every day, at least she has a swimming pool.

Later tonight, when she can't be outside anyway, she'll sit with Daddy in his TV-watching room and make orchids. Daddy said no more going to the swamp, not even with him. With helicopters still passing overhead every day, Daddy thinks they should steer clear. And now that Tia would rather swim at Nora's than run around on the banks of Halfway Creek or venture into the swamp, Jenny is left on her own. She wishes she were brave enough to go looking for Francie Farrow by herself, but she isn't. Maybe on Jenny's birthday, Margaret will appear and tell her what to do next, because Jenny doesn't know. And the best way of making sure Margaret appears is for Jenny to make as many orchids as she can. She's not afraid of doing that.

This summer, as one of the most important parts of her turning eleven, Jenny will make ghost orchids from cardboard, white satin, and pipe cleaners and hang them in the pines along Halfway Creek. They'll guide Margaret Scott and hopefully Mama, too, through the dark night and right to Jenny's house. It may not be much, making orchids, but it's something, and right now, it's all she's got.

Tia and Jenny lead the way to Nora's, and Mandy runs hard to keep up. Three sets of flip-flops slap the ground and keep them from going too fast. Even though it isn't far, Jenny's sweating by the time they get there. The morning air is the heaviest of the day, and that means the sour smell coming off the swamp is at its thickest. They all three crinkle their noses as they run up Nora's driveway, and they all three laugh at seeing each other do it at the same time.

Lily must have heard them coming. She opens the door before they can knock and sweeps them inside. They drop back to a walk as they go from the bright outside light to the dark front room where all the blinds are drawn. Jenny shivers head to toe, her shoulders shooting up to her ears as the cool air hits her damp skin. She's smiling when she glances back to tell Lily thank you. Then she stops smiling.

Mr. Banks sits on the couch, leaning forward, elbows to his knees. His head is dipped so he's looking up at Jenny from under the hood of his heavy forehead. Lily drops in behind the three girls and, with outstretched arms, hustles them toward the back of the house.

"Nora's waiting in the pool for you girls," she says, straining to pull open one of the sliding doors. "I'll bring drinks to you in a bit."

Once outside, Jenny straightaway thinks maybe today won't be so fun. Floating in the middle of the pool on a blow-up raft, Nora wears a grown-up swimsuit. It has shoestring-thin straps that tie behind her neck and another set that holds her bottoms together at the sides. And she has a grown-up body to go with it.

The Final Episode

Jenny kicks off her flip-flops and drops her towel. And then it gets worse. Tia and Mandy tear off their clothes and jump in. They don't have Nora's grown-up curves, but their suits have the same skinny straps and the same bright oranges, blues, and greens. Their suits aren't faded. Their elastic doesn't pucker. And like Nora's, their suits are two pieces. Jenny wears a one-piece with squared-off legs and thick straps. It's faded to nearly gray, and it bags at her waist.

Even before the splash that Tia and Mandy made has flattened out, Nora is smiling. It's like she already knows Jenny doesn't have a suit like everyone else.

"Go ahead, Jenny," Nora says, pulling her arms slowly through the water so she floats closer. "Show us what you got."

Slipping off her shorts, Jenny turns her back to take off her T-shirt. She's already the odd one out with her wiry dark hair and dark eyes. She takes a deep breath, her lips fluttering as she lets it out long and slow, and grabs hold of her T-shirt. She'll yank it off quick and jump in before anyone gets a look at her suit, but then she stops. Straight ahead, through the sliding glass door into the kitchen, she sees a pitcher and four plastic cups.

"I'll get the drinks," she says, leaving her shirt on and tugging it flat and long over her hips.

Once inside, she slips into the bathroom off the kitchen, closes and locks the door, and leans there. Dropping her head back, she shuts her eyes. She never once thought about a new swimsuit. When they wade into Halfway Creek, they wear cutoffs and old sneakers. This is the first summer they can swim in a real swimming pool.

Stretching the neckline of her T-shirt, she looks down on the faded, baggy, little-girl swimsuit underneath. It's even worse than she remembered. The only thing she can do is leave her T-shirt on. She'll say she has sunburned shoulders and doesn't want to make it worse. That'll work as long as Nora doesn't ask to see the sunburn. But Nora is probably the kind to ask.

Nodding because it's a good plan, the only plan she's got, Jenny opens the door. She starts to go back outside and then remembers. She takes a few steps toward the kitchen counter to get the pitcher and cups, but she stops before she reaches them. Hearing loud voices come from the back of the house, she slips into the bathroom again and quietly closes the door, but not all the way. That'll make a click, and she doesn't want to make any noise.

From inside the bathroom, she hears heavy footsteps crossing through the house and lighter, quicker steps scrambling after. There's banging, too. Something knocking against the wall again and again.

"Please," Lily says. "Stay. Levi, it won't look good."

"Guess you should have thought of that before spreading your legs." It's Mr. Banks.

There's more scrambling, and this time it ends with a loud thud and Lily crying out, but the cry is quickly muffled.

"What'll I tell Nora?" she says, her voice quivering like she's trying not to cry. "Please. It's behind us. All of it's behind us. Please, I'm so sorry. Leave your things."

When the front door flies open and the screen door slaps shut and the voices fade, it means Mr. Banks is leaving and Lily is chasing after him. Jenny peeks out. Seeing nothing, she tiptoes from the bathroom and goes straight back outside.

"Where're the drinks?" Nora says.

Jenny sits on the edge of the pool, and quickly, without making a splash or any noise, she slides in still wearing her shirt.

"Forgot," she says.

Hanging on the edge of the pool so she won't see Nora, Mandy, and even Tia rolling their eyes and laughing behind her back, Jenny squints to see the front door through the glare on the glass slider. The bright light that spilled inside when the front door stood open snaps off. She can just make out the shape of Lily in the living room. She's alone. There's no shape of Mr. Banks.

And then an engine rattles. That'll be Mr. Banks, starting up his truck. Tires crunch over the gravel. It starts off loud and gets quieter and finally fades to nothing.

The day Nora moved in, she told Jenny, Tia, and Mandy that her mama had an affair. That meant Nora's mama loved another man, a man who wasn't Mr. Banks. Nora also said the affair was over and that her family moved here for a fresh start. But what Jenny just heard didn't sound like Mr. Banks wanted a fresh start. It sounded like he didn't want to live at Nora's house anymore.

Beverley and Robert are up before five o'clock the next morning. As has become her routine, Beverley starts her day with Elizabeth. She gives Beverley a typed schedule of the day ahead and of talking points, things to be sure she says during her interviews. She's also brought a blue cotton button-down for Beverley to wear on camera.

In the bedroom where Beverley and Robert have been sleeping at the rental house, Beverley slips on the shirt Elizabeth gave her, brushes her hair, and powders her face. Standing behind her, Elizabeth gives a nod of approval.

"Have you seen Lily recently?" Beverley asks, sitting at a small table with a lighted mirror.

The days and nights are blending, and Beverley can't remember when she last saw Lily. She hasn't seen Levi recently, either, not since that first night. That feels wrong. That feels like he's hiding. She made out a list of all the men who have been to their house and gave it to Agent Watson. Levi Banks's name was at the top, but she's heard nothing more about him from the agent or anyone else.

"Not this morning," Elizabeth says, flipping through a file before tucking it away. "Someone dropped more flyers at the check-in tent yesterday. Must have been Lily."

"Must have," Beverley says.

After the interviews, Beverley will call Lily to check up on Nora. She's been wanting to do that, and if something is wrong, Beverley will hear it in Lily's voice. She's too kind to be a good liar. Beverley should write it down, a reminder to call. If not, she'll forget. Too much is coming at her too fast, and she struggles to remember if she already brushed her teeth, when she last ate, what she's supposed to say for the cameras. Yes, she needs to call Lily.

"I don't like this," Beverley says, staring at herself in the mirror and not liking that the soft lighting makes her hair glow or that the blue shirt suits her. "I don't like worrying about the color I'm wearing or the shine on my face. It feels trivial."

"I'm giving you an audience," Elizabeth says, looking over Beverley's shoulder at her reflection. Her voice is stern but not harsh. "And this is how we do it. I'm making it so people listen to you, watch you, and tune back in to hear you again. Because that is how we find Francie."

While Elizabeth digs two shoes out of the closet for her, Beverley turns away from the mirror, already exhausted and the day's just beginning,

"How did you get into this?" Beverley says, taking the shoes from Elizabeth and slipping them on. "Helping people like me? Are you with the police?"

"I'm a volunteer," she says. "I work with an organization that is spread across the country."

"Did you study this in school? Whatever this is? You're very established, very competent for being so young."

"Uniquely qualified," Elizabeth says, dropping onto the side of the bed, and for a moment, she looks her age. Carefree. Spry. "We all are. The volunteers. We've all been personally affected by a missing person. Some of us are the mothers or fathers, some are siblings, friends, extended family."

"Which are you?"

"Enough about my story," Elizabeth says, pushing back to her feet, and the glimpse at her younger self disappears.

The shift is subtle. Elizabeth crosses her arms, a sure sign she's putting up a wall.

"You were the missing child," Beverley says.

"Like I said, this isn't the time for my story," Elizabeth says, motioning for Beverley to stand and lift an arm so she can fold the

The Final Episode

cuff. "This is the time for Francie's story. And to that end, be sure to mention Robert is taking the polygraph this morning. Tell them before they ask. People want to know the husband is cooperating. They want to root for you, so let's give them that."

Robert had to be at the police station at 5:30 a.m. Climbing out of bed when the alarm sounded, he staggered and almost fell as he got dressed in the dark and left without eating. In the past few days, he's dropped enough weight to make his pants hang on his already slender frame.

"What if he doesn't pass?" Beverley says, Elizabeth standing back to check the length of Beverley's cuffs. "The polygraph. What if he fails it?"

Asking the question is easier in this room lit by only a single lamp, where only Elizabeth can hear.

"Answer me honestly," Elizabeth says, leaning until her eyes meet Beverley's.

"No," Beverley says as Elizabeth takes a breath to say the rest of what she was going to say. "I have no reason to believe he'll fail it."

"You don't have to have a reason," Elizabeth says, quietly, as if not wanting to disturb the moment. "What does your gut tell you?"

"He's a good man," Beverley says. She's sure about that part.

"That's not what I asked."

Elizabeth knows what the FBI agent knows. It's usually a parent or someone close to the child. It's rarely a stranger. That makes Beverley wonder who took Elizabeth. A family member. A family friend. The unlikely outsider.

"We argued sometimes," Beverley whispers, knowing with those first few words, she's setting something in motion. "He said I did too much for Francie and that she'd never grow up if I didn't stop. He was in such a hurry for her to grow up."

She wishes she could ask all the women who have stood where she stands . . . did you believe your husband was capable? Did you believe it but were afraid to admit it? Or did you truly have no idea? She wishes she could ask Elizabeth . . . what do you think of the person who took you? Does it surprise you? Did you think he was capable?

"And?" Elizabeth says, still in a whisper.

"And he'd never intentionally hurt her," Beverley says, her throat closing around the words, trying to stop them from slipping out. "But maybe he was . . ."

"Trying to help her grow up?"

"But it was the middle of the night," Beverley says, shaking her head because now she doesn't believe a word of what she said and doesn't know why she said it. "I put Francie and Nora to bed myself. He wouldn't take her out and about in the middle of the night. And what could he have been doing? No, it makes no sense."

"I won't tiptoe around you," Elizabeth says, her voice still stern but her eyes soft. "And I know you don't want me to. So, I'll say this. You tell Agent Watson everything you just told me today, or I will. You understand? No harm if Robert hasn't done anything. But Francie is worth a few uncomfortable conversations."

Beverley nods. Her throat is so tight, she has to strain to swallow.

"You're doing the right thing," Elizabeth says. "Robert will know that. Now, let's put you in every house in America and make it so the motherfucker who took your little girl can't hide."

Same as yesterday, Jenny eats her cereal at the living room window. She always does, so she won't miss Tia and Mandy when they come out their front door. But instead of meeting up with them today, she has to tell them she can't go to Nora's, at least not until later. And if she does go, she'll take extra shorts and a T-shirt for going in the pool.

It's supposed to rain all day. Daddy asked her to stay home so she could call him if the roof leaked. When he gets back from work, she can go to Nora's. She probably will if Mr. Banks's truck isn't in the driveway. It shouldn't be. He doesn't live there anymore. She doesn't like being happy about that, but she is. Yesterday, she didn't get to talk to Lily at all because she and Mr. Banks were arguing. And after he left,

The Final Episode

Lily stayed in her room, the door closed, all afternoon. Maybe today will be different, and Jenny will get to talk to her again. Daddy says Lily knew Mama since they were about Jenny's age, and that's a lot of stories Lily must have.

Across the road, the front door at Tia and Mandy's house opens. Even through the rain, Jenny can see it. But it doesn't open all the way. Wiping her mouth with the back of her hand, Jenny watches and waits. She smiles because Tia and Mandy are looking to see if the rain has let up. It'll have to stop altogether and the road will have to dry before Mandy will go outside.

But then they both appear, huddled under an umbrella.

The rain is no longer blowing sideways, and that must be enough to make Mandy agree to leave the house. The two of them fast-walk down the driveway to the road, hopping over some puddles, walking around others.

For the first time, Jenny isn't sure which one is Tia and which one is Mandy. Both girls wear white shorts, a thin black belt, and a blue tank top. They're both clean and tucked, and there's no skinned knee or tangled hair to give Tia away.

At the end of their driveway, still huddled under the umbrella, they stop. Jenny waves, but they don't see her. They must not, because they don't wave back.

Then they take off fast-walking again, but they don't cross the road to Jenny's house. Instead, they turn right and, hopping over puddles, they walk toward Nora's house. Twice, they look back as if checking to make sure Jenny isn't following.

Jenny watches until the front door at Nora's house opens and Tia and Mandy disappear inside. That's when she knows for sure she isn't invited. It always feels the same, like a door slamming in her face. It happens a lot back home, enough for her to know how the rest of the summer will go.

Dehlia's always telling Jenny that fitting in now may be the easier path, but it'll saddle her with fitting in forever, and fitting in is a bore. Being different, that takes gumption. Jenny likes to think she has gumption, but gumption doesn't stop her from feeling bad about getting left out.

Taking her bowl to the kitchen, she dumps the last of her cereal in the sink. In the living room, she switches on the TV and brings her tub of orchid-making supplies down from her bedroom. She has a whole day ahead with nothing to do, and someone with gumption doesn't waste the day sulking.

She starts by shaping and twisting pipe cleaners to look like two stretched-out frog legs. Next, she cuts oval bodies from white, silky fabric. By the time she's cutting slender petals from cardboard, she's stopped thinking about Nora's house altogether. Instead, she's thinking about midnight on her birthday and how brave she's going to have to be to find Francie Farrow. She'll have to be as brave as Margaret herself was.

She can't use the hot-glue gun alone, so once she's finished cutting out and fashioning all the parts, she pieces them together into piles. Each pile will make one ghost orchid. When Daddy's home, she'll glue them and tie fishing line to each, and he'll help her hang them in the pines growing on this side of Halfway Creek. She's going to make so many that they'll dangle in the trees like wind chimes, and the clatter they make will lead Margaret Scott and Mama straight to her.

At lunchtime, she makes macaroni and cheese in the microwave and eats it cross-legged in front of the television. When the show she is watching ends, the news comes on. She grabs the remote, but before she can change the channel, a woman appears on the screen. Her eyes are red and tired, and she wears a blue shirt. This is a replay. Jenny saw the same report when Daddy was still home, but he shooed her out of the room when it came on. It's Francie Farrow's mama.

"Our Francie hates the rain," Francie's mama says, her voice soft but clear. She looks right into the camera. Her watery blue eyes and long yellow hair shine. "It makes her asthma so much worse, the rain kicking up all the pollen. She has medicine, things that help her breathe. Please, to whoever took our Francie, see to it she gets what she needs. I'm sure you want what's best for her. I'm sure you understand."

The Final Episode

Jenny continues to watch as a picture of Francie fills the screen. Her mama goes on talking, asking everyone to please study the photo of Francie.

"Francie's picture has probably been in a newspaper that comes right into your own home," she says when she comes back on the screen. "For us, please, find one of those newspapers. Find a photo of our sweet Francie, cut it out, and hang it on your refrigerator. Look at it every day and one of you will see her, recognize her. I miss my little girl, and I know she misses us. She must be so lonely. Please, help us find our Francie."

Jenny sits up tall and nods, letting Francie's mama know she hears her. Jenny knows all about being lonely and not having a mama. She knows how hard those things are. This is why Margaret picked Jenny.

"It might be you," Francie's mama says, looking at Jenny through the TV. "You might be the one to spot our Francie. You might be the one to bring her home."

"It might be me," Jenny whispers, thinking this is what gumption feels like.

It's just like the flyer they saw out in the swamp. Jenny was right. The flyer was a sign from Margaret Scott. So was the helicopter that flew overhead. And now, Jenny's getting another sign. It's all a for-sure thing now.

"All of you, watching me right now," Francie's mama says. "Please, look at our precious girl's picture. Study it. Help us find our Francie."

As soon as Francie's mama disappears from the screen, Jenny starts shuffling through the mail and magazines stacked on the side tables and on the kitchen counter. Sometimes, Daddy leaves the newspaper there if he hasn't read it yet. Not finding one, she looks in the room where Daddy likes to watch baseball. Still nothing.

She checks the garage next. Daddy keeps old papers by the paint cans. Every so often he paints for his clients who are trying to rent a house or condo. But all the papers in that pile are too old. Last, she looks in the big garbage can that goes out by the curb every Friday. Tucked down in the side is yesterday's newspaper. She takes it out, and right there on page one is Francie's picture.

Back in the kitchen, she spreads the paper out on the table and grabs a pair of scissors. Once she's cut out the picture on the front of the newspaper, she looks for more. There's another article a few pages in. It's about people gathering outside Francie's house to hold candles. An entire page is covered by pictures of people holding lit candles, hugging each other, looking up at Francie's mama who's talking to them.

She presses the paper flat and cuts out the pictures, taking care to work the scissors in a straight line. There's a picture of Francie's parents standing in front of their house. Mrs. Farrow is talking to the crowd. She is tall and has long, smooth hair, just like on TV. And Francie's dad is tall, too, and wears glasses. There's a picture of police officers walking into a house, one with men wearing suits standing in a front yard, and another showing people walking through shallow water, poking it with long sticks.

She stops cutting when she reaches the biggest picture. It shows a large gathering, and near the front of the group stand three people. She trails a finger over each of the three and stops when it lands on a young girl. The girl's face is tipped down and lit only by a candle she holds.

Jenny sets down her scissors, picks up the newspaper, squints, and yes, she's sure.

That's Nora, and standing next to her are her parents.

Jenny's hands shake as she finishes cutting out the picture. Nora and her parents standing outside Francie's house means they must know Francie.

Setting the picture of Nora aside, her hands still shaking, Jenny picks up the newspaper to cut out one last picture. And when she does, she sees another familiar face in the crowd. It's a hazy face, but she's sure.

Standing outside Francie Farrow's house, holding a candle like everyone else is her daddy.

FADE OUT:

CHAPTER 7

I was still watching my backyard through the app on my phone when Arlen got to the house. I let him into my bedroom through the French doors. We stayed there, doors locked, until the 911 operator told me two officers were at my back gate.

A half hour later, I sat alone on my sofa while the two officers searched my house. Footsteps crossed from room to room, and red-and-blue lights spun outside my front windows. Aware of how little I was wearing, underwear and a tank top, I clung to the blanket Arlen had draped over me at some point.

"They're almost done," Arlen said, sitting next to me and wrapping an arm around my shoulders.

I shivered, and his arm tightened.

"Do they think someone's in the house?" I asked, the words sticking because my mouth and throat were dry.

"Think they're looking for signs of an attempted break-in," he said, glancing up at the sound of footsteps in my kitchen.

Every light in the house was on, and so much brightness should have made me feel safe, but it didn't. All that brightness in the middle of the night where it didn't belong was a sign something had gone terribly wrong. I swallowed hard, trying to chase the bile back down to my stomach.

An officer walked into the living room and sat opposite Arlen and me. He wore a stiff blue uniform, a heavy black belt, and a gun strapped to his side. And he was young. He wouldn't like someone saying he had milky skin, but he did. I stared at his boots, relieved they didn't have dirt on them. I'd still vacuum the moment they left.

I first began sorting, organizing, and cleaning the day I heard the reports of your sentencing. Sitting cross-legged on my bedroom floor, the television playing in the front room, I pulled every book from my bookshelves. I sorted them into stacks, wiped each with a damp cloth, and as I put them back, I imagined them snapping into place. I even started making the sound—*click, click, click.* I did it again and again, all of it to give my mind something to chew on instead of what I was hearing from the television. Paul Jones . . . Naples, Florida . . . real estate agent and developer . . . guilty . . . twenty-five years.

I've been organizing and cleaning and trying to snap my life back into place ever since.

"You're right about the video not giving us much to go on," an officer said as he walked into the living room. "Could have been anybody."

"The squirrels set it off sometimes," I said, readjusting the blanket to cover a sliver of my leg that was showing. The officer's eyes dropped there and then lifted back to my face. "Or cats. But this was different."

"We've checked the house," the officer said, nodding in a way that told me he had a squirrel problem too. "No signs anyone attempted forced entry. Same at the two gates to your backyard."

"I didn't imagine it," I said.

"Not at all," the officer said. "But I do wonder how secure those gates are."

"They're keyless." Arlen squeezed my hand as if to tell me I was doing good.

"And the combination?" the officer asked.

"It's my birthday," I said.

"You share that on social media?" the officer asked, jotting something in his notepad.

"I'm only online for work," I said. "Nothing personal."

"Because you're Jenny Jones from the show," the officer said, finishing my thought. "You're Paul Jones's daughter."

Since the day I was born, I've been viewed through a lens warped in one way or another. First, I was the wetland witch who killed her own mama. Then I was the girl with second sight. But being viewed through the lens of being your daughter, that has been the hardest. Once that label stuck, I stopped getting even polite invitations, the kind that went to every kid in the class. That label has followed me all the way into adulthood.

"They asked how the front window got broken," Arlen said. "That meant telling them about Beverley Farrow and that led to the show."

Arlen tried to smile at me, but it wouldn't stick. He'd told the police he thought Beverley Farrow was the one creeping around my backyard, and he knew I wouldn't like that.

"Mrs. Farrow is a sad, desperate woman," I said to the officer, "but she wouldn't go this far. And she wouldn't know the first thing about getting past locked gates or knowing a camera was watching her. Got to be almost seventy."

I was trying to convince myself as much as I was trying to convince the officer. I didn't want it to be her. I didn't want my landlord pressing charges. I didn't want police at her door. I didn't want to be the cause of any more of her pain.

"What are you talking about?" Arlen said, his tone surprising even him. He took a deep breath before continuing in a more buttoned-down way. "She threw a cinder block through your window. She's long past breaking into your yard."

"You sound sure of that," the officer said to me while silencing Arlen with a tip of his head. "That Beverley Farrow couldn't be involved."

"She's come to my house plenty of times, starting when I was a kid. And since the series began, she's been coming more regular. But she's never been one to sneak around. The opposite. She makes herself known. She comes here to get attention, my attention."

"Would she know your birthday?" The officer glanced at his notepad.

"Anyone who watches the show will know her birthday," Arlen said, immediately holding up a hand in apology for butting in again.

"Very true," the officer said, finishing the back-and-forth he and Arlen were having with a nod that said no problem. "How about we consider this . . . you mentioned Mrs. Farrow has been coming around for a long time. Why'd she escalate, do you think? Throwing a cinder block through a window is no small thing."

"Dr. Farrow," I said.

"Pardon?"

"It's Dr. Farrow. Beverley Farrow is a doctor. A psychiatrist."

She would always be Mrs. Farrow to me, but I felt obliged to correct others.

"Fair enough," the officer said. "Why do you suppose Dr. Farrow escalated to throwing a cinder block through your window?"

"I knew she'd come," I said, and now I was the one giving Arlen a silent apology because I never told him I felt that way. "After episode seven aired, I knew she would. True, I didn't expect she'd break my window, but there was no sneaking involved."

"What made you think this particular episode would bring about a visit?" the officer said, starting to scribble again.

"Because everyone who watched it saw my father turn into the villain."

If there's been one criticism about this season, it's been that the show makes you too likable. Watching the first several episodes, viewers found it impossible to imagine you could do anything that would land you in prison. Evil doesn't explode onto the scene. It creeps, they said. They wanted hints of what was to come. They wanted to see through you, but for six episodes, you were a simple, good man. The morning shows and drive-time radio started speculating about what might really have happened to Nora and who else might have taken Francie Farrow.

The Final Episode

Levi Banks was a favorite choice as the true villain, and so was Robert Farrow. A few even revived suspicions about Beverley Farrow.

But now the seventh episode has aired, and you've been revealed as the one-and-only villain. On screen. In full color. No one sees you as the good guy anymore. They're relieved, I suppose, to believe that when the final episode airs, you'll finally be held to account for all your crimes.

"And you believe seeing that made Mrs. . . . Dr. Farrow upset enough to break your window," the officer said, "but not sneak into your backyard."

I nodded, not expecting him to understand. I had twenty years' experience with Beverley Farrow. He didn't. Episode seven cemented what Mrs. Farrow always thought. You took her daughter, and she came looking for me because she couldn't get to you. But she didn't come to hurt me or scare me. She came because she had nowhere else to go.

Whenever Mrs. Farrow came to my house, she was either looking for conversation or answers, but never to sneak up on me. When she came at night, she was after answers. But when she came in the day, she wanted to talk and sometimes listen. She'd tell me about Francie, the kind of little girl she was, how wonderful she was. The hardest days were when she wanted to talk about me. During college . . . how were my grades? When I first started my business . . . was I careful about the homes I went into? When she first noticed Arlen had become part of my life . . . was he good to me? I dreaded those visits most, far more than the ones that ended with red paint or a cinder block.

It wasn't Mrs. Farrow sneaking around my yard. I was sure.

"That cinder block was her way of begging for answers," I said. "That's all she's ever wanted. Sneaking around doesn't get her answers."

"So, if not Beverley Farrow," the officer said, "then who? Is there anyone else who might have been particularly upset by the episode?"

The name snuck up on me. Dehlia would say it was my second sight rearing up. I'd say Mr. Farrow mentioning her name earlier in the evening had me thinking about her. Remembering her.

"Nora," I said.

"Nora from the show?" The officer nodded because, having seen the show, that made sense to him. "She's the one who was there when that girl got taken? That the one you're talking about?"

"Yes, Nora Banks."

"When's the last time you saw her?" the officer asked.

"That summer," I said, a familiar knot swelling in my throat. "The night my father was arrested."

"Would you recognize her?" he asked.

"Would you recognize a kid you knew for a few days when you were ten years old?"

"Anyone new come into your life lately?" the officer asked.

"All the time," I said, the officer's question making my heart pound faster. I could feel him headed someplace I didn't want to follow. "I get new clients all the time. Or I did. Not so much lately."

Pushing to his feet, the officer tucked away his pad of paper.

"Good enough," he said. "I'd suggest you keep an eye out and lock your doors and windows. Call us if you have any more trouble."

"Wait," Arlen said. "Why are you asking about new people in her life?"

"Break-in coming just a day after the show aired, that's a little telling," the officer said. "Makes it more likely it was someone with some skin in the game. Someone who, like your Beverley Farrow, was upset by the episode. But they didn't come here on a whim. They'd gone to the trouble of learning where you lived, were prepared to get past the locks on your gates, maybe even knew you lived alone. Had to find those things out somehow. Maybe means they have some sort of access to you. Or your visitor could have been a savvy neighbor looking for a lost cat."

I have no idea what that summer might have done to Nora. Did it make her bitter and hateful? Had she found a way to put it all behind her? Was she still angry that you were never charged in Francie's disappearance? What I did know . . . she'd spent the last several weeks

The Final Episode

watching you on screen getting to be the good guy. Until now. Until episode seven.

People call it being triggered these days. You'd have said that maybe the latest episode provoked Nora, set her off. You'd have said maybe it made her reach her boiling point.

Whatever the answer, Nora definitely had skin in the game.

"One last thing," the officer said, his face softening as he glanced over his shoulder to make sure the other officer wasn't listening.

"I have no idea," I said, because I already knew the question.

I got it all the time. He wanted to know if I knew what was coming in the final episode.

CHAPTER 8

After the police left, suggesting I double-check the positioning of my outside camera in the wake of someone having messed with it, Arlen stayed with me until morning. When the sun finally rose, he offered to load up his truck with the things that were ready to go, follow me to Dehlia's, and help me unpack. We were both tired, and I was still rattled. It would have been easy to say yes to him, but anything easy usually felt wrong.

"Still?" Arlen said, standing in my open door, me turning him away again. "You're still not going to let me help you?"

"I can't spring you on Dehlia," I said, partly because it was true but mostly because nothing had changed between us. "Now just isn't the time."

"Promise me something?" Arlen said, rubbing his forehead like it ached.

"Anything," I said.

"You said you thought it might have been Nora, sneaking around out back."

"I don't know why I said that."

But I knew. Like the officer said, she had skin in the game.

"That may be, but I want you to be careful. Anyone sneaking around is looking for trouble. I don't know why, and I don't care. And be careful of Beverley Farrow. No matter who she's been in the past, or who she looks like on the show, she's more desperate now. And I'm guessing she knows the way to Dehlia's place."

That was the second time Arlen warned me about taking my troubles to Dehlia's doorstep. He was right, and I knew it, but I also knew there was no prying Dehlia away from that house. Joining her was my only option. So I sent Arlen home, packed my car, and headed south.

The drive to Halfway Creek took me through panther territory. Long minutes passed without my noticing the miles I was covering. Maybe I was tired, having never gone back to sleep after the police left, and that made for two restless nights. Or maybe I was still in shock. Arlen warned me to take it slow, not to overload my to-do list. A car appearing in my rearview mirror jerked me back to where I was going and what I was doing.

It was early, but already heat rose in silvery waves off the asphalt. Seeing Belle in the back seat, I told her she was a good girl and flicked my eyes to the rearview mirror again. The car had drawn closer. I sat up straight to get a better look. It wasn't Mrs. Farrow. I was sure of that because of the shape of the car. Squinting into the sun that cut through my rear window, I tried to make out if the driver of the car was a man or a woman. A man felt safer this time. I was still thinking about Nora and that officer asking me who had come into my life recently.

At the intersection with Tamiami Trail, I stopped to wait for cross traffic to clear, adjusted my visor, and looked again as the car rolled to a stop behind me. It was a sheriff's car. The lights on the roof gave it away. And then those lights popped on and off. I exhaled, crossed the intersection, pulled over, and parked on the shoulder. The patrol car did the same. A few moments later my passenger's side door opened, and Henry Baskin dropped down on the seat. He cupped Belle's head when she stuck her nose in his ear.

You'll remember Henry and Doreen Baskin. After you went away, Henry did his best to make up for you being gone. Not all the neighbors were as supportive. In truth, he and Doreen were the only ones who stuck by us. Maybe since the two of you had known each other since you were kids, he felt obligated. Maybe he and Doreen are just kind people. Even after Dehlia decided she and I would move out of the house in Naples to the one down on Halfway Creek, Henry still came around. He mowed our yard and helped keep the white birds trimmed and the palm fronds picked up. He's the undersheriff now and getting close to retirement. After all these years, he's still looking out for me and Dehlia.

"Headed to Dehlia's?" he said.

"Where else?"

When my phone vibrated with an incoming call, I glanced down to see Mr. Farrow's name. It was his third call, and for the third time, I ignored it.

"Looks like you're staying awhile," he said, glancing at the boxes and suitcases stacked in the back seat. They left only enough room for Belle and for me to see out.

"For the foreseeable future."

"You need to get that?" he said when my phone vibrated yet again.

"It's nothing. You back to working the streets?"

I rarely saw Henry in a patrol car anymore.

"Loaner for the day," he said, taking off his hat and running a hand over his thinning hair. "Glad I caught you. Heard you had some trouble."

"You saying you being here is a coincidence?" I asked, already knowing it wasn't.

"Maybe not. Now, you were saying about that trouble you had?"

"You saw the video?" I said, forcing a smile as if I wasn't all that worried about it.

"I did," he said, shifting in his seat to make more room for the stomach that spilled over his belt buckle.

"Please don't tell Dehlia? Would rather just forget about it."

"So, it shook you up," he said, nodding that he'd keep my secret.

The Final Episode

"It did, but I recovered," I said, downplaying it as much for me as for him. He did too much, and he'd done it for too long. "Thought I shouldn't be leaving Dehlia alone. Wouldn't want the same happening to her."

"You think it was one of the girls from back then," he said, looking off into the distance and not at me. He reminded me of you in that way, not pushing too hard. "So I heard."

"That's a bit of an overstatement," I said, loosening my hands because I was clinging to the steering wheel. "I've had plenty of run-ins since the show started. Could have been anyone."

I added a shrug like I hadn't thought much about it, but I'd been thinking about nothing else. If she'd cared to, Nora could have slunk around the outer edges of my life and easily learned anything she wanted to know about me. Or she could have given herself a new name and come straight at me, and I'd have never known. I'd tried thinking back on all my clients, looking for some piece of them that matched some piece of the almost-thirteen-year-old Nora I'd known. Tia and Mandy, I'd know them anywhere, but not Nora. All I could see when I tried to conjure her was the Hollywood version. The actor who plays Nora is taller than the real one was back then. Thinner and prettier too. And definitely older playing younger.

"Whoever it was," Henry said, rearranging himself like he was getting ready to leave me, "I hope you're taking it seriously."

"This isn't proof enough?" I nodded at the bags and boxes crammed in my back seat.

I'd packed up as much as I could in a few hours, and I had no idea when I'd go back for the rest.

"Want me to look into the one gal?" Henry asked. "Nora. That's her name? Nora Banks."

"Can you do that?" I asked.

"Can give it a whirl," he said. "And you and Dehlia, you take care. Keep the doors and windows locked. The gate too."

Soon after the first episode aired, cars piled up outside the house on Halfway Creek and clogged the streets all the way into Everglades City. They were mostly fans of the show, looking for pictures. Some were reporters. To get it under control, the sheriff's office installed a cattle gate on our stretch of road. I suspect Henry Baskin paid for it out of his own pocket. It's not a perfect system, but it does keep the reporters away. The heat and the mosquitoes keep away most everyone else.

"And you have my number," Henry said, tugging his hat back on. "You need it, use it."

Giving Belle one more pat, Henry got out, and once he pulled away, I continued to Dehlia's place.

The air smelled different as I neared the swamp. After all these years, I bet you can still smell it. Even with my windows up and the air conditioner blasting, I could.

Coming up on the gate, I eased toward the side of the road, careful to avoid the soft shoulder. I put the car in park, told Belle to stay put, got out to unlock the gate, and decided to ask Dehlia if she'd kept any pictures from that summer. Feeling more at ease to think a picture of the real Nora might clean up my memories of her, I reached for the lock, but it hung loose.

I grabbed it as if double-checking might change something. The gate stood ajar, and when I pushed it, it swung open.

Dehlia was the only one still living out here, and only she and I and a few others had the combination. No one lived in Nora's house. For a while, it was a rental but had been abandoned for years. Tia and Mandy's old house had stood empty ever since that summer, too, but the yard had continued to be mowed, and a management company kept an eye on everything else. The company must have had the combination too. And Henry, he had it, which meant other deputies also had it.

But the instant I saw the lock dangling on the gate, I didn't think of any of those people. I thought of Nora. Maybe now was the time for her to come home again, same as it was for me. Dehlia would call it second sight, straining to get my attention. I'd call it a gut feeling, an instinct.

EPISODE 4

INT. JENNY'S BEDROOM - NIGHT (3 days, 18 hours missing)

A flash of lightning startles Jenny. She opens her eyes to a dark bedroom. All day it's been raining, and now another storm has rolled in off the Everglades. It's close, the thunder coming right on the tail of the lightning. Another crack brightens her window. Hoping to see nothing creeping out of a corner, she scans her room before it falls dark again. Once the thunder has quieted, she holds her breath and listens. The rest of the house is quiet too. No sounds of Daddy coming down the hall to check on her.

Keeping her blankets tucked up tight under her chin, she reaches for her bedside lamp and switches it on. Once the soft glow has sunk into her room, she grabs a flashlight from her nightstand and double-checks that it works. Nature is bigger than we are, Daddy's always saying. Think otherwise, and you'll be sorry. That means Jenny should always be prepared for things like nature knocking out the electricity.

"Daddy," she says, still huddled under her blankets. She whispers, afraid if she talks too loudly, she'll wake up who knows what. She always worries that when Dehlia smudges to chase away the spirits, she'll miss some.

"Daddy," she says again, louder this time.

She'll feel better once Daddy's awake. His being asleep when she's awake makes the house feel bigger and darker and like it isn't really hers anymore.

Tossing the blankets aside, she pushes herself up. Something crackles in her bed. It's the pictures of Francie Farrow that she cut from the paper. She didn't want Daddy to find them, so she brought them to bed with her and tucked them under her pillow. He'd put the newspaper in the garbage can that he hauls out to the road once a week, and that made her think she wasn't supposed to see it. That made her think she'd get in trouble if Daddy found out she did.

Gathering all the pictures, and the articles she cut out, too, she tucks them in her nightstand drawer. Each photo has a caption under it. All day, she read them over and over. One of them, the picture of the crowd gathered outside Francie's house, said that parents all over Florida were double-checking windows and locks, because no one wanted their daughter to be next.

Daddy sleeping while Jenny is awake makes her worry that she'll be next.

Tiptoeing as fast as she can, she crosses her room and heads down the hall. When she was younger, she checked on Daddy almost every night, wanting to make sure he hadn't died like her mama. He startled awake on those nights, wrapped an arm around her waist, and scooped her under the covers next to him. I'm not going anywhere, baby girl, he'd whisper.

In Daddy's doorway, she squints, trying to see him, but the room is too dark. She walks to his bed, pats the spot where he should be, but he isn't there.

Not knowing what to do next, she backs slowly from his room. The rain outside pounds the roof and rattles the gutters. A flash of light fills the windows in Daddy's room. Thunder shakes the floors. Wanting to find Daddy before the lights go out, Jenny holds her flashlight like a torch and checks the upstairs bathroom. Daddy's not there. She checks the one downstairs. He's not there either. Then she runs toward the TV room. That's where he'll be, watching the last of a game, maybe even asleep in his chair.

Creeping through the house and able to see the glow of the television up ahead, Jenny feels better. The stiffness in her throat loosens. Still trying to be quiet so whatever might be out there won't hear her, she tiptoes through the room to Daddy's chair. But it's empty too.

She glances at the television. It's tuned to a baseball game, and the glow flickers in the dark house. Another flash of lightning lights up the room and ends with a crack that makes Jenny stumble backward a step. She draws in a deep breath, and as the thunder rolls across the house and out over the swamp, the glow coming off the TV sputters and disappears.

The house falls black.

Jenny stares at the TV, wanting it to pop back on, but it doesn't. Wrapping herself up with her arms, she backs out of the room, testing each step as she goes. Her hair is heavy on her back and shoulders. Her neck itches. When the electricity went off, so did the air conditioner. Already, the house feels hotter. On the terrazzo in the entryway, her feet make puckering sounds. The floor is damp as if someone came or went and let the wind blow in a rainy mist.

When she bumps up against the front door, she reaches behind her, turns the knob, and pulls. The sound of rain battering the flat tin roof over the entry and spilling from the gutters grows louder. She keeps backing out of the house until the blowing rain hits her feet and calves. But outside feels safer than inside, even if it means getting wet.

She knows the rule well. Any time Jenny needs an adult, she is supposed to go to Mrs. Norwood. Legs stiff, Jenny turns toward the road. The rain soaks her shins all the way up to her knees. Sucking in a big breath as if to dive in the deep end, she looks both ways, one of Daddy's most important rules. Look left. Look right. Look left again.

Looking left one last time and ready to dive into the rain and run across the yard and then the road as fast as she can, quick before anything or anyone sees her, Jenny eases back under the overhang.

Lightning cuts through the dark sky, giving her just a glimpse, but she's sure. Someone is in the road, walking away from Nora's house. Maybe it's Daddy, but Daddy wouldn't be out in the dark. She should go now, run as fast as she can and knock on Mrs. Norwood's door, but that shadowy figure makes it so she can't move.

All across Florida, people are locking their doors so their daughters won't be the next little girl snatched out of her own bed, and now, someone is sneaking around Nora's house. Maybe Nora's about to be snatched right out of her own bed. Maybe because her picture was in the newspaper and she knew Francie Farrow.

Lightning cracks overhead again, dumping another dose of light on the road. The one person Jenny saw is really two. The man already has Nora. He's already been into her room, covered her mouth, and made her go away with him. Now, he'll take her into the swamp like he did Francie Farrow.

Since she first saw reporters on TV tell how a man took Francie from her own bed, Jenny's been wondering why a man would do such a thing. When the answer started creeping up on her, she turned away quick, not wanting to get a good look at it. She needed to be older to tackle that fact of life.

Now, seeing a man do to Nora what he did to Francie, Jenny squats on the wobbly pad of pavers outside her front door. The rain sprays her in the face. She covers her mouth over, wants to yell or run down there, but she can't move. She can't even stand. She wants to save Nora from ending up a pile of pictures cut from newspapers. Lily Banks won't be strong enough to stand in front of a camera and beg for Nora's safe return like Francie's mama did.

Jenny wipes her face and eyes. She can't really see, but she can see enough. Another flash shoots across the sky, and the two people turn into people carrying an umbrella. The weight holding Jenny down lifts. She pushes to her feet. The two people are huddled together. They aren't running. One isn't dragging the other. The other isn't stumbling behind.

The Final Episode

And it's the way the two people move, the size of one of them next to the other, the way one is resting her head on the other's shoulder, the way the other holds her, one arm wrapped around her shoulders. Wrapping her up like Daddy wraps up Jenny when she's scared. Let me wrap you up in my arms where you'll be safe, he always says.

The shadowy figures move closer and turn into Daddy and Lily Banks, Nora's mama. Maybe. Maybe it's them, walking in the rain together on a night when Levi Banks's big white truck isn't parked in the driveway.

By the time Beverley has finished yet another round of interviews with the morning shows, Robert still isn't home from taking his polygraph at the police station. It rained all night, not the gentle rain that might lull her to sleep, but the loud booming rain that startled her on and off until dawn. She's tired, and as she sits on the couch and waits, her head pounds from the aftereffects of one long lingering bad dream.

The examiner declined to administer the polygraph yesterday because Robert's blood pressure was abnormally high, he was dangerously dehydrated, and he was exhibiting symptoms of an anxiety attack. That was what Agent Watson reported to Beverley. She in turn told him everything she'd told Elizabeth about the disagreements Beverley and Robert had over how to manage Francie's conditions as she got older.

"I believe he'll pass," she said. "I really do, but that's surely what every wife says. I just thought . . . it's best for Francie, for me to tell you."

"We'll try again tomorrow," Agent Watson said, nodding that she'd done the right thing. "He needs fluids and make sure he sleeps. I'm not looking for trouble where there isn't any. I want a good examination. One worth doing."

Same as he did yesterday morning, Robert left the house before dawn, and since Beverley's final interview ended, she has been sitting on the sofa, her eyes pinned to the front door, waiting. And the longer she waits, the more she wonders if Robert knows what she told Elizabeth and Agent Watson. Though she doesn't really care. She's numb to feeling anything. If he passes, she should feel guilty, but she won't. And if he doesn't, she'll wish she'd said something sooner.

She has no idea how long a test—not test, examination—should last, but she's pretty sure the longer it takes for him to come home, the worse the results.

"Mrs. Farrow?"

Beverley startles, not realizing she slipped into a daze as she sat, staring at the front door. She looks up.

"Ma'am?" It's a man wearing neatly pressed street clothes. No uniform. No badge. He has dark hair and a kind face. "Hate to disturb. My name is Paul Jones. I manage this property, this house."

"Yes," Beverley says, her eyes darting to the front door when it opens and someone walks in.

It isn't Robert.

"I just wanted to let you know I have a plumber upstairs, working on that leaky faucet."

"A faucet is leaking?" she asks.

The man looks at a clipboard.

"Elizabeth Miller contacted me. I believe you've been working with her. She apparently noticed it. We won't be long. Be out of your hair real soon."

"I'm sorry," Beverley says, trying to shake off the cloudy feeling she hasn't been able to get rid of. "Who are you?"

"I manage this house for the owners," the man says, laying his card on the coffee table. "Paul Jones. I'm a childhood friend of Lily's. She called me about you all using the house."

"Yes, she mentioned you," Beverley says. "Mentioned that you helped. Thank you. For this. The house."

"We're all just real sorry about this happening to you and your family," he says. "I have a daughter of my own, Jenny, and I can't imagine."

The Final Episode

"Thank you," Beverley says. "Lily's been a godsend. I can't thank her . . ."

Her voice trails off. She's too tired for emotion. She can only handle the bare essentials of what she has to do. Getting up in the morning. Eating. Brushing her hair before going on air. Wondering if she was right to put her own husband on the list of suspects alongside a man like Levi Banks. She's strong enough to handle those things, but not to handle the soft touch of another person's kindness. Those good feelings only remind her how much she's lost. They're too sweet.

The man nods, understanding why Beverley can't finish her sentence. Like he understands all too well how kind Lily is.

"Ma'am," he says, dipping his head in that way southern men do, and turns to go.

The front door opens again. This time it's Agent Watson. As the two men pass, one coming, one going, they shake hands. The man who knows Lily gives Agent Watson his business card before disappearing out the front door.

Beverley reaches for the card the same man left her. Paul Jones. Lily's friend. When she looks up, Agent Watson stands over her. One hundred and one hours since she found Francie missing; she's counted every one of them, and this man's name is the only one other than Elizabeth's she can remember. She and Agent Watson have adapted to each other's rhythms. She knows his focus is Francie and not her. And he knows to get right to the point with Beverley. Like Elizabeth, he trusts Beverley to manage what's coming.

"You doing all right?" he says. He smiles and tilts his head, letting on that he's concerned about what he sees.

He has the same rumpled look as most of the people who have been in and out of the house over the past few days, though he had that look on the first day they met. No one is sleeping or eating.

"Yes, I'm fine," Beverley says, adding some spark to her voice as she holds up the card that reads *Paul Jones*. "Apparently there is a leaky faucet in the house."

If the agent sees weakness, he'll keep the hard things from her, and someone might try to give her pills again.

"May I speak with you for a moment?" he says.

"Robert's not back yet," she says.

"I'm aware," he says. "But I have to drive up to Tampa shortly."

"Is it bad, how long the test is taking?" she asks.

"They take time," he says. "Doesn't mean anything."

Beverley sinks back into the sofa. She hears in his tone that he's going to tell her something she doesn't want to hear. It's become a reflex already. Her muscles stiffen, and her stomach hardens, readying her to take the blow.

"The screen that was destroyed was a ruse," he says. "And the unlocked window was an attempt at misdirection."

"You've known that from the beginning," Beverley says. "If you listened to me, you've known that."

She told them on the first day that the window wasn't accidentally left unlocked. Because the windows were never opened. None of them. Whoever came into her house unlocked the window after he was inside. He didn't tear the screen to get in. He got in another way and tried to make it look like he came in through the window.

"We now believe it's possible the intruder was inside the house, perhaps for hours," the agent says. "A second possibility, and one we've already discussed, the intruder may have had access to a house key. A third, someone let him in. All are viable, given there is no forced entry."

"That's why you think it was Robert," Beverley says, shifting in her seat because she suddenly can't breathe. "Because he was already in the house."

"That's a set of facts we have to explore," the agent says. "That's all it means. Any person who gained entrance using a key would know the pool of people with that kind of access would be small. It would explain the effort to stage the window as the point of entry. He wanted it to look like a break-in."

Robert would have the same interest in staging a break-in.

The Final Episode

"I want you to know I really don't think Robert could have been involved," Beverley says. "I really don't. Elizabeth said leave no stone unturned. But I worry I made it sound like we argued about Francie."

Maybe she backpedals because it's too hard to believe Robert might have done this. If he did, she doesn't see how she'll survive. But if he were guilty, that would also mean she had an answer. That's the struggle. She doesn't know which will be harder to survive. Her husband being a monster or living her entire life with no answer.

"And you didn't argue?"

"We did, I guess," she says. "But he was only doing what a father does. He was pushing his daughter, guiding her to grow up, be independent. That's what fathers do. Isn't that what fathers do?"

"I really wouldn't know," Agent Watson says. "What I can say . . . you and Robert both gave a list of people who frequented the house and those few who had keys. Most have been easily dismissed. That's good. That's progress."

"Most?"

"One name is being stubborn."

Across the room, Lily Banks appears at the front door. Beverley meant to call her yesterday, and just as she knew she would, she forgot. But here she is. Lily. She glances around the house, and seeing Beverley, she smiles and starts toward her. Beverley lifts a finger, signaling for her to wait a moment.

"We're treating Levi Banks as a person of interest," the agent says, following Beverley's stare. He turns and sees Lily too. "That information won't be made public. I need to make that very clear to you."

"What does that mean?" Beverley asks, trying to swallow, but her throat catches and makes her cough. She shifts in her seat so Lily can't see her. "Person of interest?"

"Means we're looking at him very closely," the agent says. "But it doesn't mean he's guilty. To date, he's cooperated as to questioning, but he's declined our offer to take a polygraph."

"Declined your offer?" Beverley says.

"We can't compel him to take it," the agent says, tucking away his small pad of paper and pen, a sign he's preparing to leave. "But when a person refuses, we have to question why."

"And in the meantime?" Beverley asks.

"In the meantime, we continue to consider all avenues, his included."

"You said someone might have let him in," Beverley says, realizing the agent said something she's not considered before. "Did I hear that right?"

"No forced entry," the agent says. "And we have your sound recordkeeping and our investigation telling me it's highly unlikely that window was the point of entry. With no signs of forced entry, there are only so many ways in."

Earlier this morning when Daddy's footsteps stopped outside her bedroom, Jenny pretended she was asleep. Smelling like a hot shower and spicy cologne, he whispered that he was headed to work and would be gone all day, but she didn't answer. After she heard the front door close and his car drive off, she waited a long time more, staying in bed, eyes closed, even fell back to sleep, just to be sure he was gone.

That was almost two hours ago. Now, certain Daddy's gone for the day, Jenny dresses, pulls her hair into a sloppy ponytail, and heads downstairs for breakfast.

She didn't lie to Daddy. Pretending wasn't the same as lying. Even as she was doing it, she wasn't sure why she lied, pretended, but when she stacked up all the little pieces of what she'd seen yesterday and last night, she was certain Daddy didn't want her to know any of it. But she didn't know why.

After seeing Daddy with Lily Banks on the road the night before, Jenny went back inside, even though she was afraid of being in the dark house alone. She ran all the way up the stairs and into her room, put on dry clothes, stuffed the wet ones in her closet, and crawled into bed.

When the front door opened, she buried her face in the sheets and pinched her eyes closed. The sound of the rain grew instantly louder. Daddy should have stepped inside and closed the door quick, not wanting to let in any more rain, but that didn't happen. Instead, the door stayed open, as if maybe something made him stop what he was doing. As if maybe he noticed Jenny's wet footprints on the floor. Then the door closed.

Next, the bench in the entry creaked as Daddy sat to remove his shoes. There was another pause. Jenny could feel him looking at the terrazzo floors, at the rest of the dark house, maybe at the carpeted stairs. Maybe they were dented by her wet footprints. And then another creak as he stood.

Jenny rolled away from her bedroom door, balled herself up, and still hiding her face in the sheets, she breathed in the hot air she exhaled. The stairs squeaked.

"Jenn?"

Daddy stood in her doorway. She knew from the sound of his voice.

"You awake, hon? Sweetheart?"

Jenny held her breath.

"Just had to do a quick favor for Mrs. Banks," he said, still whispering.

Daddy did favors for Mrs. Norwood sometimes. Maybe Lily's roof was leaking. Maybe those gutters Daddy warned Mr. Banks about finally backed up. That was what Jenny hoped, but her seeing Daddy down at Nora's house, his arms wrapped around Lily, was a knot she couldn't unravel. She didn't know what to think.

"Lights are out," Daddy said. "Flashlight is in your top drawer if you need it. We can talk tomorrow."

Now, standing in the kitchen, Jenny wishes the daylight could wash away her seeing Daddy and Lily huddled together on the dark road. She closes her eyes, tips her face into the bright, warm light coming through the sliders. But then, she slips her hand in her back pocket and pulls out the pictures she cut from the newspaper yesterday. There are six in total. One is the picture of Daddy holding a candle outside Francie Farrow's house. Another shows Nora and her mama and daddy.

Much as she wants it to, the bright light can't wash away the pictures or articles she cut from the newspaper. It can't wash away her seeing Daddy with his arms wrapped around Lily Banks either.

Jenny drags a chair from the kitchen table over to the counter and climbs on. Daddy keeps the cereal he likes in the top cabinet where she can't reach it. He's been telling her lies or at the very least pretending. Never, not once, did he say he knew Francie Farrow or her family. He never once said he liked Lily enough to wrap her up in a hug and let her put her head on his shoulder. For that, she's going to eat his cereal and not feel bad about it.

When there's a knock on the door, she stumbles, nearly falls off the chair.

From the room where Daddy watches baseball, she looks out the front window. That's the rule when Daddy's not home. It's Tia and Mandy standing at the door. They look up at the window and wave. They know the rule too.

Just like yesterday, Jenny can't tell which one is Tia and which is Mandy. The smile she had when she first saw them fades. The two of them sneaked past her house yesterday and went to Nora's without her, and she spent the whole day alone.

"Hey," she says when she opens the door, chewing on her bottom lip instead of smiling.

"Hey."

One word is enough. That's Tia on the right.

"Your dad at work today?" Mandy asks, though she already knows he isn't home because his car isn't in the driveway.

Tia and Mandy both wear white shorts and tank tops with skinny straps. Tia looks different because her hair is combed smooth and pulled back from her face, and her tank top is tucked all the way in. Mandy looks different, too, because of the tilt of her head and the wide smile that pops into place the moment she's done talking.

"For a while, he is," Jenny says. "Why?"

Jenny's wearing a tank top, too, but hers has regular straps. She's been the different one from the beginning, and she's fallen even further behind. They have skinny straps. She has thick ones.

Tia and Mandy look at each other. Tia gives a nod like Mandy should go on.

"Nora says she's sorry for not asking you down yesterday," Mandy says. "She wanted us to come get you for today. She says we can go look for orchids if you want."

Jenny shrugs. She made eight orchids yesterday, all except the hot gluing part. And she can make that many more today. She'll have so many by her birthday, it won't matter that she never saw a real ghost orchid.

"I don't think I want to do that," Jenny says.

"Then what do you want to do?" Mandy says, stepping forward when Jenny starts to shut the door. "Whatever it is, we'll do it."

Tia and Mandy sneaking past Jenny's house yesterday hurt more than when the kids at school did the same. The kids at school were never her friends. She didn't miss any of them when they left her out.

"I'm going to make orchids," Jenny says. "Did the same yesterday. Got a lot made."

She's glad she didn't waste time moping. She kept so busy making orchids, she only felt bad about getting left out for a short while. Then she forgot about it, almost, until now.

"We can do that," Mandy says, nudging Tia so she'll say the same. "Nora can come here. That's perfect. She isn't really supposed to leave the house. But her mom's not home right now, and she said she would for you. To show you how sorry she is."

Jenny looks to Tia. She's hardly said anything since Jenny opened the door. She almost looks like she's sorry about something, and that makes Jenny wonder what she's sorry about.

"Is that okay?" Mandy says with that same wide smile. "If Nora comes here to your house?"

Dehlia says second sight is akin to intuition. She says sometimes it's hard to tell the two apart. They're both about knowing what is coming your way before it's come. It's about seeing the world for what it is, and you can only do that if you're not too busy thinking about yourself.

Having second sight means smelling trouble when it's still on a low simmer. And Jenny smells trouble.

As Agent Watson shakes Beverley's hand, tells her they'll talk again soon, and leaves, Lily approaches. Beverley lowers back onto the sofa, still thinking about what the agent told her. Levi Banks is a person of interest. She doesn't understand the difference between being a person of interest and a suspect, and she doesn't care. To her, they're one and the same.

Lily pauses to exchange a few words with Agent Watson. Her eyes are cast down the whole time, and she hugs herself, creating a barrier between them. Lily glances up at him long enough to smile and continues toward Beverley. At the sofa, she sits and gathers Beverley's hands. Like always, Lily's fingers are cool and light, and she smells like sunscreen. She's been out in the sun and fresh air. She's still coming and going because her life has continued.

"I brought more clothes for you and Robert," Lily says as she clings to Beverley's hands and glances at the front door.

Beverley looks too. Levi Banks stands in the entryway, looking larger than she remembered. Leaning against the threshold, his arms crossed, he looks like he's standing guard. When he catches Beverley looking at him, he dips his head in her direction.

"And a few other things I thought you might want," Lily says, talking to her lap now. She holds her head at an odd angle, slightly off center, as if she doesn't want to look Beverley in the eye.

As Lily continues to update Beverley on all the things she's done and brought and taken care of, Beverley studies her. If Levi weren't standing at the front door, Beverley would touch Lily's chin and turn her face so Beverley could see what she's hiding. Because she's definitely hiding something.

"Thank you," Beverley says when Lily is done, and instead of turning Lily's chin, she rubs her thumbs over the backs of Lily's tiny hands. "Thank you for everything. But I have to ask something else of you."

The shift is subtle. Maybe Beverley imagines it, but Lily seems to pull away, ever so slightly.

"I'd like to ask you to tell me what happened to your face," Beverley says.

As she waits for an answer, she keeps her eyes down so Levi won't guess that she's asked Lily about her swollen cheek, because that's what doesn't look quite right. It would be easy to miss. Lily has skillfully covered what must be a bruise, but she couldn't cover the slight swelling.

"It's nothing," Lily says, unable to stop herself from glancing in Levi's direction.

"It's not nothing," Beverley says.

She's seen the signs before and even asked Lily if she needed help on a few occasions. But there was always a well-rehearsed excuse. Not wanting to scare Lily off, Beverley would offer her help but not force it. She always ended those conversations by telling Lily that Beverley's was the number she could call anytime, day or night.

"Ran into a door is all," Lily says, delivering the excuse she most certainly had at the ready. "When I was here, in fact, just yesterday. All the people and equipment, I just tripped. But it's nothing. My own clumsiness."

"Lily," Beverley whispers, because Lily's lips roll in each time she pauses. She's hiding something, trying to trap the truth behind her tight lips. "Why did Levi hit you?"

"Your faucet should be fixed by now," Lily says, instead of answering Beverley. Her voice has shifted, her vocal cords tightening from the stress of the lie she told.

"Did he threaten you? Has he done something you want to tell me about?"

"And I've put more food in the refrigerator," Lily says, again ignoring Beverley's question. "There are also fresh sheets on your bed and clean towels in the bathroom."

"Do you know Levi refused a polygraph?" Beverley says, jostling Lily's hands so she'll look up. Her face is like a doll's, with her tiny chin and wide eyes and long, slender neck. Perfect, except for the slightly swollen cheek. "Before you answer, Robert is taking one. Today. Probably done by now. He has nothing to hide and has been asking to take it since day one."

Beverley has been clinging to those facts. As she told Agent Watson and Elizabeth about Robert pushing for a more normal life, she kept reminding herself that Robert agreed from the beginning to take the test. That has to be a good thing. That has to matter.

"But Beverley, Levi's already answered all their questions," Lily says, her eyes flicking in Levi's direction without her head moving. "He has nothing more to tell them."

"And if that were true, he'd take it."

"You don't know that," Lily says. "You don't know our family."

"You'll stay with us," Beverley whispers, the words barely clearing her lips. "Here, among all these police officers and FBI agents. You and Nora both. You'll be safe. You can stay with us forever if need be."

"You can't possibly think Levi would . . ."

"I do think," Beverley says, though she says nothing about Levi being a person of interest. She also doesn't say she's willing to consider her own husband, so considering Lily's is easy. "Prove me wrong. Convince him to take the polygraph. He'll be crossed off the list. That'll be an important step."

The Final Episode

Six months ago, Levi Banks helped Robert install a new garage door. He's cleaned their gutters, resodded the backyard, done countless repair jobs on their sprinkler system. Beverley pulled all the paperwork and the canceled checks. Levi and Lily are always in need of extra money. Beverley and Robert often spent time over dinner thinking up jobs they could give him. Having the Banks family close meant having Nora close, and Nora meant Francie had a friend.

"Levi was home with me that night," Lily says. "We went to bed at the same time. I've already told the police that, the FBI, everyone. He was with me when you called us. I know it, so what good would it do, him taking a test like that?"

Agent Watson calls it the window of opportunity. It's the time during which someone could have taken Francie. For some parents, it's the time when their child would have been walking home from school. For others, it's the amount of time they left their child home alone. For Francie, it was the hours she was asleep in her own room.

When first questioned, Nora told one of the detectives that she had no idea how long she laid in bed after the man took Francie. She had no idea if she fell asleep or lay awake the whole time, waiting for the first sliver of sunlight. Robert and Beverley went to bed at eleven o'clock, same as every night. Nora woke them the next morning. Right before dawn.

The window of opportunity for someone to have taken Francie is broad.

"And if all that's true," Beverley counters, though she does it softly, still rubbing the backs of Lily's hands, "if Levi was with you the whole time, what harm could the test cause?"

What she really wants to say is . . . how could Lily possibly know Levi was home? She was sleeping. He has access to a key to Beverley and Robert's house because Lily has one. He wasn't the imaginary intruder who waited in the house for hours after having snuck in. He was the one who used a key. He could have left Lily's bed and come back hours later, and Lily would never have known.

The window of opportunity gave him plenty of time.

There's also the possibility that Lily is lying because she's afraid. It's possible Levi wasn't home when she went to bed, and she knows it. Or it's possible she woke to find him gone and then heard him creep back to bed. But she'll also know from experience the price of making her husband angry.

"You're a good person, Lily," Beverley says, wanting to touch the swollen spot on Lily's face but knowing she can't. Levi will see. He'll know what they're talking about. "You don't deserve this. You don't want Nora to think it's acceptable, normal. You don't want her going through the same someday."

"You don't know what I've . . . ," Lily says, a breathy stream of words Beverley can barely hear. "You don't know what I deserve."

"Then tell me so I can help you," Beverley says, clinging to Lily. "Please. This is Francie we're talking about."

"And I will do everything I can to help find her," Lily says.

Beverley bites her bottom lip to stop herself from shouting at Lily.

"But you're not doing everything you can."

Lily pulls her hands from Beverley's and rests them in her lap.

"I wanted you to know," Lily says, her voice stronger, like she wants Levi to hear now. "We've moved out of our house. Temporarily. A few days ago. There were reporters all over us, and our phone wouldn't stop ringing. Levi said it wasn't good for Nora. I'm sorry I didn't tell you sooner."

"You moved?" Beverley says. "Where? Did you tell the police? Agent Watson?"

"We're staying at my parents' old place south of Naples," Lily says, straightening in her seat and looking forward instead of at Beverley. Her tone has shifted, gone flat. "I'll come back as often as I can to help you."

"You can stay here," Beverley says, and she can't help looking at Levi. She needs to stop Levi Banks from slipping away, stop them from leaving, though it sounds like they've already gone. "And the polygraph.

Please. Get Levi to take it. It'll help the police move on to other people. You should want that. Levi should want that."

But Beverley doesn't think anyone will move on because she thinks Levi did it. More so now than before. He's beaten Lily, maybe so she'll keep her mouth shut. He's moved his family away. He's desperate and on the run.

"I'm so sorry," Lily says. "We have to do what's right for Nora. I hope you understand."

Lily crosses the room quickly, never looking back. As she nears Levi, still standing at the front door, he latches on to the back of her neck. It's the same move he used the night of the candlelight vigil. Beverley thinks again that Lily looks like a doll. Next to Levi, she's tiny, her arms thin, her shoulders narrow and frail. And he's monstrous, thick in the chest, a head like a bulldog.

Before following his wife outside, Levi meets Beverley's eyes. She pushes to her feet, and as she does, Levi cocks his brows and dips his chin. He knows Beverley has given his name as a man with close ties to the family and its comings and goings.

He knows Beverley is onto him.

When Jenny opens the front door again, Nora stands between Tia and Mandy. Nora takes one big step, drawing the other two along with her as she walks into Jenny's house.

"We don't want Mrs. Norwood to see us," Nora says, pushing the door closed. "She knows my mom's gone, and I'm supposed to stay home. You don't mind, do you?"

Nora's thick, sweet perfume crowds Jenny, forcing her to take a step back.

"Look what we did," Nora says. She lifts both hands and wiggles her fingers, showing Jenny her long pink nails that glitter.

Mandy wiggles her fingers, too, but Tia shoves her hands in her pockets.

"Show me your lovely house," Nora says, sweeping up alongside Jenny, linking arms. She's always talking about being too scared to go outside, but she doesn't seem scared now. She doesn't seem mad, either, which must mean she didn't see her mama and Jenny's dad huddled under the umbrella last night.

Mandy links arms with Jenny on the other side. Together, they turn Jenny toward the stairs. Tia trails behind, and when Jenny glances back, she's looking at the ground, her hands still stuffed in her pockets.

"Show her your room," Mandy says. "Jenny has the best room, Nora."

But Jenny doesn't have the best room. She has an ordinary room. She starts to say so, but Mandy and Nora have already led her halfway up the stairs. She tries looking back at Tia again, hoping she'll say or do something. But the closer they get to the top stair, the farther Tia falls behind.

"I have a confession to make," Nora says, stopping outside Jenny's room.

"A confession?" Jenny says.

Her face feels hot, meaning it's turned red, and she's sweating. This is what being in over your head feels like. Daddy's always saying that if she finds herself in over her head, she should hightail it to higher, drier ground. But standing in her own hallway, outside her own room, Jenny isn't sure where to find higher, drier ground.

"We want to see what's in the owner's room," Nora says, pulling Jenny down the hall and waving at Tia to catch up. "Is that it? The one with the lock on it."

"I don't have a key," Jenny says. "Nothing to see in there anyway."

Nora nudges Mandy and gives her a wide-eyed look as if she wants Mandy to say something.

"You don't need a key," Mandy says. "You said you can get in any time you want."

Same as Tia has started dressing differently since Nora moved in, Mandy's changed too. She stands taller, sounds stronger, like she probably wouldn't be afraid to go into the swamp anymore.

"We just want to see," Nora says. "That's no big deal, is it? Mandy says your dad has stuff for hunting alligators in there. We just want to see it, that's all."

"We know you can get in," Mandy says. "Right, Tia? You've done it before."

One time, Jenny showed Tia how to sneak into the owner's room, and when Daddy caught them, they got a long lecture about how dangerous it was. They both promised to never do it again.

Hearing her name, Tia shrugs and nods. Jenny was hoping Tia would land on her side. But she doesn't.

"If you're really our friend," Nora says, playing her winning card, "you'll take us."

When Tia still says nothing, Jenny leads them all down the stairs, through the kitchen, and out the sliding glass doors to the lanai. She might have said no if Tia hadn't gone along with Mandy and Nora, but she did go along.

In the backyard, Jenny stands at the bottom of a ladder leading to the flat roof over the lanai. There's a sign screwed into the side of the house that reads . . . **USE ROOFTOP PATIO AT YOUR OWN RISK**. She rattles the ladder, making sure it's still anchored to the side of the house, then she makes a sweeping gesture as if to say . . . who wants to go first?

Tia steps forward. She's climbed the ladder before and wouldn't be afraid even if she hadn't. Nora goes next, smiling and not at all skittish. She's like Tia that way.

As soon as Nora reaches the flat roof, Mandy grabs hold of the ladder. For the first time since Nora moved in, Mandy looks like herself, like she's scared and wants to go home. But the look comes and goes in the amount of time it takes Mandy to draw in one deep breath. That's how much Mandy wants to be Nora's friend. She grabs the ladder and climbs it. Her wanting Nora as a friend is stronger than the fear that has followed her every day of her life.

Jenny is the last one to go. When she reaches the flat roof over the lanai, she nods at the small window on the second floor.

"We're going all the way up there?" Nora says.

"Yep," Jenny says. "Unless you don't want to. I mean, if you're scared . . ."

"It's okay if you don't, Nora," Mandy says, pressing against the house. "I'm not going any higher either."

"I didn't say I wasn't going higher," Nora said, spitting the words at Mandy.

"All right, then," Jenny says, squinting in the sun that shimmers on the black shingles. "Do just what I do. Exactly what I do."

Positioning her hands carefully on the two slanted roofs that meet to make a valley, Jenny takes a deep breath like Mandy did before climbing the ladder. The roof is hot under her hands, so she moves quickly. She wedges one foot in the valley. With her other foot, she bounces three times, pushing harder each time so the third bounce is enough to land her on the slanted roof. Once there, she swings around, sits, and looks back.

"Once you start," Jenny says, crouching so she can crab walk up the roof, "don't stop."

The three of them half crawl, half walk up the roof while Mandy stays behind, pressed tight against the house. At the small window, Jenny works her fingers under the bottom sill and pushes it open. She climbs through first, showing Tia and Nora how to slide through on their stomachs.

When they're all inside, Jenny stands in the middle of the room, the wall of shelves that holds Daddy's hooks, ropes, and spears behind her.

"This is it," she says, dropping down on an armchair with torn cushions. "He doesn't use any of it anymore. All rusty and stuff."

When neither Tia nor Nora say anything, Jenny glances at them, ready to apologize that it isn't better to look at. If Nora isn't happy, they'll all like Jenny less than they did before she got them into the owner's room.

"Where's he keep it?" Nora says to Tia, turning her back as if hoping Jenny won't hear.

Nora doesn't seem like someone dealing with troubling times anymore, like she was on the day she moved in. She seems like someone looking for trouble.

"Where's he keep what?" Jenny says, asking Tia because Nora asked Tia.

Tia crosses her arms, shifts from one foot to the other, but she doesn't answer. She doesn't answer even when Nora gives her a wide-eyed stare.

"The liquor," Nora says, turning to Jenny. "He keeps it in here, right?"

Jenny stares at Tia, but she won't meet Jenny's eyes. The one time Jenny and Tia snuck into this room together, they found bottles of liquor. It was two summers ago, and they didn't really know what it was. When Daddy walked in, he found them both sniffing a bottle they'd opened and making funny faces. He snatched it away, put it back, and made them both promise to stay clear. That was the same day he bought a big storage cabinet at a garage sale, one that had a lock on it.

"Yes, he keeps it here," Jenny says, trying not to look at the cabinet. "He's got lots of stuff in here."

"Show us," Nora says, standing too close to Jenny.

Even though she doesn't want to show them anything, Nora standing that close makes Jenny afraid of what comes next if she doesn't.

Pulling a stool over to the door that leads to the hallway, Jenny slides a hand along the top molding, knocking a small key to the ground. Her hands are shaking as she waves Nora and Tia out of the way and steps up to the cabinet. She works the key into the lock.

"Why's he got to lock it?" Nora asks, pushing past Jenny to yank open the cabinet door. "Room's already locked."

"In case a kid got in here, some stuff still needs to be locked up. He puts guns and stuff in it."

Jenny steps back as Nora shifts the bottles around, looking at the labels and lifting them to test how heavy they are. She pulls out a clear bottle that's full.

"This'll taste like water," she says. "And no smell either."

"You're taking it?" Jenny asks, looking from Nora to Tia and back again.

Tia is already at the window, climbing on the plastic tubs to get out.

"Why else would we come all this way?" Nora says as if Jenny should have known all along.

Going down is easier for everyone except Jenny because she carries the bottle. On the walk back to Nora's, Jenny carries it, too, keeping it hidden under her shirt. At first, it's heavy and slows down every step, but as they fall into a group of four and Nora is happy because her mama's car still isn't in the driveway, Jenny starts feeling like for the first time a door that slammed shut has opened again.

Once they're in Nora's bedroom, Nora holds out her hand, palm up. Jenny passes off the bottle, damp from having been pressed against her skin.

"You did great, Jenny," Nora says, grabbing Jenny's hand and squeezing, and nothing has ever felt so good so fast. "We all think so."

And then Nora goes on and on, recreating for Mandy the part of the trip she skipped by staying behind. She makes it sound like her greatest adventure ever.

"You should have seen Jenny," Nora says. "She was so amazing."

Most of what Nora is saying is made up, but Jenny still loves hearing it. She loves pretending she was amazing and brave. And Tia pretends, too, because she nods along and smiles like it's all true.

"We can't do a sleepover tonight, because my dad is going to be home," Nora says. "But tomorrow night we can. Is tomorrow night all right with you, Jenny?"

The Final Episode

The summer is back to being a good summer, one with friends and things to do. And being invited back to Nora's also means Jenny might hear more stories about Mama. Even after seeing Lily huddled up next to Daddy out in the rain, she still wants to hear those stories.

"And I'll hide the vodka in my closet," Nora says, holding the bottle up to the sunlight for a better view. "That way, we'll have it for later."

Just like that, Jenny is back to worrying. Nora is going to hide the bottle of vodka so they'll have it for later, and Jenny is afraid of what Nora will want to do when later comes.

FADE OUT:

CHAPTER 9

Driving through the gate and locking it behind me, I rolled slowly past the house where Nora lived for less than two weeks that one summer. I looked for any signs she was inside. The cracked driveway was empty. The weeds that had taken over the sidewalk leading to the front door were undisturbed. I let my eyes slide across the dark windows on the front of the house. But same as it had been for the past twenty years, the house was still and quiet. Even when it had been offered up as a rental, not many people bit.

Once past Nora's, I next got a good look at Tia and Mandy's house up ahead and knew exactly why the gate hung open. I let out a long breath that made my lips flutter and rolled my shoulders to loosen the tension I always carried there.

A set of muddy tire tracks ran down the middle of the Norwoods' drive. Someone from the property management company must have come early that morning to check on the place. It had rained first thing, and they tracked mud onto the driveway. When they left, they didn't remember to lock the gate.

Nearing Dehlia's drive, I moved from worrying about the lock on the gate to worrying how to explain to Dehlia why I was suddenly moving back in with her. I'd need to tell her something that didn't include Mrs. Farrow and her cinder block. I was also thinking of all the projects that needed doing at Dehlia's, because unlike the Norwoods' well-tended place, at Dehlia's, plants were growing in the gutters, the paint was peeling, and the yard was mostly weeds.

As much as I liked order and checking things off my list, doing anything at Dehlia's place was a challenge. It was hard for me to be there, and it was hard for Dehlia to see anything change. She'd rather see it broken and unchanged than fixed and new. She didn't want any part of you painted over, replaced, or even fixed.

Pulling into the drive and already overwhelmed by how bad the place had gotten, I hit the brakes hard. Robert Farrow's sedan was straight ahead. Again.

Throwing the car in park, I scrambled to clip Belle's leash to her collar and jumped out. Stumbling first over Belle and then over the pavers leading to the front entry, I unlocked the door. Once inside, I set Belle loose and called out to Dehlia.

Mr. and Mrs. Farrow had never shown up at Dehlia's house, not once since I moved into my own place. It was an unspoken agreement. Or so I assumed. I also thought Beverley Farrow would never throw a cinder block through a window. I was wrong about the cinder block and wrong about the Farrows never troubling Dehlia, so maybe I was wrong about Mrs. Farrow breaking into my backyard.

Getting no response from Dehlia, I crossed the entryway. My flip-flops slapped the terrazzo floors, echoing in the quiet house. In the kitchen, I found two empty chairs and two coffee cups. One was half full of black coffee. The other, orange juice. Dehlia always took her juice in a coffee cup, and that meant only one guest. That meant only Robert Farrow had come.

Continuing to call out, I looked in the TV room. The chair where you always sat to watch ball games still stood in the middle of the room, empty. Somewhere nearby, Belle was whining. While I hadn't found Dehlia, Belle had. I followed her whine back to the kitchen. She stood at the wall of sliders that looked out on the backyard, her tail wagging.

Nudging her aside so she didn't slip out of the house, I stepped onto the screened-in porch. Dehlia and Robert Farrow stood near the creek, under the shade of an oak. Dehlia was pointing, and Mr. Farrow was hunched over as if trying to get a better view of something deeper in the swamp. They both turned at the sound of my flip-flops popping off my heels. They were smiling, and when Dehlia saw me, she clapped her hands.

"And right there she is," she said. "Just a few more days and we'll have another chance. Jenny's birthday is right around the corner. Margaret will come this time. Isn't that right, Jenny? This will be the year for sure."

I walked across the grass, arms crossed. Robert Farrow stepped forward. I shook his hand. It was cold, even though the day was already hot and muggy. He took another step, putting us closer than we had ever been.

He smelled like a fresh shower, like soap and warm water. Near his left ear, he'd missed a dab of shaving cream. I wanted to wipe it away because I used to do the same for you. But all I could do was stare at it. That small splotch of white cream paralyzed me.

"Your grandmother was just telling me that your father will be home soon," Mr. Farrow said, smiling down on me as if he were happy about the news. "She says it's your doing. I'm curious about what you've done to make that so."

"It's her destiny," Dehlia said. "It's the same for all the Scott women. Jenny's one great thing will be bringing my Paul home."

Robert Farrow dipped his head at me, squinting in the morning sun that filtered through the oak's thick canopy.

"Is that true?" he said. "Is your father coming home?"

Staring down on me, he pressed a kerchief to his nose to block out the stench coming off the swamp.

"I'm wondering what you know," he said, "that I don't."

CHAPTER 10

Mr. Farrow and I left Dehlia near the creek where she was still looking for something out in the trees. It had been twenty years since Dehlia and I last sat on a blanket in the backyard, waiting for Margaret Scott to appear out of the swamp. I truly thought she'd steer me toward a future where I'd do something as great as she'd once done.

Dehlia still believes the blood in our veins matters. I know it doesn't.

As Mr. Farrow and I neared the house, I directed him around the side yard instead of taking him inside.

In the driveway, I guided him into the shade. I could feel him looking at me, waiting for me to say something. But I had questions of my own.

"It wasn't Beverley," Mr. Farrow said before I could ask. "She did not come to your house last night."

"You sure about that?"

Robert Farrow being at Dehlia's made me angry, and my being angry made me more inclined to believe it had been Mrs. Farrow I saw on my camera.

"I am," he said. "The police came to see us early this morning. Asked us about our whereabouts."

"And how can you be so sure? She goes off all the time without you knowing it."

"I took her keys yesterday after supper," he said. "Like you asked. She doesn't know it yet because she hasn't tried to go anywhere."

"Why are you here, Mr. Farrow?" I said, the harsh tone of my voice making him take a backward step and calm me with two raised hands.

"I've been calling, but you wouldn't answer. The police suggested I not return to your house, so I drove down here just hoping to check in with Dehlia. I was worried after learning what happened to you from the police."

"Did you tell Dehlia?" I glanced over my shoulder to make sure she wasn't listening.

"No," he said. "Were you hurt? Did they get inside?"

I shook my head, stared at him, and studied his eyes. They reminded me of yours, a father's eyes. Concern. Relief. He was telling me the truth, and his kindness was making it hard for me to stay angry.

Mr. Farrow would have told me if Mrs. Farrow was the one sneaking around my backyard. He'd have told me so I wouldn't be frightened. That left Nora. Or a stranger. Or a neighbor with a cat. Which meant it could have been anyone. Except I had this instinct, this bad feeling—certainly not second sight—making me circle back to Nora's name every time.

"I didn't intend to come inside," Mr. Farrow said. "Dehlia opened the gate, invited me up to the house. Insisted. She wanted help looking for a key of some sort. One that belonged to your father, according to Dehlia."

"I'm sorry she troubled you," I said, disappointed to hear Dehlia had lost something again. I worried every time something of hers turned up missing that it was because of more than just carelessness. I worried time and age were getting the better of her.

"No trouble, but it's concerning, her inviting me in like that. I thought you'd want to know."

"I'll talk to her about it," I said, trying to be patient but also wanting him to leave.

"And your father coming home?"

"None of what she said is true," I said, trying to look him in the eye so he'd be convinced I was telling the truth and leave. "He isn't coming home. Not until his sentence is done."

I didn't want him to sense the one small part of me that hoped you would. I hoped it even though I had no reason to.

I didn't want him to know about all the times I sat in the prison parking lot, not even trying to get through security because I knew the guards would look on your list and not see my name. I couldn't tell him that you wouldn't see me because you wanted me to go on with my life. I couldn't tell him about all the letters I've written to you, either, letters that include ones written with the wobbly handwriting of a child all the way up to the one I write now. All of them, letters I keep writing though you'll never read them. Because after all these years and everything I know, I still can't let you go.

That's the part that haunts me most. I don't think I'm supposed to struggle like this. I think hating you is supposed to be easier and feel just. And I guess it would if all of me could believe you were guilty.

"Your grandmother, she seemed adamant," Mr. Farrow said, pivoting from concern back to suspicion. "I feel there's something I should know."

"He's her family. She believes in him. Believes he's innocent, that he'll be released early. It's wishful thinking."

"And do you believe in your father like Dehlia does?"

"What I believe doesn't matter," I said, crossing my arms.

He studied me as if he knew everything I was hiding and feeling, as if he knew I couldn't let you go and he was deeply disappointed.

"Beverley is afraid of losing you," Mr. Farrow said after a long pause. "You should know that. Afraid the final episode will leave her hating you. We've watched you grow up. She's given you thought and worry she couldn't give her own daughter. Maybe she didn't even want to, but she couldn't help it. She knows she's caused you pain and that she's scared you. But she loves you too."

His words swirled around me, squeezing until I could hardly breathe. I'd been carrying their sorrow, trying to lighten their load, since I was eleven years old. Instead, I'd made it heavier by being a walking, talking reminder of Francie. They'd had to watch me grow up in the spot where their daughter should have been.

"I am really trying, Mr. Farrow. I have no idea how painful it's been for you and Mrs. Farrow all these years. But please, no matter what we learn when the final episode airs, don't come back."

He nodded, deeply and slowly to let me know he understood and to give my request room to breathe.

I heard the whine first, the screen door over at Tia and Mandy's being pushed open. It was like an echo that traveled across twenty years to land at my feet. I knew the slap that would follow as Tia, because Tia always walked out first, let the door fall closed behind her.

My eyes slid from Mr. Farrow to Tia and Mandy's house. A young woman walked out. She had long blond hair and wore tan shorts and a simple white T-shirt. Tia. I knew it was her and not Mandy, same as I knew it when they were kids. They looked exactly alike and yet they were entirely different.

Mr. Farrow turned, looking where I looked. He raised a hand, not at all surprised to see Tia standing across the road. He'd already seen her, talked to her.

"I only want to give my wife some peace," Mr. Farrow said, looking like he wanted to reach out and squeeze my arm, to comfort me like a father would. But he didn't. "All these years, we've wanted good things for you. I hope we can want the same after we all find out what really happened that summer. I'd be sad to feel differently."

CHAPTER 11

After Mr. Farrow left, promising again he wouldn't come back, no matter what played out in the final episode, Tia and I stood in the middle of the road, same as we did every morning of every summer before those summers ended. I was swept back to being ten years old. I smelled sunscreen, felt sticky bug spray on my arms and legs, and my insides swelled with the feeling of waking to warm sunlight every summer morning and wondering what new thing Tia and I would do that day.

"You haven't changed," Tia said.

"And you . . . you remind me so much of your mama."

In the years since Tia and I last saw each other, she'd grown to look like a blond version of her mother. Petite and strong like a gymnast, yet because of the way she held herself, she didn't seem small.

Tia is a public defender now, which won't surprise you. Dehlia told me that a few years back. Not sure how she knew.

"How is she?" I asked. "Your mother?"

"Still remembers me," Tia said. "Usually. I've been coming down here about once a month to see her for the last year. Always stay at the house in Naples. I would have called . . ."

"But your plate was full," I said, giving her an out.

You probably don't know that Mrs. Norwood was diagnosed with early-onset Alzheimer's a handful of years ago. I've been to see her a few times. She's still in there, the mom who always had the camcorder running. I sometimes wonder if she was so intent on capturing every memory back then because she somehow knew she'd lose hers one day.

"I'm bringing her up north with me," Tia said. "Before things get really bad."

"I hope you'll tell her hello," I said.

"It was nice of you to go see her," Tia said. "The nurses told me."

I nodded, and we stood in that awkward silence that swells between two people who were once close but had grown into strangers. We were both grasping for the one thread we could tug that would draw us back together. As we tried, we glanced around at the familiar landscape, her looking one way, me the other.

"Think he's still there?" Tia asked, nodding toward the end of the road.

That was all she had to say. She'd tugged the perfect thread. Twenty years vanished in a *poof*, and we tumbled right back into the familiar rhythm we'd carved out as children. Tia, the bold one. Mandy, the voice of caution and reason. Me, somewhere in between. I'd fit there so perfectly, and feeling it again, I realized I hadn't fit anywhere since that last summer. Not quite. Not in that same perfect way.

"Dehlia still sees him sometimes," I said of the alligator who had to have been ancient even when we were kids. "But who knows if it's the same one."

"I still have nightmares about him," Tia said, shivering as if remembering.

I took a breath to say what was next . . . that it was good to see her, that she was the last best friend I had . . . when the good feeling withered and a question pushed its way to the front. The change must have shown in my face. Maybe I even took a step away.

"It wasn't me," Tia said before I could ask. "Flew in just this morning. Drove straight here and got in just in time to see Robert Farrow pull in Dehlia's drive."

"And he told you about my overnight visitor?" I asked.

"He did," she said. "And he asked me the same thing you were about to."

"I'm sorry," I said. "Whole thing just has me on edge."

"What did the police say?" Tia leaned close as if not wanting to miss anything I said. It was a glimpse of what she must have been like in her work life. Focused. Thorough.

"Said it was telling that the break-in happened the night after the show aired," I said. "They also said it might have been a neighbor looking for a cat. So, who knows?"

"I don't think it was a neighbor with a lost cat," Tia said. She didn't smile. She wasn't making a joke.

"You know something I don't?"

"I think it was Nora," Tia said, not shy about barreling ahead. She never was. "And I'm guessing you do too."

"Maybe," I said, not willing to let on that I kept circling back to Nora's name for no good reason. "Seems a little far-fetched, though. Why me after all these years? Why now?"

"How often have you been asked if you know what's going to happen in the final episode?" she said.

"More than I can count."

"There you go," Tia said. "Maybe she's looking for a little inside information on how it's all going to end. Maybe she's worried about what might come out."

"So not revenge?" I said, because that was what the police officer in my living room first suggested, if not in his exact words. It was in the way he dipped his head at me and punctuated his warning. Keep an eye out, he had said. Lock your doors and windows.

"Could be, but in my experience, people are more motivated by saving their own ass than by getting revenge."

"But what did she expect to learn creeping around my house?"

"No telling. Point could have been to scare you, which is exactly what happened."

"Did Mr. Farrow tell you she got in trouble for stealing?" I said. "Hasn't been seen since? It's been ten years, he said."

"So, she's no saint," Tia said. "That surprise you? Also means she's most likely going by a new name."

"Police said Nora had skin in the game," I said, shaking my head, because no, I wasn't surprised she was no saint.

I struggled to remember what Nora looked like, but I remembered the feel of her, the way she filled a room, the way she worked the people in it. Being around Nora was like walking on a sharp-edged knife. One wrong step, you either fell off or got cut. Both had happened to me in the time I knew her.

"When's the last time you saw Nora?" Tia said.

"The night my dad was arrested. You?"

"At the hospital the day after," Tia said.

There it was again. After.

"Mandy went into her room, sat with her for a while," Tia said, glancing back at her house like she was expecting someone to walk out the front door. "I stayed in the hall. Didn't want to see her, not after what she did to Mandy. Mandy was much kinder than I am. Always was. Too kind, probably. I could tell it scared her, seeing Nora, talking to her. And after that day, she went on being scared of Nora. And I never knew why."

Another silence opened up, like we were both stuck thinking about that summer and couldn't find our way back. Tia gathered her hair and lifted it off her neck. I used a sleeve to dry the sweat running down the sides of my face.

"How long you staying?" I finally said.

"Until I can get this place on the market," Tia said. "Figured it was time to sell."

"And Mandy?" I said, glancing at Tia's house, expecting to see Mandy walk out, arms crossed, moving slowly, hesitantly. "How's she feel about selling?"

The Final Episode

Tia looked away and cringed as if something in her gut hurt. That was enough. I knew what came next, and I pressed a hand over my mouth. Tia had given me a hint by talking about Mandy in the past tense. Mandy was so much nicer than me, Tia had said.

"Oh, Tia," I said. "I'm so sorry. What happened?"

"Four weeks ago," Tia said, and her face changed. Her jawline sharpened. Her lips pressed into a hard line. "It was that damn show. And a whole lot of pills."

Even as a kid, Mandy struggled to hold on. She was constantly trying to outmaneuver whatever frightening thing might pop up next. She must have been so tired.

"She talked to one of the producers, I guess," Tia said. "Back when they were still doing their research, still trying to decide if Francie's case was something they'd take on. They tried to talk to me, too, but I said no."

"I'm sorry, Tia," I said again. They were weak words, but the only ones I could manage.

"She called out of the blue, shortly before she died," Tia said, and she began shifting from side to side as if uncomfortable with something she was about to say. "I didn't hear much from her these past years. Really, since college. And she didn't say much the day she called, either, only that she wished she'd never met Nora. And she also asked me to tell you that she was sorry."

"Me?" I said. "Why would she apologize to me?"

I hadn't seen Mandy in over twenty years, Tia either. But Mandy was thinking about an apology to me in the final days before she took her own life. And that scared me.

"Everyone thinks the show found Francie Farrow," I said slowly, inching up on the reason for Mandy's apology.

Tia nodded, meaning she thought so too.

"Mandy must have known something about Francie's case," I said. "She must have told the show the thing that will finally implicate my dad. And that's why she was sorry."

I stared at the end of the driveway where Mandy always stood, feet planted squarely on the ground, arms crossed, afraid but trying her best not to look it.

"Part of me always thought it was Levi Banks who took Francie, and that Nora was covering for him," I said. "But that wouldn't explain why Mandy felt she owed me an apology."

Tia let out a long sigh like she thought the same.

"Don't make too much of it," she said, but that was just her being kind. "You can't assume anything. But I had to tell you. I promised her."

Since the series dropped its first episode, I've had the silliest notion, one that won't let me be. Wishful thinking, I suppose. I thought . . . what if the final episode sets you free? Somehow. Someway. Free from all of it. Free from what you did to Nora. Free from what so many think you did to Francie. That was what the show did last time. It set an innocent man free.

Now, hearing about the toll Mandy's secrets took on her, that's a notion I don't think I'll have anymore. Mandy must have felt the need to apologize to me because she knew she had sentenced you to death when she sat down with the show and finally told someone all her secrets.

You did it. You took Francie. You killed her. That has to be what Mandy told the show. And my wafer-thin hope that you're the father I once thought you were is lost.

EPISODE 5

**INT. RENTAL HOUSE - BEVERLEY'S BEDROOM - DAY
(5 days missing)**

Beverley sits on the end of her rental-house bed, staring at her shoes. They're mismatched. She didn't have Elizabeth to help her pick them out today. She spent her entire morning talking to people across the country on three different networks, and she had been wearing two different shoes.

Today, as she settled in front of the camera, Elizabeth told her to be more vulnerable. Show the stress, the pain. We need people to stay engaged. That meant people were drifting. They were moving on to other concerns, leaving Francie behind. So Beverley did what Elizabeth suggested. As she spoke to the black shimmer that was the camera lens, she tried to imagine it was her best friend. But her best friend was Francie. And when that thought slipped into her mind as she was stumbling through an answer about the thousands of acres of swampland in southern Florida, she realized her mistake.

She put Francie in the past tense. Francie is Beverley's best friend. Dear God, *is*, not was.

By the time the interview ended, she was sobbing and apologizing to the black lens, begging it to forgive her. And then she was screaming, afraid Francie couldn't hear her.

Someone ended the broadcast. She doesn't know who. When she finally lifted her head and lowered her hands from her face, Elizabeth was sitting next to her, and the room was cleared.

"That's all for today," Elizabeth said. "I think you need to take some time. I'm *certain* you need to take some time."

Now, Beverley's sitting on the end of the bed, two different shoes on her feet. Though the sun is full in the sky, the bedroom is dark. Neither she nor Robert bother opening the blinds when they get up in the morning. Or maybe they keep them closed because signs of sunlight are signs of another day they must face without Francie.

"Come in," Beverley says to a quiet tap on her door, staring at the chair where Robert will drape his clothes at the end of the day.

She knows it's Elizabeth even before the door opens. She heard the footsteps coming down the hall. Heavy, fast. Elizabeth is always in a hurry, and that's one of the reasons Beverley trusts her. No matter how tired Beverley gets, Elizabeth is running on high.

"Wanted to let you know that you and Robert can go back home," she says, standing in the open doorway. "Police are done over there."

Beverley glances up and squints. The light flooding in from the hallway strains her eyes.

"Not sure which is worse," Beverley says. "Staying here or going home."

"Either way, you should wait a bit before going back," Elizabeth says. "A few volunteers are over there now, doing some cleaning. Dust from the fingerprint work. Some muddy footprints you won't like."

Stepping into the room, Elizabeth closes the door behind her. The room falls dark again.

"I think we need to get you out of here," Elizabeth says, grabbing a black shoe from the closet that matches one of the shoes Beverley is wearing. "Get you a little fresh air. This morning, that was tough. You're not taking care of yourself."

"Did I look pale?" Beverley asks, because pale doesn't play well on camera. She's been told that a few times already.

She wonders why. Does pale make her look insincere? Detached? Guilty?

"I'm not talking about the camera," Elizabeth says, handing Beverley the shoe and lingering near the door. "You should come down to the check-in site with me. It would do you good to get out of this house and see how many people are looking for Francie."

She's taking more care with Beverley than usual. That's a sure sign this morning was really bad. Seeing Beverley have a breakdown like that, one that seemingly came out of nowhere, people will wonder what brought it on. What is taking its toll? they'll wonder. Is it sorrow? Is it pain? Is it maybe guilt? Guilt can take an awful toll. They won't understand the pain of a simple slip of the tongue.

"Robert is managing better down there," Elizabeth says. "If nothing else, you'll see some familiar faces. People want to help you, support you. Let them."

"You should take them all that food, the volunteers," Beverley says. "People are still bringing it, and the freezer's full."

"Robert's results should come back soon," Elizabeth says, nodding that she'll see to the food. "From the polygraph."

"So I've heard."

That's why Beverley has been sitting here in the dark. She's been waiting for someone to come and tell her. When Robert came back from the police station yesterday, he said that the examination went better than the day before, that he kept it together. He looked relieved. She was terrified.

Robert being relaxed meant that soon, he'd be cleared. And once he was, there was no other path. Agent Watson only talks about physical proof and alibis, and he puts no stock in the deep-down feeling Beverley has about Levi Banks. We don't arrest people on a feeling, he keeps saying. If there is no trail leading to Levi and if Robert is cleared, then Francie is lost. The police, the FBI, they have no one else.

"How old were you?" Beverley asks. "When it happened to you?"

"This isn't a good idea," Elizabeth says. "My experience isn't Francie's."

"But you're here," Beverley says. "That says something. It says there's hope."

"I'd like to think there's always hope."

"Was it a family member, a family friend?"

Elizabeth shakes her head. She's closing herself off again. Crossing her arms, leaning against the closed door, putting space between the two of them. Beverley is causing her pain by asking her to conjure the name of the person who took her, but Beverley needs to hear it. She needs reassurance that the statistics are true. It's almost always a family member or someone close to the family. Almost always. They can find someone who's close.

"Have you seen Lily Banks today?" Beverley says when Elizabeth doesn't answer.

"No," Elizabeth says. "Might be down at the check-in. Want me to find her, send her here?"

"I don't think she's at the check-in," Beverley says.

Lily won't be out in the heat because the makeup would wear off her bruise. She's been hit before, and she'll know how to keep her secret safe.

"Can you get me a car?" Beverley says, standing and smoothing her skirt. "I have no idea where my keys are."

"Got my car. Can take you wherever you want to go."

"I have an address," Beverley says. "Probably take about an hour to get there."

Beverley found the information on the appraiser's website. The house is in Lily's name now, not her parents. That's where Lily will be, where no one will wonder how she got that black eye.

"Is something going on, Beverley?" Elizabeth says. "Anything I need to be concerned about?"

Beverley shakes her head. Agent Watson already said that he couldn't force Levi to take a polygraph. They questioned him. He cooperated. And Lily's story matched up with his. They went to bed together at just past midnight. And he was lying next to her when Beverley called in the morning. The agent said it like there was nothing else he could do.

The Final Episode

But there is something more Beverley can do. Levi Banks is someone close to the family, and it's almost always someone close to the family.

Jenny sits on the floor of Nora's room, all her orchid-making supplies spread out before her. For the second day in a row, Nora is conditioning her hair, and Tia and Mandy are helping. They did the same yesterday after they stole the vodka. Every so often, Jenny takes a break from her orchid making and glances at the closet. She can feel the vodka bottle in there where Nora hid it, sitting in a dark corner, ready to explode into a mess of trouble.

Same as yesterday, Tia is in charge of making sure the towel doesn't slip off Nora's shoulders, and Mandy is making sure every strand is coated with the silky, coconut-scented conditioner. When they finish the hair conditioning, they're going to page through all Nora's magazines and look for the cards that have perfume on them so they can rub it on their wrists.

When Jenny got invited back today to spend the afternoon and stay for a sleepover, she brought her orchid-making tub. She didn't care about rubbing perfume-scented postcards on her wrists, and she for sure didn't want to do it for the second day in a row.

Now, she's finished making eight piles, each one with everything a ghost orchid needs, and she's ready for the hot-glue gun. But the rule about gluing is the same at Nora's house as it is at Jenny's.

Pushing to her feet and shaking out her one foot that tingles from being asleep, Jenny grabs two piles, all she can carry by herself. Tia jumps up and helps her by opening the door and then goes back to her towel-holding duties.

In the kitchen, Jenny drops the parts and pieces on the table. Lily Banks stands at the counter where she's leaning into an orange slice as she grinds it on a juicer. Staring at a blank spot on the wall, she doesn't see Jenny at first. When she does, she pops a smile in place.

"You can plug in over there," Lily says, continuing to lean on the orange slice.

Plugging in the hot-glue gun, Jenny begins sorting everything into piles again. She's hoping to hear more about Mama but is afraid to ask.

"Not interested in painting your nails?" Lily asks, glancing up from her work.

"It's hair conditioning right now," Jenny says.

Maybe she's supposed to want to rub thick white lotion in her hair and perfume on her wrists, but she doesn't. She didn't think Tia would like those things, either, but so far, she does.

"You know, your mama used to like this cake," Lily says.

"She ate one of your cakes?" Jenny pushes back from the table and sits up tall, ready to grab hold of every word Lily says about Mama.

Daddy hardly ever talks about Mama. It makes him sad, and he never says things about what she ate or what she liked. He just says how much she loved Jenny, which doesn't seem likely since she was dead before getting a single glimpse of her baby. The moment part of Jenny seeped into Mama's blood, she started to die. Mama was allergic to her. Daddy doesn't like to say it that way, but that's what happened. Jenny seeping through Mama's veins is what killed her.

"It was her favorite, as I remember," Lily says, swiping the hair from her eyes with her forearm and taking care not to touch herself with her sticky hands. She makes a funny face, as if she hit a sore spot when trying to push her hair aside. "She liked anything that made her pucker a bit."

That's the same as Jenny. She likes things that are just sour enough to make her eyes pinch closed, her shoulders pop up around her ears, and her whole body shiver.

"This area, all of Naples, was a small town back then," Lily says, grinding on a second orange half. "Everyone knew everyone. We went to the same school, your mama and me. I like remembering her, having a reason for talking about her. I imagine it's bittersweet for your daddy to see you growing up to look so much like her."

Jenny picks up a pipe cleaner and a piece of felt, but she can't touch them together in the right spot because her hands are shaking so bad.

The Final Episode

She stops thinking about Lily and Daddy out in the rain and instead hopes Lily never runs out of stories.

"She loved you up one side and down the other," Lily says, taking a break from grinding the orange as she says it. "She'd be real proud of you, the young lady you're becoming."

Lily stares off at that blank spot on the wall again as if she's thinking more about Jenny's mama, and Jenny wishes she could see everything Lily is seeing and know everything Lily knows.

"She was like you," Lily says, turning to study Jenny. "Had your same hair and coloring, of course. But she had the same quiet way about her, too, quiet but strong. She listened more than she talked and always seemed to know what came next. Like she saw more when she looked at the world. That's like you, isn't it?"

Even though Lily doesn't know it, as she describes Mama's way of seeing the world, she's describing second sight. She's telling Jenny that Mama had second sight for sure. Lily also said she thinks Jenny, like Mama, sees more of the world. Jenny's never thought of herself that way, but maybe she does see more. She's been wondering when she'd know for certain she had second sight, and now, maybe she does.

Second sight has always been confusing to Jenny. Her wanting something and being afraid of it at the same time doesn't make much sense. What isn't confusing . . . she can't let on that she has it. Already, Jenny covers up the second sight simmering inside her. She misses test questions on purpose and turns the pages slow when she reads. Her being too good at anything ends with finger-pointing and name-calling. Be proud of who you are, Dehlia is always saying, but be careful who you turn your back on. People can be hateful toward things they don't understand.

When the doorbell sounds, Lily wipes her hands and starts toward the door. The lost, faraway look on her face vanishes and is replaced by a puzzled look, like she doesn't know who it could be. Whoever it is, Jenny wants them to go away so Lily can go back to a place where she's remembering Mama.

"Might be your daddy," Lily says, the confused look replaced by a smile. "He was going to bring by an extra sleeping bag."

Jenny leans on the table, the felt and pipe cleaner still in hand, hot glue dripping from the tip of the glue gun. She doesn't want to move until she thinks hard on everything she's learned about her mama and tucks it in good and tight so she never forgets it.

"Beverley," Lily says when she opens the door. "My goodness. How are you? Please, come in. And Elizabeth. Yes, please, both of you, come in."

Jenny swings around in her chair, and there is Francie Farrow's mama standing in Nora's living room, a real live person. She looks exactly like she looks on TV and in the newspaper. She glances in Jenny's direction. Jenny sinks into her chair and stares, wondering if it could really be her.

Mrs. Farrow looks like a woman from an old movie. She's beautiful and tall, and her hair falls in loose, soft curls down her back. Except for her sadness. Like thick, chalky smoke, it trails her into the house, rolls around her feet and across the floor. Jenny clings to her chair, afraid of what will happen when the sadness reaches her.

"This is Jenny Jones," Lily says, sweeping a hand in Jenny's direction. "She's been a good friend to Nora. You met her father. He's the real estate agent handling the rental. Jenny, this is Mrs. Farrow and Miss Miller. Come in, please."

The two women glance at Jenny, but they don't say anything. Jenny doesn't know what to do. Should she smile? Should she say she's sorry about Francie? Should she tell Mrs. Farrow about her birthday and her one great thing that is going to be finding Francie?

But before Jenny can do any of that, Mrs. Farrow closes her eyes and takes a deep breath. She's readying herself to do or say something, and it's going to be something bad.

"We won't be long," Mrs. Farrow says. "I think it's best we don't come in."

The swelling is down on Lily's face. That's the first thing Beverley notices when she steps into Lily's living room. The blinds on all the windows are tilted to filter the midday sun, but they let in plenty of light to see by.

The house is small, a single-story cinder block. The furniture is tattered and too large for the small space with its low ceiling. The walls are a drab olive color, but the terrazzo floors shine, and the windows behind the tilted blinds glitter from being so clean. It's all Lily's doing.

"I think the girl should leave," Beverley says.

She's already forgotten the girl's name, but whoever she is, she doesn't need to hear this conversation.

Lily shrinks, backing away as she wraps her arms around herself.

"Of course," she says, and nods at the girl, a gesture meant to send her away.

The girl slowly stands—Jenny, that's her name—her eyes darting around the room. As she walks past Lily, she pauses like she wants to take Lily with her. Lily cups the girl's face and ushers her along.

"Is he here?" Beverley says, glancing around for any sign of Levi.

Lily shakes her head.

"Levi hit you," Beverley says, just like that because she doesn't have time for being sensitive anymore. "And I want to know why."

"I explained what happened," Lily says, looking smaller here in her own home. "You're making something out of nothing."

Beverley used to think Lily looked like a ballet dancer, even asked her once if she ever studied. Her thin neck and long, slender limbs used to look elegant. Now, instead of looking delicate but strong, she looks fragile. Broken.

"That swelling is not nothing," Beverley says, leaning to get a look at Lily's face. "I can still see it. Was he threatening you?"

"Threatening me?" Lily says. "Why would he be threatening me?"

Elizabeth takes Beverley's arm and leans in as if to whisper something, but Beverley nudges her away before she can get it out.

"I don't know, Lily," Beverley says. "You tell me. Maybe he wants to be sure you keep your mouth shut."

"It's not like that," Lily says, rubbing her head as if she can't keep it all straight. "It's not what you think."

Beverley wants to grab her and shake an answer out of her because time is something she does not have. Since Francie disappeared, the minutes pass quicker than they did before. Every one that ticks by means less chance that her little girl will ever be found.

"Then tell me what I should think," Beverley says. "Why are you protecting him?"

Elizabeth is trying to draw Beverley back to the door, whispering to her that this isn't the way. But Beverley is not leaving until she gets the truth, because if it's not Levi, then they have no one else. The second Robert's polygraph comes back clean—and it will—the police have no other leads. The FBI has no other leads.

"I'm not protecting him," Lily says, her eyes closed, her arms still wrapped tightly around her chest. "He's protecting me."

"Protecting you?" Beverley says, her throat closing on the words. "Lily, my God. What did you do?"

Pressed against the wall near Nora's room, Jenny leans just enough to see the three women standing inside the front door.

"Answer me, Lily," Mrs. Farrow says, steadying herself with a hand on the back of the closest chair. "What did you do?"

The woman who came with Mrs. Farrow steps forward, putting herself between Mrs. Farrow and Lily.

"Let me get the police down here," the woman says. Miss Miller, that was her name. "Let's let them handle this."

Mrs. Farrow moves the woman aside with a stiff arm. She's steady again and seems to grow taller.

"Where is she?" Mrs. Farrow buckles her hands into fists and shouts it at Lily. "Where. Is. Francie."

The Final Episode

Those few words send Lily stumbling backward. She presses a hand over her mouth and smothers a sob. Jenny does the same and closes her eyes. She wants the two women to leave so she can go back to hearing about Mama and the things she liked and didn't like.

"That's why you're hiding down here," Mrs. Farrow says, still spitting her words at Lily. "That's why you all but disappeared. I want an answer, now. What did you do to my daughter?"

"I didn't do anything, and I'm not hiding," Lily says. "It wasn't my idea to move down here. It was Levi's."

"Go on and tell her, Mom."

Jenny swings around. Nora stands behind her, but she's not pressed to the wall. She's not hiding like Jenny. Instead, she stands in the middle of the hallway where everyone can see her.

Lily hurries toward Nora, a hand outstretched, but Nora shakes her head and crosses her arms. As if Nora slapped her, Lily flinches and eases away.

"Tell her," Nora says again, taking a few steps past Jenny. "Tell her what you did. Tell her why Dad moved us here and why he doesn't live with us anymore."

Mrs. Farrow grabs Miss Miller's hand. They both stare at Lily, waiting for her to say something.

"Levi doesn't live here anymore?" Mrs. Farrow asks. "Why not? Where is he?"

"I was having an affair," Lily whispers. "Levi moved us here because I was having an affair. There were so many reporters and police, and he didn't want people to find out. He was protecting me. He didn't do anything. I did."

Jenny covers her ears. She wants to run into the living room and push Mrs. Farrow out the door so she'll stop asking questions. Jenny saw Daddy and Lily Banks together, walking through the rain, their arms wrapped around each other, and that makes her afraid that Daddy's name is going to be the next thing out of Lily's mouth.

Miss Miller steps forward again and takes a big deep breath as if trying to get Mrs. Farrow and Lily to do the same.

"We need to leave, Beverley," she says. "We need to leave right now. I will get officers down here immediately. But we need to leave."

"You were having an affair?" Mrs. Farrow says. "That's why he hit you?"

"I'm so sorry I've made a terrible time worse," Lily says.

Mrs. Farrow stares at Lily as if still trying to make sense of what she's said and then turns to leave. Jenny takes a deep breath, relieved. No more questions. No more answers.

"Tell her who you had the affair with, Mom," Nora says. "Tell Mrs. Farrow. Or are you too ashamed?"

"No," Jenny says, the word bursting out before she could stop it.

She knows all about affairs because Tia and Mandy's daddy had one, and for one whole summer, Tia and Mandy cried a lot and Tia didn't want to go outside as much. Jenny doesn't want Daddy to cause anyone a whole summer of crying.

"Shut up, Jenny," Nora says, pressing a flat palm in the center of Jenny's chest and pushing her down the hallway.

Jenny tries to scramble in front of Nora, but she keeps shoving Jenny backward. She doesn't want Lily to say Daddy's name. She doesn't want it to be true.

"Go on, Mom, tell her," Nora says. Her voice trembles in the same way Jenny's sometimes does when she's trying not to cry. "Tell Mrs. Farrow who you were having the affair with."

"What are you implying, Nora?" Mrs. Farrow's eyes widen and her head tips off-center as she tries to unravel what Nora is telling her.

"If anyone deserves to know," Nora says. "It's Mrs. Farrow."

The woman, Miss Miller, tries again to pull Mrs. Farrow toward the door. She is shaking her head and trying harder this time to get Mrs. Farrow to leave. Maybe Miss Miller is like Jenny. Maybe she sees things coming before they come, because she seems to have figured out what Jenny has figured out.

The Final Episode

"We need to go, Beverley," Miss Miller says. "The police will come take statements. We need to . . ."

"It can't be," Mrs. Farrow whispers, shoving the woman away, and her eyes roll from Nora to Lily.

Lily shakes her head, slowly and then faster.

"Oh, Beverley," Lily says. "Wait. No . . ."

"You were my friend," Mrs. Farrow says.

"Beverley." Lily reaches for her. "Please, wait."

Mrs. Farrow waves her off as she stumbles out the door. Miss Miller signals Lily to stay put and follows Mrs. Farrow.

Nobody said a name, but it was all right there, in the empty spaces between. It was right there in the way Nora said what she said and the way Mrs. Farrow's eyes stretched wide and the air drained from her body. Lily Banks's affair wasn't with Daddy. It was with Mrs. Farrow's husband. Francie Farrow's father.

When Jenny saw Daddy and Lily in the rain, Daddy was just being a shoulder for Lily to cry on. That's what he is for Jenny sometimes. When she's sad about something, he wiggles one shoulder and then the other and says . . . which do you want? They're both good for crying on.

When the door slaps closed behind Mrs. Farrow and the woman who came with her, Nora swings around and marches back to her room. She doesn't look at Jenny, doesn't seem to notice her standing there. Jenny is stuck, not knowing if she should go home or follow Nora. Standing in the middle of the living room as if she's lost, Lily motions for Jenny to go with Nora and mouths the words . . . I'm sorry, over and over.

At her closed door, Nora stands with her hand on the knob, air rushing in and out of her nose. Jenny comes up behind her and starts to rest a hand on her shoulder but is afraid to. Nora is like a hot stove. Jenny will get burned if she gets too close.

"I'm sorry, Nora," Jenny whispers so Tia and Mandy won't hear. She doesn't think Nora will want them to know what happened.

"What are you sorry about?" Nora says, swinging around and sending Jenny stumbling backward.

"About your mama," Jenny says, hugging the wall. "And I saw your picture in the paper, holding a candle for Francie. I didn't know you knew her. I didn't know that was the troubling thing your family had. I'm sorry about that too."

Nora stares for too long. It seems she'll never say anything, and Jenny wonders again if she should go home.

"Don't be sorry about my mom," Nora says, stepping up to Jenny and looking down on her. "At least I didn't kill mine."

The drive from Lily Banks's house on the swamp back to Beverley's takes a good hour. When Elizabeth finally pulls into Beverley's driveway, Beverley throws open the door before the car has rolled to a stop.

Forgetting she was cleared to live in her own house again, Beverley starts across the lawn toward the house next door, but Elizabeth calls to her.

"They've already moved your things," Elizabeth says. "You're back home again."

Beverley changes directions, puts her head down, and cuts across the lawn to her sidewalk, staying well ahead of Elizabeth. At her front door, Beverley slaps her pockets for keys, reaches for a purse she hasn't carried in days, and then, out of options, braces herself with a hand to the door. She holds it there, like she's feeling for a pulse, but the house is cold and dead. It's her first time back home since Francie disappeared, and she's coming home to nothing.

Footsteps come up behind her, a hand rests on her shoulder, and another dangles keys near the side of her face.

"Take your time," Elizabeth says. "You need to take a deep breath before you walk in that house."

Beverley steps aside as Elizabeth sorts through the keys for the right one, but before she can find it, the door opens.

Robert stands there, freshly showered, still rubbing his hair dry. His face is sunburned from spending his days searching. His lips are

The Final Episode

chapped. His eyes are red, but when he sees Beverley, a full sigh lifts his chest. As he exhales, he smiles and reaches for her. She recoils. She can't move forward because now the house is vibrating from being so empty, and she can't turn to leave.

She stares at him, squints. It's her husband, and yet she isn't certain she recognizes him. The man she's known for half her life fizzles and another version slides in behind.

"Everything all right?" he says, sounding the same but he isn't.

"Was it just an affair?" Beverley says, studying the new version of her husband. She wonders when this replacement slithered in. Or was he never the man she thought he was? "Or did you love her?"

Robert stands back as Beverley and Elizabeth enter the house.

"What are you talking about?" Robert says, looking to Elizabeth for an answer. "What is she talking about?"

"Agent Watson will be here tomorrow," Elizabeth says. "Let's put this on pause until then."

Robert tosses the towel aside and grabs a shirt hanging from the back of a kitchen chair. As he pulls it on, Beverley walks into the middle of her kitchen and slowly turns. It looks like it did the night she last put Francie and Nora to bed. It's clean. The windows shimmer. The floors shine. It even smells the same, crisp and sharp. It's as if the past several days never happened. A bad dream. A nightmare. She looks to the top of the stairs, expecting to see Francie there, both arms dangling over the banister as she calls out . . . what's for dinner?

"Lily Banks moved," Beverley says, still staring at the empty spot near the top of the stairs and wondering how she got this far. How did she become the woman who never saw it coming? "Her whole family moved. They're practically living in the swamp because her husband found out she was having an affair with you. And now our little girl is gone."

Robert laughs at first and then, rubbing the spot between his eyes, goes silent.

"I was having an affair with Lily Banks?" he says. "Is that the latest theory?"

"Has it been the whole time, the whole two years she worked here?" Beverley asks, closing her eyes and listening for the sounds of Francie overhead. Of her jumping on her mattress. She gets to do that because of everything she doesn't get to do. And then two feet hitting the floor at the same time, a thud, as she jumps off her bed, hands stretched high overhead, a gymnast sticking a perfect landing. Beverley and Robert watching from the doorway, huddled together, happy, clapping, shouting out ten, ten, ten.

"Are you really asking me this?" Robert says.

"And I want an answer."

Elizabeth reaches for her, to stop her from saying anything more, but Beverley slaps her hand away.

"Is this what happened to you, Elizabeth?" Beverley says, staring at Robert as she spews the question. "Was it your father? Because that's who it usually is, isn't that right?"

"I told you to slow down," Elizabeth says, backing away from Beverley and shutting down like she did the first time Beverley asked her about being abducted as a child. "I told you to listen, to wait."

"Good God," Robert says, a look passing over his face as if he just fully pieced together what Beverley is accusing him of. "You think . . . I can't even say it. You think I did something to our daughter because I was having an affair?"

"That's exactly what I think," Beverley says, still listening and hearing not one footstep overhead. She wants to scream at her house to say something, anything. She wants it to give her a sign Francie will come back. But there's only the hum of the air conditioner and the click of the ceiling fan spinning overhead.

"Lily never said it was Robert," Elizabeth says, stepping into Beverley's line of sight and trying again to take hold of her hands. This time, Beverley lets her. Elizabeth squeezes, saying listen to me. "You realize that? She never said his name."

"But Nora did," Beverley says, jerking her hands away because she doesn't want to listen. "She wouldn't lie. She probably barely even understands what it all means."

"You're right," Elizabeth says. "Nora implied the affair was with Robert, but you didn't give Lily a chance to speak."

"You think I'm having an affair with Lily Banks," Robert says, running his fingers through his damp hair, "because a child said so? Is that where we are?"

"You haven't denied it," Beverley says, dropping down at the kitchen table.

She's exhausted, and as much as she needs to be in this house, the emptiness is piling on top of her, crowding out the air, making it so she can barely breathe. She already lost Francie here, and now she's lost her husband here too.

"Then how about this for a denial?" Robert says, planting his hands on the table and pressing close to Beverley. "Fuck you and fuck Lily Banks and whoever she was having an affair with, because it damn sure wasn't me."

Jenny sits on the edge of the pool in Nora's backyard, her feet dangling in the water while the other girls float around on blow-up rafts. They drift lazily from one end to the other. The sun is low in the sky, and Jenny scoots every so often to stay in the one sliver of shade that keeps moving. Same as it's been all afternoon, no one is talking. A heavy silence settled in after Francie Farrow's mama came and went.

As Tia floats past Jenny, she meets Jenny's eyes and gives a nod in Nora's direction as if to ask, yet again, what happened to make Nora act like she's been acting. Jenny answers with a blank stare, same as she has every other time.

Soon after Mrs. Farrow left, Lily tapped lightly on Nora's door and suggested Tia, Mandy, and Jenny go home.

"Maybe this isn't a good day for a sleepover," she said, her eyes watery and red.

Jenny started to stand because she wanted to leave. Nora had said a hateful thing to her about Mama being dead and Jenny being the one to kill her. It had stung like a slap across the face must sting, and it still stung.

"You've ruined absolutely everything," Nora had said. "And now, you're going to ruin my sleepover too. You're going to make my very best friends leave?"

"I'm not going to make anyone leave," Lily said, letting out a long sigh as she gave in to Nora. "Are you all right, Jenny?"

Everyone looked at Jenny. Tia and Mandy looked because Lily's question made them wonder what happened to upset everyone so much. Nora looked because she was warning Jenny to keep her mouth shut. And that's what Jenny did. She kept quiet and went right on being relieved her daddy wasn't the one causing all the tears. Francie Farrow's daddy was the one doing that. He was the one having the affair with Lily.

Near suppertime, Daddy drops off hamburgers but says he isn't staying to grill them. Instead, he lights the charcoal, gives Jenny a hug, and looks her over like he knows Mrs. Farrow came to the house and is worried about Jenny. When Jenny says that she's fine, he cups her face and gives her a long, lingering hug. She holds on tight, her face buried in Daddy's chest, happy to feel like she got her daddy back.

After Daddy gets the grill going and leaves, Mrs. Norwood shows up with a marshmallow fluff salad. Sitting at the kitchen counter, the four girls eat fat burgers that drip juice on their fingers, french fries Lily baked in the oven, and the creamy fruit salad. After dinner, they eat warm-from-the-oven brownies and ice cream that's like sweet vanilla soup in their bowls.

The whole time they eat, Nora flips through a magazine, acting like she doesn't want any of them there even though she called them her very best friends.

After dinner, they go to Nora's bedroom. Jenny rolls out the sleeping bag Daddy dropped off when he lit the charcoal. Tia and

The Final Episode

Mandy roll out theirs too. The same silence continues, making Jenny wonder if it will last the rest of the summer. Tia and Mandy must think the same because they start exchanging looks. They give head tilts, shrugs, and wide-eyed stares like they sometimes do, carrying on an entire conversation without saying a word.

Tia is thinking about going home, same as Jenny, and Mandy is telling her no.

"You first," Nora says, interrupting the silent debate as she hands a red cup to Jenny.

"Me first, what?" Jenny says.

"Drink it," Nora says, whispering and watching her bedroom door like she's afraid someone might walk in. "Before the ice melts. That'll ruin it."

"Ruin what?" Mandy asks, leaning to look in the cup.

"It's mostly lemonade," Nora says.

"Mostly lemonade?" Jenny says, tipping the cup so she can see inside without getting too close.

"And vodka," Nora says. "Since we got it at your house, you get to go first."

"You want me to drink it?"

Jenny gives the cup a shake, the ice inside rattling. She holds it to her nose. It smells sharp and sweet.

"No big deal," Nora says, and uses Jenny's own words against her. "Unless you don't want to. I mean, if you're scared . . ."

That's exactly what Jenny said to Nora when Nora was afraid to climb from the flat roof up to the window in the owner's room.

Looking to Tia for help, not getting it, and feeling trapped into doing what Nora wants her to, Jenny presses the cup to her mouth and tips it. The lemonade touches her bottom lip first. It's cold. And then it rolls across her tongue, mixing with the toothpastey taste that's still in her mouth. Her lips pucker. Her mama would have liked this taste, and that makes her take another sip. It's tart and tastes mostly like lemonade should taste, except when she swallows. As it slides down her throat, it leaves a burn on the back of her tongue.

She smiles because that wasn't so bad and hands the cup to Nora so she can go next.

"That one's yours," Nora says, blocking the cup with a flat hand.

"Thanks," Jenny says, and reaches to set the cup on Nora's nightstand. "But you guys can try too."

Nora steps between Jenny and the nightstand, not letting her set down the cup.

"You can't leave that in here," she says. "That's yours. You have to drink it. All of it. Or you'll get me in trouble."

"Nora," Tia says. Finally says. "Maybe we shouldn't. She can just pour it out."

Mandy steps close enough to look down into the red plastic cup again.

"There's not even much in there," she says, shrugging like she's drank more than that. "Just drink it."

"What do you know?" Tia says.

"More than you, according to every report card ever," Mandy says.

Tia's face turns red, and she and Mandy suddenly look nothing alike. Mandy looks hard and mean. Tia looks broken.

"You don't have to drink it if you're scared," Nora says, flashing a smile at Mandy. "You can go home, but when my mom finds it, I'm telling her you brought it."

"Just drink it," Mandy says, again talking as if she knows all about it.

Nora drapes an arm over her shoulder. "Like Mandy said. Just drink it."

Tia tried, and that means she and Jenny are still friends. That's a powerful thing. Powerful enough to make Jenny brave enough to drink it all.

In ten gulps, the lemonade is gone. Mandy was right about it not being that much. The ice made it look like more. When Jenny swallows the last mouthful, she sets the cup down and wipes her mouth. Her throat burns, maybe from the cold lemonade or maybe from the vodka.

Nora grabs Jenny's hands and studies her eyes. Tia and Mandy cover their mouths like they can't believe Jenny did it.

Now it's Jenny's turn to act like it's no big deal. She wipes her mouth and belches. That makes everyone laugh. Even Nora. Even Jenny.

"How do you feel?" Nora says, leaning close as if still looking for something in Jenny's eyes.

Jenny shrugs, feeling the same as always, but all three girls stare at her like something is different. She presses both hands to her face. It feels hot. She looks at all of them looking at her and starts to feel scared.

"She should sit down," Tia says.

Jenny lets them lead her to a spot on the floor. They all sit, and everyone leans forward to stare at her again. She stares back, wondering what they think is going to happen. Her throat still burns from the icy cold lemonade, all the way down her chest and into her lungs, but she feels good. She feels tired too. It's been a long day, and they ate a big dinner of fat hamburgers. She must say out loud that she's tired because Tia helps her lay down. She stares up at the ceiling. It shifts and rolls like waves crashing on the beach.

"What do I look like?" Nora says.

She stands over Jenny, hops from side to side, and waves her hands.

Jenny lifts her head and tries to follow Nora with her eyes but can't. Wanting Nora to stop, Jenny tries to grab an ankle, but Nora yanks her feet away before Jenny can get hold of them. And then she's circling Jenny, and bouncing and twirling, her arms stretched wide.

"You getting dizzy?" Nora says, first from behind Jenny and then from near her feet.

Jenny closes her eyes. Seeing Nora spin and twirl makes her feel like she's spinning and twirling. Tia lies next to her. Jenny rolls her head toward Tia so they're staring at each other, their noses almost touching.

Tia rests a hand on Jenny's cheek. Jenny reaches up with one finger and taps the tip of Tia's nose.

"You're my very best friend," Jenny says.

The room is dark and quiet when Jenny opens her eyes. Tia is asleep next to her, one hand on Jenny's arm. Mandy sleeps on the other side of Tia. Gritty blues plays on a record player. It's soft and Jenny can barely hear it. It's Daddy's music, swamp blues with a slow walking bass and a meandering saxophone. He says the notes sound as lost as we all sometimes feel. To Jenny, the music sounds lonely, but Daddy says it makes him feel less alone to know everyone feels a little lost sometimes.

Picking up Tia's hand by taking hold of her index finger, Jenny gently moves it off her arm and sits up so she can see Nora's bed. But Nora isn't there. The room is dark except for the glow leaking around the drapes on Nora's sliding glass door. Jenny turns to face them, and one end of the sliding door glows more than the other. Nora is sitting on the floor, the curtain pushed aside so she can see onto the pool deck.

The soft glow spilling inside flickers and then turns steady again. Somewhere out over the Everglades, a storm is rolling in and bringing with it distant lightning. It happens almost every day. The rain, the lightning, the thunder.

It happens again, a burst of light falling on Nora's face. She turns to Jenny. They sit like that for too long, staring at each other. Then Nora lets the curtain fall, and she turns into a shadow.

"I'm sorry about today," Jenny says, her mouth dry and the words scratching her throat. "I'm sorry about Francie too. I know that was her mom who was here today. I guess you knew her. I guess maybe she was your friend, and I'm sorry."

"I was with her when she disappeared," Nora says, her voice flat. "I was the one in the room. Are you sorry he didn't take me instead? Is that what you're sorry about?"

The Final Episode

"No," Jenny says, wishing she'd gone home when she first wanted to. "I didn't know that was you. I don't wish that."

Daddy's always saying you never know what's going on with a person. Jenny sure never thought Nora was the little girl who the news reporters said was having a sleepover with Francie when she disappeared. That's why she doesn't like to go outside, and maybe that's why she isn't always so nice. Maybe she's afraid she'll disappear next.

"I bet you do," Nora says, and crawls back in bed. "I bet you wish he took me instead of Francie."

The bed creaks as Nora slides under the covers. Jenny sits in the dark for a few minutes and then, trying not to make any noise, she crawls to the spot where Nora had been. Even though she doesn't really want to, it feels like that empty spot is waiting for her. It feels like it's drawing her in.

She pushes aside the curtain, the tiniest amount she can so she doesn't let in too much light.

The pool's underwater lights are on, throwing a soft glow on the decking. At first, she sees only shifting shadows. They're tucked around the side of the house where Jenny can hardly see them, but now that she knows they're there, she studies them. They're dancing, moving to the slow, rolling blues. The sky stays dark, but Jenny still knows. She can tell by the shape of them, same as she could tell when she saw them walking with the umbrella. It's Daddy and Lily. And because of the way one face is tipped up and pressed to the other, she can tell they're kissing.

This is what Nora saw too.

Jenny lets the curtain fall closed.

"You know what that means?" Nora says. "What you see out there, you know what it means?"

Her voice floats out of the darkness.

"It means it was your dad all along," she says. "He's the one who had an affair with my mom. And my dad, my stupid dad, moved us here and doesn't even know what he did."

FADE OUT:

CHAPTER 12

I don't know how long Tia and I stood in the middle of the road. The sun had risen full in the sky, and the drier, lighter air was no longer strong enough to carry the rot coming off the swamp. As the tart, rancid smell faded, the sweetness of the night-blooming jasmine broke through. Sweat streamed down the sides of my face. My shoulders burned where the sun hit them full on.

"It's going to happen," I said, feeling as if I couldn't fully inhale. "Isn't it? It's going to be my dad. He's the one who took Francie Farrow."

"It might, yes," Tia said, brave enough to be honest. "You know Mandy loved your dad. After ours bailed, Paul was the only part of being at the swamp that she liked. That's probably what tore her up so bad. It's confusing, right? It must be for you, wondering how he could be two different men."

"Dehlia's going to fall apart," I said, not wanting to let Tia into my battle with the two halves of you. I was too ashamed about the silly notions I'd had, about the hope I'd held out that you were the man I thought you were. So I changed the subject instead. "I don't know how she survives this."

"Do you talk to him often?" Tia said, taking my arm and guiding me toward my house. She must have seen I was unsteady on my feet. "Has he ever talked about that night? What happened?"

Outside Dehlia's door, I stopped and pointed so Tia would take care not to trip on the pavers. The grout was breaking down, and the pavers were uneven. It was another job to add to my list of things that needed fixing. The last thing we needed was for Dehlia to take a fall.

At the door, Tia reached across me to open it, but I took her by the forearm, stopping her.

"I haven't seen my father in over twenty years," I said. It was a husky whisper, one I had to force out. I'd never said it out loud.

"Twenty years?" Tia said. "You haven't seen him once since . . ."

The look she gave me, wide-eyed shock that melted into sympathy, was why I never told people. I didn't want sympathy. I didn't want pity. But part of me was always afraid that one day, I'd regret so many lost years. I didn't have that worry anymore. All my hope had drained away. Instead, I felt sick, thinking of all the times I missed you and worried about you. Thinking how you didn't deserve those things. Instead, I needed to spend not one more moment missing you, and I needed to figure a way to help Dehlia survive what was coming.

The door opened. The cool air from inside rushed over Tia and me, causing us both to pull back. If we were still kids, we'd hug ourselves, jump up and down, and squeal. But we weren't kids anymore.

"Good Lord in heaven," Dehlia said, grabbing Tia and pulling her into a hug.

Dehlia stood barefoot, her long gauzy skirt brushing her ankles, her single braid trailing over one shoulder. She drew Tia into the house and held her at arm's length.

"You are a little bit of a thing," she said as Belle darted between our feet and jumped on Tia. "Just like your mama. Oh, bless her heart. How is she? Come in."

Dehlia's excitement was big. It curled around Tia and me and pulled us up and out of being sad. We both smiled to see Dehlia smile.

"It's Tia, right?" Dehlia said. "I always know Tia because you're not so fussy as Mandy."

Dehlia hustled me inside as an afterthought and looked past me like she was looking for Mandy.

"Mandy isn't with me," Tia said, ruffling Belle's ears.

She and I exchanged a glance. It had been years, two decades in fact, but we still knew each other. No need to tell Dehlia just now, Tia was saying in that one glance. No need to ruin the mood.

Leading Tia toward the kitchen, Dehlia looked over her shoulder at me.

"Keep an eye out for your daddy's key," she said, and continued toward the kitchen, chatting with Tia about how nice her house looked and what a beautiful way to honor her mama by keeping it in such good shape.

I gave Dehlia a wave, my way of telling her I'd keep an eye out. Since Mr. Farrow first mentioned her search, I'd been thinking about it. She was probably looking for the key to the door that led from the house into the garage. We hadn't had a key to that door for years and never locked it. Without a key, it was too easy to lock ourselves out. One more thing to add to my to-do list.

"And if you're going to be living here," Dehlia said, again talking to me over her shoulder as she and Tia disappeared into the kitchen, "no more folding my towels like you folded them last time. Just because all those clients want you messing about in their closets, doesn't mean I want you messing about in mine."

I'd heard it before and knew better than to argue with Dehlia, but her mention of my clients reminded me that I wanted to follow up with Eva about my résumé.

"Be there in a minute," I called into the kitchen. "Need to make a quick call."

I slipped outside, sat on the front steps, and dialed Eva.

"Hi, Jennifer." It was Eva. I imagined her in her office, surrounded by clothes, shoes, and handbags that I could put in perfect order. "Got your résumé. Thank you."

"Good," I said. "Just wanted to follow up. Be sure you didn't have any problems opening it."

I couldn't see Dehlia and Tia from where I sat outside, but I could hear Dehlia rattling around as she pulled out a skillet. It made me smile because nothing made Dehlia happier than feeding people, and I hadn't seen her happy for a long time.

"I believe I mentioned I've already started interviewing," Eva said. "You're kind of coming in on the tail end of the process."

"Yes," I said, managing an upbeat tone as if I didn't know what those few words really meant. She was letting me know in a gentle, roundabout way to prepare for the worst. "Of course."

I stood and leaned against the door where I could get more shade and look inside through the sidelight window. Dehlia crossed through the entry, her arms full of photo albums she was carrying into the kitchen. She was smiling, and she'd even let her braid slip over her shoulder and trail down her back, something she never let happen.

"I'll give you a call," Eva said. She took a sip of what was likely sweet tea, ice crackling as she tipped and lowered the glass. "In a few days."

"One more quick thing," I said, certain there would be no call in a few days. "If you don't mind my asking."

I knew the sound of a polite brush-off. The polite part was for Eva, so she didn't feel guilty. That's how it always went. I had nothing to lose, because it was already lost.

"What's on your mind?" she said.

"Do you do background checks on your assistants?" I said.

"You're worried about a background check?" Eva said, each word coming slower than the last.

I've grown accustomed over the years to people watching out for signs of you in me. That's what I heard in Eva's question. She was wondering what was in my background that I didn't want her to see.

"No, I'm not asking about my background check," I said. "I'm curious about Tanya's."

It only occurred to me in the span of the phone call that Tanya, the fired assistant I was hoping to replace, was a relatively new person in my life. Something the police told me to be on the lookout for. She was about the right age, give or take, and she reminded me of Nora. At least the things about Nora that I thought I remembered. Tanya had Nora's blond hair, her curves, her big personality. And the last time I saw her, she had torn off her Verifiably Vintage polo and tossed it out her car window. That was the kind of thing Nora would have done.

"I can't discuss someone's background check with you, Jennifer," Eva said. "I'm sure you understand that."

"Would you mind telling me her last name?" I said. "It's kind of important."

"I don't think I'd better do that either," Eva said. "It's sounding like you're having some kind of problem, and I'd rather not get mixed up in it."

Through the phone, I could hear that Eva was on the move, the leather sandals she always wore slapping the floors in her house. She'd had enough of our conversation and was ready to get on to other things.

"Sure, I understand," I said, and if I'd had any chance at the job, I'd just ruined it. But I hadn't had a chance. "We'll talk next week when I'm back again."

And the line went dead. My regular appointments with Eva Oakley had come to an end. I'd get a text in the next day or two, one much like all the others I'd gotten since the show began. Eva would tell me, politely so she didn't have to feel guilty, that she could handle her own closets and pantries going forward but would reach out if she needed my assistance again.

Back inside, I walked into the kitchen where Tia and Dehlia were flipping through old photo albums. Dehlia stopped making them after that summer, so as she and Tia leaned over the pages, pointing and smiling, I knew they were looking at older pictures. Joining them, I smiled, too, not wanting to let on that I was worrying and wondering how I was going to pay the bills going forward.

I was also left worrying and wondering if Tanya could really be Nora. I didn't know why she'd be sneaking around the fringes of my life unless Tia was right. Maybe Nora was afraid of what the final episode would reveal. Plenty of people think I know what's coming. Maybe Nora thought the same.

CHAPTER 13

In the excitement of having Tia in the house and reliving all the good memories, Dehlia never asked why I was suddenly moving in. She didn't ask what brought Tia back after all these years either. It was as if she'd been expecting us. She even had sweet tea ready, and if you remember anything about Dehlia's sweet tea, you'll remember it takes a few days to make.

While Dehlia and Tia continued flipping through old albums, I lugged boxes and suitcases to my old room. By the time I finished unpacking, coffee and eggs had turned to iced tea and tomato salads and Dehlia had stacked the albums in the corner. We ate at the kitchen table, Tia and I sitting in the same chairs we'd sat in as children, and the chair where Mandy always sat stood empty.

As we ate, making more happy sounds as we tasted the sweet, fresh tomatoes and sipped the sugary tea, I told Tia about my business that had suffered a quick death and lied by saying I had a good chance at a full-time job with a client. She told me about life as a public defender and how she walked away from it the day Mandy died. Except she didn't say the part about Mandy out loud. Instead, she said she'd quit four weeks ago and couldn't be happier and, at the same time, sadder. And I knew why. Too much stress, she said. Too many cases. She did her time and couldn't do any more.

When the light in the kitchen dimmed, a sure sign clouds were rolling in from the Everglades and dousing the worst of the afternoon sun, Dehlia made old-fashioneds in her best cut-glass highball glasses and dropped a Luxardo cherry in each. Same as when we were kids drinking soda instead of whiskey, Tia and I fished out the cherries with our fingers and popped them in our mouths. They were sweet and rich, another echo from childhood.

Tia felt it, too, the echo. As she slowly chewed, she laid her head back and smiled. And then the smile wilted, and her chin buckled as if she might cry. Just as quickly, the smile returned. She was thinking about Mandy, and so was I. Tia and I would eat our cherries first thing, before we'd even taken a sip. Mandy would always save hers until the end.

Sitting on the screened-in lanai, Belle curled up at my feet, we watched the rain move in over the swamp and sipped our bourbon. We listened to quiet jazz that I streamed through a speaker and told stories of orchid hunting, fishing with fat earthworms, and wading across the creek. Eventually, we fell silent, each of us listening as the rain dripped from the cypress branches and splattered off Halfway Creek.

It had been a long time since we'd had a happy moment in the house, and I wanted it to float on top as long as possible.

"I'd better go," Tia said when we had a break in the rain. "I have another one of those drinks, I may well forget the way home."

Giving Dehlia a hug and telling her not to get up, Tia headed for the front door, and I followed.

"You can stay here," I said as we walked outside. I didn't want her to leave and end what could be one of our last happy times. "Your house might seem kind of empty."

"Thanks, but I'm good," Tia said, staring across the road at her house like she wasn't good at all.

"What happened after college?" I said, feeling Mandy was close, almost like she was standing right here with us. "You said that was when you started to lose track of Mandy."

"Partly on me," she said, turning her back on the dark windows at her house. "I took off for Boston, and she ended up in Tampa, working some bullshit bartending job. Seemed every time she called, she had a new number and a new job, and was living in a new town. Every one of them farther away from home. Then she stopped having a phone altogether. That left me waiting around for the next call."

I nodded, and we were back to one of those awkward moments.

"Dehlia seems to be doing well," Tia said, trying to return to a happier subject.

"She has mostly good days," I said. "We'll have a little adjusting to do, with me being back here and all."

When a crack of lightning rolled across the sky, Tia glanced overhead.

"Does she still do it?" she said, meaning did Dehlia still squat out in the middle of a storm and scream up at the sky. "Got to admit, scared me the first time I saw that picture of her in a newspaper."

"She stopped about the time I turned eighteen," I said. "I don't really think about it anymore."

I don't know why I lied. I still wince when I hear thunder or see a distant flash of lightning. I only saw Dehlia do it a few times. To me, she always looked like a wounded animal that had been rooting in the mud. She looked like someone I didn't know, and that scared me. I was afraid what happened to her in the rain would leak into the rest of our lives, and I'd lose her all together. And then I'd have no one.

I still fall asleep to every storm with my hands pressed over my ears, not wanting to hear the sliding door open and close, not wanting to imagine her out there.

"I saw that same picture not long ago," Tia said, drifting toward her house. "And seeing it now—as an adult, I guess—I thought she looked more sad than scary. I thought she looked like she was in pain."

I nodded but said nothing.

"And I thought," Tia said, glancing up at our house, "maybe she was out in that rain, crying and screaming because all that pain over losing first your mom and then your dad had to go somewhere, but she didn't want you to hear it. Like she could scream as loud as she wanted, and you wouldn't hear her over the rain."

Tia shrugged like maybe she was right, maybe she was wrong and headed toward her house. I stayed in the middle of the road, still sorting through what she'd said.

When that picture of Dehlia first showed up in the paper, some kids at school cut it out and brought it to show the whole class. They asked if I howled at the moon too. It was one more thing that made them certain they were right to call me the wetland witch.

I was angry at Dehlia for a long time after that and ashamed of her, too. I hated the way she looked. I hated that she still talked about us having Margaret Scott's blood coursing through our veins. I hated that she still thought I was going to do something great one day when I knew I never would. The girl whose daddy is in prison and who killed her own mama doesn't do great things. All I wanted was to be like everyone else, and that hatred for Dehlia stuck with me for a long time.

But I've been wrong all along, and Tia was right.

Dehlia wasn't crying out for guidance or worshipping the moon or thinking we were special. Dehlia screamed into a dark, rainy sky because her pain had to go somewhere, and she was keeping it as far from me as she could.

CHAPTER 14

After saying good night to Tia, I went back inside and rummaged around in my things until I found the camera that had been mounted outside the back door at my rental. I set it up in the entryway near the sidelight so it would catch any motion out on the front patio. Pulling up the app on my phone, I tested that it was working and then went up to bed.

In my room, I flopped down on my mattress, a move from my teenage years. Hugging a pillow, I inhaled the scent of the fresh linens Dehlia had put on. She put them in the washer before I even called to tell her I was coming. Somehow, she'd already known.

It's been a decade since I called the bedroom at the Halfway Creek house mine, and in all that time, it hasn't changed. I've tried to get Dehlia to put in new flooring, get a fresh coat of paint, replace some furniture, but she never would. It was as if she thought the wait for you to come back home wouldn't be so long if she could stop time by keeping things just as they were.

Rolling off my bed, another move from my childhood, I walked down the hall to tell Dehlia thank you for the fresh sheets and the tomato salad and the sweet tea and the fancy cherries. She'd done her crying out in the rain to protect me, and I needed to tell her thank you more often. But there was no sliver of light under her door and her bedroom was quiet. She was already asleep.

Back in my room, I propped up my pillows, snapped off my light, draped an arm around Belle, and stared across the road at Tia's house. One by one, the lights in her windows went out. I liked knowing I'd see her again tomorrow. We'd managed to save some of what had been good from those summers. That was something to be happy about on a day when a lot had gone wrong. And it would be something to hold on to in the days ahead.

When my phone chimed, I pushed to a sitting position. I took a deep breath, readying myself for it to be Arlen. Instead, it was Eva.

Wanted you to know I've hired an assistant. I'd like you and me to transition to an as needed schedule. Given that, I've asked my asst to pick up your key. Please let me know a good time and where she should pick it up. Wishing you the best. You're my first call if I'm ever in need again.

I'd already known this was coming, but this one was tougher. It was the final nail. I didn't have a business anymore. I had nothing. Next step, waiting tables maybe. Bartending. More likely, I'd have to take a remote job, something I could do from my computer where no one would recognize me.

I sent a text back to Eva, telling her the assistant was welcome to pick the key up tomorrow morning any time after eight o'clock and giving her the address. I used to have a bulletin board filled with hooks and all the keys to all the front doors of all my clients who trusted me with one. Eva's was my last.

When Eva didn't text back, I started to bring up episode one. It was habit. In past weeks, I'd fast-forward until the sweeping shots of the Big Cypress Swamp came on screen. Then, against the backdrop of your swamp blues, a car would pull into the drive of a house meant to look like this one. I'd close my eyes, waiting to hear your voice, feeling young again when I did. Feeling good. Feeling safe. But I couldn't do it now. Not anymore. The man in that car who looked back at his

The Final Episode

little daughter to say . . . the old place fared well . . . he didn't exist. He never did.

I put my phone on the nightstand, rolled over, and wondered if I'd ever go to sleep.

Something woke me. Music. Gritty blues. I fumbled with my phone to turn it down, but the screen was dark. The music wasn't coming from it. I tapped on it, bringing it to life, and checked the time. 1:35 a.m. I'd been asleep for at least a few hours.

Pushing up in my bed, I let the sheets fall away and listened. It was slow and sultry, gravelly just like you always played. You used to say it had a way of seeping inside, rooting around your heart and soul, and toughening up your glossy insides. That's what life does to us, you'd say. It toughens up our glossy insides.

I wonder if you remember that like I do, like it was yesterday.

I rested both feet on the floor and slowly stood. Same as when I was a kid, I didn't want to make noise. I always felt something in this house was waiting for me to wake it.

At my closed door, I listened. The music was muted. Maybe Dehlia was playing it. Maybe same as she only cried when the storms would drown her out, she only played your music when she thought she was alone. Or it could have been coming from outside, from Tia's house maybe.

I put Belle in her kennel so she wouldn't follow and opened my bedroom door a few inches.

The hallway was dark. The music grew louder but just barely. I felt the bass notes in the center of my chest. They moved slowly, like a heartbeat. I looked toward Dehlia's room. The seam under her closed door was still dark.

Holding tight to the banister, I took the stairs slowly, giving myself time to measure where the music was coming from. It seemed to change direction with almost every step. Or maybe the volume was changing, growing louder and softer and louder again.

When I reached the bottom step, the entryway was dark, only a sliver of moonlight reflecting off the terrazzo floors. The music stabilized but was faint, and I recognized the song. I crossed toward your baseball-watching room. If Dehlia was sitting in there, playing your records, she was doing it in the dark.

"Dehlia," I whispered, stepping into the room. "You in here?"

As my eyes adjusted, I saw that your turntable was closed, and your chair was empty.

I took a few careful steps toward the kitchen. The music grew louder and beat stronger in my chest, and then it stopped.

Someone must have been floating down Halfway Creek, playing music that the water picked up and amplified. Between the strange way water played with sound and the single-pane windows in the house and the middle of the night having a way of amplifying things, too, the music must have sounded like more than it was.

I turned to head back upstairs but stopped when it began again. It was louder, clearer. This time, I was certain I knew the song.

Everyone who watched the show knew the song. It opened episode one.

I stood in the entrance to the kitchen, listening. The music was steady. It didn't swirl around me anymore. I'd latched on to it, or it on to me. Walking my hands along the counters, I made my way to the sliding doors and pushed apart the heavy drapes Dehlia closed every evening.

The rain had stopped, and the full moon cloaked the lanai and backyard in a misty, soggy glow. Our whiskey glasses still sat on the side table where Dehlia, Tia, and I had been only hours before, and the Bluetooth speaker we'd been using sat on the table too. The small red light on the speaker's base, bright enough to cut through the hazy night, meant it was on.

Stepping back from the doors and pulling out my phone, I swiped a finger across the screen to open it. I wasn't the one streaming music through the speaker. That meant someone else was. And they weren't streaming just any music. It was your music. Whoever was streaming it was also close enough to maintain the connection to the speaker and adjust the volume. I'd done the same as we sipped our old-fashioneds earlier in the evening. When the rain had first started up, causing a loud rattle on the roof over the lanai, I'd tapped the volume button on my phone, turning up the sound.

Opening the drapes again, I looked the length of the lanai. The door that led from the screened enclosure to the backyard was closed, but I also knew it had no lock on it. Anyone could have come onto the lanai and turned on the speaker. I scanned the yard, watching for the shadow of someone creeping past. When the air conditioner clicked off and the house fell silent, I pressed an ear to the glass door and listened for the crackle of footsteps, but I could only hear the music, the slow, meandering music.

Dragging a chair to the doors, I stood on it to get a better view of Halfway Creek. There was no boat drifting past, a lantern on its bow glowing in the dimly lit night. No outline of a fisherman with his pole tipped in the air. Crouching on the chair, holding the drape open with one finger, I let my eyes settle on the speaker. The small red light still glowed. I stared at it, not knowing what to do. If I called the police, there was nothing I could tell them.

I didn't have an emergency or a break-in or even someone creeping through the yard. I had music playing on a Bluetooth speaker. I didn't even want to call Henry Baskin. He was a half hour away at best. And I couldn't call Arlen. Not again.

Letting the drape fall closed and staring at my phone, the music still filling the dark kitchen, I settled on calling Henry. I'd ask his advice only, wouldn't let him get in his car and drive down here. He'd have an explanation, maybe a few, and that would be enough to make me feel better.

And then, the music stopped. I listened, waiting for it to start up again, but the house stayed quiet. Keeping my eyes on the small red light at the base of the speaker, I decided against bothering Henry, pushed the chair aside, slid to the floor, and with the drapes still open only a sliver, I watched the dark backyard and listened for what would come next.

EPISODE 6

INT. FARROW HOUSE - KITCHEN - DAY (6 days missing)

Beverley stands at the windows looking out on her backyard and stares at the torn screen. It's well past the time Robert would normally be up and around for the day, but he has yet to come down since Beverley accused him of having an affair with Lily Banks. It's also possible he packed up and left in the night while she was asleep on the sofa. She hasn't checked the drive to see if his car is gone.

She's been here, first sleeping in the living room and now standing at the kitchen windows, all night. Elizabeth stayed with her until it seemed certain Robert wasn't coming back downstairs.

"I'm here to help you and Robert find your daughter," Elizabeth had said before leaving. Since Beverley used Elizabeth's past to make Robert look guilty, Elizabeth had barely spoken. "And I will do everything I can to do just that, but please do not raise my case again. The man who took me, he's never been found. He's still out there. And that's all I want to say about it. My life, from here on out, it's off limits."

Unlocking the window, Beverley slides it open, probably for the first time in ten years. He did this, the man who took her little girl. He tore the screen and left it for Beverley to find. It's like a piece of him is still here, living in her house.

The Final Episode

With one long nail, she scratches at the jagged edges of the screen and then picks at them, trying to yank them from the frame. When that doesn't work, she grabs a knife and digs out the rest. Bits of wood flutter to the ground at her feet as she pries the last of him from her house.

She stops and lays the knife on the table when the front door opens and closes. A few moments later, Agent Watson stands in her kitchen, filling a glass with water.

"The wife," he says, downing the glass. He's winded as if he ran from the car to the house. "On me every day."

"Is that always your opening line?" Beverley says.

"Most people don't catch on so quick," he says, sitting across from her. "But it's true about my wife and the water. Just keeping the peace at home."

"Robert's not having an affair," she says, "is he?"

In the middle of the night, when the house was quiet, quiet in a way she didn't know quiet existed until Francie disappeared, she realized it. She'd known it when she stormed out of Lily Banks's house and when Elizabeth trailed her to the front door, begging her to think before she spoke. She knew it as she spit accusations at Robert. But the thing is, she wanted it to be true.

If Robert had been having an affair and that made him take Francie away, for whatever reason, Beverley would have had an answer. And an answer meant a chance to bring Francie home. That's all she wanted, all she cared about. Bringing her little girl home. Even if her only chance to do that meant she lost her husband and spent the rest of her life hating him. Dear God, she wanted it to be true. She would give up anything for a chance to bring Francie home.

"We've been through every nook and cranny of Robert's life," he says. "Yours too. Far as I can tell, Robert is not and never has had an affair. Same goes for you."

"You were already considering the possibility," she says.

"It's often a strong motivator."

"For women too?" Beverley says.

"Not everyone's gifted with the same compass," he says.

Beverley glances at the staircase, wondering if Robert is upstairs or if he's already gone. She'll have to apologize to him, but when she does, it'll sound shallow because it will be. She's relieved he wasn't having an affair, but disappointed too. No, she's disheartened. Robert being the good, faithful husband has taken away her last chance. What an odd twist. She's not sure she can love him anymore now that he's done that, taken away her last hope of bringing Francie home.

"Should I call Robert down?" she says, certain Agent Watson has come with a purpose.

"Why did you ask Elizabeth Miller to take you to the Bankses' house?" Agent Watson says, shaking his head about Robert.

"Because Robert told me his polygraph went well," she says.

"Results aren't back yet."

"Doesn't matter. Robert was relaxed when it was over. Never once tried to pave the way with excuses for why the results might be bad. He took it and forgot about it because he had nothing to hide."

"I don't follow."

"Robert had nothing to hide because he was innocent," Beverley says. "And you had no one else on your radar. After everything I told you about Levi Banks, it still wasn't enough to arrest him. I was terrified of a dead end. So I went there, to Lily's, looking to find out something about Levi Banks that might finally get your attention."

"And you go, and you say what to Lily Banks?"

"I asked again why Levi hit her. You must have seen her face. I knew it meant something. I just knew it. So I asked her, and that's when she admitted the affair."

"What made you think the affair was with your husband?" the agent says, rubbing his forehead.

Beverley explains about Nora saying Beverley deserved to know the truth about the affair. And there was only one reason Beverley would deserve to know.

The Final Episode

"I believed Nora only because I wanted to," Beverley says. "I just wanted an answer. But clearly Robert hadn't done anything. He wouldn't have been so calm about the polygraph if he'd been having an affair. I know that now."

"All right, then," the agent says, pushing away from the table and nodding like he finally understands. "I'm saying this once. Do not go to that house again. And for sure, don't try talking to Levi. If you want to help Francie, you'll let me do my job."

"Why would Nora know who her mother was having an affair with?" Beverley says, ignoring the agent because her mind is still churning through the things that happened in Lily's living room. "Lily is a good mother. She'd never tell Nora something like that. She'd never carry on in front of Nora either."

Leaning on the sink, Agent Watson crosses his arms and says nothing. Even when Beverley leaves silence for him to fill like he's done so many times to her, he says nothing. He's already figured it out. Maybe he got there long ago.

"Nora was wrong about Robert being the other man," Beverley says. "But her being wrong doesn't matter. What matters is that Nora thought the other man was Robert, and that means there's a good chance Levi Banks was thinking the same."

"That may all be well and true, but your theories won't help me with this case. You can help by letting me be the one to ask the questions."

"Levi Banks thought his wife was having an affair with my husband," Beverley says, dropping back in her chair, limp as the last few pieces fall into place. "And he took our little girl to punish Robert, to punish us. I've watched Levi lord over Lily for almost two years. Even if she tried to tell him it wasn't Robert, if he thought it was, that would be all he needed. He's arrogant, cocky. I know it. I know it in my heart. Levi Banks took my little girl because he thought Robert was the other man."

"Dr. Farrow," Agent Watson says, taking a deep breath like he's already exhausted and he only just got here. "I did notice Lily's face, and we're not as far behind as you think we are. Please, let me do my job."

Jenny sits in her bedroom window, her cheek pressed to the warm glass and watches Nora's front door. Lily and Nora are coming for sure, but she doesn't know when. The not knowing, that's the hardest part.

Lily appears first. Nora comes next. Lily tries to wrap an arm around Nora's shoulders, but Nora dips out from under it, and the two of them continue toward Jenny's house.

Jenny has been watching and waiting for them since she came home from Nora's this morning. When Jenny woke in Nora's bedroom after drinking vodka the night before, she was alone, and the house was the kind of quiet that made her feel she'd been left behind. She dressed, rolled up her sleeping bag, and walked toward the kitchen.

Reaching the end of the hallway, she knew right away that something was wrong. Lily sat at one end of the dining room table, both hands resting lightly on top. Tia, Mandy, and Nora sat at the other, none of them willing to look at Jenny. And sitting right in the center of the table . . . the bottle of vodka they stole from Daddy's cabinet.

"Your daddy wants you to head straight home," Lily said, her voice soft like she was trying to cushion Jenny's hard times ahead. "The two of you have some talking to do. Then we'll all talk later this afternoon."

That's when Jenny knew. Nora told her mama about the vodka, and she said Jenny did the stealing all by herself.

Ever since, Jenny has been sitting in her bedroom window, waiting. And now Lily and Nora are headed this way, and Lily is carrying that same bottle of vodka.

"Better come on," Daddy calls from downstairs because he sees them too.

The Final Episode

Jenny blows out a long breath that makes her lips flutter. As she turns to leave, Tia, Mandy, and their mama walk out their front door. Holding each of her girls by an arm, Mrs. Norwood marches them toward the road. At the end of their drive, they stop to wait for Nora and her mama. Tia and Mandy stand, heads down, arms limp at their sides. They stand like they're in trouble, too, but they shouldn't be. When Daddy asked Jenny if everything the other girls said about Jenny stealing the vodka and drinking it was true, Jenny said yes. She took all the blame, even though it was a lie.

Daddy wouldn't like that she did that, but he also wouldn't understand that lying was easier than losing every friend you had.

Down on the road, a large white truck pulls up behind Nora and Lily and parks on the shoulder. Mr. Banks steps out. He wears dark jeans, cowboy boots, and a white T-shirt. He's thick and tall, and his ball cap is pulled down over his eyes, making him look angry even from where Jenny is, way up on the second floor. She hopes he's only mad about the vodka and that he hasn't figured out his wife and Jenny's daddy were dancing and kissing by the pool.

Mr. Banks yanks the vodka out of Lily's hand and makes a motion with his thumb, sending her and Nora back home. Then he turns toward Mrs. Norwood, Tia, and Mandy and gives them the same signal. Then he walks toward Jenny's house.

"Jenny," Daddy calls out a few minutes later. "Come on down. Mr. Banks is here to see you."

Jenny creeps from her bedroom and down the stairs. In the entryway, Daddy stands in the open door, blocking Mr. Banks from seeing inside. Jenny stops on the bottom stair, sits, and wraps her arms around her knees, making herself small again.

"Tell Mr. Banks what you told me," Daddy says.

Biting her bottom lip, Jenny pushes to her feet, but Daddy shakes his head.

"Stay where you are," he says. "And tell Mr. Banks what you told me."

"I took the vodka from upstairs," Jenny says, sitting where Mr. Banks can't see her. All she can see is the side of Daddy's face as he stares straight ahead at Mr. Banks standing outside. "I took my daddy's key, and I got into the cabinet where he keeps it. I took a bottle and brought it to Nora's. I drank from it too."

That's what she told Daddy because that's what Nora said and Tia and Mandy too.

"We got trouble enough," Mr. Banks says, casting a shadow that falls across the entry and lands near Jenny's feet. "Don't need your kid causing more."

"Understood," Daddy says, and behind the door, where Mr. Banks can't see, he motions for Jenny to go back upstairs.

"That's it?" Mr. Banks says. "You ain't going to even have the girl come tell me to my face?"

"You heard what you needed to hear," Daddy says. "She said what she needed to say. Won't happen again."

"See that it don't," Mr. Banks says.

Daddy stumbles and when he closes the door, he holds the vodka bottle by its throat. Mr. Banks must have shoved it at him, but Daddy didn't shove him back.

Jenny wants to smile because Mr. Banks is gone, but Daddy isn't smiling, and that means she shouldn't either.

"We'll stay through tomorrow to celebrate your birthday," he says. "You're to stay home until then."

"Yes, sir," Jenny says.

"Mrs. Banks already has a nice lunch planned for tomorrow," Daddy says. "Went to a lot of trouble, so we'll go, assuming we're still invited. And then we're going back to town. We're done with the swamp for this summer. Already told Dehlia to expect us."

Daddy looks down on Jenny for a good long time, as if making sure his talking-to sunk in, and then as he lowers onto the step next to her, his face softens.

"Just doesn't seem like you," he says. "Stealing from me like that. Can you help me understand?"

Jenny rests her head in her hands and doesn't say anything. Daddy wouldn't understand that once you have a friend or two, sometimes lying for them is more important than telling the truth to your daddy.

"Do I still get to stay up with Dehlia tonight?" Jenny says, trying not to let her voice crack on the way out. "Can we still wait for Margaret Scott?"

"I'm saying yes only because you don't get a do-over on your eleventh birthday," Daddy says.

"Will you help me hot glue before Dehlia gets here?" Jenny asks, snuggling in next to Daddy, tucking up under his arm. "And help me hang the orchids."

Daddy drapes an arm over her shoulder and pulls her close.

"We'll hang so many orchids, Margaret Scott won't stand a chance of missing this house."

Jenny leans hard into Daddy, not even caring that she has to go back to their house in Naples and miss spending the rest of the summer at the swamp. It's warm next to Daddy, and she'll like spending every day with him at his work. Maybe when they come back next year, Nora will be gone, and the swamp will be like it was before.

"Dehlia says Mama saw Margaret Scott on her eleventh birthday," Jenny says, resting her chin on her knees. "But I don't think that's true."

"And why is that?"

"Because Mama never did her one great thing."

"Sure, she did," Daddy says, smiling even though his eyelids droop like he's still sad.

"What did she do?" Jenny says, thinking she's going to hear something she's never heard before and not wanting to miss a single word.

"You think on that for a while," Daddy says. "See if you can figure it out."

Sitting this close to Daddy, no space between them, feels so good that Jenny doesn't even care Daddy didn't give her an answer.

"Mr. Banks doesn't live with Mrs. Banks anymore," she says when Daddy stands. "Does he?"

She's been wanting to ask Daddy a question ever since she saw him and Lily by the pool. If she doesn't do it now, in this quiet time, she doesn't think she ever will. And she has to ask him because she has to warn him.

"No," Daddy says, lowering himself back down, closing the space between them again. "He doesn't live with his family anymore."

"Because Mrs. Banks had an affair," Jenny says.

Daddy cringes as if Jenny using those words is like her throwing a handful of rocks in his face.

"Yes, she did," he says.

"And Mr. Banks knows."

"He does."

"But he doesn't know the rest, does he?" Jenny asks.

"The rest of what?"

"That you're the one who loves Mrs. Banks," Jenny says.

Daddy dips his head, hiding his face from Jenny.

"I saw you and Mrs. Banks by the pool last night," Jenny says. "And so did Nora."

"That was a goodbye you were seeing," Daddy says, letting out a long sigh. "Sure didn't intend for you to see it. Sure didn't intend for Nora to see it."

"I'm glad we're leaving," Jenny says.

"You've had to do way too much growing up," Daddy says, touching his forehead to Jenny's. "That's on me, and I'm sorry. Suppose we both have something to spend the rest of the summer making up for."

Jenny rests a hand on Daddy's stubbly cheek. He pinches his eyes like her touching him hurts.

"Daddy?" Jenny says in a husky whisper. Their noses almost touch, and she has to ask him again because he still hasn't answered her. "Does Mr. Banks know?"

Silence fills the house and presses on them both, not letting them move. And the longer it presses on them, the heavier it gets, until it finally squeezes an answer out of Daddy.

"No," he says. "Mr. Banks doesn't know about me and Lily."

"Even if last night was goodbye, Nora still saw," Jenny says. "I think for sure she's going to tell her daddy. I think she'll tell him real soon."

Beverley stands in her backyard. The sun burns her neck, and sweat drips between her shoulder blades. She gathers her long hair, twists it on top of her head, and pulls on a ball cap. It's a quiet morning. The daily grind of trucks rattling down gravel access roads and nail guns firing and circular saws churning through lumber is still on pause. It's as if the entire neighborhood and the next and the one after that are holding their breath, waiting to see what happens next. Tugging her hat low on her forehead, she stares at the chain saw sitting on the ground.

Elizabeth keeps trying to get her to go down to the check-in site. She says it'll be good for the morale of the volunteers. She says it'll be good for Beverley. But she doesn't understand. Now that Beverley is back, she can't leave this house. Francie is here, in every room, in every corner. She's in her favorite chair, the closet filled with her clothes, the brush in the upstairs bathroom, the shoes that wait for her just inside the front door. Beverley might never leave this house again.

But the swings in the backyard, they have nothing to do with Francie.

Nudging the chain saw with her toe, Beverley looks up at the swing set. A tower with a slide anchors one end, and a crossbar holds two swings. It can't be that hard. One cut on the top support beam should bring down the entire side where the swings are attached. But she's never started a chain saw.

She'd never torn out a window screen, either, but she figured a way.

Feeling as if she's being watched, she glances up at the house. Someone stands in the back windows. It might be Robert. His car was still in the driveway. She saw it when Agent Watson left to go next door to the rental where he still has people working. She's ready with an apology, but she'd do it again. She'd put them through any nightmare if it led them back to Francie. But an apology is the right thing to do. She and Robert need to reset, put up that united front Elizabeth is always talking about.

The person in the window disappears. The back door off the kitchen opens, and Agent Watson walks out. He looks like a man who might know how to start a chain saw.

"Back so soon," Beverley says, squinting up at the swing set, still considering how best to attack it.

Beverley was pregnant when she and Robert bought the house, and the wooden swing set was already here. They kept it, imagining their little one would play on it one day.

Ten years later, it hasn't been touched, not once.

"What you got going on here?" Agent Watson says, slipping off his suit coat and draping it over one arm.

"Know how to start one of those?" Beverley says, nudging the chain saw with her toe again.

"Mind if I ask what you have in store for it?"

"It was cruel of us," Beverley says. "Robert and me. Leaving this swing set here all these years. Francie never played on it. I guess we kept hoping one day."

"That's not cruel. That's optimistic."

Beverley shakes her head. "No. It was cruel. For a long while, she'd ask to play on it. We said no so many times, she stopped asking."

"Let's go hustle up Robert," Agent Watson says. "Get his opinion."

"Think he's sleeping," she says, and just as she says it, Robert appears at the back door.

He crosses the yard to stand next to Beverley. The two men greet each other, and they all stare at the swing set.

Robert rests a hand on Beverley's shoulder as if he's about to encourage her to go inside. But instead, he gives her a squeeze like he already knows just what she has planned and picks up the chain saw. Agent Watson drapes his jacket over the single chair on the back patio, unbuttons his cuffs, and rolls up his sleeves.

"Here's hoping," Robert says, and gives the chain saw one good yank.

It starts up on his first pull. Surprised by the sound of the motor, a rumble she feels in her throat, Beverley backs away. Agent Watson steps under the swing set, reaches both hands overhead and presses them on the underside of the crossbar where the swings hang, ready to support its weight. Robert lifts the chain saw. He gives the agent a look, an are-you-ready look, and when Agent Watson nods, Robert plants his feet wide, reaches up, and presses the blade to the length of wood.

As Robert eases the blade deeper into the cut, his shoulders shake. The wood begins to smoke, and Beverley wants to lay her head back, scream, and never stop. Instead, she presses both hands over her mouth. A sob erupts in her throat. Her eyes fill with tears. She blinks, clearing her vision because she doesn't want to miss a moment of this.

When the blade cuts through, Robert switches off the chain saw, sets it down, and quickly slides up next to Agent Watson. Together, they lower the section Robert cut free.

"I'll call someone to come finish the job," Robert says, turning his back on the carnage. "Haul it off. Maybe donate it."

"No," Beverley says. "Leave it."

One half of the structure now lays on the ground, the two swings a tangle of rusted chains. The wooden tower is all that's left standing. She wishes they'd taken it down years ago. Maybe somehow, someway if they had, Francie would still be here. Having to look at it, day in and day out, that'll be her and Robert's punishment.

Back inside, Agent Watson, having sweated through his shirt, sits at the kitchen table. Beverley hands him a damp cloth. He wipes his face as Beverley and Robert sit across from him. Beverley's hand is in Robert's. He took it when they sat, must have, but she didn't feel it. Their fingers are laced together. They skipped over the part where Beverley apologized for her accusations. He didn't need to hear it any more than she needed to give it.

"Well," Agent Watson says. "That was a first."

His news isn't fatal. He'd come at it a different way if it were. But it's big enough to sit them both down.

"You have something to tell us?" Beverley says, clinging to Robert's hand.

"The report came in regarding Robert's polygraph," Agent Watson says. "No deception indicated."

The pressure of Robert's hand on Beverley's doesn't change. He knew it all along.

"And?" Robert says, his posture softening slightly as he exhales. Maybe he was more worried than Beverley thought. But now, he's relieved.

"We received a letter at the PO box that was established for Francie's case," Agent Watson says. "I mentioned it a few days ago, that we set it up."

"Just one?" Robert says.

Beverley traces their fingers with her eyes, letting them roll from Robert's to hers and back to Robert's.

"One in particular," the agent says. "Given extenuating circumstances, it got our attention. The letter appears to have come from a child."

Beverley lifts her eyes.

"A child?" she says, and then a sharp intake of air fills her lungs as a thought blindsides her.

"No, not from Francie," the agent says. "My apologies."

The air draining from her body leaves Beverley dizzy. She clings to the table, a habit that began only a few days ago but will likely stay with her the rest of her life.

"What did it say?" Robert asks, his voice steady. He takes Beverley's hand again.

"It was short," the agent says. "Just a few words."

"Which were?" Robert says.

"Francie won't come home. I know you'll miss her. I'm sorry."

"It's a prank," Robert says, pushing away from the table, nearly knocking his chair over.

Beverley grabs it before it falls.

"You think Nora wrote it," she says. "You think Nora knows her father took Francie, and she wrote that note. Trying to be kind, she wrote that note."

As he pieces it together, Robert bends forward, hands to his knees, as if suddenly dizzy himself.

"Because Levi Banks thinks I was having an affair with his wife," he says. "Because he thought that, he took our little girl."

As his understanding sinks in, he squats to the ground, dips his head, and wraps his hands over it.

"The letter is being analyzed," the agent says, staying on a flat plane despite Beverley's and Robert's ups and downs. "The zip code is in line with the possibility. And so you don't go storming down to the Bankses' house, Lily Banks gave permission for Nora's school to provide us with a variety of writing samples."

"And she understands why you need them?" Beverley says.

"She does."

"How long until we know?" Robert says, pushing to his feet, steadier now, but just barely.

Beverley goes to Robert and wraps her arms around him. She rests her head on his chest. Like hers, his heart is racing. Francie is the thing that bound them together, more so even than the vows they took. And now, to lose her, it could tear them apart. Or it could bind them closer. She knows the research. It can go both ways.

"Depends how nuanced the process is," the agent says.

"Do you know where Levi is living?" Beverley says, sliding into the crook of Robert's arm, hoping the two of them survive this. Hoping they're strong enough.

"We do," the agent says. "But I'll remind you, even now, Lily Banks maintains her husband was home with her the night Francie disappeared."

"What now?" Robert says. "What next?"

"Next?" the agent says, standing and filling a glass of water. "We wait to see what the handwriting tells us."

When Dehlia's car appears at the end of the road, Jenny pushes off the front patio and runs to the drive to meet it. Throwing open her car door, Dehlia climbs out, arms stretched wide, and twirls, showing off the panels of her flowing skirt that spread like the petals of a flower.

"Come, my daughter of Margaret Scott," she says, sweeping Jenny up in her arms. "We have much work to do."

Dehlia smells of sweet, musky sage. Her long braid hangs over one shoulder, and she's woven slender, fuzzy feathers into it. Jenny runs her hand over the braid, careful not to touch its tip. She's glad Dehlia is here and that they still get their night of waiting up for Margaret. She's also glad she and Daddy are going home. She even hopes Lily changes her mind and cancels the birthday party. Home will feel better, safer, and next summer, they'll all start over.

"Daddy helped me hang the orchids," Jenny says. "He says we hung so many, we might as well hang Christmas lights too."

"You're making a believer out of him," Dehlia says. "Good for you."

The Final Episode

Drawing in a deep breath of Dehlia's sweet, musky smell, Jenny straightens her shoulders and lifts her chin, readying herself to tell Dehlia about her plan.

"I know where Margaret Scott is going to guide me," Jenny says. "She's been guiding me since the day we got here. I know what my great thing is."

She clamps her lips down tight, startled by how quickly the words spilled out.

Dehlia pulls a casserole dish from the trunk and hands it to Jenny. She makes the same macaroni and cheese every year for Jenny's birthday.

"You know already?" Dehlia says. "Shouldn't be surprised. You've got more second sight than any Scott woman I've ever met. Go on, then. Tell me."

"I'm going to find Francie Farrow," Jenny says, thinking that by saying it out loud she's trapping herself into doing it. "Right here in the swamp maybe."

"What do you mean, find . . . ," Dehlia says, her smile wilting. "You're talking about the girl from the newspapers?"

"Yes, Francie Farrow from Fort Myers."

"Darlin'," Dehlia says, squatting to look Jenny straight on, her long, gauzy skirt pooling at her knees. "Finding that poor girl, that would be a great thing. But Margaret wouldn't want you out there in the swamp, looking where it isn't safe"

"But she does," Jenny says. "She's left me signs."

Jenny's been holding on through all the hard times, just like Dehlia said she should. She's been holding on until her being different turned into something good. She's been holding on until the day the kids stopped calling her the wetland witch and being afraid of her because she killed her own mama. She's been holding on until now, this day, when she would be strong enough to do something as great as Margaret Scott. And she's ready for the holding on to come to an end.

"What signs, darling?" Dehlia says, looking like she doesn't really want to know.

"Margaret Scott didn't leave me a ghost orchid," Jenny says, ready to tell Dehlia the thing that will convince her for sure. "But she left me something better. She left me a flyer with Francie's picture on it. Right across Halfway Creek. Right where we always go for orchid hunting. And the man who took Francie said he was taking her into the swamp. Margaret Scott is leading me to Francie."

Dehlia dips her chin. She puckers her lips and starts taking quick, deep breaths through her nose like she's working herself up to tackle a steep set of stairs.

"If that sweet girl is lost out there," Dehlia says, "the helicopters will find her. Or the police. Not me. Not Margaret Scott. And for sure not you."

"But Dehlia," Jenny says, deciding to use Dehlia's own words to convince her. "This is my occasion to rise up. This is when I can outfox them and bludgeon them with their own hatred. This is when I can bend history."

Still kneeling, Dehlia drops forward to her knees like she's getting ready to pray, except Dehlia doesn't pray.

"You listen to me, Jennifer Anne Jones," she says, looking hard into Jenny's eyes like she's pounding the words into Jenny's brain. "Margaret Scott did not leave any flyer for you. She is not leading you anywhere. And you will not go looking for Francie Farrow."

Waiting isn't much fun. That's mostly what Jenny thinks as she and Dehlia sit on a blanket spread out in the backyard. But it isn't all bad either.

Jenny took a nap so she could stay up late, and now, it's full on dark. The night air is sticky hot. Clouds of mosquitoes buzz overhead, searching for a crack in her bug spray. Those things, she doesn't much like. But she does like the tiki torches Daddy drove into the ground. He lit each one, and now the flames dance and flicker. Their reflections sparkle in Halfway Creek, making the black water come alive instead of lying there dead like usual. And overhead, the white ghost orchids she made shimmer in the dark trees. Those things, Jenny likes.

"Close your eyes and listen," Dehlia says right in the middle of neither of them saying anything for a long time.

The buzzing mosquitoes have grown louder. Cicadas whine out in the dark trees. Somewhere deep in the swamp, a limpkin screams.

"I'm hearing all kinds of things," Jenny says. "What am I listening for?"

"Footsteps," Dehlia says.

"Footsteps?" Jenny says, her eyes popping open. She hugs her knees and stares into the shadowy trees on the other side of Halfway Creek.

Sitting straight and tall from doing yoga most every day, Dehlia closes her eyes.

"Sometimes you'll hear Margaret before you see her," she says. "It's almost time. It's nearly midnight."

Jenny plants her chin on top of her knees and looks as hard as she can, letting her eyes roll from left to right and back again. She listens hard, too, for any crackle or rustle. She's hoping for two sets of footsteps. One will be Margaret. One will be Mama.

The night air grows thicker. Most of the sounds coming from the swamp trail off, leaving behind only the steady buzz of the cicadas. Every once in a while, Jenny stretches her eyes wide, trying to force them open. Her arms feel heavy. Her head wants to roll off to the side like it's lying on a pillow. She jerks a time or two, shakes off the sleepy feeling, and pries her eyes open, but then they're heavy again. They close and open, staying closed longer each time.

She jerks upright when something takes hold of her arm.

"Up," Dehlia says, yanking Jenny to her feet. "Inside. Now."

Half standing, Jenny stumbles backward.

"What is it?" she says.

Dehlia yells at her to get herself inside, grabs the kitchen ladle they brought with them when they laid out the blanket, and douses the first tiki torch.

"Is it time?" Jenny says, backing toward the house, the damp grass prickly on her feet. "Is it happening?"

Dehlia goes from torch to torch, snuffing them out and waving at Jenny to get inside. Jenny keeps backing toward the house. The smoke from the snuffed-out flames sticks in the heavy, wet air, making her cough.

Once inside, Jenny slides the glass door closed and looks around for Daddy, wishing he were here. But he isn't. He's upstairs in his room. He promised to give the Scott women their privacy. He'll be asleep by now.

Out in the backyard, Dehlia's long skirt glows as she hurries from one torch to the next. When she's darkened the last one, she looks out across Halfway Creek. Keeping her eyes straight ahead like she's afraid something is going to charge her, she backs toward the house.

"To bed," she says once inside.

"Dehlia. Grandma. What was it? What did you see?"

"Never you mind what I saw," she says, waving Jenny away with a flick of her hand. "To bed. And not a word of this to your daddy. Promise me, not a word."

"I won't promise. Not until you tell me what you saw. Was it Margaret? Did you see her? Was my mama with her?"

"No," Dehlia says. "It wasn't Margaret. It wasn't your mama. It was another kind of something. We made it too easy. I did. I made it too easy, lighting up all those torches. You have to promise me you won't go poking around out there, looking for that girl. That Francie. You promise me, right here and now. Margaret isn't out there, hoping to help you. Something evil is out there, hoping to hurt you. Hoping to hurt us all."

With her hands pressed to the glass, Dehlia stares into the dark yard. Jenny looks, too, but doesn't see anything, not even the moonlight shining on Halfway Creek. Clouds must be covering the moon, and without its light and the light from the tiki torches, the night is so black it seems the world falls away right outside the sliding doors. It seems the only thing left behind is them and this house.

"I see danger out there," Dehlia says. "There's nothing for you on the other side of Halfway Creek. You promise me you understand. You'll do something wonderful one day, I know it like I know my own name, but Margaret sent a warning tonight instead of a calling. She's begging you to stay put and stay safe."

Mandy lifts onto her knees when the springs in Nora's mattress squeak. The bedroom is dark. The whole house is asleep, except for Mandy and Nora. As Mandy's eyes adjust, soaking in the little bit of moonlight that seeps into the room, she can just make out the shape of Nora. She's sitting up in bed, hugging her knees. The red numbers on the clock on her bedside table read 12:43 a.m.

"Do you think Jenny saw her grandma Margaret tonight?" Nora whispers.

"I don't know," Mandy whispers back, not wanting to wake Tia.

Mandy likes her time alone with Nora. That's when they share things no one else can hear.

"Do you believe all that?" Nora says. "The stuff about Jenny being like her grandma, being able to see things other people can't?"

"It's real about Margaret Scott," Mandy says. "She's Jenny's grandma and was hanged for being a witch. That's written about in books. It's real about her doing a great thing and stopping anybody else from getting hanged too."

"But the second sight," Nora asks. "Now that Jenny's eleven, will she have that? For real?"

Mandy shrugs, but Nora probably couldn't see.

"Maybe," Mandy says because sometimes she thinks Jenny already has second sight. Jenny says it's been simmering since she was born, and that when she turns eleven, it'll be fully cooked.

"Is it like reading minds?" Nora asks.

"Sort of," Mandy says, wishing Nora didn't like talking about Jenny so much.

"What does 'sort of' mean?" Nora says, spitting the words like she knows Mandy could tell her more if she wanted to.

"She says when things happen, they don't only leave a trail behind," Mandy says, sharing the one thing Jenny ever told them that she understood. "They leave a trail out ahead too. It's like a trail of pictures, parts of pictures, fuzzy sometimes, clearer sometimes, leading right to what's going to happen. That's how it's supposed to be."

"Is it that way for Jenny?" Nora asks, sounding more worried now than interested. "She knows about things before they happen?"

"I don't know," Mandy says. "She just said that's how it's supposed to be."

Nora gets quiet, maybe thinking over what Mandy told her.

"I have to tell you something," Nora says.

Mandy crawls to the side of Nora's bed, rests both hands and her chin on the mattress and sits back on her knees.

"You can tell me anything," Mandy says.

"Remember the night Francie got taken away?" Nora says. "What I told you?"

A few days after Nora moved in, she told Mandy a secret, one she had to cross her heart and promise not to tell anyone. Nora asked if Mandy knew about Francie Farrow, and when Mandy said yes, Nora told her that she was the girl asleep in the room when Francie Farrow was taken. She also said she felt real bad that Francie was gone and would never come home again. Other people were still looking for Francie. Other people were still hoping she'd come home. But not Nora. She already knew Francie was gone for good. Mandy didn't like knowing that secret.

Wishing Nora wanted to talk about something else, Mandy presses her mouth into the mattress, and in a muffled voice says, "I remember."

"There's something else," Nora says, staring across the room at nothing. "Something no one knows."

Mandy doesn't want to hear anything no one else has heard, but that's not something she can tell Nora.

"The man who came into Francie's bedroom," Nora says, and takes a long pause like she's working up the courage to say what she has to say, "he was there to get me."

"Get you? Instead of Francie?"

"I had to tell someone," Nora says, pulling back like she thinks Mandy is angry at her. "You're my best friend. I don't know what to do. Please don't be mad at me."

"I'm not mad," Mandy says, reaching for Nora's hand, but Nora pulls away. This is a secret Mandy definitely doesn't want to know. She wants to wad it up and give it back, and that isn't what a best friend should want to do.

"He came to my bed first," Nora says, covering her mouth with both hands like she can't believe she said the words out loud. "He grabbed my ankle. He shook me. But I pretended I was asleep."

Mandy closes her eyes and swallows the sour swirl that leaks up from her stomach. Then the song she can't shake starts playing in her head. Francie Farrow. So much sorrow. Hope she comes back home tomorrow. It runs through her head every night when she's trying to sleep.

"He knew my name," Nora whispers. "He said, 'Nora, get up.' I was so scared, but I kept my eyes closed. He knew my name, Mandy."

Air rushes in and out of Mandy's nose. She squeezes the edge of the mattress with both hands and dips her forehead so her whole face is hidden in the sheets and blankets. She wants Nora to stop.

"And then Francie must have heard him," Nora says, looking off toward nothing. "She was too young. She didn't know to pretend she was asleep."

Mandy lifts her eyes, the only thing she can manage.

"I guess he grabbed Francie out of bed, because I heard her ask where they were going," Nora says, her hands sliding up over her eyes. Mandy sometimes does the same when something gets too scary. "And that's when I looked, just the littlest bit."

"You saw him?" Mandy says, glancing back to see if Tia is still asleep. "You saw who took Francie?"

This time, instead of hoping Tia was still asleep, Mandy wishes she'd wake up. She wants to reach across the room and shake her until she does.

"I did see," Nora says, digging her hands in the sheets that are crumpled up around her. "I saw him. I saw who took Francie."

Mandy's head sinks into her shoulders. Nora's secret keeps getting bigger, and Mandy can't hold it up any longer.

"Nora," she says, exhaling a whisper. "You have to tell someone."

"I can't," Nora says, pulling the sheet up over her chin, mouth, and nose. Only her eyes peek out at Mandy. "You're the only one I can tell."

Mandy doesn't know what to say next, but she knows what Tia would say.

"You have to," Mandy says. "For Francie, you have to tell an adult. Your mom. You should tell your mom."

"I can't," Nora says. "I'm afraid."

"Do you know his name, Nora?" Mandy says, the room thinning at the edges like a bubble ready to burst. "The man you saw, do you know his name?"

Letting the sheet slide from over her face, Nora leans in.

"I'm afraid if I tell, what happened to Francie will happen to me," Nora says, her voice turning breathy, like she has to say what needs to be said quick before all her air runs out. "I'm scared, Mandy. I'm really scared."

Mandy has one more question to ask, but she's too afraid. She can't even take Nora's hand to make her feel better. She can't even crawl back to her sleeping bag. She can't even move her lips. But if she could, she'd ask Nora if it was her own father she saw in Francie Farrow's bedroom that night. She wants to ask if Levi Banks took Francie.

The Final Episode

Jenny opens her eyes to a bright bedroom. The light is always safer than the dark. She smiles at first, thinking about today being her birthday, but then she remembers she didn't see Margaret Scott last night. She also didn't see Mama, never even worked up the courage to ask Dehlia if she might. The next time her birthday rolls around, she'll be twelve, and there's nothing special about turning twelve. She'll never see Margaret. She'll never see Mama.

In the bathroom, she splashes cold water on her face and washes her arms up to her elbows, all of it to scrub off the feeling she is stuck with being ordinary. Because, one way or another, she's not going to let that happen.

Her face still dripping wet, she pushes away from the sink, gathers her dark, wiry hair and pulls it over her right shoulder. Last night, Dehlia said she saw something evil out in the swamp. In that moment, Jenny believed her, and she was scared. But after having all night to think it through, she's starting to think Dehlia was lying about it all. Still, she's going to be careful just in case, and the braid will help her do that.

Beginning on the left side of her head, she carves off a layer of hair, divides it into three sections and weaves the strands together. The hair slides from her fingers and hangs in her face. She tries again, but the braid is too loose and falls apart.

"Want me to help?"

Dehlia stands in the doorway, her own long braid hanging over her right shoulder and falling nearly to her waist. It's tight and perfect and looks like a long sisal rope. Jenny holds out the only brush that will go through her hair.

"You having this braid to protect you doesn't change the promise you made me," Dehlia says, drawing the brush through Jenny's hair. "You can't be running around in that swamp, searching for that young girl. It's not safe out there."

Staring down at the counter and not at Dehlia, Jenny nods as if to say she'll stand by her promise. But she doesn't think she's going to.

More than once, Dehlia has said doing great things sometimes means breaking rules. Margaret Scott told a lie when she said the governor's wife was a witch, but that lie saved countless women and their daughters and sons. Jenny wanting to save Francie Farrow, a great thing for sure, makes her lie to Dehlia a lie worth telling too.

Starting on the left side, Dehlia parts Jenny's hair and splits it into three sections. Her fingers move quickly and smoothly as she weaves Jenny's hair together, picking up more sections as she moves across her head and toward her right ear.

"Did you make it all up?" Jenny says, afraid to ask but knowing she has to.

"Did I make up what?" Dehlia's fingers pause before going back to work on Jenny's braid.

"You didn't really see something evil out there in the swamp. You only said that, so I won't go looking for Francie."

There's another pause, longer this time.

"All I know is what I saw," Dehlia says, but because she puckers her lips and lifts her chin, Jenny is certain she's lying. "We'll try again next year."

Jenny was right. Dehlia didn't see anything out in the swamp last night. She only pretended she did so Jenny would promise not to go looking for Francie Farrow.

"You know, being eleven isn't an ending," Dehlia says, still trying to convince Jenny. "It's a beginning. You have a lifetime to do your one great thing, and you never know when Margaret will find her way to you."

Reaching the tip of the braid, Dehlia ties it off with a black band and washes her hands with soap and water. Watching Dehlia, Jenny forces a smile like she's happy to wait until next year. She smiles like she's happy to stay away from the swamp and forget about Francie Farrow. She smiles like she's happy to end up being Dehlia's age and still having not done anything great with her life.

The Final Episode

But she isn't happy to do any of that.

"This braid will snag all evil that comes near you," Dehlia says, placing her hands on Jenny's shoulders. "The evil'll get confused in all these twists and turns and have nothing to do but drain onto the ground."

Dehlia might be lying to Jenny, but she does weave a good braid. Jenny feels safer with it. Safer and stronger. She feels ready. And she'll need all the protection she can get because she isn't staying put like Dehlia wants her to.

"Mind you don't step on your shadow," Dehlia says, studying Jenny's reflection in the mirror as if she knows what Jenny's thinking. "That'll be good as stepping in all that evil. Don't let it drain down your back either. It'll follow you forever if you do."

Again, Jenny nods. She already knows all the rules of Dehlia's braids.

"And never," Dehlia says, swinging around and looking Jenny straight on. "Never touch the tip."

"And if I do," Jenny says, "wash with soap and water."

"But listen to me and listen to me good," Dehlia says, her fingers squeezing Jenny's shoulder, kneading the warning into Jenny. "If enough evil comes your way, that one braid won't be able to snag it all. You still have to steer clear. That means no wandering off into that swamp because you think you can save that young girl."

Jenny nods like she promises, but again, she doesn't say it out loud.

The whole rest of the day is still Jenny's eleventh birthday, and then tomorrow, she and Daddy are going back to town. She's glad about that. Getting Daddy away from the Banks family is a good thing. But for today, she's still at the swamp, and she can do what needs doing.

Hopefully, one more day is all Jenny needs. Hopefully, one more day will be enough, but not too much.

Toting macaroni and cheese, sliced rolls, and everything to make homemade ice cream, Daddy, Dehlia, and Jenny walk to Nora's house for Jenny's birthday lunch. Jenny keeps sneaking peeks at Daddy and Dehlia to see if they're watching her extra close. They walk as if it's any other day, Dehlia asking Daddy did he remember the salt for the third time and Daddy not answering, but instead, eyeing her over the top of his sunglasses. They're not watching Jenny any closer than any other day.

Being a daughter of Margaret Scott wasn't something Jenny learned. It has always been part of her, like her wiry, dark hair or her second toe being the longest. Dehlia must have started telling her the story of Margaret Scott the day Jenny was born. Jenny likes it best when Dehlia tells her the part about the eleven-year-old girl who was sitting in a prison and waiting to be hanged after they finished hanging Margaret. Instead, Margaret slung her accusations at the mayor's wife, the trials ended, and that little girl went free. She was the first person Margaret Scott saved. That little girl grew up and had children of her own, and they've been trickling through history ever since.

Every daughter of Margaret Scott knows the eleventh birthday is the most important. And for the rest of today, it's still Jenny's eleventh birthday.

"Good to see you, Jenny," Lily says when she opens the door to the three of them. Her voice is cheery, as if she's forgotten about the vodka. "And happy birthday to you. I understand it's a very important one."

Daddy flicks his eyes at the spot where a white pickup truck is parked whenever Mr. Banks is at the house. The spot is empty, meaning Mr. Banks isn't here. Jenny feels better knowing that, and she hopes the empty spot stays empty.

"Thank you, Mrs. Banks," she says. "Lily. And thank you for having us today."

Lily wraps Jenny in a hug. She smells like frosting, like sugar and vanilla. She holds on a long time, letting Jenny know there are no hard feelings.

The Final Episode

"The girls are back in Nora's bedroom," she says when she finally lets go. "Why don't you go ask them to come on out? I want to get some pictures."

The four girls gather under the oak tree in the front yard. Lily brings out Jenny's birthday cake so it can be in the pictures, too, apologizing that it isn't quite done yet. Dehlia snaps pictures, and Mrs. Norwood flips on her camcorder. Daddy stands off to the side, laughing as the girls jockey for position.

"No sense taking video if you girls are just going to stand there," Mrs. Norwood says, squinting as she looks through her viewfinder. "You're in back, Nora. You're the tallest. Have some fun already."

At first Jenny doesn't do much but stand still and smile. She's thinking about Francie Farrow and wanting to get busy trying to find her, except now she isn't sure how to do that. On the walk from her house to Nora's, the swamp seemed to grow a whole lot bigger. But as everyone else starts twisting and turning and having fun, she does too. She makes silly faces and what she thinks are grown-up faces.

When the cameras are shut off, the spell is broken. The laughing, strutting, and posing stops, the adults head back inside, and Nora and Mandy peel off by themselves.

"That braid mean you're like your grandma now?" Nora says, keeping her distance as her eyes slide down the braid trailing over Jenny's shoulder.

"I guess," Jenny says.

"That mean you can read my mind?" Nora says, now studying Jenny top to bottom.

Jenny shakes her head. "It's not like that."

"Probably a good thing you can't tell what I'm thinking," Nora says, then gives Jenny one last once-over and takes Mandy's hand. "See you guys later."

More than once, Daddy has told Jenny to be patient with Nora. He said people who go through difficult times sometimes become difficult people. They need a thick hide so the pain they're going through doesn't sting so bad. Being difficult, even nasty, is a way of growing a thick hide.

"You didn't want to go with them?" Jenny says to Tia, shuffling her feet in the bristly grass as Nora and Mandy walk toward the trailhead at the end of the road.

"Na," Tia says. "Nora was mad her mom invited you, said she and Mandy were leaving if you were coming."

Jenny thinks about telling Tia that Nora has a thick hide to protect herself and that maybe she's sometimes nasty for a good reason, but she decides not to. She's not sure if Tia knows about Nora being the girl in Francie Farrow's bedroom, and she's not going to be the one to tell her. Also, part of the time Nora was being nasty, Tia was too. And Jenny doesn't want to make Tia feel bad.

"Did Margaret Scott come last night?" Tia says, digging a toe in the dirt instead of looking at Jenny. "I stayed up until twelve thirty, thinking about you and Dehlia."

"She came with a warning that it wasn't safe to look for Francie," Jenny says, happy to know Tia stayed up that late for her. It makes her feel like they're almost friends again. "That's what Dehlia said anyway."

"But you don't believe her," Tia says, smiling and already walking toward the road. "You're going to go looking for Francie anyway."

"Want to come?" Jenny asks, having to run after Tia, who is already on her way to the spot where they can cross Halfway Creek.

They both know going back to where they saw the flyer is the place to start. Jenny isn't certain what comes next, but she's counting on Margaret Scott to show her.

Everything is snapping into place, and that feels so good that it's almost easy to think of Nora as weaving a thick hide with all her meanness instead of being plain old mean.

FADE OUT:

CHAPTER 15

I woke on the kitchen floor, the house dark and quiet. Lifting onto my knees, I looked out on the lanai. Nothing was out of place, and the power light on the speaker was dark. Across Halfway Creek, the tops of the cypress trees glowed orange with the beginnings of sunrise. Not wanting Dehlia to catch me sleeping on the floor, I stood, tiptoed upstairs, and slid back into bed. I stayed there, drifting in and out of sleep, until Dehlia woke and went downstairs to the kitchen. When I heard her filling the coffeepot at the sink, I got up and let Belle out of her kennel, knowing Dehlia would feed her and take her out.

In the shower, the hot water relaxed my back and shoulders, both sore from sleeping on the hard terrazzo. As the pain eased, I hoped the strangeness of that music playing in the middle of the night would ease as well. But it didn't. It felt like part of you had seeped into the house through those slow, wandering notes right when I was trying to let you go.

The more I thought about Mandy's apology to me, the more certain I was you were about to be outed as the man who took and killed Francie Farrow. Somehow, I needed to prepare Dehlia, but I didn't know how to do that. No matter what I told her, she would go on believing in you. I settled on bringing the speaker inside once I was done in the shower and checking around the house for any signs someone had been here. I couldn't prepare Dehlia, but I could protect her.

When the water turned cold, I dressed and headed downstairs. The smell of bacon and freshly brewed coffee drifted out of the kitchen and so did voices. Dehlia was talking to someone, and it sounded like she was talking to Arlen.

Walking into the kitchen, I nearly stumbled over plastic containers and lids scattered on the floor. Kneeling in front of an empty cupboard, Arlen looked up at me.

"Sorry about the mess," he said, pushing back on his knees and nearly falling over when Belle jumped on him. He smiled, but his eyes were heavy, making him look tired. "Didn't intend on coming inside. Your grandmother is very persuasive. She was kind enough to get breakfast going for me too."

Standing at the counter on a step stool, Dehlia pulled spices from an overhead cupboard as bacon simmered and popped on the stove.

"She is persuasive," I said, wishing I weren't so happy to see Arlen. But I was. "What's she got you doing?"

"Helping her look for a key," Arlen said, flicking his eyes in Dehlia's direction and giving me a shrug as if he wasn't altogether sure why or what key.

"He brought your furniture," Dehlia said, stepping off her stool to flip the bacon. "You left your phone there on the counter. He was texting for you to open the gate, so I let him in."

"Hope you don't mind," Arlen said. "Texted you a while ago. Probably should have waited to hear back. Loaded up the things I knew wouldn't fit in your car and wanted to drop them off before I got on with my day."

"It's great to see you," I said, an awkward thing to say even if it was true. "I mean, I appreciate your help. Thank you."

"Told him unloading could wait," Dehlia said.

Same as Dehlia had seemed to know I was moving back and same as she had sweet tea ready for Tia, she seemed like she'd been expecting Arlen. I'd never told her about him, yet she was as at ease with him as

The Final Episode

she might have been with her own grandson. He was equally at ease with her.

"You shouldn't be bothering Arlen," I said, annoyed with Dehlia for dragging Arlen into her mess. "If you're looking for the key to the garage door, we don't have one, remember? I have to get a whole new lock."

Dehlia raised her brows because she hated when I used that word . . . remember. She didn't like the implication, but sometimes she did forget. Sometimes, she chose not to listen.

"Don't think it's the one to the garage," Arlen said, speaking up as if to ease the tension. "Think it's one of your dad's. Ring a bell?"

He held my glance an instant longer than necessary, a sign he wondered if there was something concerning about Dehlia looking for your keys.

"Daddy's keys are in his room, Dehlia," I said, even more annoyed that Dehlia was wasting Arlen's time by looking for old keys that didn't go to anything anymore. "What do you need them for?"

Shoving jars and small tins of spices back in the cupboard in no particular order, Dehlia yanked open the next. I stepped in to try to help, because I wanted her to stop so Arlen could get on with his day. I also wanted her to stop because her haphazard approach was like a leaky faucet that was going to torment me until I stopped the drip. But she brushed me aside.

"I'm not talking about those keys," Dehlia said. "The spare. That's what I'm looking for. The spare from the extra room."

Arlen took my hand, gave it a squeeze, and mouthed the words . . . it's okay . . . because he knew I was frustrated with Dehlia.

"I got time," he whispered.

"She's talking about the owner's room," I said, squeezing his hand in return to say thanks and then taking the bacon off the burner. "From when we used to rent the place. Mostly old furniture in there. All junk by now."

"Room is full of liquor, is what it is," Dehlia said, and hands to her hips, she studied the kitchen as if deciding where to look next. "As

Jenny here well knows. Been looking for that key for three weeks. Ever since she swiped that vodka."

I stopped laying out the bacon on a paper towel to think about what Dehlia just said. This was a first, Dehlia losing two decades. It surprised me, and it scared me.

"I think you're remembering not quite right," I said, taking care with what I said next. "I was ten when I took that vodka. It's been twenty years, not three weeks."

Crossing her arms, Dehlia slowly squared up to me, and I clung to the smile I'd managed. I was waiting for her mistake to swoop down on her and bracing for how she'd react when it did.

"I know damn well it's been twenty years," she said, her tone knocking the smile from my face. "I'm talking about the three weeks since I saw you do it on that show."

"You're talking about the series?" Arlen said, nodding as he put together Dehlia's train of thought. "Yeah, you stole it in episode four."

He smiled as if we should be happy Dehlia had been making perfect sense. And I was. I was relieved, too, but her scolding still stung. I didn't get many of those as a kid, but when I did, Dehlia always said having a daddy in prison meant I had to be twice as good as every other kid. She said I'd get one strike in life, and I'd better never expect a second and for sure not a third.

"That's right," Dehlia said. "You stole it in episode four. Now, let's get busy and find that key."

"There was no spare key to the owner's room," I said. "Just the one. And it's probably still on Daddy's key ring."

"Yes, Jennifer," Dehlia said, using my full name as another way of scolding me. But right on top of it, she used a softer tone. "And I used that key a few weeks ago to get into the room. Seeing you swipe that vodka, that's what made me think of it."

Arlen slid up alongside Dehlia and helped her empty a bottom drawer of bowls and plates. He gave me another look like he was just fine being here in the middle of this mess.

The Final Episode

"You went into the owner's room?" I said.

More than any other part of the house, the owner's room filled with all your things has stood still, waiting for you to come home. I never went inside. Being so close to you and so far at the same time was too painful.

"And you know what I didn't find in there?" Dehlia said, squeezing Arlen's arm in thanks for emptying out the drawer. "That spare key that's supposed to be hidden up over the door. The one you used on the show to steal the vodka."

"You're talking about the spare key to the cabinet," I said.

"That's right," Dehlia said, slapping her hands together, happy I'd finally caught on. "The original key to the cabinet is on your daddy's key ring, right where it belongs. But that spare, I saw you return it to its proper hiding place on the show. Now, it's not there."

Other than my birth causing amniotic fluid to leak into Mama's system and kill her, my decision to steal that vodka had been the one truly bad thing I did in my childhood.

"That was a long time ago," I said. "Police probably took it when they searched the house."

Dehlia jabbed a finger at me like I was onto something. Pressing that finger to her lips, she let her eyes slide around the kitchen. Settling on the small desk where she paid bills, she pulled open the bottom drawer.

"Take a look," she said, slapping a folder on the table.

Arlen stood behind me, a hand on my shoulder. I placed mine over his out of habit, but once I did, it felt good. I held it so he'd know I wanted him to stay and flipped open the folder.

A receipt was tucked inside. It listed everything the police took from the house when they searched it the night you were arrested. A small check mark in red pencil was next to each item.

"There," Dehlia said, pointing at an entry that read . . . set of five keys on ring. "They took your daddy's keys and returned them. That's what the check mark means."

"You checked off things as the police gave them back?" I said.

"I did. Made sure every single thing came back to us."

"There's no entry for a single key," I said, sliding my finger down the list of items. "Just the key ring."

"Precisely," Dehlia said.

I glanced at Arlen as if he might know what Dehlia was getting at. He shook his head, meaning he didn't. I'd gone from feeling like he was an outsider who I had to protect from all our dirty secrets to feeling like he and I were a team. I started wondering if I was unwilling to give second strikes to anyone because I had never expected any for myself. I hadn't given Arlen a chance to explain what happened with the jobs he lost before I swooped in with a solution on strike one. I hadn't considered a second strike for him and me. And I wanted that for us, had since the moment I sent him away, but I still didn't want to saddle him with me and my name.

"Do you think this proves the police didn't take the key?" I asked.

"I do," Dehlia said. "If they took it during the search, it would be on this receipt."

"I'm a little confused," Arlen said. "Why does that key matter?"

"I'm confused too," I said. "It's been twenty years, Dehlia. It got lost in the shuffle. I don't know why we should care."

"Right now, I'm not altogether sure why either," she said, cupping my chin. "But you will figure it out. Same as the mess I've made in this kitchen is gnawing at you, that missing key will gnaw at you until you put all the pieces together."

Dehlia still thinks too much of me. It makes me sad every time she lets on that she does, and every so often, it makes me angry. I do what has to be done, and that's what matters. I pay the bills. I work hard. I do unto others by being kind. But that has never been enough for her. She still thinks too much of me despite a lifetime of me being nothing special.

I love Dehlia, but I'm worn out from living with her expectations. Sometimes I want to tell her, enough already. Her expectations are nothing but constant reminders of all my failures. I can't bear to tell her she's setting me up to fail once again, because I have no idea where the key is or why it matters.

CHAPTER 16

I led Arlen into the garage, him shaking off yet another of my apologies about Dehlia and her missing key. I hit the button, opening the door, and sunlight and hot, muggy air flooded in.

"That the ladder you used to get on the roof and steal Dehlia's vodka?" Arlen asked, nodding at a ladder propped against the far wall.

"The vodka *we* stole," I said, wagging a finger at him. "All four of us."

We were teasing each other, almost flirting. It had been the same when we first started dating. We'd circled the friendship for weeks, testing each other's interest. This felt the same, except it couldn't end the same. I'd lost my business and a chance for a steady job, all because of my name. And I didn't want the same to happen to Arlen.

Nothing had changed for us, not yet. But the anger and frustration were gone.

"Want me to get another key made?" he said, lowering the tailgate on his truck as I rearranged a few things to clear space in the garage. "Put Dehlia at ease?"

"Might need to do it to put me at ease," I said. More easy conversation that felt like it used to. "Apparently, that lost key is going to be my undoing if I don't find it."

Arlen laughed as he moved around the truck, loosening the tie straps he'd used to secure my things.

"You were right to move back here," he said, pausing as if thinking something over. Then he nodded and moved on to the next strap.

"I'm not so sure," I said, checking the yard for signs someone had been to the house the night before. There wasn't even a stray branch on the ground.

Curious about what I'd said, Arlen stopped what he was doing and faced me.

"I think you may have been right about trouble following me," I said, straining to look him in the eye. "But it's not like I had a choice about moving back."

"Something happened," he said.

As I explained about the music, Arlen stayed quiet and tried his best not to let his anger show, but he forgot about his jaw. It flexed as he clenched his teeth.

"Mind if I take a look around when we're done here?" he said, and now he couldn't look me in the eye. He was that angry.

"I lost my last client yesterday," I said. "I don't think . . ."

I intended to tell him again that I was still afraid of him losing clients. But already knowing what I was going to say, he raised both hands, surrendering the argument.

"I get it," he said. "Just asking to take a look."

"And if I asked you to stay? At least until this is over? For Dehlia, in case more trouble shows up?"

"For Dehlia?" He winked. Another lighthearted moment.

"And me. And if we keep measure of things, namely your clients, and they don't bail, maybe we keep on? Go back to the way things were before? But we go slow, we wait to decide."

"Which is to say, I'll be sleeping on the couch," he said, keeping on with our playful tone.

"For the foreseeable future, yes."

Across the street, Tia walked out her door. Her hair was pulled back, making her look more like Tia from twenty years ago. Really, more like Mandy.

I thanked her for coming over to help, and after introductions, we began unloading the truck. Arlen kept a comfortable distance, letting Tia and me work together and pretending not to notice Tia's silliness as she jabbed and teased me about him. With so much worry hanging over all of us, a little fun felt good. It felt normal.

When my phone chimed, I set down my end of a coffee table Tia and I were carrying.

"I got to go deal with this," I said, wiping the sweat from my face with the tail of my T-shirt and digging my keys out of my pocket.

Eva's new assistant was down at the gate, right on time to pick up my copy of Eva's house key.

"I'll come with," Tia said, hustling down the drive to catch up to me.

On the short walk, I explained that I'd not only lost my last client but I'd also lost a shot at a steady job. Then I fessed up to asking Eva about Tanya's background check because it had occurred to me that Tanya was a new person in my life. It occurred to me that she could be Nora.

"Doesn't sound like a crazy thought to me," Tia said, our footsteps on the gravel falling in perfect time, just like when we were kids.

"But what sense would it make?" I said, working Eva's key off the key ring. "Why would she go to the trouble of getting a job with Eva just to befriend me?"

"She ever ask you about the show?" Tia asked, stopping as the gate at the end of the road came into sight.

Tia had first raised the possibility on the day she arrived at Halfway Creek. Revenge could be a motivator, but so could fear. If Nora was afraid of something coming out in the final episode, something like her having covered for her dad all those years ago, she might come looking for information from someone like me. But then I circled back to Mandy and her apology. Something was coming in the final episode that Mandy knew about and that made her want to apologize to me. I thought that meant you were guilty. Maybe I was wrong to assume that, or maybe there was no Nora. Maybe I was looking for something or someone who didn't exist anymore.

"We talked about it a few times," I said. "But almost everybody I talk to these days asks me about the show."

"Somebody tried to break into your house," Tia said, smiling and waving as if she knew the girl who climbed from a car parked on the other side of the gate. "Maybe it was Tanya. Maybe it was even this girl."

Tia stayed a few steps behind as I met the girl at the gate. Eva was trying someone a little older again, still trying to find that work ethic none of her other assistants had. The girl was tall and slender and everything about her made me think her life had always been easy.

"Eva said to tell you thank you and good luck," the girl said, smiling as if Eva instructed her to do that too.

I handed her the key. She took it, taking care not to let her fingers touch mine, or maybe that was my imagination.

I'd returned many keys over the last six weeks. I have a spreadsheet where I keep track of the date I receive a key, the date I return it, and the name of the person I hand it to. One disagreement that ended with me having to pay to get a house rekeyed taught me the lesson. I had every reason to do the same now.

"Do you mind sharing your name with me," I said, glancing at Tia. "I keep records. Since Eva isn't picking her key up, I'd need to make note of who is."

"No problem," the girl said. "Christine Brighton."

I watched until Christine drove away, and when I turned, Tia already had her phone out. She cupped her screen to cut down on the glare.

"Good idea," she said. "You just whip that up on the fly?"

"Sort of," I said. "But that wasn't Nora Banks. Way too tall, right? And she didn't hesitate to give me her name."

Tia nodded for me to follow her into the shade that fell along the side of the road.

"She's all over social," she said, flashing me her phone. "Christine Brighton. Here she is with three older sisters. You're right. She's not Nora."

"So, that leaves Tanya," I said. "Or someone else altogether."

Tia tucked away her phone, and we started back toward the house.

"I'll poke around tonight," Tia said. "See if I can drum up anything online about someone named Tanya who worked for . . . what was the company called?"

"Verifiably Vintage," I said. "Tanya with Verifiably Vintage."

EPISODE 7

EXT. GRAVEL ROAD on HALFWAY CREEK – DAY (7 days missing)

Leaving Nora's house without telling the parents where they're going, Jenny and Tia head straight for the trailhead at the end of the road. They'll cross Halfway Creek there and stick to the main trail, and that'll take them right back to the flyer with Francie Farrow's face on it. Then they'll look until they find the next sign from Margaret.

They run as far as Jenny's house and then slow to a walk, both of them red faced, breathing hard, but mostly smiling and happy.

"Look who beat us here," Tia says, nudging Jenny and pointing straight ahead.

Nora and Mandy stand in the shade of the pines at the end of the road. Nora has a hand cupped to Mandy's ear and is leaned in as if whispering to her. She keeps whispering until Jenny's and Tia's footsteps make her turn.

"Let's go to my house," Mandy says, sneaking a look at Jenny like she doesn't want to be around her.

"We don't have to leave," Nora says, crossing her arms.

"Nobody said you did," Tia says, walking past Nora and Mandy.

At the spot on the bank where they always slide down to the creek below, Tia looks left and right for any sign of the Old Man. Stepping up alongside her, Jenny can still feel Mandy's eyes darting in her direction. Something is causing a tingle on the back of Jenny's neck, but it isn't the Old Man. It's Mandy. She's looking at Jenny like she's scared of her.

"What do you think?" Tia says, nudging Jenny and pointing down on the creek. "Can we still try?"

After so much rain, the stones they use for crossing are all underwater.

"We've done it before," Tia says, poking Jenny this time because she isn't paying attention.

Instead, she's listening to the sound of rustling and crunching. It's coming from Mandy. She's high-stepping through clumps of wire grass as she makes her way toward the road. Nora takes a quick look at Tia and Jenny, maybe decides it's too hot to stay and watch them try to cross Halfway Creek, and follows Mandy.

Glancing over her shoulder, Mandy smiles as Nora falls in behind her. When she turns back so she can continue through the bristly clumps of grass, she stops.

Tia is still going on about the stones in the creek being down there even if they can't see them, but Jenny isn't listening. Something is wrong because Mandy is standing like she's stuck in wet cement. Something has scared her. Jenny scans the ground and the trees, and then she sees it.

"Tia," Jenny says. And when Tia doesn't hear, she says it again. "Tia. Look."

Straight ahead, beyond the wooden sign that marks the trailhead, the Old Man is stretched out on a grassy patch of ground. The sun hits him full on, making his black hide shimmer like a suit of armor. Or maybe like he's chiseled from black stone.

Sometimes the Old Man floats in the middle of the creek, his green eyes piercing the black water's surface. Other times, he's on the far side of Halfway Creek, stretched out on the soft, muddy bank. But today, he's no more than ten steps away. One green eye is closed, but the other is open and pointed at Mandy.

"Everybody just back up," Tia says, wrapping a hand gently around Mandy's arm.

Jenny takes Mandy's other arm. Together, she and Tia take small backward steps, taking Mandy with them.

"Is it dead?" Nora says, sliding in behind Jenny where she can see the Old Man without being too close.

Nora's voice is loud, like she's talking right in Jenny's ear.

"Just a few more steps," Tia says, whispering in a slow, even tone to Mandy. "Nice and easy."

"It's not moving," Nora says, still right in Jenny's ear. "I think it's dead."

Jenny wishes Nora would stop talking so loud. Daddy always says to be quiet, stay calm, and back slowly away if they ever come upon a gator. They're more afraid of you than you are of them. But Nora's being loud. Too loud. She'll wake it, or worse, she'll startle it. And the Old Man doesn't look at all afraid.

"You're okay, Mandy," Jenny whispers, talking as much to herself as Mandy.

Still shuffling backward, Jenny and Tia lock eyes and move at the same speed. The crackling grass turns to gravel crunching under their feet. The gravel feels safer.

It feels like they're almost home.

Jenny and Tia drop Mandy's arms. Mandy's shoulders soften. She exhales a puff of air.

"Somebody see if it's dead," Nora says, again breaking the silence.

"It's not dead, Nora," Jenny says. "Nobody's checking anything."

"You chicken?" Nora says.

"No, Nora. I'm not chicken," Jenny says, trying her best to remember about difficult times making difficult people. "I'm just not stupid."

"Shut up, Jenny," Nora says.

"You shut up," Jenny says. "You don't know anything about anything."

Tia stands at Jenny's side, the two of them shielding Mandy from Nora.

"What do you think, Mandy?" Nora says, staring at Jenny but talking to Mandy. "You want to see if it's dead?"

Same as Mandy has been looking at Jenny in a new way today, so is Nora. But Nora is looking like she hates Jenny. Nora saw her mama and Jenny's daddy dancing by the pool and maybe she saw them kissing, too, but she doesn't know it was goodbye. Probably, she wouldn't care.

"Well, Mandy?" Nora says, still glaring at Jenny. "You want to see if it's dead?"

"Sure," Mandy says, the word barely squeezing out.

Nora came only a few days ago, but Mandy's whole life has changed in that time. It started when Nora took Mandy's hand, looked her straight in the eye, and told her she was so pretty. Right away, Mandy stood taller. She lifted her chin, held her head just so. Nora liked her best, and that was the one thing Mandy had never had. Tia was everyone's favorite. She was fun and made people laugh and was never scared of anything. Now that could be Mandy because she wasn't scared when she was with Nora.

"We can use this," Nora says, bending to pick up a palm frond. It's brown and dry and as long as a broomstick. "Just give it a poke. Make sure it's still alive."

Holding the palm frond by its spine, Nora waves it. The brittle leaflets rattle. More of what might wake the Old Man.

"Show them how brave you are, Mandy," Nora says, passing the palm frond to Mandy.

Mandy's eyes jump between Tia and Jenny on one side to Nora on the other, maybe deciding which side to choose.

Choosing Nora, like Jenny knew she would, Mandy wraps both hands around the palm frond, jabs it straight ahead and shuffles her feet until it's pointed at the Old Man.

"You're so amazing, Mandy," Nora says, smiling at Jenny. But it's not a happy smile. It's a hateful smile. "Show them why you're my best friend."

Hurting just Jenny isn't enough for Nora. Instead, she's going to hurt Jenny more by hurting Mandy.

"You don't need to do this, Mandy," Jenny says. She understands about doing almost anything to have a friend.

"Yeah," Tia says. "You know he isn't dead."

With her arms crossed, Nora cocks a hip out to the side and smiles. Everything about the way she stands and looks says to Mandy . . . go ahead. It's no big deal.

Sweat drips down Mandy's forehead. Her arms quiver from the weight of the palm frond. Taking a few steps toward the Old Man, she works her hands to the end of the palm frond's spine, stretches her arms as far as they'll go, and tips at her waist.

When she's still not close enough, she takes another step. Both Jenny and Tia take the step too. The Old Man is only a handful of steps away now. His sides push out and fall in, a sure sign of his breathing. The fuzzy tip of the frond bounces in the tall, brittle grass. Jenny wraps her hands around Mandy's to take some of the palm frond's weight. Tia does the same.

They can't stop Mandy. She needs this too much. But they can help.

As Mandy stretches, Jenny and Tia stretch. Their skin sweats where they're pressed together. Mandy's entire body shakes. She tips forward so far, she nearly falls. Just one more step and they can touch the Old Man's snout.

Something sails past Tia's head, making her swing around. Mandy falls, dropping the frond, and Jenny goes down next. A rock lands to the right of the Old Man's snout. A perfect shot. And the statue carved from stone comes to life. As Mandy is scrambling backward, screaming and pushing at Jenny who is scrambling, too, the Old Man lunges, his head swings to the side as he snaps at the sudden movement near his mouth.

Someone yells. Maybe Tia. Mandy is sobbing. Jenny is pulling Mandy through the bristly grass.

And someone is laughing.

Once Jenny reaches the gravel, crawling there as she pulls Mandy along with her, she drops onto her back. Lifting onto one elbow, she looks straight ahead as the tip of a black tail disappears over the bank and the Old Man slips into Halfway Creek.

"It's gone," Jenny says, Mandy lying next to her.

Tia stands over them, staring at something. And that's when Jenny notices Mandy isn't sobbing or screaming anymore. She's frozen again.

Jenny pushes off the ground and brushes her hands together. Once she's steady on her feet, she bends over and touches a raw spot on one knee. Blood drips down her shin. Then she looks down on Mandy.

"We have to do something," Tia whispers.

Mandy's arm hangs limp, and her wrist doesn't look right anymore. It's an odd shape, and one of her fingers is bent the wrong way.

Jenny and Tia look at each other, neither of them certain what to do. They gather Mandy to help her off the ground, telling her over and over, it'll be okay. It'll be okay. Once on her feet, Mandy begins to scream again.

And somewhere nearby, Nora is still laughing.

Jenny runs back to Nora's house, not knowing what's wrong with Mandy but knowing it's bad. She runs the fastest she's ever run, losing her flip-flops on the rocky road and not even cringing as she runs barefoot the rest of the way. She's never seen an arm bent the way Mandy's was bent.

By the time she reaches Nora's house, her lungs burn and sweat runs down the sides of her face. She throws open the door, not bothering to knock. Once inside, she leans forward, her hands to her knees, and sucks in the cold inside air. It burns and makes her gasp. When she's able to talk, she says . . . Mandy's been hurt.

Picking potato chips from a bowl, Daddy sits at Lily's kitchen table. Mrs. Norwood sits at the other end where she's leaned over Jenny's birthday cake, piping letters on top. Lily stands at the stove, cooking up the base for the homemade ice cream.

Hearing Jenny, they all swing around to face her. Daddy jumps to his feet, his chair toppling over behind him.

"Where?" he says.

"The trailhead."

Jenny points at the open door, and Daddy runs outside, the screen slapping closed behind him. Mrs. Norwood follows Daddy, and Lily sweeps up alongside Jenny. With a wooden spoon still in hand, Lily guides Jenny toward the screen door where they can see outside. Milky white ice cream mixture drips down Lily's wrist.

"What happened?" she says, stepping into the front windows for a better view of the road where Daddy and Mrs. Norwood disappeared.

Hearing footsteps outside, Jenny turns. Nora stands on the other side of the screen door. Her eyes jump from Jenny to her mama, looking like she's trying to figure how much Jenny already told Lily.

As Nora pulls open the screen door and steps inside, Jenny points a finger at her.

"It was Nora's fault," Jenny says. "She made Mandy touch an alligator, and Mandy fell. I think she broke her arm."

Nora drops her head off to one side and looks to her mama. She's giving Lily all the space she wants to say something.

"Nora," Lily says. "Is that true?"

"She used a branch," Nora says, making a face that means it was no big deal. "Not my fault she fell. I didn't push her."

"She threw a rock at the alligator," Jenny says. "It snapped at it, and that made Mandy fall. It was Nora's fault. All her fault."

Lily runs her hand down the length of Jenny's braid.

"Are you okay?" she asks Jenny. "Did you get hurt?"

Keeping her eyes on Nora, Jenny shakes her head, her chest pumping up and down as she sucks cold inside air through her nose. She feels it all the way down, and it helps her stand tall.

"That is not how we behave, Nora," Lily says, still holding Jenny close. "You owe the girls an apology. And Jenny's dad and Mrs. Norwood too."

"How should I behave, Mom?" Nora says, her head still tipped off to the side, her eyes stretched wide as she waits for an answer. But there's a lot more hiding inside Nora's question than it sounds like at first. "Should I behave like you?"

Nora is saying that since Lily had an affair, she shouldn't be telling Nora how to behave.

"Don't get smart," Lily says, shooing Nora away from the door so she can go outside. "Go on to your room."

Jenny sinks into Lily's side as Nora walks past. Once Nora's bedroom door slams closed, Lily pushes open the screen and runs outside, leaving Jenny alone in the middle of the living room.

She wraps her arms around herself, shivering with the cold air hitting her sweaty skin, until another pair of arms wraps around her. They're warm and sturdy.

"You're all right." It's Dehlia. Jenny forgot she was here. "You did real good. Your daddy will take care of Mandy."

When Jenny says nothing, Dehlia checks her over, top to bottom, to make sure she isn't hurt.

"You hear me? You're all right. You're safe."

Jenny nods, and Dehlia leads her to the front window.

"See there," she says. "Your daddy has Mandy. They'll get her to a doctor. They'll see to it she's taken care of."

Cradling Mandy in his arms, Daddy takes long smooth steps down the middle of the road. Mrs. Norwood hurries alongside him, brushing the hair from Mandy's face with one hand and holding tight to Tia's hand with the other. She's smiling as she talks to one girl and then the

The Final Episode

other, but both she and Daddy are walking as fast as they can without breaking into a run.

When the group gets near the house, Lily runs back inside, drops the wooden spoon on the living room floor, wipes her sticky hand on the front of her dress and grabs her keys from the kitchen table.

In the front drive, Lily unlocks her car, throws open the back door, runs around to the other side and starts up the engine. By the time Daddy reaches the driveway with Mandy in his arms, the car is ready to go. Lily holds open the back door while Daddy sets Mandy inside. Mrs. Norwood slides in next to her, and Daddy jumps behind the steering wheel. And then they're gone.

"Already on their way," Dehlia says, hugging Jenny as they stand in the front window. "She'll be fine. You'll see."

Out in the middle of the yard, watching as the car drives away, Tia stands alone. Lily reaches out to her as if to lead her back to the house, but Tia shakes her head and says something to Lily. She's probably saying just what Jenny said. That it wasn't an accident. That it was Nora's fault. Then Tia turns on one heel, marches over to the oak that straddles her yard and Nora's and sits in its shade.

Lily comes back inside and disappears into Nora's room, and Jenny and Dehlia join Tia under the oak tree.

"You picked a real good spot, Tia," Jenny says, sitting next to Tia. She sits so close that when they crisscross their legs, their knees touch.

Dehlia brings them lemonade and sprays them down with bug spray, and Jenny plans to sit here with Tia all night if need be. They'll sit here together until Daddy brings Mandy home.

Sitting behind the steering wheel of her parked car, Beverley stares up at her dark house. She's left the driver's side door open, but the heat will eventually drive her back inside.

Robert thinks she's sleeping beside him, and the last two nights, she's tried. But both nights, every time she started to drift off, the wind in the attic vents or the ice maker dropping a load of ice woke her. She began to wonder . . . If I can hear all that, how did I not hear a man take my daughter from her bed? Not able to bear another reminder of what she didn't hear and with nowhere else to go, she escaped to the front seat of her sedan.

Next door, a lone patrol car sits in the driveway. No one has said the police are tapering their search, but they are. She's still doing interviews, but more and more, Elizabeth is asked what new information will be reported before the interview is booked. Everyone is turning to the next story.

When the rearview mirror catches the reflection of a set of oncoming headlights, she shifts around in her seat. A dark sedan parks on the street behind her. Its door opens and slams closed. She steps out of the car and stands.

"Is it the note?" she asks.

She and Robert have talked of little else since Agent Watson told them about the note they received in the PO box. It was the key to everything making sense. Nora had been covering for her father because what daughter wouldn't? But she was a good girl. She couldn't keep lying, so she did the best she could. Thinking it would be a comfort to Beverley, Nora sent an anonymous note. Beverley and Robert couldn't be happy that they were closing in on the answer because nothing in the answer guaranteed Francie was still alive. But the note was the first step toward finding her.

Agent Watson startles. He left his suit coat in the car, and his sleeves are rolled up.

"Are you just getting home?" he asks, leaning to see if anyone else is in the car.

"Easier to spend my nights out here," she says. "Decent breeze tonight. It's not so bad."

"You're not sleeping out here," he says, looking at her over the roof of the car.

"Sleeping, no. But I like the quiet."

He nods as if he understands, but he doesn't.

"Guessing you've stopped by for a reason," Beverley says.

"Here about the note."

"I should wake Robert," Beverley says, closing her car door.

The police have probably picked up Levi already. This is the beginning of finding Beverley's little girl. Levi wouldn't kill her. He couldn't. He did it to punish them, not destroy them. Resting her hands on the roof of the car, she takes a deep breath, readying herself for everything to change. When she starts for the house, Agent Watson meets her at the front of the car.

"Not sure you need to disturb Robert," he says. "Don't see the need."

Beverley shakes her head, slow at first and then faster. She drops back against the car. Her shoulders slump. Her head drops.

"It wasn't Nora?" she says.

"No, it wasn't," Agent Watson says, his voice sounding as if it comes from far away. "I'm told there was no question. Unfortunately, we can't control what comes in. My guess, a well-meaning child. Parents probably didn't know she did it."

"So, a girl wrote the note?" Beverley asks, lifting her head. "Then maybe it was Francie. Did you ever check? Let me see it, the note. I know her . . ."

But Agent Watson is shaking his head.

"Francie was the first person we eliminated," he says. "Even before I told you about the note. I'm so sorry. I know you were counting on this."

"And Levi," Beverley says, staring up at the dark house. Now she'll have to tell Robert in the morning. "Is he crossed off the list now?"

Agent Watson rocks backward a step and blows out a long breath. After only a few days, a week, Beverley knows him so well. More bad news is coming.

"A few days ago, Levi provided mileage records for both the cars he owns," the agent says. "We've been analyzing them."

"That's convenient," Beverley says.

"Tax records," the agent says. "Daily mileage because he and Lily are both self-employed. He had entries up to and including the trip he and Lily made to your house the morning you called them."

"And that's proof?" Beverley says. "He's saying he's accounted for every mile, and it doesn't include an extra trip to kidnap my daughter?"

"The records go back years," the agent says. "Mostly, it's Lily's handwriting. She seems to be the organized one. Mileage to jobs is separate from other car trips."

"So he borrowed a car, rented one." Same as she's felt the manpower next door slipping away with every passing day, she feels the agent slipping away too.

"Perhaps," he says. "But we have to find proof of that to make it so. Can't wish it into existence. I know you see Levi Banks being a perfect fit, but you seeing it isn't enough. I wish it were. We have no evidence of him being in that room. No prints on the doors or windows. Nothing. I need proof, and right now I don't have it. And I can't promise you I ever will."

"Are you telling me Levi Banks is no longer a suspect?" Beverley says.

"I'm not telling you that," he says. "I'm not done with anyone or anything. If I get new information, I'll follow it. Back to Levi or onto someone new. But Beverley, the vast majority of these cases, I mean the vast majority, are runaways."

"And the vast majority are older than Francie," Beverley spits back. "The vast majority were abused. The vast majority had ongoing conflicts with their parents. None of those parts fit."

The Final Episode

"I know you don't believe Francie would run away but consider another word. Perhaps she wandered away. Strayed too far."

"That's what you've thought all along," Beverley says. "How much was missed, I wonder, because that's what all of you thought all along? And now you're done? Is that what you're here to tell me?"

"After a few days, memories start to fade," the agent says. "We may still get new information, but the best has likely already found its way to us. And time is not our friend here. I'm sure you know that."

"It's over, then?" Beverley says.

She's already seen the drop in officers at the rental next door. Robert says people are still showing up to search, more every day, but they're searching for a body now. No one will say that to Beverley, but it's true. For most people, hope is too slippery to hold on to for long.

"It's not over," the agent says, and pauses, leaving Beverley to say the rest.

"But we may never know," Beverley says.

"I hope that's not the case," the agent says. "But preparing for it might make your life the littlest bit more bearable."

Daddy kneels next to Jenny, smooths her blanket, and kisses her on the forehead. Up in Mandy's bed, Mrs. Norwood does the same to Mandy. Then she takes a giant step over Jenny, who's sleeping on the floor between the two beds, gives Jenny a quick kiss on her way past, and ends by tucking in Tia.

When Daddy and Mrs. Norwood got back from the hospital with Mandy, Tia and Jenny and Dehlia were still waiting under the oak. The sun was down, and Jenny and Tia were asleep on the blanket Lily brought out to them. Dehlia got in her car and went home, Jenny and Tia each showered, and no one said anything about how Mandy got hurt. Daddy and Mrs. Norwood said that could wait until morning.

At the door, Daddy flips off the light.

"You three get some sleep," Mrs. Norwood says, squeezing past him and looking in over his shoulder. "I'll try not to wake you girls when I check on Mandy."

Daddy backs from the room, slowly pulling the door closed on his neck until he pretends he's stuck. He lets his head droop and dangles his tongue out the side of his mouth. This makes Tia and Jenny laugh, and Jenny is happier than she's been all summer. Even with Mandy's arm being hurt. Jenny is happy like she might not sleep at all tonight because she doesn't want to miss out on one moment of this feeling. She's almost as happy as the first day at the swamp, when she and Daddy pulled up to the house, when the helicopter hadn't flown overhead yet, when she hadn't met Nora and it was still just her, Tia, and Mandy. Because now it's just the three of them again.

Until just now, she forgot today is still her birthday. It's almost over. She hasn't thought about it once since she ran back to the house to get help for Mandy's broken arm. She even forgot about Francie Farrow, and she feels bad about that. She'll have to ask Dehlia if there's a chance Margaret Scott might come on another night or maybe show up in the backyard at the house in Naples.

"Sweet dreams, all," Daddy says, pulling his head free of the door and leaving it open just enough for a sliver of the hall light to spill into the room.

Tia and Jenny both laugh at Daddy again, but Mandy doesn't. Instead, she rolls onto her side without saying good night to anyone.

As happy as Jenny is about having her friends back, Mandy probably feels like she lost her only one.

The house is dark when a telephone rings. Jenny opens her eyes. From somewhere far away, a bed creaks and footsteps hit the floor. Down the hall, a light pops on. More footsteps, coming this way. Jenny sits up. The hall light comes on next, a sliver of it falling across Jenny. Her eyelids flutter. She scrambles backward when Tia and Mandy's door flies open.

"Are you here?"

The Final Episode

It's Mrs. Norwood. The overhead light switches on. Her long red hair is a tangle that frames her face, and the oversize T-shirt she wears hangs nearly to her knees. Jenny squints and holds up a hand to shield her eyes. The covers on Mandy's bed drop to the floor as she kicks them off, and Tia's mattress creaks when she sits up.

"What?" Tia says. "We're here. What is it?"

Tiptoeing through the blankets and pillows scattered across the floor, Mrs. Norwood plants a palm on the top of Jenny's head for balance. She checks Tia over, touching her just long enough to make sure she's real, and then Mandy. She takes another look at all three and then takes in the rest of the room.

"Nora," she says. "Is she here? Has she been here?"

She crosses over Jenny's makeshift bed again and grabs the closet door, throws it open, and pulls the string that makes a single light bulb pop on. Pushing aside the hanging clothes, she leans to get a closer look. Next, she yanks on the bedroom door, checking behind it. When the doorbell rings, followed by someone banging, she runs from the room. Jenny starts to stand, but before she can untangle herself from her sheets, Daddy rushes in. Like Mrs. Norwood, he checks Jenny over, touches Tia's foot, Mandy's knee.

"Stay put," he says, and runs from the room.

All through the house, doors bang open, furniture topples, and over and over, Daddy and Mrs. Norwood call out Nora's name.

"She's not here," Mrs. Norwood shouts from somewhere downstairs and again from farther away. Every time she says it, she sounds like she's having a harder time squeezing out the words.

And every time she says it, Jenny pinches her eyes closed and clamps her hands over her ears. She doesn't want to hear Mrs. Norwood sounding so afraid, because that makes it real. Nora is gone.

Gone, just like Francie Farrow.

Over the past several days, again and again, Jenny has read the many articles she cut from the newspaper, so she knows exactly what's happening. Nora is gone, and now she'll be the headline, and people will poke at the ground with sticks as they search for her. They'll shout her name, hang flyers, and her parents will go on TV and beg whoever took her to bring her back.

When Daddy and Mrs. Norwood return to Tia and Mandy's room, they're breathing heavily, their faces shiny from sweat. Like Mrs. Norwood did, Daddy looks around the room and then behind him into the hallway. He pushes his hair from his face. He doesn't know what to do next or where to go.

"This is no time for messing around," he says, shaking his head in case any one of them had any idea about lying to him. "I need you three to listen to me. Do you know where Nora went?"

Jenny hugs her knees to her chest, feeling safer all balled up. She shakes her head, quickly and only a few times. Being scared is weighing down her voice, and she can't answer with words. Daddy's eyes go from Jenny to Tia, and she must shake her head, too, because Daddy gives a quick nod. Then his eyes slide to Mandy.

Mandy scoots up in her bed, wedging herself in the corner where the headboard butts up to the wall, and hugs her knees. Like Jenny, she wants to be small, so whatever got ahold of Nora won't get ahold of her too.

"Nora's gone?" Mandy says, her voice squeaking as she forces out the question.

"Do you know where she went, sweetheart?" Mrs. Norwood says, sitting softly on the edge of Mandy's bed, taking care not to bump up against her arm and the new cast on it.

Mandy leans so she's hidden behind her mama. When she doesn't answer, Mrs. Norwood tries again.

"Tia, Jenny, Mandy, you too," she says. "Mr. Jones is right. This is no time for messing around. Did Nora say anything, tell you anything about wanting to run away? Was she upset, do you think, by what happened to Mandy?"

"I'm glad she's gone," Jenny says, the words tumbling out before she felt them coming, but once they're out, more start piling up behind.

The Final Episode

"Jenny," Daddy says. "You mind that mouth of yours."

"She really hurt Mandy," Jenny says, feeling like she's saying what she's been holding in since Nora first came to the swamp. "And she did it on purpose. And she lies. I didn't steal the vodka, she made me do it. She lies and she's nasty and I'm glad she's gone."

"Not another word," Daddy says, jabbing a finger at Jenny when she starts to open her mouth again. "You all stay put. I'm going to go call Lily back."

"Honey, your daddy and I see a lot more than you think we do," Mrs. Norwood says once Daddy is gone. Reaching down from her spot at Mandy's side, she strokes Jenny's head. Jenny buries her face in her pillow to hide that she's about ready to cry. "But right now, I need you girls to think, because Mrs. Banks is scared to death. Did Nora ever talk about a favorite place? Did you all like to sneak off somewhere special?"

"I don't think she ran away," Mandy whispers, looking at Jenny over her mama's shoulder and then cupping her mouth like she doesn't want anyone else to hear.

But Jenny hears. She stops thinking about how she can reel in all those hateful things she said about Nora and starts wondering why Mandy is hiding from her. Same as Mandy spent all afternoon being afraid of Jenny like she was the gator hiding in the wire grass, she's doing the same now.

"Why do you think that, sweetheart?" Mrs. Norwood says.

"Because I think someone took her."

Keeping her eyes fixed on Mandy, Jenny pushes slowly to her feet and backs away. Mandy saying someone took Nora is stirring up a terrible feeling inside Jenny. Maybe this is what she gets for saying she's glad Nora's gone. Whatever it is, the feeling is like a balloon, growing slowly bigger, pressing on her chest, squeezing up into her throat, ready to bust wide open, and she wants to get away from it. She wants to get away from Mandy.

Daddy calls up the stairs, saying they all need to hurry up and get going. Mrs. Norwood yanks clothes from two drawers, throws shorts and a T-shirt to each of the three girls, and helps Mandy change while Tia and Jenny dress. She doles out shoes next and ties off three ponytails in three quick motions before shooing them all from the room.

"Hold the railing," she says as they hurry down the stairs. "Follow Jenny's dad. Watch your step."

Jenny's legs ache like they want to run but she has to go slow and be careful. Her feet hurt, too, because Tia's shoes are too small, and that thing growing inside her like a balloon is making it hard to breathe. She clings to Tia's sweaty hand as they fast-walk out the front door into the black, quiet night. She keeps looking back to make sure Daddy is behind them. Mrs. Norwood is in front, waving for them to hurry up and calling out to be careful. Hurry up. Be careful. Hurry up.

Once they all reach the drive, Daddy runs ahead to the Bankses' house. Across the road, Jenny's house is dark, but at Nora's, every light is on. Every one of her windows is like a wide-open eye watching them as they creep across the dark lawn.

Inside Nora's house, Lily is on the telephone. At seeing them all walk in, she presses a hand to her mouth and turns away. Mrs. Norwood starts to take Jenny, Tia, and Mandy back to Nora's room, but Daddy stops her.

"They shouldn't be in there," he says and glances at Lily to make sure she isn't listening. "In case the police need to search her room."

Mrs. Norwood nods at Daddy and glances around the brightly lit house as if wondering where else she might take the girls. She decides on Lily's bedroom. She sends Jenny and Tia first and walks alongside Mandy, tugging at her sling and asking if she's in any pain.

Lily's bedroom is large, and the bed is much bigger than Nora's. On one side, the white comforter is smooth, and on the other, it's slung back and the sheets are rumpled. Lily was sleeping there. Mr. Banks wasn't.

Switching on a lamp, Mrs. Norwood hurries the girls into a corner and tells them to sit on the floor where they can look out on the pool, as if that's a fun thing to do while they wait.

Tia sits first. Jenny sits next to her, and Mandy steps over them both to sit on the other side of Tia where she won't be near Jenny. Again, Mandy is acting like she's scared of Jenny, and wondering why is making Jenny feel like she's running out of room to breathe.

Once the three girls are settled on the floor, all of them cross-legged and staring up at her, Mrs. Norwood turns in a slow circle. With two fingers pressed to her lips and her eyes closed, she is thinking. She stops when she faces Mandy, opens her eyes, and bends to the floor. Settling on her knees, she takes Mandy's one good hand.

"You said something, sweetheart," Mrs. Norwood says. "Back at the house. You said you thought someone took Nora."

Mandy chews on her bottom lip and shakes her head.

"You did," Mrs. Norwood says.

Mandy shakes her head again and scoots away from Tia, but because she leans back to look at Jenny, she's scooting away from Jenny.

Mandy being afraid of Jenny means something bad is coming. Jenny knows it like she can see it out in the distance, like photos tumbling over the horizon and floating this way. Like a deck of cards somebody sprayed into the air. They're too small and too cloudy at first, but she keeps watching, knowing they're coming closer.

"It's all right that you said it," Mrs. Norwood says, giving Mandy's good hand a kiss. "I would just like to know why."

The lamp Mrs. Norwood switched on throws a soft glow that makes Mandy's eyes shimmer. Looking up at her mama, she blinks. A tear rolls down her cheek and disappears in the crease of her nose. Mrs. Norwood wipes it away with her thumb.

"No need for tears," Mrs. Norwood says, manufacturing a smile for all of them.

More light spills into the room when the door opens. A police officer walks in, taking off his hat as he does. Daddy comes up behind him and leans in the doorway.

Pushing off the floor, Mrs. Norwood joins the two men. As they talk in whispers, Tia drapes an arm over Mandy's shoulder and whispers to her that everything is okay. Over and over, she says it, and Jenny pretends Tia is saying it to her too.

When Mrs. Norwood turns to walk back to where the girls are huddled, the police officer follows and so does Daddy. Jenny starts to stand so she can go sit with him, but the officer stops Daddy, waves him back to the doorway, and says something to him. Instead of sitting on the floor like Mrs. Norwood does, Daddy nods to the officer and backs out of the room. Jenny wants to lunge for him and tell him to stop, come back.

"Be right outside," Daddy says. "Everything's going to be okay."

"You tell them out there that I want eyes on Levi Banks," the officer says to Daddy. "ASAP, Levi Banks."

Then the officer walks into the room. Daddy leans in one last time. He smiles at the three girls, and when he reaches Jenny, he holds her eyes and nods because he really believed what he said.

He really thought everything was going to be okay.

When the door closes on Daddy, Mrs. Norwood settles herself on the floor with the girls and scoots them closer together as if posing them for a picture. She cups Jenny's cheek like Jenny is one of hers. Pressed tight against Tia, Jenny fixes her eyes on the bedroom door. She wants to see Daddy the second he comes back.

"Do you think this is Levi's doing?" Mrs. Norwood says to the officer. She turns a shoulder on the girls as if they won't hear.

But they hear.

The Final Episode

"Let's start by one of you telling me about the cast on this young lady's arm," the officer says, reaching down to give Mrs. Norwood's arm a squeeze instead of answering her question. "Which one of you smart young ladies would like to tell me what happened?"

That's his way of not saying anything about Levi Banks. Jenny felt it the first day she saw him. He was the kind of thing that would come slithering up behind if a person didn't keep her eye on him.

The officer looks like a grandpa. He's tall and slender with thick silver hair and two bushy eyebrows. Taking off his hat, he lowers to the ground with a groan. As he waits for one of the girls to say something, his eyes move slowly over each of them. Mandy's knees are drawn up tight, and her face is buried in them. Jenny hugs her knees, too, and lets her eyes float to the floor so the officer won't pick her.

"How about you?" the officer says to Tia. She's looking at him like she's aching to tell him about Mandy's arm. "It's Tia, right? You look like you know what's what."

Tia straightens her back, lifts her chin, and crosses her arms over her chest. Jenny's supposed to be the one to do something great with her life, but Tia is the one rising up to be strong.

Tia starts slowly, but as she tells the story, it tumbles out. Jenny nods each time the officer asks if that is how she remembers it. Nodding isn't a great thing, but it's something. Mandy doesn't even do that.

Tia finishes by telling that Nora threw the rock that scared the Old Man and made Mandy fall.

"And how did Nora feel about Mandy getting hurt?" the officer says.

"She was glad," Tia says. "She laughed and didn't help Mandy at all."

"Fair enough," the officer says. His silver hair sparkles in the dim lighting. "How about this . . . today or any other day, did Nora say anything about wanting to run away?"

"She didn't like to go outside," Jenny says, starting to think that helping the officer will make this all end sooner. "She was scared to."

The officer nods and smiles at Jenny like she said a smart thing. She shifts around, her feet tingling as blood reaches them again. The questions are easy enough, and the officer is happy with what they're telling him. Jenny starts hoping their answers will help the police find Levi Banks and that she'll get to go home soon.

"Thank you for sharing that, Jenny," the officer says, then his eyes slide to Mandy. "I'm real sorry about your arm. It hurt much?"

Mandy's head sinks into her shoulders. She crosses her arms over her chest and shakes her head the littlest bit.

"Glad to hear it," the officer says. "Would it be all right if I asked you a few questions?"

Still hunched up like she doesn't want the officer to see her, Mandy nods.

"You told your mama you thought someone took Nora," the officer says. "Why do you think that? You mind telling me?"

"Nora was afraid," Mandy says, her words muffled because her face is buried in her knees.

"Can you tell me why she was afraid?"

"She was with Francie Farrow when she got stolen from her bed. Nora thought she would get stolen next."

Mrs. Norwood glances at the officer. "You're aware of Nora's involvement with Francie Farrow?"

Nodding at Mrs. Norwood to show that he already knows all about Francie Farrow, the officer stretches his legs out in front of him. Using the toe of one foot, he flips off a shoe. Then he flips off the other.

"Good, that's real good, Mandy," the officer says. "You mind? Been on my feet all day. Promise to tell me if my feet stink?"

Mandy pinches her nose. The officer lays his head back and laughs.

"No wonder Nora likes you so much," he says.

Next to Jenny, Tia's shoulders bounce as she laughs. She nudges Jenny, wanting Jenny to laugh too. She manages a smile and looks at the bedroom door, wishing it would open and she'd see Daddy again.

The Final Episode

She was hoping all these questions would get them home faster, but the officer hasn't asked one thing about Levi Banks.

Pretending he's embarrassed by his stinky feet, the officer puts his shoes back on and tugs on the laces of one like he can't remember how to tie a bow.

"Makes sense to me that Nora was afraid," the officer says. The loops of his bow keep falling apart. "What else did she tell you about that night with Francie?"

"She told me the man came for her," Mandy says. "Not Francie."

"And when did Nora tell you this?" the officer says.

"During a sleepover," Mandy says. "Tia was there, too, but she was asleep."

"But not Jenny," the officer says, winking at Jenny. "She wasn't there?"

Mandy shakes her head quick without looking at Jenny.

"And why did Nora think the man came for her?" the officer says.

"He said her name. He said it when he tried to wake her up, but she kept her eyes closed. She was smart. Francie wasn't."

"And that's why the man took Francie?" the officer says, starting a new bow with two new loops. "Because she didn't pretend to be asleep?"

"Nora said the man had to take Francie or she would have told on him," Mandy says, her eyes following the officer's thick fingers as the waxy laces slip through them.

It feels like the whole room is holding its breath. Tia grabs Jenny's arm. She feels it too. Jenny wants Mandy to say the man's name. Say Levi Banks. Say he was the one who took Francie Farrow and left Nora behind. But Mandy won't say it, and the terrible feeling ballooning inside Jenny is blocking off her throat and she has to rock forward to make herself swallow. Out in the distance, fuzzy photos are starting to spin closer and float to the ground.

"Do you mind giving me a hand?" the officer says to Mandy, flicking the shoelaces he can't seem to tie.

Mandy crawls toward the officer, but she keeps an eye on Jenny like Daddy sometimes keeps an eye on a stray dog who wanders onto their road. All day, that's what Mandy's been doing. Looking at Jenny like she's a stray dog. Not the sad kind of stray, but the kind that might bite.

"You said the man knew Nora's name?" the officer says, smiling as Mandy ties a perfect bow for him. He sticks out his other shoe, its laces dangling loose too. "Did I hear that right?"

Mandy ties the second shoe, and as she gives the bow a tug to pull it tight, she looks up at the officer.

"And she knew his name too," Mandy says.

Mrs. Norwood lets out a gasp and quickly covers her mouth. Tia buries her face in her hands like she can't bear to watch. And Jenny presses her hands to the floor because something inside is telling her to get ready to run.

"And when did Nora tell you this?" the officer says, lifting a finger to silence Mrs. Norwood. "At your sleepover?"

Crawling into her mama's lap, taking care with her arm, Mandy lifts her eyes to the officer. In the softly lit room, they shine like blue glass. She shakes her head. The air sizzles, like someone lit a firecracker. Jenny can smell the chalky smoke in the air. Get ready to run. It's time to run.

"Today," Mandy says, her eyes rolling back to the officer. "Before I hurt myself, Nora whispered to me some more."

"And can you tell me the man's name?" the officer says. "The name of the man Nora saw in Francie's room?"

Mandy buries her mouth in her mama's shoulder and looks at Jenny. This makes the officer look at Jenny too.

Clouds fill Jenny's head, making it hard to think. She doesn't want to hear anymore. Mandy is supposed to say Levi Banks. But she hasn't. She won't.

Jenny has known trouble was coming since the day Nora moved in. She hasn't been able to get a good look at it, because it's been way off in the distance, so far away that she squinted and still couldn't see it. If this is the second sight Jenny is supposed to have, it hasn't been at all

The Final Episode

like a dream, like Dehlia said it would be. It's been more like snapshots, flipping past so far away Jenny couldn't make sense of them. Flipping past so quickly they made her dizzy. But now, they're slowing down and piling up.

Tia is squeezing Jenny's arm and burying her head in Jenny's side because she doesn't know what's coming, but Jenny does. It's so close now that it's spinning right overhead. Spinning so close, it makes the room spin with it.

"Nora said the man wanted to get rid of her," Mandy says. "So he could have Mrs. Banks all to himself."

Mrs. Norwood bites down on her bottom lip, her chin crumpling, her head shaking. She turns her face away so Mandy can't see and strokes Mandy's hair, slowly, steadily with one hand.

"Nora was afraid he would take her next because she knew his name," Mandy said. "As soon as she moved to the swamp, she recognized him."

One last picture flutters to the ground at Jenny's feet.

"Nora said Jenny's dad took Francie Farrow."

FADE OUT:

CHAPTER 17

I got up early so Arlen and I could leave the house before Dehlia woke. I took Belle out, fed her and then found Arlen waiting for me in your baseball-watching room. He slept on the couch, which will tell you something about him. And his sheets and blanket were folded and neatly stacked. That'll tell you something else.

Pressing a finger to my lips, I grabbed my shoes and motioned for him to follow. Once we were outside, stepping into the soggy morning air like stepping into a sauna, we continued toward the car, still in silence. I didn't want to have to explain to Dehlia why we were leaving the house so early.

Across the road, Tia's house was quiet. I hadn't seen much of her since we finished unloading my things from Arlen's truck. She was busy sorting and packing and getting her house ready to be put on the market. I offered to help, told her weeding out was my specialty, was even fun for me, but she said she needed to do it alone. The house was full of memories of her mama and Mandy, same as Dehlia's house is full of memories of you.

"Thank you for coming with me," I said when Arlen got back in the car after having opened and closed the gate.

"Who needs sleep anyway?" Arlen said, feigning exhaustion. But he did look tired.

"It's the only thing I could think of," I said, glancing at the time. "Tanya was strict about one thing . . . her morning workout."

The Final Episode

The drive to the gym where Tanya worked out took less time than I thought. There wasn't much traffic at six thirty in the morning. I backed into a parking space, giving us the best view of the gym's front door without being too close, left the car running so we'd have air-conditioning, and sat back to wait.

I'd spent most of the previous day looking through all Dehlia's old pictures, hoping to find one of Nora, but I never did. My memory of her was skewed by all the years that had passed and by the actor who portrayed her on TV. Every time I tried to recall the real Nora, the TV version shoved her aside. I was hoping an old picture would rebuild the real person so I could look at Tanya with a better set of eyes.

Pulling out his phone, Arlen propped it on the dash.

"What are you doing?" I asked.

"Tell me when she walks out," he said, repositioning his phone for a better shot. "And I'll start filming. Give you something to watch later if you're still not sure."

At a few minutes to seven, people began to file in the front door. The class Tanya took every morning ended soon, and the new arrivals were there for the next class. I sat up and leaned forward, wanting to get the best look I could.

Over the next few minutes, the flow of people into the gym slowed and reversed. People drinking from water bottles, blotting their faces with towels, or with eyes buried in their phones pushed through the door.

"There," I said and with both hands gripping the steering wheel, I leaned over it. "Red tank, black shorts. That's her."

As Tanya pushed through the door, she slipped a band from her ponytail, and her long, blond hair fell around her shoulders.

Arlen hit play on his phone.

"Not a great shot," he said. "Too far away."

"Should I get out?" I asked. "Try to get a closer look?"

"Take this," he said, handing me his phone and cracking his door.

"What are you doing?" I tried to keep my eyes on Tanya as she paused to say something to the person behind her. "Arlen. I'll go."

But he was already outside the car.

"I'm going to talk to her," he said, leaning in but keeping his eyes on Tanya as she stepped from the curb. "Play the prospective gym member. See what I can get out of her."

He was gone before I could stop him.

He jogged around the car to walk down the aisle behind us. I shifted in my seat and tried to keep him in sight. The top of his head was visible, and I could tell when he stopped, but I couldn't tell who he was talking to. Still holding his phone but getting only a shot of the car next to me, I took note of the time. Arlen's head was still in the same place. He laid it back the way he does when he laughs.

After six minutes and forty-nine seconds, he started weaving through the cars, making his way back to mine. His door opened, and he dropped down in the seat.

"Well?" I said.

"Not her," he said, leaning toward the air-conditioner vent and fanning his shirt.

"You're sure?" I said, straining to get another look at Tanya, but she was gone.

"Moved here with her parents several years ago," he says. "Loves the gym. Said the whole family goes here. She's the baby. Five kids in all."

"The baby," I said, another surefire sign Tanya was just Tanya. Nora had no older siblings.

Arlen nodded. "Like I said. Not her."

Arlen and I were back at Halfway Creek before Dehlia woke up. Taking care to be quiet again, we sat at the kitchen table, coffee in hand.

"I don't think there is a Nora," I said, staring out the back sliders. "I mean, I know there is. Somewhere. Maybe. But not here. I wouldn't even be thinking about her right now if not for the whole mess with the security camera and the police and all."

The Final Episode

The sun had cleared the cypress trees on the other side of the creek, and the black water shimmered as it crawled toward the Gulf. Everything I said, that was what I wanted to believe. I wanted to cap off that one worry and not think about Nora anymore.

"Then again," I said, because I still couldn't silence the feeling that she was circling. "A person can be whoever she wants to be."

"I don't understand," Arlen said, looking at me over his coffee cup.

"Tanya said she was the baby of the family," I said. "But she could have told you anything and you wouldn't have known the difference."

"You think she lied to me?" Arlen said, glancing at the time and taking his last sip of coffee. "You still think Tanya might be Nora Banks?"

"I don't know," I said. "And I'm pretty certain that's the point. I don't know if she lied to you, and neither do you. I don't know anything more than I knew before we went. Not really."

CHAPTER 18

Arlen was away at work most of the weekend, and I kept busy with projects around Dehlia's place. When Arlen was gone, I took Belle on early morning walks to avoid the heat of the day and did things I didn't want Arlen to see, my obsessive, nitpicking things. Things like alphabetizing the canned goods, scrubbing the grout lines in both bathrooms and refolding every one of Dehlia's towels, sheets, and blankets, despite her telling me to stay out of her closets.

In the evenings when Arlen got back to Dehlia's, he'd spend a few hours scraping the stucco siding and getting it ready to be repainted. Tia spent her days packing, a job she continued to insist on doing alone. And when it got dark, she joined Arlen, Dehlia, and me for cocktails on the lanai.

We were all doing our best to keep busy until Tuesday. Waiting for the final episode to air was like preparing for lab results we worried might bring bad news. The blood was drawn and all that was left was the waiting.

I tried not to think too much about Mandy or the apology she passed on to me. For the time being, Dehlia had a full house, and she was happy. I wanted her to have that, to be happy as long as she could.

I tried not to think about Tanya, too, and when a few days passed and nothing else odd happened, that became easier. She wasn't Nora. I wasn't being stalked. I never was, not by Nora. Not by anyone else.

The Final Episode

The incident at the rental house had been a one-off. It probably was a neighbor looking for a lost cat.

There were no more visits from Mrs. Farrow, either, which meant no more arguments about her with Arlen.

When Monday rolled around, Arlen and Dehlia reminded me that it was my birthday. Dehlia said . . . I know, I know . . . even before I said no orchids in the trees. Arlen worked a half day, Tia came over, and we had burgers on the grill to celebrate. The smell of the charcoal when Arlen first lit it surprised me. It sent me reeling back to our summers at the swamp. It made me miss you in a way that stuck in my throat. It made me angry too.

That's the thing about our good memories. I don't know if they deserve to be enjoyed. They're all tainted by you. And yet, they badger me every day, these memories of you before. They are why I write these letters. They are why, even though you've never let me visit you, I can't give up. I feel the fool so often, holding onto hope. I've even let myself hope that somehow, someway, Francie will come home. Alive. That's how badly I want to believe you didn't do it. Any of it. I feel weak thinking that way. I feel ashamed. I feel I'm betraying the victims. But my wafer-thin hope, it just won't let me be.

When Arlen left for work on Tuesday morning, I rode with him to the gate. I gave him a quick kiss, smiling so he wouldn't think I was worried about the final episode that would air later that night. Then I opened the gate and waved as he drove on to work.

The last few days had been nice, him and me having coffee, him going off to work, me getting ready to settle into my own projects. All the ordinary moments we'd shared had mended us. Now, it was down to the waiting. I was hoping he and I would get a second chance at something beyond friendship, but that would depend on what kind of anchor I turned into after the series ended.

I started to close and lock the gate behind Arlen, but stopped when a patrol car appeared, passing Arlen's truck on its way out. Henry Baskin pulled through, reached across his front seat, and popped open the passenger's side door. I jumped in and rode with him back to the house.

"Want to tell me about that?" Henry said, pulling into Dehlia's driveway. He hitched his thumb in the direction Arlen had driven.

"We used to date," I said. "Friends now. He's helping keep an eye on things."

"So he's living here?"

"Not exactly," I said, answering him like I would have answered you. "Staying temporarily. On the sofa."

Standing in the driveway, Henry studied the road from end to end and waved off my offer to come in for coffee.

"Just wanted to touch base," he said, mopping his face with a kerchief as his attention landed on Tia's house. "And let you know I talked to some fellows up in Fort Myers about Nora Banks. Seems they're already looking for her. Have been for some time. Producers of the show shared something with police up there that gave them cause to want to talk with her. But so far, haven't tracked her down."

"Do you know what they shared?"

He shook his head. "Pretty tight lipped about it. Didn't seem to put much stock in what the show brought them, though."

"Meaning the police in Fort Myers think the show got it wrong this time?"

"Darlin', I don't know what to tell you. It's TV, right? Just remember that when you're watching tonight."

"Thank you. I appreciate you letting me know."

I'd thought a lot about what the show might reveal, but I hadn't thought much about how reliable it would be. They'd gotten it right the first season. I'd been hoping, one way or another, the final episode would be the end for us too. Maybe not a good ending, but an ending. Now, I thought maybe it wouldn't and we'd end up saddled with more doubts, not less.

"What about over there?" Henry said, nodding toward Tia's house. "That causing you any trouble?"

The Final Episode

"Gather you know Tia's back," I said. "It's fine. It's been nice actually, seeing her again."

"She staying?" Henry asked, his eyes still fixed on her house.

"Getting the place ready to sell," I said, not liking the suspicion in his voice. "What are you expecting to see over there?"

"No expectations," he said, giving me a wink. "Just taking it in."

First the blinds in Tia's front window moved. I recognized the motion. It was another remnant of our summers here. Next, the front door opened, and Tia walked out, carrying a cardboard box. Once she crossed the road, careful to avoid the potholes Arlen had already added to his to-do list, she set down the box.

"Tia Norwood," she said to Henry, shaking his hand.

"Henry Baskin."

"Don't mean to intrude," Tia said. "Found a stash of old videos my mom took. Got another few boxes inside. You have something that'll play them?"

"In our house where nothing's changed in twenty years?" I said. "Yeah, we do."

"Something to keep us busy," Tia said, and what she didn't say was . . . while we wait for the last episode to air.

"Henry is with the sheriff's department," I said, drawing Henry back into the conversation. "Family friend too."

Henry eyed Tia's waist. "Know what you're doing with that?"

"I do," Tia said, her posture stiffening. It was surely a move she used often in the courtroom, a way of making up for her smaller size.

"What are you talking about?" I said, looking between the two of them.

His eyes still pinned on Tia, Henry said, "Your friend here is carrying."

"T's are crossed," Tia said. "I's are dotted."

I wasn't sure what that meant. It seemed to pacify Henry. It did not pacify me.

"I'll let you all get on with your videos," he said.

"Lock the gate?" I called after him as he pulled away.

He gave a wave through his open window, meaning yes.

Then I turned to Tia.

"A gun?" I said. "You know how to shoot a gun?"

"Might come a time you're glad I have it," Tia said, gathering the box and following me inside. "You did just have a break-in."

"I had a prowler."

"And how do you think break-ins begin? Who knows what would have happened if you hadn't had the boyfriend two doors down. Just because nothing came of it, don't make the mistake of thinking nothing ever will."

"Point taken," I said. "But really, Tia. A gun makes me nervous."

"Let's drop these at your place," Tia said, jostling the box of tapes and giving an eye roll that was another throwback to our summers together. "Then come back with me. I have a few more boxes and something you need to see."

CHAPTER 19

While Dehlia took a bottle of pine cleaner and a rag to the VCR and began organizing the first box of videos, Tia and I went to her house for the rest. Nearing her door, I fell back a half step, same as I did when we were kids. Tia yanked open the screen, and we filed through before it fell closed.

"Will you tell me now?" I said.

I'd asked twice already what Tia had to show me, and each time she said we'd talk about it when we got back to her house. That meant she didn't want Dehlia to hear.

We jogged up Tia's stairs, same as when we were kids. At the top, I hoisted myself up and over the last few steps by grabbing hold of the newel post and landed two footed. I expected to see Mrs. Norwood come around the corner from the kitchen, her long red hair popping free of the loose ponytail she always wore. I even smiled until remembering she was in a room where she didn't remember any of this or any of us.

Tia peeled off toward the kitchen, and I looked to my right. It was another reflex. Back when we were kids, Mandy would have been sitting in her favorite chair, knees tucked under her as if afraid something might nip at her feet, a book open in her lap. But her chair was empty.

Mandy was always warning Tia and me back then. No going in the swamp alone. No baiting your own hook. No crossing Halfway Creek when the water's too high. But that chair being empty was the loudest warning she'd ever given. Maybe the police didn't think much of what the show had found, but Tia and I both knew that whatever was coming in the final episode had broken Mandy. It was going to be bad.

"You really should let me help you with all this packing," I said, joining Tia in the kitchen crowded with boxes, tubs, and garbage bags.

"Perfectly organized," Tia said, sitting at the table and resting her fingers lightly on a notepad. She nodded for me to sit too. "Boxes are to give away. Everything else is trash."

As I sat, I stared at the notepad. Tia was barely touching it. Whatever was in those pages was toxic.

"Going to tell me what this is all about?" I said, smiling as if that would ward off whatever bad news was coming.

"First of all," she said. "Haven't found anything about a Tanya with Verifiably Vintage. Not all that surprising. Small business like that. But I gave it a try."

I nodded, knowing something else was coming.

"Did some other digging," Tia said, hesitating and then sliding the notepad toward me. "Called in a few favors from some people I know out on the West Coast. Seems Robert Farrow was right about Nora having gotten herself into trouble."

I only glanced at the page of scribbled notes, afraid of what I might see.

"She did move out to California after that summer," Tia said. "It says on there the exact year. I think she first enrolled in a California school in 2004. Maybe took a year off after everything with the trial. Parents got divorced. She graduated and got into UCLA but looks like she only attended for a few months."

I trailed a finger under the scribbles and nodded as if I were following along, but I wasn't. The letters melted together, and the words only popped off the page as Tia spoke them. 2004. Divorced. UCLA.

"Then in 2013, a complaint is filed," Tia said.

"What does that mean?" I asked, pushing the notebook aside. "A complaint."

The Final Episode

"With the police. Seems she cleaned out some bank accounts," Tia said. "A few different people were targeted, all family members. The boyfriend Mr. Farrow mentioned and his parents."

Her voice is different. It's stiff, forced, like one she might use when representing someone she knew was guilty but had to represent nonetheless.

"And after the complaint," I said, "she disappeared?"

"Yes," Tia said. "So either she took off for obvious reasons, or the boyfriend found her."

"Meaning?"

"Who knows. But if he found her, and she hasn't been seen since, use your imagination."

"What does all this tell you?" I said, figuring the dates and filings meant more to Tia than to me.

"You understand there's no record of her since 2013, right?" Tia said. "You get that she wiped out the boyfriend's entire family, as far as money goes? You understand what it means that she hasn't been seen in years? What the boyfriend may have done?"

"Yes, you think she either took the money and disappeared with it, or the boyfriend found her and killed her."

Tia flipped the page in her notepad and slid it to me again. She wanted me to see it in writing.

"I got a name for the boyfriend," she said.

"And?" I said, but like it so often happened, I already knew.

It was a flash. A spark. A picture that flipped over just before.

"It's Arlen, Jenny," Tia said. "The boyfriend is Arlen."

But I already knew.

CHAPTER 20

When Arlen sent a text, telling me he was pulling up to the gate, I ran through the steps I had already laid out for dealing with him. I've lived my entire life that way, particularly the hard parts. I have a plan for what to do when someone screams at me in the grocery store for being Paul Jones's daughter or pushes me out of line at the pharmacy because to hell with me if I won't tell the Farrows where their little girl is. It's another way of organizing, which is to say it's another type of control. It takes out the emotion, leaves no room for second-guessing.

Slipping on my flip-flops was step one. Then before opening the door, a few deep breaths and a reminder to keep it short. The list quickly fell apart when Tia followed. I'd only planned for me and Arlen. I hadn't planned for Tia to be part of the showdown.

"I'll be all right," I said, already thrown off course, off script. Once that happened, it was never as easy to stay numb. And staying numb was the whole point.

"Sure you will," Tia said. "But I'm still coming with."

Walking down the drive and onto the road, I couldn't remember one thing I was supposed to do or say. Tia's footsteps crunching in the gravel next to mine distracted me. Instead, everything I'd been trying to keep at bay came crashing down. It buried me with the feeling that I was a fool. I was bait. I was a pawn in a game. I was nothing.

By the time we reached the top of the rise and could see the gate, Arlen was already there. He could have unlocked it himself but was waiting for me to do it, his way of not rushing me when it came to the two of us. I stopped short of the gate and crossed my arms. My heart raced. My throat clamped down, making me think I wouldn't be able to speak.

"What is it?" he said, shielding his eyes so he could better see my face. He already knew something was wrong.

"Were you ever going to tell me?" It was all I could manage.

He draped his hands over the gate and let his head drop between his arms.

"A hundred times."

"And yet, not even that morning at the gym. You thought it might be her, didn't you? You thought Tanya might be Nora."

I couldn't get enough air. I was feeling lightheaded. I had wanted to be curt with him, businesslike, pretend he'd meant nothing to me like I'd meant nothing to him. But I was failing. The hurt was all over me.

"I did," he said. "Damn sure wasn't going to let you go alone."

"Because what might have happened?" I said.

"You have no idea," he said.

His voice turned harsh, but he quickly raised a hand to apologize. I wasn't ready for him to push back. If Tia hadn't knocked me off course, Arlen's harshness would have.

"Can I assume you didn't kill her?" I said. "Since you went there looking for her."

He stared at me, leaned closer like he wasn't sure he'd heard me correctly.

"If I'd have ever gotten the chance, I might have."

That was enough for me. Remembering at least one part of my plan, I kept it short and turned to leave.

"I had to drop out of med school because of Nora Banks," Arlen said, waiting for me to turn back before continuing. "My parents had to start over. She took every cent they had, and I brought her into their lives. If I'd have seen her walk out of that gym, I'd have called the police and made damn sure they got her. But it wasn't her, and I told you as much so you didn't go on thinking differently."

"Was I bait to you?" I said. "You thought she'd come looking for me eventually?"

"At first," Arlen said. Honesty. More of what threw me off course. "Then, it became about you and me. I didn't think about her again until the show came out. You started losing clients, and people were saying terrible things online, and Beverley Farrow threw a damn cinder block through your window. I just wanted to keep you safe, and you were making it so damn hard."

His head dropped again, and he rubbed a hand across his eyes. He did it like he'd said too much.

"It was you," I said. "You set off the camera that night."

"That wasn't my intent," he said, that same tired look on his face that used to make me afraid he'd leave me for being too much trouble. "You wouldn't do anything about Beverley Farrow. Instead, you threw me out."

"So you scared me into letting you back in?"

"No," he said. "I was there, at your house that night, in case Beverley Farrow showed up again. I couldn't just sit home and do nothing. I was walking around your place and forgot about the camera until it caught me. Then you texted."

"And you told me to call 911?"

"Damn right, I did," he said. "I wasn't even thinking about Nora at that point. But Beverley Farrow could have killed you. You know, all this might come down to her. She's acting like a woman about to get outed for killing her own daughter, and you are blind to it. At least, the police have record of her now."

"And the music," I said. "That was you too?"

He shook his head.

"Don't expect you to believe me," he said. "My guess, it was Dehlia. She can't make heads or tails of the app that controls the speaker. Helped her disconnect her phone from it a few times, just since I've been here."

I glanced back at Tia. Her expression had changed in the short time we'd been standing there. She'd gone from rolling her eyes at what Arlen said to nodding along.

"Why did you come here?" I said. "To Naples, my neighborhood?"

"I spent years trying to track Nora down," he said. "She'd been using her mother's maiden name. Soon as I knew who I was really looking for, I learned what happened to her as a kid and about Francie Farrow. Even tracked down her mother, who hadn't seen her in years. She was begging me for answers."

"So, you randomly moved next to me, thinking you'd find Nora?"

Arlen turned away, giving himself a moment to step back from the frustration creeping into his voice.

"Naples was the only place she had any ties to," he said in a calmer, easier tone. "That made it the only educated guess I could make. And you were the only connection to what happened back then. I never hid my name from you."

I stopped any more excuses with a raised hand.

"I didn't plan any of this," Arlen said, not bothering to wipe away the sweat that left muddy trails down his face. That's how tired he was of worrying about me. "The two of us, that just happened. I didn't play you."

I cocked my brows because he did play me. He played me enough that two police officers searched my house, inside and out.

"You let me believe it could have been Nora at my house that night," I said. "Told me I was bringing trouble to Dehlia's front door, putting my own grandmother at risk."

"You are putting Dehlia at risk," Arlen said, tipping forward to look me in the eye. "Beverley Farrow is a danger. Yes, I misled you, but I did it to get that woman out of your life. As far as Nora goes, you raised her name the night of the break-in. Not me."

"Stop it," I said. "Just stop it with Beverley Farrow. Because of that night, because I had police searching my house, I've been seeing Nora in every new face I come across. Jesus, Arlen. There is no Nora. Hasn't been for ten years. She's either dead or she's long gone."

I wanted the feeling that Nora was circling me to stop, and blaming Arlen for the feeling was easier than blaming myself. Maybe it wasn't fear that kept bringing her to mind. Maybe it was guilt. By holding on to you, I had been trampling on what she'd suffered. How could I still love you, knowing what you'd done to her?

"Maybe she is gone," Arlen said, shaking his head at me as he opened his door. Yes, he'd finally had enough. "Dead even. I don't know. But I do know I stopped caring about getting even with her years ago. Just cared about you. Still do."

He dipped his head at Tia, ducked inside his truck, and drove away.

CHAPTER 21

As I watched the road until Arlen's truck disappeared, I set my jaw and clenched my fists, both things to hold on to my anger. I even shook my head as if to get in the last word, but it was all just for show. No matter how much anger I mustered, it was no replacement for the pain I was feeling.

"He's not wrong, you know," Tia said. "Nora's no victim."

"Maybe," I said, starting back to the house and not wanting to hear what Tia was saying. No matter what came later in her life, Nora was a victim. She was your victim.

"No maybes," Tia said, stopping me with a hand to my forearm. "After that last summer, Mandy and I, we never saw Nora again, but for years, she kept calling Mandy. Only now and again, but it got so Mandy wouldn't answer the phone. Ever. That's how afraid she was of Nora. Never knew why, but I knew she was afraid."

"I'm truly sorry about that," I said. "But I . . ."

"I don't need your sorrys," Tia said, her harsh words cutting me off.

I pulled back, Tia's tone one I'd never heard. It got my attention. It snapped me out of thinking only about my anger and got me thinking about hers.

"When I tell you Mandy is dead because of Nora," she said, "I mean it. It's not my grief looking for someone to blame. She saddled Mandy with something that tortured her until it killed her. And I wish to hell I'd been more like Arlen. He was just trying to keep you safe, from Nora or Beverley Farrow, or whoever. If I'd done that for Mandy, tried as hard as he did, maybe she'd still be alive."

We walked the rest of the way to the house in silence. Part of me always knew Arlen would eventually let me down. Not in the way you did, nothing that horrendous, but I knew. Being up close to what happened to Francie Farrow at such a young age changed me deep down. That was the first time I wondered why men did the things they did, and I was far too young to wrestle with that question. I wondered why a man would want to take a little girl from her family, her mama, her home. I didn't know why those things happened back then, but I knew enough to be afraid of the answer. I know now.

Men do it, some men, because they can. They do it because they're weak enough to want to.

All along, I've been waiting for Arlen to show his weakness, and now he had. No matter what Tia said, Arlen used me because he was weak enough to want to.

When we reached the front door, I stopped, thinking I'd try to tell Tia I was sorry again, but before I could, she gave me a nudge. It was the kind of nudge one kid gives another when they don't have the words to say what needs saying.

"I know you probably have a lot of guilt around what your dad did to Nora," Tia said, landing another nudge. "But don't let her ruin you like she ruined Mandy. Give it some time, and then call Arlen. I mean it, Jenn. She's nobody's victim."

I nodded, wanting to believe that. If Nora was nobody's victim that would mean you never hurt her. That was what I really wanted. But I didn't say those things to Tia. Instead, I nodded as if I'd think about giving Arlen a call, and as I reached for the front door, it flew open.

"You're not going to believe what I found in those videos," Dehlia said.

Grabbing hold of us both, she dragged us into the house and into the TV room.

"There," she said, pointing at the screen. "Look."

The Final Episode

Tia and I stepped up to the TV where we could get a good look. A grainy image of four girls filled the screen. Off to the side of them, Lily Banks held my eleventh birthday cake. She was smiling and showing it to the camera. It didn't have my name written on it yet, and it never would because Mandy broke her arm before anyone could finish decorating it.

Us four girls—me, Tia, Mandy, and Nora—were striking a pose. I stood with one hand on a hip, my head tossed back. I was happy because Tia stood next to me, an arm draped over my shoulders. Mandy stood on the other side of Tia, her arms dangling loose, her eyes looking at something off screen. And Nora, the tallest, stood behind us, her arms stretched overhead and her back arched as if she were getting ready to do a backbend.

"Didn't you say you'd been looking for pictures of Nora?" Dehlia said. "Well, right there she is. Have about fifteen minutes that include her."

I stared at the frozen screen. After seven episodes of watching the fake Nora, I'd forgotten more about the real one than I'd thought. She seemed so much older than the rest of us back then, but looking at her on screen, she looked so much the same as us. So much more ordinary.

"The show starts in three hours," Dehlia said. "And we have plenty of videos to keep us busy until then. I sure do wish Mandy could have come with you, Tia. I sure would like to see Mandy again."

Dehlia was smiling because she had believed all along that the final episode would lead to something good for you. She didn't know about Mandy sharing her secrets with the show. She didn't know those secrets destroyed Mandy and made her feel the need to tell me how sorry she was. Mandy's secrets were going to destroy all Dehlia's hopes for you too. She just didn't know it yet, so she was still smiling.

THE FINAL EPISODE

INT. COFFEE SHOP - DAY (19 years missing)

For thirty minutes, Mandy has been sitting at the small table, waiting. She's kept herself busy by folding, creasing, and pinching thin paper napkins until she turned a half dozen of them into orchids. Now, they're scattered across the tabletop like a haphazard centerpiece, and her hands still haven't stopped shaking. If anything, they're worse than when she first sat down. Pressing both flat on the laminate surface where they're surrounded by the paper orchids, she draws in a deep breath that rattles in her chest as she exhales.

The small coffee shop reminds her of one she went to as a child with Tia and Mother. Tia and Mandy liked the cherry turnovers at that place and the black-and-white checkered floor. They'd leap from square to square, trying to balance on one foot. Mother liked to sip her coffee from the giant mugs the café served it in.

The bell over the coffee shop's entrance chimes. Combing her fingers through her hair, Mandy does her best to smooth it. Her hands tremble, and not even pressing them flat again helps. She draws both into her lap, shifts in her seat to sit taller, and smiles as someone lowers slowly into the chair opposite her.

From behind the counter, a phone rings. A wall phone. An old-fashioned ringtone. Mandy clenches her fists, inhales to the count of three, exhales to the count of three. It isn't her phone. She doesn't have a phone. Whoever is on the other end isn't calling for her. Nora isn't calling for her. She thought she drank enough before coming here to stave off the shakes, but maybe she didn't.

"Mandy?" the woman sitting across from her says. "Mandy Norwood?"

The woman can't help the surprise that flashes across her face when she gets her first look at Mandy. Mandy's seen the look before on many different faces. When it does happen, the expression always comes and goes quickly. People don't intend to be unkind. Tia is the standard. Tia, with her shiny hair, bright skin, strong petite frame. Tia, who is successful, articulate, well adjusted. She is what people expect to see when they meet Mandy, but instead, they get a withered, frail version of Tia with brittle hair, sunken eyes, and pale skin. Tia is a few months shy of thirty. Mandy, the identical twin, is decades older inside and out.

"And you're Elizabeth," Mandy says, extending a hand. It trembles. "You've barely changed."

Using only the tips of her fingers, the woman lifts one of the paper orchids and cups it in her hands as gently as if it were real.

"Ghost orchid?" she says.

"A passing resemblance of one," Mandy says.

Mandy was ten, almost eleven, when she first saw Elizabeth Miller on the television. Back then, her job was to help Francie Farrow's parents. She was the person off to the side during the TV interviews, ready with a tissue or a bottle of water if Mr. or Mrs. Farrow needed one.

"I have to ask," Elizabeth says, and as if giving Mandy the space she needs, Elizabeth leans back. She has the same dark shoulder-length hair, the same strong look about her, the same smooth, casual way of moving that puts a person at ease. "Did you and I meet back then, when you were a child? If we did, I'm embarrassed to say I don't remember."

Mandy wraps her hands around her iced tea. The tall, slender glass sweats cold beads of water. The cold focuses her.

"No, we never met," she says, straining to lift her eyes because that's what people do when having a conversation. But she's not used to this anymore, talking to another person.

It didn't happen all at once, her slipping away from everything and everyone. As she withered physically, she withered in other ways too. Fear has been working on her for her entire life, and a good while ago, it won. Or maybe she gave in. It has been chipping away at her ever since.

"Got to ask then," Elizabeth says, sliding a stack of letters across the table. "Why send all these to me?"

"I remembered you from the interviews Mrs. Farrow gave back then," Mandy says. "She always thanked you, said how much you helped her, how she couldn't get through it without you. She trusted you, so I did too. And I was hoping the letters might make their way to her, to Mrs. Farrow."

Elizabeth fans the pile of envelopes across the table like a hand of playing cards. Mandy started writing to Elizabeth when she and Tia moved away for college. They didn't go far, but far enough. They went to Florida Gulf Coast University in Fort Myers, and Elizabeth Miller was right there in the phone book. Mandy would sit in her dorm room alone, and later in the apartment she and Tia shared, and write the letters over and over until she got them just right. She labored over every detail, making sense of the story as she wrote, finally convincing herself that every terrible thing she'd been afraid of was worth being afraid of.

"I'm glad you sent them," Elizabeth says. "But I have to be honest. I didn't go to Beverley Farrow with them. I took copies to the police. I felt I had to, even though nothing you say in these letters is new information. Not as far as the police are concerned. And whatever we discuss today, I won't go to the Farrows with that either. The show shares everything we find of significance with the police. They decide when and if to share that information, when and if to act on it. Just want to be clear about that."

"Understood," Mandy says, disappointed Mrs. Farrow never read her letters.

The Final Episode

Even though Mandy always addressed the letters to Elizabeth, as she wrote them, she imagined she was telling the story to Francie's mother. She also imagined that one day she'd be brave enough to tell Mrs. Farrow what really happened. Now, Elizabeth is telling her that the Farrows may or may not ever know how the story ends. It'll be up to the police. Will there be enough proof? Will they believe Mandy? Will they ever find Francie Farrow?

"I reached out to Tia not long ago," Elizabeth says, leaning forward now, setting her cell phone on the table and touching Mandy's hand. "Did you know that?"

Mandy nods and resists jerking away from Elizabeth's touch, from the cell phone. She shakes from straining so hard not to move. When the strain gets too great, she slides her hand into her lap. But the phone is still right there. Another deep breath. Another reminder that it isn't her phone. No one will call, saying . . . Long time, Mandy. How's things?

"So you also know I work with *Inspired by True Events*?" Elizabeth says. "You know that's why I contacted Tia. We've been looking into Francie's case for quite some time."

Elizabeth eases her phone away as if sensing Mandy's struggle and puts her hands in her lap too. She must have been the same with Francie's mother, always knowing exactly what she needed and how to give it to her.

"Does that mean you'll make a show about all of this?" Mandy says. "About what I tell you?"

"Don't know yet. We're still looking into the case. It takes a while. Your letters, they're what made me pitch the idea in the first place. Landed me the job, if I'm being honest. Francie's story never left me, and reading all your memories made me certain there was more out there to be uncovered. I want you to know, I really appreciate you meeting with me."

Mandy nods and draws one finger up and down the side of the glass.

"But Tia refused to talk to me," Elizabeth says. "You'll know that too. She said you wouldn't talk either. Just trying to be up front with you."

"Did you tell Tia about the letters?" Mandy asks, her fingertip going numb as she swirls it through the cold drops of water.

"I didn't," Elizabeth says. "I hope it helped you deal with that time, writing it down and sending it off."

"I think you can tell it didn't help enough," Mandy says, trying to laugh at herself but the awkward moment leads to a long silence.

"Is that why we're here now?" Elizabeth says. "Do you have more to share, maybe something that will be enough to help you deal with it?"

"The last letter I sent you," Mandy says, "that wasn't the end of the story. The afternoon I broke my arm because of the alligator, that wasn't the last time I saw Nora."

"And you'd like to tell me the rest of your story?" Elizabeth says.

Mandy nods, still trailing her finger from one drop of water to the next. Connecting all the dots.

"Yes, I would."

Mandy sits on her driveway, just close enough to the road to see Jenny's house. The rot coming off the swamp is strong, like the swamp has crept closer. Sometimes, Mandy imagines that is happening. After dark, when the lights are out, she imagines the swamp creeping across Halfway Creek, creeping toward her house.

Three police officers stand at Jenny's front door, each of them holding a flashlight that cuts a yellow line through the darkness. They're at Jenny's house because Mandy told the officer that Nora saw Jenny's dad take Francie Farrow. After she told, more officers came and one of them walked Mother, Tia, and Mandy back home and told them to stay put.

The Final Episode

The officers have knocked once so far, and now one of them is shouting for Paul Jones to open up. But Jenny's dad isn't in there. The house is dark, and he's out looking for Nora like everyone else.

Tia sits next to Mandy. Bugs click and pop overhead, swirling around the one streetlight. The air is sticky, and dust and grime cling to Mandy's face and arms, making her feel gritty all over. Mother doesn't know Tia and Mandy are out here. She's inside, too busy packing to go back to the house in Naples to notice they aren't helping.

When the door over at Jenny's house doesn't open, one of the officers waves the other two aside and drives a foot into the door. Tia and Mandy link hands and scoot until they're pressed close to each other. The officer drives his foot into the door again and again. When it flies open, Mandy and Tia jerk backward, Tia surely thinking like Mandy that Nora will come tumbling out. She doesn't.

The three men disappear inside. As the lights pop on in Jenny's house, men's voices rise up. They're calling out for Nora. Scooting farther down the drive but stopping before they reach the glow now coming off Jenny's house, Tia and Mandy stare at Jenny's front door. It still stands open. The distant sounds of a radio crackling come from inside the house.

The two girls scramble backward when another set of headlights sprays across the road. It's an ambulance. It rolls to a stop and parks. Two men climb out, bags in hand, and disappear inside Jenny's house.

"The ambulance means they found her," Tia says. "We have to go. We have to go back inside."

Tia doesn't say it like she's happy they might have found Nora. She says it like she's scared of what comes next. For once, Tia is afraid of the same thing as Mandy.

"Look," Tia says, sucking in a quick breath because something surprises her.

She points down the road where the light from Jenny's house barely reaches. It's dark, but Mandy sees it. It's two shadows, people walking down the center of the road. As they get closer to the glow spilling out of Jenny's house, the shadows turn into two men. One has hold of the other with one hand. Just before the two cross the seam between dark and light, they stop. The one man drops to his knees. His head rolls forward.

"That's Jenny's dad," Tia says, pushing to her knees for a better view.

Mandy wants to push to her knees like Tia, but she can't move.

"Go inside, girls." It's Jenny's dad.

He sees Tia and Mandy, and he's talking to them.

Tia looks down on Mandy, wide eyed, asking without asking . . . did you hear that?

"Both of you." His voice is louder but not angry. "Please, girls, go inside. Now."

The man standing over Jenny's dad shoves him to the ground and drives a boot in the center of his back.

Tia jumps to her feet and grabs Mandy, pulling her toward the house.

"You two girls," someone shouts. It's a police officer walking down Jenny's driveway. He's pointing at Tia and Mandy. "Inside. Now. And stay there."

Behind them, the front door flies open. Mother gathers the girls with an arm around each and steers them toward the house. She stops when another police car rolls up. She pulls the two girls close, trying to cover their eyes with her hands, but Mandy still sees.

"Oh, that poor girl, that poor, poor girl," Mother whispers, and Mandy wonders if Mother is talking about Jenny or Nora.

As two officers stuff Jenny's dad in the back seat of the patrol car, he looks up at the three of them. He doesn't hang his head. He looks them straight on like he wants to be sure they hear him.

"I didn't do this," he shouts, and one of the officers throws an elbow that catches him in the mouth. And then not as loudly. "You tell Jennifer. Tell her so she'll know."

The Final Episode

The door slams closed. The car pulls away without any sirens or lights. Just like that, Jenny's dad is gone.

Mother hustles them inside and up the stairs. She puts Tia to work packing the things from the refrigerator in two coolers. She sends Mandy upstairs to pack all the clothes in her and Tia's room, and everything they'll ever want because they're never coming back.

In her bedroom, Mandy leaves the lights off and closes her door. She flips open one of the two suitcases Mother gave her, but instead of packing, she lifts a single blind at the window and looks down on Jenny's house.

Every window is still brightly lit, and the front door still stands open. Mandy sets her eyes on the open doorway, because if they did find Nora inside, that's where she'll come out.

Mother told Mandy that she was brave for telling Nora's secrets to the police, that she might have saved Nora's life. But Mandy doesn't feel like she saved anything. She feels like she struck the match that set the whole world on fire.

Mandy presses close to the window when the two men who came in the ambulance walk out the front door down at Jenny's house. They pause and look back. As if someone has motioned for them to keep going, they continue onto the sidewalk. Two officers walk from the house next. They each extend a hand inside as if coaxing someone to keep coming. And then, Nora appears. Clinging to the doorframe, she waves at the two officers to keep going like she doesn't want them anywhere near her. She keeps waving until they've reached the drive.

Nora wears the same blue shorts and pink T-shirt she always slept in. Her white socks glow under the patio light, and her hair hangs in her face. Seeing her from the second floor, Mandy thinks she's never looked small, but she does now.

Still clinging to the doorframe, Nora seems to tilt her head as if to look up at Mandy's window. Mandy falls backward, letting the blind close. Sinking to the ground, a hand to her chest, she listens for any outside sounds. Another radio squawks. A car door slams shut. Pushing to her knees, she lifts the same blind the tiniest bit she can.

One of the officers who coaxed Nora from the house is walking toward the end of Jenny's driveway as he talks into a radio. Another one stands on the sidewalk, a hand extended to Nora. Still hovering, she shakes her head and pulls back like he's frightened her. He lifts his hand, an apology, and turns his back to her like the other men. That's when Nora starts to take her first step.

With one foot out the door, she looks like she's testing the water. Maybe she's finally scared for real. She lets go of the doorframe, takes another step, and sinks to the ground. Mandy lifts onto her knees for a better look. It wasn't a fall. It wasn't a stumble. It was like she melted.

Once on the ground, Nora pulls one knee to her chest. She balls herself up and wraps a hand around her ankle as if she's twisted it. And then, she cries out, but the cry wasn't timed right with the fall. It was like when the voices on TV don't match the moving lips.

All four men lunge for her. She waves them off to signal that she's okay and pushes slowly to her feet. She must say something, because one of the two men from the ambulance steps up to help her. She takes his arm and limps down the short sidewalk and onto the drive, one of the men pointing at the ground as if to warn her to be careful. The officer with the radio still lifted to his mouth jogs the rest of the way down the drive. Looking up and down the dark road, he takes a few steps toward Nora's house.

At the ambulance, Nora lets one of the men help her into the back of it. She disappears inside as Mrs. Banks appears down on the road. She's part running, part stumbling. Mandy watches the dark road for Levi Banks. He should come next. A father should be here with his daughter, even in the middle of the night. But he isn't. Jenny's dad never scared Mandy, not once in all the summers they spent here. Nora's dad scared her from the first day she saw him. She wonders if Levi Banks is really the one who belongs in the back of a police car.

The Final Episode

When Mrs. Banks nears Jenny's house, all the lights fall on her. One of the officers helps her into the ambulance. The doors close and the ambulance drives away with Nora and Mrs. Banks inside. But no Mr. Banks.

Nora always talked about being scared, but she never was. That's the thing about Nora that never fit quite right. Mandy didn't see it at first. She liked too many other things about Nora to pay attention to that one thing. Nora liked talking about being scared as if it made her special, as if it meant the rest of them had to be extra nice and always do what she wanted. And they were extra nice. They did always do what she wanted.

Mandy hid being scared as best she could. From everyone. She hid it with excuses, like her allergies were acting up or the mosquitoes were too bad or she had a stomachache.

Mandy knew all about being scared of things, and she knew Nora was never scared of anything or anyone. Not really. Not even tonight. She for sure was never scared of her own dad.

Beverley knows the way to Lily Banks's house, but Robert drives. He insisted. She didn't argue. She braces herself with a hand to the dash, squints ahead, and tells him they're close. It's so dark on these roads, it's hard to see. Slow down. We're close.

Beverley wasn't supposed to hear what she heard, but once she did, there was no unhearing it. She'd fallen asleep in the car after Agent Watson left, having told her the note sent to the PO box wasn't written by Nora. Most anything will wake Beverley these days, even an unusually deep breath from Robert, but the crackle of a radio was like a slap in the face. Her eyes popped open when she heard it. Through her open windows, she heard it again. Louder. Someone was standing near the end of the driveway at the rental house, the red tip of a cigarette glowing in the night. An agent catching a smoke break.

The radio crackled again.

"All units. All units. Be on the lookout for twelve-year-old female. Blond hair. Blue eyes. Name, Nora Banks. Last seen southeast of Naples near . . ."

Beverley lunged across the passenger seat to hear better. The alert sounded again, and she was certain. It was about Nora Banks, and she was missing.

Inside the house, Beverley woke Robert. He dressed, grabbed the keys, and on the way out the door, he said that he was driving. He said it like Beverley better not argue.

"It's just up ahead," Beverley says as they take the last turn.

Beverley points at an open spot on the shoulder, and Robert pulls over. Patrol cars and people crossing back and forth clog the road. Red-and-blue lights spin. Staring straight ahead, the lights making his eyelashes flutter, Robert switches off the ignition. The engine shuts down. The air-conditioning and radio turn off. Inside the car, it's suddenly quiet.

Beverley sucks in a deep breath as if she's been underwater and just surfaced. Robert grabs her hand. She's afraid to get out now that they're here. The thin layer of silence inside the car is the last veil between their old life and what lies ahead. Once they step out, they'll never be able to go back to before because the answer to what happened to Francie is out there in all that chaos.

"You all right?" Robert says, patting her knee and her arm, checking her over.

She nods as the dome light of a car parked in front of them pops on. The driver's side door opens. Agent Watson steps out and lifts a hand. The passenger's side door opens next, and Elizabeth appears, this time dressed in shorts and an oversize T-shirt. She came here straight out of bed.

"Nora's been found," Agent Watson says, meeting Robert and Beverley at the front of their car. "She's with her mother at the hospital."

Beverley grabs Robert and holds on.

The Final Episode

"She's okay?" Beverley says.

"Nora is safe. She's fine," the agent says. "And Paul Jones has been arrested."

"He's the man who . . . ," Elizabeth starts to say, shielding her eyes from the headlights Robert never turned off.

"We know who he is," Beverley says. "He's Lily's friend, the agent handling the rental. And you've arrested him?"

"Nora was found in his home," the agent says.

"And?" Beverley says, because she knows Agent Watson too well. It's the way he blew out a single deep breath. This is the part of the job he hates.

"And Nora has identified Paul Jones as the man who took Francie," Agent Watson says, taking Beverley by the arm as if that might cushion the blow. "Nora told as much to a friend. Said she recognized him after moving into this house."

"He took our little girl?" Robert asks, dropping back against the car. "He took our Francie?"

"And we believe he took Nora tonight to keep her from identifying him," the agent says. "That is our thinking, though it's only a theory at this point."

Robert takes a step, drawing Beverley with him, both of them getting a clear view of the house farther down the road.

"But why Francie?" Robert asks. "We didn't know him. He didn't know Francie."

"We can't be certain of his reasons," the agent says. "But it seems Nora might have been his intended target that night. We're not sure why, though he was having an affair with Nora's mother. Apparently, Francie woke up so she saw him. Nora, on the other hand, feigned sleep."

"So he took our Francie because she saw him and Nora didn't," Beverley says, staring at the house straight ahead.

Agent Watson nods. "But I'll caution you again, these are theories only."

"And he lives there?" Beverley whispers, studying each brightly lit window, looking for a shadow, something slipping past. "That's where they found Nora?"

She takes another step, leaving Robert behind and waiting for Agent Watson to tell her yes to everything. Yes, he's the man who took Francie. Yes, he lives there. Yes, that's his house. Yes, they found Nora there, so maybe . . .

Her heart is pounding in her ears. She's inhaling too fast, and the air sticks in her throat.

"Is Francie in there?" she says, gagging on the words as someone takes her by the wrist. She yanks but can't pull free. "Is my daughter in that house?"

At first, Beverley thinks it's Robert who wraps his arms around her. She fights to pull free. She doesn't want to let the house out of her sight. Not ever. But it isn't Robert who holds her. It's Agent Watson, and he's whispering in her ear.

"She's not there. No, Beverley, not yet. We didn't find her. Not yet."

He says those words over and over. No, Beverley, not yet. He says them until she stops pulling away from him and trying to run down the road toward the flashing lights. When she's calm, he holds her at arm's length and draws in a deep, exaggerated breath, so she'll do the same.

"A search of the house has turned up no sign of Francie," he says, quietly, now holding her by both hands. "Found a few articles about her investigation cut from a newspaper in the daughter's room. A bunch of pictures too. But no, Francie is not in that house. I'm sorry, Beverley. Robert. We'll continue the search. We'll continue to question Paul Jones. We're not done, but there's been no sign of your daughter. Not yet."

His glance moves from Beverley to Robert and back again as he speaks. Elizabeth slips in front of Beverley, taking Agent Watson's place. She wraps both arms around Beverley and clamps on tight.

"But he took her," Beverley says. "Nora saw him. He did it. He took Francie. So he'll tell you now where she is?"

The Final Episode

Agent Watson lifts a finger, silencing her questions, and steps away, a radio pressed to his ear.

"I don't understand," Robert says, shouting after Agent Watson and then turning to Elizabeth. "You said you cleared him. You said you looked at Paul Jones."

"They did look at him," Elizabeth says, resting a hand on Robert's arm. "They did clear him. Early on, along with several others."

"I need to look in that house," Beverley says, closing her eyes as if behind her dark lids she'll see Francie. "I need to see for myself."

"No, Beverley," Elizabeth says. "You can't. You know you can't. The two of you need to go back home. The police have a lead now. A good lead, and the first priority will be getting information regarding Francie. I'll keep you updated. I promise. But you can't do anything here but get in the way."

"But, Elizabeth," Beverley says. "If Francie isn't in that house, then where is she? You have to make him tell us. You have to make Paul Jones tell us where our little girl is. Make his daughter tell us. You said she had the newspaper articles. She must know. Make her tell us."

Jenny is in the back seat of Dehlia's car, huddled on the floor, her face buried in her arms, but she can still hear Dehlia shouting at the officers. When she thinks she hears a familiar voice, she lifts up, hoping to hear it again. Strangers are walking in and out of the front door of her house in town. Not seeing a single face she knows, she slides back down on the floor and wraps herself up.

When she and Dehlia first pulled up to the house in Naples, two police cars were already parked out front, their lights spinning. The front door was open, every light was on, and police were filing in and out. Dehlia told Jenny to stay put, rolled down a window to let in some fresh air, and threw open her door.

"Might as well get back in your car," an officer said before Dehlia could say anything. "You're not going in until we're done."

That was when Jenny slid off the seat onto the floor, curled up, and pressed her hands over her ears, but she could still hear the shouting. Dehlia shouting that they better damn well take care, they better hurry up about it, they better let her get her granddaughter to bed. The police telling her to calm down, let them do their job, it'll be over sooner if you stay calm.

But they said calm one too many times.

"Don't you tell me to fucking stay calm," Dehlia screamed.

Jenny pinched her eyes closed and pressed on her ears until she couldn't feel her hands anymore. She didn't unravel until the shouting stopped, and she heard a familiar voice for the second time.

"Dehlia, listen to me." It's Mr. Baskin from next door. He's a deputy who wears a uniform and sometimes talks to Daddy out in the front yard about flood insurance or dollar weed. "I'm going to help you, but you got to listen, and you got to calm down. They're taking care with your things, you can trust that."

"What do they want?" Dehlia says. "What are they doing?"

"They have a search warrant," Mr. Baskin says, speaking quietly, as if not wanting anyone else to hear, but Jenny can hear because they're talking right outside the car. "For this house and the one down on the creek. Dehlia, they have reason to believe Paul is responsible for the abduction of Francie Farrow as well as the young girl tonight. They'll be looking for any number of things. Anything they take will be documented, and you'll get a receipt for it. I'll help you go over it. You understand? You have any questions?"

Jenny peeks out the window when Dehlia doesn't answer. She wants to hear that Dehlia understands because Jenny doesn't. Then her door opens, and damp night air spills into the car, chilling her sweaty skin.

"I'm sorry, Jenny." Mr. Baskin reaches in and pulls Jenny out in one smooth motion. "I didn't know you were just there. I'm sorry you heard that."

The Final Episode

Mr. Baskin is strong like Daddy, but his spicy smell is different. She clings to him and buries her face in his shoulder as he takes off walking. His skin is damp, and his breathing turns fast and heavy, but he never slows down, not for a step.

Dehlia walks next to him, her hand on Jenny's back. Jenny wants to reach out and grab Dehlia's hand, but she can't make her arms let go of Mr. Baskin.

At Mr. Baskin's house, Mrs. Baskin opens the door for them. And when Mr. Baskin sets Jenny on a small bed and snaps on a bedside lamp, Mrs. Baskin sits next to her, putting her hand where Dehlia's had been.

"I'll be just down the street," Dehlia whispers. "I'm going to see to taking care of everything. Taking care of your daddy. We'll be okay. We'll all be okay."

When Dehlia and Mr. Baskin begin backing away to leave Jenny in the small bed, Jenny lifts her head. She wants to tell Dehlia that she's wrong. Jenny already knows, even if Dehlia doesn't. None of them will be okay for a very long time.

Mandy grabs Tia's hand when they step off the hospital's elevator with Mother. Tia pats Mandy's shoulder, a sign there's nothing to be afraid of. Then they link hands and follow Mother.

Mandy wore her best shoes, and as they wind through the hallways, looking for room 225, her hard soles *click, click, click* over the tile floors. Mandy doesn't like it and wishes she'd worn sneakers like Tia. The click of every step is a reminder that they're getting closer to Nora's room.

As they pass rooms 217 and 219 and are certain they're almost there, Mother keeps hurrying them up. Ever since last night, Mother has been in a hurry. A hurry to pack, a hurry to lock up the house on Halfway Creek, a hurry to visit Nora in the hospital, and a hurry to get back to the house in Naples and never go to the swamp again. Mother has been in a hurry to leave all this behind. Tia too. But not Mandy.

Not quite. She isn't ready to lose her best friend and go back to being afraid all the time.

And as soon as they reach room 225, that's what is going to happen. She's going to lose Nora.

"Go on in, girls," Mother says in a whisper. "I'm going to go see to Nora's mother, make sure she doesn't need help."

At the end of the hall, where she talks to a man wearing dark pants, a white shirt, and a tie, Mrs. Banks is leaning against the wall as if it's the only thing holding her up.

As Mother walks toward Mrs. Banks, Mandy reaches for Nora's door, but Tia doesn't move.

"You go," Tia says. "I'll stay out here."

Mandy pushes open the door. The air inside is instantly warmer. It feels good, and for a moment Mandy is happy to get Nora all to herself. Then she remembers what happened to Nora, and she shivers like the air is still icy cold.

As Mandy takes a step into the room and the door falls closed with a soft thud, Nora's head rolls toward Mandy. At first her face is hard and looks more grown up than it ever has. But when she sees Mandy, all the hard lines soften, and she smiles.

"I thought you were my mom," she says.

Mandy stops just inside the door. Taking even one more step is like trying to get herself to step on the spongy swamp floor. Her body just won't let her do it. Even though she thinks she wants to.

"Sit down," Nora says, nodding toward a chair next to her bed. "You're my first visitor."

Nora's hair is all bunched up behind her, and usually she wouldn't let that happen because it would lead to split ends, but she must not care about broken, frizzy hair anymore. Mandy thought she'd look different after getting taken right out of her own bed and stuffed in a locked cabinet inside a locked room, but she doesn't. She looks smaller in the bed, but otherwise the same.

This morning, Mother took a phone call where she listened for a long time. When she hung up, she sat Tia and Mandy down and told them nothing had been done to Nora. She said it twice and then asked if Tia and Mandy understood what she was saying. They both shook their heads because they didn't.

"Jenny's daddy," Mother said, swallowing hard like something was having a tough time going down, "didn't do anything violating to Nora."

Pushing off the closed door and thinking that "violating" is about the worst word she's ever heard, Mandy leans forward, and her feet follow. Grabbing the back of the chair near Nora's bed, she falls into it. She feels bad being afraid of Nora. Mother told them that Nora was still the same person. A bad thing was done to her, but that didn't make her bad.

"Got to ask you something," Nora says. "Did you tell the police what I told you about Jenny's dad?"

She crosses her hands in her lap and lowers her eyes like she's the one who's afraid. Mandy sits taller in her chair. Seeing Nora afraid makes Mandy want to be strong. Maybe that's why Tia is always strong. She's strong because she has to be for Mandy.

"You mean about him being the one you saw take Francie from her bedroom?" Mandy asks, whispering because Nora whispers. "Yeah, I told. Mother said I had to."

"You saved me, Mandy," Nora says, scooting up in her bed and reaching for Mandy's hand. "You know that? They knew to come looking for me in that house because you told them. You're a hero."

Since Mandy and Nora first met, Nora has been making Mandy feel taller, braver, smarter, prettier, funnier. She's feeling the littlest bit of that now—taller and braver—and that's what she wants more of.

"Did he really stuff you in the cabinet?" Mandy says, swallowing hard, not sure if she's allowed to ask.

Nora nods. "I was all twisted up in there," she says.

"And you couldn't get out?"

"Not once he closed the doors," she says, pinching her eyes tight like she's trying not to remember. "No one's supposed to be on the inside. No handle. No nothing."

"But the police got you out," Mandy says. "That's good. That's real good."

"You're my best friend," Nora says, nodding and squeezing Mandy's hand like she'll never let it go. "My only friend, really."

"You're mine too," Mandy says.

"Can I ask a favor?" Nora says, glancing at the door before continuing. "One I couldn't ask anyone else."

Mandy nods and looks at the door, too, wondering who Nora is hoping won't come in, because that's what it feels like. Whatever Nora has to say, she wants to say it while they're still alone.

"I lost something, and my mom is going to be real mad at me," she says. "More mad. She's already mad because I got Jenny's dad in trouble."

"She'd never be mad about that," Mandy says.

"She loves him, you know," Nora says. "I told you that. She loves him more than she loves me. So will you help me find it?"

"I'll help."

"It's nothing, really. My house key. I think I dropped it at Jenny's house the day you, me, and Tia went there, just outside her door. My mom will know I left the house if she finds out I lost it there."

Mandy nods. She remembers. It was the day they took the vodka from Jenny's house. But she's back to slouching in her chair because she doesn't want to go to Halfway Creek ever again, and she sure isn't going back to Jenny's house. Slouching is her only way to hide.

"We already packed," Mandy says, ashamed that she couldn't hold on to being strong long enough to help Nora. "We're going back to Naples from here. I don't think I can go look for something at Jenny's house."

"But you have to," Nora says, pinching her brows and getting that hardened expression that makes her look grown up again. "Unless we're not friends anymore."

"We are friends, but your mom won't care about a key," Mandy says, slipping, slipping, slipping all the way back to the person she was before she met Nora. "But I can't go to that house again. I just can't. I'll explain to your mom. I'll . . ."

"I did everything for you, and you can't do this one thing for me," Nora says, turning away like she can't stand to look at Mandy anymore. "You can't even pick me over Jenny's dad. You think you know him, but you don't. Everybody knows he's bad. You know it. I know it too. I've known it since the day we moved to the swamp."

Mandy slides to the edge of her seat. Her being afraid is bigger than her wanting to be friends with Nora. That's been Mandy's whole life. She measures things by how much they scare her. Nora's the same way except instead of measuring fear, she measures her friends by how much they do for her.

"I remember the day you moved in," Mandy says, standing and backing away from Nora's bed.

Nora shrugs, keeping her back to Mandy.

"Before we met you," Mandy says, her chest getting heavier with every word. "Jenny's dad told us how he'd known your mom since he was a kid."

Mother's always saying how amazed she is by all the things Mandy knows and by how much she reads. She's always saying Mandy sure is a smart one, but right now, Mandy wishes she weren't so smart. She wishes she hadn't figured it out. But she did. Nora started it when she said Mandy didn't really know Jenny's dad, as if Nora knew him better. And Mandy filled in the rest.

Nora gives another shrug, but the air changes. It sizzles and crackles like bacon when Mother fries it on the stove.

"He told us we'd like you," Mandy says, taking more backward steps toward the door. "He told us you liked to read just like me. He told us he'd met you several times, and every time you were nicer than the last."

"So," Nora says, turning enough to look at Mandy with a sideways glance.

"You said you didn't know the man when you saw him in Francie's bedroom," Mandy says, stopping when she bumps up against the door. "You said you didn't know it was Jenny's dad until you moved to the swamp and first saw him."

Nora looks Mandy full on. Her chest lifts and lowers, making Mandy afraid she's going to rise right up out of the bed.

"You already knew Jenny's dad before you moved to the swamp," Mandy says, her chin quivering and tears pooling in her eyes.

One more time . . . "So?"

"You said you didn't know the man in Francie's room. You said you saw him plain as day, heard his voice plain as day, but still you didn't know who he was. If it was really Jenny's dad in Francie's room, you would have recognized him from the very beginning."

"You tell anyone that," Nora says, smoothing her hands over her hair, "you'll be sorry."

"I won't be sorry. You should never be sorry for telling the truth."

"Then I'll tell you this," Nora says, setting her stare on Mandy. "If you don't want to end up like Francie Farrow, you'll keep your mouth shut."

"How do you know how Francie Farrow ended up?" The words come out on their own, but as soon as they do, Mandy knows it's a brave thing to say. So she says it again.

"It was her idea to sneak out," Nora says, sliding her legs over the edge of the bed. "It was her fault. When she got herself stuck, I told her to quit crying and squirming. I got out just fine."

Nora slides off the bed until her toes touch the floor. She is going to push to her feet, cross the room, and come for Mandy.

Mandy's breath rushes in and out of her lungs, making a swishing sound that roars in her ears.

"You got out of what just fine?" Mandy says.

"I even tried to help her, but she kept clawing at all that dirt and sand and crying, and I told her to stop."

"What dirt and sand?" Mandy asks, but she already knows enough.

When there's sand, a hole more than elbow deep is too deep. That's the rule for every trip to the beach, every summer at the swamp.

As Nora tells about the dirt and sand and how Francie ended up too deep in it, Mandy presses tight to the door, hoping someone will come in. She closes her eyes, but that doesn't stop her from hearing every word.

Nora and Francie Farrow ran until they found a chain-link gate with a loose-fitting lock. They squeezed through, and once on the other side, they threw rocks and clumps of dirt. When they got tired of that, they jumped down into deep trenches, laid in them on their backs, made themselves long and straight like pipes, and stared up at the dark sky. When it was time to go home, Nora climbed out. Francie couldn't.

"You have to tell," Mandy whispers when Nora's finished telling her story. "Francie's mama, you have to tell so she'll know. It was an accident, just an accident."

"You want me to go to jail for the rest of my life?" Nora says, pulling her long hair over one shoulder. "Figures that's what you would want."

Mandy shakes her head. She doesn't want Nora to go to jail. It doesn't seem right that she would, but Mandy doesn't know much about what sends a person to jail.

"You might go to jail too," Nora says. "Because you knew all along and never told. It'll be like Francie died because you never told."

Mandy wants to say that's not true, but her throat snaps closed. Standing in this room that's suddenly turned cold and staring at Nora sitting in that bed is like standing at the end of the road on Halfway Creek and staring at the Old Man. They both lie still, their empty eyes looking at her, making her wonder if anything inside is living or if everything that matters is already dead.

"I'll call you in a few days," Nora says, "to make sure you found my key."

Mandy nods and pulls open the door without turning her back on Nora.

Jenny's daddy always said to leave the Old Man well enough alone and he'd leave them well enough alone. As Mandy backs into the hallway, letting the door fall closed, Nora turns her mouth into a smile, and Mandy doesn't think Nora will ever leave her well enough alone.

Mandy stops talking when the waitress tips a pitcher and refills her drink. As full cubes of ice spill into the tall glass, she tries to latch on to one with her eyes and follow it as it bounces and twirls in the dark tea. Elizabeth nods when the same waitress offers to freshen her coffee. Neither of them speaks until the waitress's footsteps fade and the chatter of the other customers fills in behind.

"Despite the way Nora handled it," Elizabeth says, "it sounds like it was an accident. Is that what you think? She should have gone for help, no doubt, but if it happened as you described, it would have come too late."

"Nora taking that little girl outside was no accident," Mandy says. "But no, I don't think she intended to kill Francie. I also don't think she tried to save her. I don't know if that's a crime or not, but I know it's wrong. I know it's wrong to not try."

"Had they done it before, do you think?" Elizabeth asks, scribbling in a small notebook and avoiding eye contact with Mandy. "Snuck outside?"

This is why Elizabeth was so helpful to Beverley Farrow in the days, weeks, and months after Francie disappeared. Though they just met, Elizabeth already knows eye contact is hard for Mandy.

"I think it was the first time," Mandy says, taking a sip of her tea. She chokes down the urge to gag. "Nora didn't want her mother to work for the Farrow family anymore. So she took Francie outside to prove she didn't need all that babying. Nora's word. She wanted to prove Francie wasn't all that fragile."

Elizabeth thinks for a moment, tapping the end of her pen on the table.

"Nora wanted her mother out of that house," Elizabeth says, pointing the pen at Mandy and smiling at first, but her smile quickly fades. "Because she thought her mother was having an affair with Francie's father."

Mandy nods and tucks her hands under her legs so she won't use them to push herself up and out of the booth. Each breath is harder to find than the last.

"And then she realized at some point," Elizabeth says, "that her mother's affair was with Paul Jones."

Mandy nods, thinking of riding on Jenny's dad's shoulders and pointing up into the trees. She never did find a ghost orchid for Jenny.

"Can I ask you?" Elizabeth says. "And I swear, no judgment. Just curiosity."

"Why didn't I tell someone?" Mandy says.

"Well, yeah."

"After seeing Nora in the hospital," Mandy says, "I started lying to the police. I told them I didn't remember what Nora said about Paul Jones. I told them I didn't know if she saw him in Francie's bedroom. I told them I didn't remember what I said before. It's what I said in court too. It was the best I could do. And it was the truth in a roundabout way. I was too afraid of anything more. I still am. It's like she's always watching me, like I feel her eyes in the center of my back every moment of every day."

It's like the nightmares she still has about the Old Man. She dreams he'll slither through her bedroom window, drag her out in the night, and bury her under the dark waters of Halfway Creek.

"But you're not too afraid," Elizabeth says, starting to take Mandy's hand and then thinking better of it. "You're telling me now. That's something. That's a lot. What you did, how you handled it, likely kept Paul Jones from being charged in Francie's disappearance too. Maybe even her murder."

"She told me I could go to jail if I told anyone," Mandy says. "I know that's not true now, but I didn't as a kid. And the longer I kept it to myself, the more I was just as guilty as Nora."

Elizabeth's eyelids close for a long stretch, so long Mandy thinks they might not open again. Then taking a deep breath as if to reset herself, she opens them.

"We'll look into outstanding permits at the time," Elizabeth says, jotting something more in her notebook. "Given what Nora told you about sneaking through a fence, it sounds like they were playing on a construction site, in a trench of some kind. There was a lot of construction back then. Not sure how much we'll be able to narrow it down, but you've made it so we might be able to give Francie back to her parents."

"Mother was always afraid of us digging holes," Mandy says. "It was our number one rule. Sand is heavy. So heavy. No deeper than our elbows. That was our rule."

"We're almost done," Elizabeth says. "I promise."

Mandy forces a smile. She needs something to wash away how she's feeling. She needs a drink. It's right there in her purse. Just one, something to slide down her throat and leave a trail that burns all the way down. The trembling will stop. The ache in the center of her chest that has been slowly working its way up into her throat will fade.

"A letter was sent early on, soon after Francie disappeared," Elizabeth says. "From a child. It was sent to a PO box."

Mandy nods before Elizabeth can finish her question.

"That was me. I didn't want Mrs. Farrow to keep hoping. I wanted her to know Francie wasn't coming home. I knew, long before Nora told me all of what happened, that Francie wasn't coming home. I think I knew almost from the beginning that Nora knew exactly what happened to Francie. She was never scared enough."

The Final Episode

"Do you remember what you wrote?" Elizabeth says. "The more I can confirm, the better."

"Francie won't come home. I know you'll miss her. I'm sorry."

Mandy stands, pulls two singles from her pocket, and lays them on the table. She dabs her face with a napkin, knowing her skin is damp and shiny. And the spot over her nose is throbbing. Soon it'll spread behind each eye. And her hands. She tucks them in her front pockets to stop them from trembling.

"How do you feel about Paul Jones?" Elizabeth says. "Given what he did to Nora."

"What I feel," Mandy says, "I can't prove. And yet I know it. Paul Jones did nothing to Nora. Somehow, she did it all to him."

Elizabeth finishes the thought.

"Because in the end, Paul Jones was the man having the affair with Nora's mother. You think Nora wanted to punish him."

Mandy nods.

"Last question," Elizabeth says, holding up a just-one-more finger. "Did you ever go back to look for the key Nora was so worried about? Ever go back to Jenny's house?"

Mandy shakes her head. "Never. Even to this day, I've never been back."

"Does Nora know that?" Elizabeth says, raising her brows in that way someone does when they want to warn you of danger but can't quite put the warning into words.

"No," Mandy says. "She called me after that day in the hospital. A week or so later. I told her I found it and threw it in the swamp. I thought that would make her leave me alone, but she kept calling, off and on, for years. I always said the same."

She knows the warning Elizabeth is giving with her raised brows, and while Mandy is still scared of Nora, she would welcome anything Nora might do to her. Whatever it might be, it would never be as bad as what she did to Francie Farrow or Paul Jones.

"It's important what you've told me," Elizabeth says. "It'll matter to a lot of people. I hope you know that. I hope this helps you move on."

Mandy nods, not wanting to disappoint Elizabeth. She's disappointed everyone else. Her mother. Tia. Herself. If Mandy had been brave enough, she would have never let all these years pass. But she was never the brave one. That was always Tia.

"I just wish I'd told in the very beginning," she says. "Thank you for meeting me."

"Can I get a number?" Elizabeth says. "In case I need to follow up, get some clarification?"

"Don't have a phone," Mandy says, turning to walk away.

"Wait," Elizabeth says. "Your orchids."

"Those are for you," Mandy says. "Something pretty to remember me by."

Crossing the small café, Mandy resists the urge to hop from one black tile to the next. When she's half a block away and Elizabeth and the old-fashioned phone ringing on the wall have both been left safely behind, she slips the bottle from her purse. One long swallow and warmth spreads through her body. It moves through her chest, down her arms, along her legs. She takes another.

Sometimes she manages to drink enough that she doesn't dream about the story Nora told her. Most nights, no matter how much she drinks, it's not enough. Mandy knows the story well, every detail. She feels it, smells it, hears it.

It's as if every night of her life is spent following Francie Farrow to her death.

Two little girls creep out a back door and into a dark night, the littler girl following the older girl. The little girl stops just outside the door before she pulls it closed. Going into the backyard is against the rules. Going without a parent, without checking the weather, all of it is

The Final Episode

wrong. But then the older girl circles back. She grabs the little girl's hand and squeezes it. The older girl is smiling. Her eyes are wide. She's trapping her laughter between lips that roll in on themselves. The little girl smiles too. It feels good to be out, just once, for only a little while. No one will know.

Somewhere in the distance, a sprinkler hisses and spits. The damp night air is rich with the scent of night-blooming jasmine. The little girl closes her eyes and draws the sweetness into her lungs. This is air she's never breathed before. Rich, full, sparkling air. In the dark, where no one's watching, it's like a secret she finally gets to hear. One breath after another rushes in and out of her lungs. The sweet air fills her up as she runs, pumping her arms, doing her best to keep up with the older girl.

The little girl has never run through damp grass. It's cold and prickly, and her toes are numb as she and the older girl near the edge of her lawn. Her lungs begin to burn, her deep breaths rubbing against her insides. The sugary sweet air has turned grainy. When the older girl isn't looking, she pops her inhaler in her mouth and inhales sharply. It helps but not enough.

The farther they run, the more the little girl falls behind. The older girl pulls ahead, her long blond hair floating in the night air, shimmering in the moonlight. She spins, jumping and leaping, waving her arms at the little girl to hurry up.

When they leave the cool grass and cross over onto dirt and gravel, the little girl slows to a walk because that's what the older girl does. Trying to quiet her breathing and imagine the air moving smoothly in and out of her tender lungs, she keeps smiling. But imagining doesn't work and smiling is hard because it's hard to do anything when breathing hurts. The older girl looks back, and the little girl waves and stifles a cough.

When the older girl squeezes through a gate in a chain-link fence, the little girl follows. They're walking now, and the burn in the little girl's lungs quiets. And then the two of them, the little girl and the older girl, are down in a trench. It's sandy, damp, and cool on the little girl's back, and her shoulders brush against the sides of the long narrow hole.

Looking up at the night sky, she rubs the sand between her fingers, and she's happy again. She and the older girl lay longways in the trench giggling, arms pressed tight to their sides, legs long and straight, both of them pretending they're pipes. Usually, the little girl does all her pretending alone. It's fun to pretend with someone else. When the dirt and sand start to warm beneath them, the older girl sits up. She's worried they've gotten dirty. It's time to get back.

The older girl scrambles to her feet, awkward in the narrow space. She plants both hands on solid ground, swings a foot around, and in one giant step, she's out of the trench. She's older, taller, stronger than the little girl and makes it in one try. She stares down on the little girl, and as she tells the little girl it's her turn, the sandy earth breaks away under the older girl's feet.

The older girl stumbles backward, causing more earth to break free. Cool, damp sandy dirt drops in clumps on the little girl's slender shins, nearly covering them over. She sits up, pulls her knees to her chest, and brushes the dirt and sand from her skin and from the lacy pajamas she only wears when company comes over. The sand clings to the silky fabric. She's afraid now because the older girl is right. She's gotten too dirty and will get in trouble for sure. Mama will see the dirt and know the little girl has gone where she isn't allowed to go.

Trying to push to her feet, the little girl begins to cough. The night air is filled with things that clog her lungs and tickle her throat. She plants her hands on the edge that is almost as high as her armpits. More earth crumbles in her fists. It buries her feet. She kicks it away just as more sand buries them. She can't stop coughing and that makes it hard to stand straight. She tries to swing a leg up and plant her foot on the ground above, but she falls, and more earth tumbles down with her.

The sides crack and cave. She's on her back, trying to push the sandy dirt away with her hands but it's like trying to stop running water. It keeps flowing. It flows through her fingers, around her arms, over her face, into her mouth. She coughs and spits the grit and grime. She's crying for the older girl. She claws at the sides of the trench where she pretended to be a pipe, and the earth gives way one last time. Everything goes dark.

The older girl stares down into the trench. Where there was a little girl before, now there is none. Just like that, there's one less person. The damp sand shimmers in the moonlight. The mound is still, like no one is underneath. Like it's already a grave. Nothing moves, except one foot that sticks out. The toes curl and straighten. Curl and straighten. The older girl jumps into the trench. A small plastic tube, bent like the letter *J*, lies where the little girl's hand used to be. The older girl stuffs the inhaler under the sand and dirt where no one will ever see it. And as the tiny toes stop moving, she dumps a handful of dirt on them so no one will see them either.

With one giant step, she's back on solid ground. She turns and runs. No one cries out after her. No one has to know.

Before going back inside, the older girl brushes the sand from her arms and legs as best she can and tears a screen from a window. Inside the quiet house, she thinks through all the other things that need doing, and she does them. She unlocks the same window, leaves the back door unlocked, cleans footprints from the kitchen floor and washes off the rest of the sand in the downstairs bathroom. She runs only a trickle of water so no one upstairs hears. With paper towels, she cleans the floors and wipes down the sink. She even straightens the hand towel when she's done. There isn't really much to do. It isn't really all that hard.

The very last thing . . . she stuffs her dirty pajamas and the used paper towels in the bottom of her backpack and puts on a T-shirt and shorts.

When the window in Francie's bedroom glows with its first bit of orange, the older girl creeps from the dark bedroom out into the hall. She walks slowly, taking deep breaths. It's okay that she's scared. She's supposed to be scared. No one will know the difference between being scared of one thing and not the other.

At the parents' bedroom, she stands in the quiet doorway, knowing if she stares long enough, the mother will wake. And she does.

"Are you okay, sweetheart?" the mother says. "Nora, sweetheart, are you okay?"

The older girl wraps her arms around herself, lets her shoulders round forward. She wants to look small and frightened. She lets her head droop.

"Bad dream?" the mother says, resting a hand on the older girl's cheek.

The mother knows nothing. She doesn't even know her husband has been loving another woman. He's been loving the older girl's mother. But not for much longer. The older girl and her mother, they won't have to come to this house anymore. If there is no little girl, there is no reason to ever come back.

The older girl lifts her chin just so, letting the shine from the hallway's single night-light catch in her blue eyes. She buckles her chin the way she does when she cries.

"What's wrong, sweetheart?" the mother says, kneeling and drawing the older girl into her arms.

The little girl's mother never noticed her husband was in love with another woman. She doesn't notice the older girl is wearing different pajamas either. No one ever will.

"Francie's gone," the older girl whispers into the mother's neck.

FADE OUT:

IN LOVING MEMORY OF
FRANCIE MAY FARROW (2/4/1993–5/26/2003)
and
AMANDA (MANDY) GRACE NORWOOD
(8/12/1992–4/27/2025)

CHAPTER 22

The house was dark by the time the final episode ended. We stared at the screen—me, Tia, and Dehlia—as real pictures of Mandy and Francie Farrow appeared on the TV. The where-are-they-now statements came next. LILY AND LEVI BANKS DIVORCED IN 2005, AND BOTH CONTINUE TO LIVE IN SOUTHERN CALIFORNIA. PAUL JONES WAS FOUND GUILTY IN THE ABDUCTION OF THEIR DAUGHTER, NORA BANKS, AND IS CURRENTLY SERVING A 25-YEAR SENTENCE IN FLORIDA.

Staring at the screen while all our names rolled across it, I pushed up from my chair. As I grabbed my phone, Tia walked from the room.

"They said it was an accident," Dehlia said, jabbing at the screen. "No one said Paul did it, that he did anything to Francie? Is that right?"

"Yes, Dehlia," I said as I fumbled with my phone, trying to enter the passcode correctly. "Daddy didn't do it. He didn't hurt Francie."

"So Nora lied," Dehlia said, settling back into the couch, looking from the TV to me. "She said she saw Paul in Francie's bedroom. She told the police that. She lied on purpose. Is that what she did? She lied to hurt Paul?"

"I just need a minute, Dehlia," I said. "Just, please, let me do this."

"What does it mean?" Dehlia said, still staring at me. "Jennifer, tell me. What does that mean for Paul?"

Dehlia's face turned blank, a flat expression that sometimes overtook her when too many things came at her at once.

"Jennifer, why did Nora lie? And where is Mandy? Why did they put her name on the TV like that?"

I set my phone down and forced a few deep breaths.

"I'm not sure yet what this means for Daddy," I said to Dehlia, my hands trembling. "But if you'll help me, I think I can find out."

My hands first began to tremble when I watched Mandy's character on screen share the story of how Francie Farrow died. It was an accident that Nora covered up to spare herself. And then we watched it play out, Francie dying alone in the dark. I ached for Beverley and Robert Farrow, but I couldn't linger there. The parts and pieces were tumbling into place. I sifted through them, sorted them, put them in order, and when they settled, I knew.

The only evidence the police ever had was Nora's testimony and a room and a cabinet that only you could unlock. But none of those things were true.

Nora had lied when she ID'd you as the man who took Francie, because there never was a man. She didn't misspeak. She didn't mistakenly identify you. She lied, on purpose, with purpose. And there wasn't only one way into that room or that cabinet.

My notions, my wafer-thin hopes, had come true. You didn't do any of it.

I was trembling harder. I believed you were innocent of it all in that hard way you believe in something you know to be true. Two plus two equals four. The earth is round. Water is wet. But my believing wasn't enough.

"Can you help me?" I said, rubbing the backs of Dehlia's hands with my thumbs as I tried to get her to focus again. "Can you do something for me?"

You won't know this, or maybe you do. Dehlia is older, and while she's still Dehlia, things have changed for her. Sometimes, she needs things to slow down just long enough for her to latch on.

"What do you need?" Dehlia said, her watery eyes clearing and snapping back to normal.

"I need the receipt the police gave you from the search that happened here," I said. "Remember, you showed Arlen and me just a few days ago. Can you get that for me?"

Dehlia nodded and disappeared into the kitchen as I sent a text to Henry Baskin. I should have felt guilty, asking him to come at this time of night, but I didn't. I also thought he'd probably been waiting by his phone since the show began.

He texted back . . . Be there in 15. His being that close meant he had been expecting to hear from me. He was somewhere nearby, waiting. He wouldn't have known why, but he'd have wanted to be close whatever the reason.

I found Tia in my bedroom. She sat on my bed and stared at her house across the road.

"She did what she could do," I said to Tia's back. "She did the best she could for Francie. She couldn't have changed what happened."

Tia turned. Her face was like Dehlia's. Her expression flat. Too much coming at her too quickly had overwhelmed her.

"And Tia," I said, pausing, wanting to make the most of what I was going to say. "She saved my father. By changing what she told the police, by not backing up Nora's story, she saved his life, kept him from being convicted in Francie's abduction."

Tia nodded and smiled, just a hint of one. She knew the same, and she was proud of her sister.

"That was hard to watch," she said, and cleared her throat, her way of regaining control. Belle lay next to Tia, her chin resting on Tia's leg. "That actress, she was too good, you know?"

"I think they showed Mandy in a good light," I said. "She was so young back then. No one will think poorly of her."

"What about your dad?" she said. "Nora tried to set him up for Francie's disappearance. And what about the rest, what happened to Nora."

"I need your help," I said, cutting her off before she went down the same line of reasoning I had gone down. I didn't want to wait for her. I wanted to barrel ahead.

And same as I did for Dehlia, I gave Tia simple directions that would pull her back to the present. I sent her into the garage to gather some tools.

Back downstairs, Dehlia met me in the entryway. She held the receipt in both hands to show me she'd found it. I opened the front door but stopped Dehlia from walking outside.

"Henry is coming," I said. "And I need you and Tia to stay in the house."

Tia walked up in time to hear the last of my instructions to Dehlia. She set a few large putty knives, heavy-duty screwdrivers, and hammers on the terrazzo floor. Get anything we can use like a chisel, I had told her.

"What's going on?" she asked.

I held up a finger as headlights appeared down the road. I couldn't say it out loud. Not yet. The thought of what might happen was making my heart pound. My body sizzled inside, like electricity popping and crackling.

"Not yet," I said, pulling up my phone and pausing notifications from the motion-detection camera. We were going to be working in its path, and I didn't want my phone constantly buzzing with notifications. "Keep Belle in the house, and you two stay here. Please, just stay here."

Before I tucked my phone away, a text from Arlen popped up.

Your father didn't do it. Your father didn't do any of it.

Arlen had watched the final episode and had seen what I had seen. He thought what I thought. Not thinking about anything that had come before but only thinking that I wanted him with me, I texted back.

I know. Come over. Come right now.

The headlights belonged to Henry. I met him in the drive. He turned off the engine and stepped out slowly, taking in the surroundings. He was making sure we had no unwanted visitors.

"What's going on?" he said, closing his door quietly.

He could see it in my face. I wasn't smiling. Not yet, because I didn't know for sure. Then he leaned to look past me at Tia and Dehlia standing in the open doorway, the hot, humid night air spilling into the house, along with the mosquitoes. They both clung to the doorway, leaning as far as they could without stepping outside.

"Do you remember the grout you put in for us?" I said. "Long time ago? I was headed to college, and you did that repair work for us. Remember?"

"Knees still hurt," he said, glancing at the sidewalk where he'd squirted mortar between the pavers like he was squirting piping on a cake.

"We're going to undo all that," I said. "I want you here, officially. I want you to do whatever you have to so it's legal or whatever. Either I dig it all out, me and Tia, or you get people here to do it. Either way, we're digging up those pavers."

Arlen arrived next. He'd been close by, too, same as Henry Baskin had been. And then four more deputies arrived. They were on duty, unlike Henry. And unlike Henry, they didn't have knee problems.

"Darlin'," Henry said. "I really need you to tell me what we're doing. I got a whole lot of men here, and I'm running on faith alone. I need to know what we're looking for."

"A key," I said, looking to Arlen. He was nodding because he already knew. "We're looking for a key."

CHAPTER 23

As the deputies began chipping away the grout Henry laid in more than ten years ago, more men arrived with more tools and Arlen set up folding chairs for Dehlia and Tia. They came outside through the garage, Tia remembering the bug spray. Once they were all comfortable, Arlen sitting next to them on the ground, I told Henry that I was ready to explain.

"Can we do this in the kitchen?" Henry said. "The bugs are killing me out here."

"I'm not taking my eyes off this sidewalk until they're done," I said, gesturing toward the men huddled at my front door who were chipping away the grout.

"Okay, then," he said. He tapped on his phone, pulled up a recorder, and gave me a look as if to okay its use with me. I nodded.

"Tell him what you've been looking for, Dehlia," I said. "And why you went looking for it now."

Dehlia had been overwhelmed by learning about all Nora's lies and by seeing the news that Mandy had died, but right there in our cracked driveway, she was bursting with life again. She was the Dehlia from my childhood. She ran her hands over her long braid, taking care not to touch the tip, and lifted tall in her seat.

She started with the night she watched episode four and saw me stealing the vodka. That's what got her thinking about the key. It was right there in the show, how a spare key for the locked cabinet was kept over the door. But when she went looking for it after the episode ended, it wasn't there.

Next, after sending Arlen into the house to get her folder, she showed Henry the receipt the police had given her after the house was searched following your arrest. She handed it to him so he could see for himself that a single key was not removed by the police. She'd been looking for it ever since she watched episode four. Where was that key? Where did that key go?

"And you think it's under those pavers?" Henry said once Dehlia was done.

"I think it's been there for over twenty years," I said. "I think it's been under that grout, secure, untouched, for the last ten. You laid the grout. You should know."

I wanted it to be clear. We didn't put that key there on a whim. We didn't do something to outsmart the system. It had been there all along because Mandy never went looking for it when Nora asked her to. Henry's grout had sealed it in place. His grout had stopped time.

"Darlin'," Henry said, shaking his head like he already doubted me. "What does that key matter?"

"You saw the show tonight?" I asked.

"I did. Nora said she lost a house key. Wanted Mandy to find it so she didn't get in trouble. You think you're going to find Nora's house key under those pavers too?"

"Nora *said* it was a house key," I said, shaking my head. "But I don't think it was. I think it was the spare to the cabinet where the police found Nora. The same key Dehlia discovered missing."

"Still not sure I understand," Henry said, letting out a deep breath and looking like he was about to land a blow he didn't want to land. "Your daddy had his keys on him when he was apprehended. He was the only one who could have unlocked the room and the cabinet and put Nora in there. Don't matter about the spare key."

Dehlia got to the end all on her own. She was smiling like you've never seen her smile. And I knew what she was thinking. She was thinking she knew it all along. This was my one great thing.

"Remember episode four," I said. "The way all of us girls stole the vodka. We all climbed onto the flat roof, in through the window, and I took the key from the molding over the door and unlocked the cabinet. Nora was there. Nora saw me do it."

"And you think that's what Nora did the night she disappeared?" Henry said.

"She knew how to get into that room without a key," I said. "And she knew how to open the cabinet. She climbed on the roof, in through the window, took down the spare key, unlocked the cabinet, and stuffed herself in. She even fed Mandy the story about seeing my daddy take Francie Farrow. She made certain the police would come looking for her in this house. All of it because she knew about her mom and my daddy. She wanted to punish him, and that's what she did."

Henry studied the house as if something he saw might help him better piece it all together.

"That's a lot of supposing," he said.

"But if we find the key," I said, "all that supposing will mean something."

"And why do you think we'll find it down here?" one of the deputies said, a chisel in hand and having already shed his uniform shirt.

"She had to get rid of it," I said, glancing back at Tia, Dehlia, and Arlen. They all three nodded, urging me to keep on. I was breathless and struggling to get the words out. "If she had unlocked the cabinet, put the key back, and then closed herself in, we'd have found the key right where it belonged, hidden over the door. But it isn't there. I think she closed herself in and then realized she still had the key. And once inside, I guess she couldn't get out. She was stuck with the key."

"Doesn't answer the man's question," Henry said. "Why do you think the key is out here?"

The Final Episode

"Answer was in tonight's episode. The night Nora disappeared, the police found her in our house. When they brought her out, they brought her through the front door. She stumbled, remember, but in an awkward way. Might even be a line in a report somewhere, saying she suffered a sprained ankle. She must have had the key hidden on her, in her sock maybe, and dropped it between the pavers. That's what the awkward stumble was all about. It was Nora getting rid of the key. And then she asked Mandy to go find it."

Another of the deputies who was chipping out the grout and removing the pavers lifted a hand. The other three stood and backed away.

"I think we're about to find out if you're right," Henry said.

A different deputy, one who had taken pictures of the sidewalk before the work began, stepped in, squatted, and took a picture of something on the ground. He took a few more, asking the four men to light the picture with the flashlights from their phones. And then a sixth man, wearing a pair of gloves, picked up a small key, barely an inch long, and dropped it in a small envelope.

The last step . . . Henry slipped a glove on his right hand, and after the key was logged by the man who retrieved it, Henry and I walked upstairs.

"Assuming the key opens that cabinet, it's not a guarantee your daddy's getting out," he said. "We'll have to see how accurate the rest of Mandy's story is."

"You mean you think it'll matter if they find Francie's body where Nora said it would be?" I asked.

It mattered because finding Francie's body would prove that the things Nora told Mandy were true. It would prove Francie died in a trench and that Nora lied when she said she saw you in Francie's bedroom. It would prove you committed no crime and without a crime, you'd had no reason to silence Nora.

"Finding that poor girl's body will be a damn good start," Henry said. "I'd tell you not to get your hopes up, but I don't generally bother with advice I know won't be followed."

Standing next to Henry Baskin, I used your keys to open the door to the owner's room. The bulb in the overhead light didn't work because we have rarely gone in that room since you went away.

Pulling out my phone, I flipped on the flashlight and lit the way.

It only took one try. The key fit. The cabinet where they found Nora Banks twenty years ago opened.

The last thing I did . . . I called Tia upstairs. She was smaller than me and not much taller than Nora probably was back then. She balled herself up inside the cabinet, and we closed her in.

"Won't open," she called from inside the cabinet. The doors rattled as she felt for a way to open them. They rattled again and kept rattling as she kept trying. I could hear the smile in her voice. "There's no latch. There's no handles. There's no way out."

Once Nora had stuffed herself inside the cabinet, she likely tried to get out so she could return the key to its hiding spot. She tried to open the doors, but she hadn't been able to. It was her only mistake.

Henry Baskin warned me not to get my hopes up. Like he said, my theory was a whole lot of supposing and making it all true began with finding Francie's body under the countless roads, houses, and parking lots that had sprung up in the past twenty years. But we would find her, and once we did, we would know there never was a man in Francie's bedroom. Once that lie, one of many that Nora told, tumbled, her entire story would come crashing down.

CHAPTER 24

Before Henry Baskin left, he told me to be patient. There were no guarantees. Things didn't always work out, and even when they did, justice moved slowly.

Promising Henry that I heard everything he was saying, I closed the door behind him and leaned there. Though it was almost one o'clock in the morning, the house was brightly lit, almost every light having been turned on, and it smelled of freshly brewed coffee. Braced against the door, I could hardly hold myself up. I locked my knees so I wouldn't collapse, closed my eyes, and let out a long breath. The house felt like a home again.

Since the day you went away, I've been clinging to the one sliver of hope that you were the man I thought I knew. Though I didn't realize it as it was happening, I was afraid that if I loosened my grip for even a moment, that hope would slip away and be lost forever. I had so many doubts about loving you, so much guilt, but even in those darkest moments, some part of me fought to hold on to hope. But now, I could hope freely. The doubts that tormented me, they were gone. The longer I stood there, the door holding me, the greater my hope grew. Not one of Henry Baskin's warnings could change that from here on out—I could love you and miss you and want you to come home as much and as big as I wanted to.

No matter what disappointments or delays or roadblocks might lay ahead, my loving you would never again be a hardship.

We gathered in the kitchen, all of us sitting around the table. I thought it would take some time to explain it all to Dehlia. Tia went first, explaining that Mandy was gone but that she'd done the most courageous thing by telling the truth.

The coffee quickly gave way to old-fashioneds, and as I sipped mine and listened to Tia talk about how proud she was of Mandy and how much she missed her sister, my hands wouldn't stop trembling. When Arlen asked if I was okay, all I could do was smile and nod. And then it was my turn.

"You were right about the key," I said to Dehlia, taking another sip, the bourbon burning the back of my tongue like never before. Not in a hurtful way, but in a deep-seated way that gave the sharp, full taste time to travel my entire body. That was my first clue that I had a whole lot of new feelings ahead of me.

I didn't know how numb I'd been all these years until that moment.

"Of course, I was right," Dehlia said.

I smiled, giving her that win.

"I know I promised no orchids on your birthday," Dehlia said, cutting me off before I could say anything else. "But a day here or there doesn't matter. I've been telling you all your life you'd do something great. You are a daughter of Margaret Scott, and I knew she wouldn't forget you."

"What did you do?" I said.

Dehlia stood and flipped a switch, flooding the backyard with light. Two dozen construction paper ghost orchids dripped from the trees, sparkling as a gentle breeze kicked them around.

"You don't have to explain a thing to me," Dehlia said, taking in the sight of all those orchids. "Your daddy is coming home, and it's your doing that he will. I knew it. I always knew you'd do it."

Dehlia eventually went to bed, waving off all of Henry Baskin's warnings that I tried to share with her. She wasn't wasting her time with a single one of them. Tia lay down in my room. Insisting that she was all right but also happy to stay over, she took Belle with her for company.

The Final Episode

That left Arlen and me.

We didn't bother with anything that happened before. He gave no more apologies, and it no longer mattered to me why he came to Naples and moved into a house near me. Because what happened between us once we got to know each other had been real. It was still real. Too much good had come our way to squander it by wallowing in the past.

The whiskey and the late hour made us tired, so we sat down to watch videos from the summers you and I spent together on Halfway Creek. I wanted him to get to know the real you. I wasn't certain yet if the final episode would be enough to stop clients from leaving him, but I was hopeful. It was a new and wonderful feeling, like the bourbon on the back of my tongue. I'd tasted hope before, but nothing like this. Nothing so sweet and strong.

When we reached the video from the summer I turned eleven, Arlen leaned forward in his seat, elbows to his knees, getting a closer look at the screen. The house was quiet and dark, and the light from the video flickered on his face. His jaw was sharp, as if his teeth were clenched. His hands were buckled into fists. And when Nora appeared, he dropped his head as if the sight of her pained him.

After a long moment when he kept his head lowered and his eyes pinched closed, he looked again. It was the part of the video where us four girls were posing for the camera. He shook his head at seeing Nora as a child.

"Does she look the same?" I said.

"Sort of," he said, his words sounding as if they hurt him. "She moves the same. But her hair was different when I knew her, and she had sharper features."

He turned away from the TV and closed his eyes again.

"Can you turn it off?" he said, still not looking.

I paused the video, knelt next to him, and took his hand. His strong reaction to seeing Nora as a child surprised me, but only for a moment. And then it made sense.

"Did you go with me to see Tanya that day because you thought she might be Nora?" I said, and took a deep breath, easing up on my next question. "Or did you go so I'd stop chasing a ghost?"

"I told you why I went," Arlen said, taking a sideways look at the frozen screen. "If the woman we saw had been Nora, I'd've called the police."

"You were always worried about Beverley Farrow," I said. "But were you ever really worried about Nora? Why was that?"

"I don't understand."

The grainy, childhood version of Nora was still looking at us from the screen.

"You can tell me, Arlen." In the dark, quiet house, no one else would hear. "Is Nora dead?"

"If she is," he said, looking me in the eye, "it isn't because I killed her."

After a long silence, he stretched out on the couch. I wanted to ask him the question again. I wanted him to feel he could tell me the truth. I wanted him to understand that I'd love him even knowing he killed Nora. Instead, I lay next to him. It was an easy decision for me. I was certain I could live the rest of our lives together pretending he'd told me the truth. I'd asked. He'd answered. I would choose to believe him. I would choose to believe he didn't kill Nora, even though in that quiet room, him being too pained to look at her on the screen, I knew he did.

It didn't matter to me when he did it or how he did it. Nora was dead, and that was the end of her.

With my head resting on Arlen's shoulder, I stared at the image of us four girls trapped in that single moment in time. They were vaguely familiar, as if I recognized them but couldn't tell you their names.

Closing my eyes, I found myself looking down on Francie Farrow's house, an aerial view I'd seen on the news countless times. So many roads and streetlights and barrel tile roofs. Somewhere under a city of cement lay Francie Farrow, and finding her body was the first step toward bringing you home.

CHAPTER 25

Beverley was afraid to see Elizabeth Miller again. Elizabeth had been a lifeline in the days after Francie disappeared, but now she was the worst kind of reminder. She would bring twenty-year-old memories with her, and nothing scared Beverley more than memories. Beverley had also spent many years resenting Elizabeth because she got to come home while Francie didn't. But when Beverley opens the door, Elizabeth has brought only good things. She's brought her strength and commitment, same as she did all those years ago, and Beverley instantly feels stronger, more ready for what lies ahead.

Pulling Elizabeth into a hug, Beverley wants to ask if they're close to finding the man who took her. Beverley knows the whole story now. She sat at her computer one day, typed in Elizabeth's name, and it was all right there for the taking. But she doesn't ask. In this very kitchen, Elizabeth had been clear on that point. Her past was off limits.

Agent Watson has come too. He no longer works out of Tampa but is living somewhere up north. He finally dropped those few pounds, maybe too many, and his clothes are still rumpled. Like Elizabeth, he came back because he never stopped thinking about Francie.

After the final episode aired, Beverley spent days walking her neighborhood. She stood on curbs, at intersections, sometimes in the middle of a street. Closing her eyes, she'd will herself to feel Francie nearby. She thought a good mother, a real mother, would feel her daughter's presence.

Day after day, she walked no matter the heat or the rain or the fading light, but she never felt her little girl. She chided herself for being not good enough. Over and over, she walked the same streets, and when she could walk no more because her blisters were bleeding and her feet were numb, she went home and fell into bed even though she dreaded sleep. In her dreams, she finally saw her little girl again, but not in a way that comforted her. She saw her Francie under a mound of wet sand. One small foot stuck out. Five tiny toes wiggled. Wiggled. Wiggled. And then went still.

Day after day, Beverley walked, even when Robert begged her to take a break. She didn't stop until a man reached out to the phone number that ran at the end of the final episode.

His name was Rodney, and twenty-two years ago, he left his home early to get to his construction job. They started early during the summer months so they could finish before the hottest part of the day.

He remembered the morning well. He started with coffee at the gas station near Beverley and Robert's house. Then he drove on to the site where he'd been working. He wasn't the first there that morning. Two others had stopped for coffee, too, and were sitting on the back of a truck.

It was quiet. That was what Rodney remembered most. He remembered the sun was barely up. He sat on the truck's tailgate with the other two men for a few minutes, sipping his coffee, enjoying the stillness. Then he got right to work.

He started up his loader. His job was to backfill. It was nuanced work. No one had quite the touch he had. He was quicker, safer than most. He worked for maybe twenty minutes before he stopped. A patrol car pulled up, its lights being the thing that got his attention. If the siren had been running, he hadn't heard it over his loader.

The officers explained about a young runaway. None of the three men had seen anyone matching her description. They hadn't seen anyone at all. Rodney showed his driver's license and answered a few questions. He gave his address, a brief work history, the name of his wife and daughter who both saw him off that morning. The other two fellows gave the same. After taking note of Rodney's license plate, the officers sent him and the others on their way. Rodney waited outside the gate until the last man left. Then he locked up. He didn't go back there to work for almost two weeks.

"It's possible, I think," he said, according to the police report that was shared with Beverley and Robert, "that I covered over her poor body in those few minutes I was on the job. I was working a trench, just like it said on the show. I remember that day because for weeks after, we heard about that poor little girl on the news. But I sure didn't know about the girls playing in the trenches back then. I can show you just where it was, if it might be of help."

The small group waits to leave the house until the sun has dropped low in the sky. It's still hot outside, but the sun isn't as likely to burn them. Someone suggests they drive, but Beverley wants to walk, and Robert agrees.

At the back door, Beverley and Robert link hands and take the first few steps their Francie took twenty-two years ago, almost to the day. Elizabeth, Agent Watson, and the officer who is accompanying them walk ahead, giving Beverley and Robert their privacy.

The landscape outside Robert and Beverley's house is different now than when Francie last walked across their yard. The swing set still stands in ruins. None of the neighbors has ever complained.

The house directly behind Beverley and Robert hadn't been built yet back then, so the people who live there have opened the gates to the fence that surrounds their backyard. They've done it so the group—Beverley, Robert, Elizabeth, all the rest—can walk where Francie most likely walked. The homeowners have placed a bouquet of flowers at the back gate where the group enters and at the side gate where they exit to continue across the next street.

Letting Robert lead her, Beverley closes her eyes and tries to envision Francie running across this very stretch of ground that would have been dirt and gravel back then. She tries to feel her like she did when she walked the streets in the days right after the final episode, and she does. She feels Francie, can see her smile, can hear her laughter rolling on the late-day breeze.

They cross the front yard of the first house and the street, and then they walk through another open gate on the side of another house and through another back gate. There are more flowers, a small pink teddy bear, three pink balloons. They do it all in silence, as if on their way to the funeral Francie never received.

Once they've exited the back gate on the second house, the group stops. The officer points straight ahead because they've reached the spot.

Beverley smooths her hair, as if readying herself to see Francie again. She wants to look her best, doesn't want to look tired, worn down, old, all the things she feels. She wants Francie to recognize her, be proud of her. She wants to show no sign of what the past twenty years have been like.

Robert knows what she's doing. He always knows. He squeezes her hand.

"You look nice," he says. "You look real nice for our girl."

Still standing at a distance, Elizabeth, looking so much like she did all those years ago, glances back. She's waiting for a nod from Beverley. She lifts her chin, a signal only Elizabeth would understand. Yes, Beverley is ready.

They've draped white tarps over the section of road they had to tear up. Someone has laid more flowers. Beverley had already been warned that they wouldn't be able to get too close, and they only had a short time in which to make the visit. The police had their policies, their procedures.

The officer tells them where they must stop. They can only see the white tarps, but that's enough to prove that it's real. That is the spot where their little girl's body rests. Everything Mandy Norwood shared was true. Francie died because Nora Banks thought her mother's affair was with Robert.

The Final Episode

The funeral will come in the days ahead. It will be small. Neighbors who remember Francie will come. Elizabeth. Agent Watson. But this is Beverley's goodbye.

She turns toward the west. It's a perfect moment to spend with a setting sun. The drier air of a Florida winter usually makes for the best sunsets, but today's is the best. Even with the sticky, hot air that isn't as good at splashing the sky with all the colors. Somehow, the soft oranges are at their most beautiful. The last sliver of the sun is at its brightest. She holds up a hand to watch the yellow speck disappear below the horizon and spots a small group standing off to the side. They're at a distance where they can't possibly see anything. They all back away at seeing Beverley turn toward them.

Beverley lifts a hand and whispers to Robert that she'll be right back.

She invited them, Jennifer and Dehlia, and as Beverley nears the threesome, she recognizes Tia Norwood as the third.

It's an awkward moment for all of them, except for Dehlia. She knows exactly what to do. Despite all the years that Beverley hounded Dehlia and Jennifer for a truth they didn't have, Dehlia wraps Beverley in a hug. It isn't a polite, loose-fitting hug. It's a tight-knit hug meant to mend everything that went wrong.

When they separate, Beverley keeps hold of Dehlia's hand and reaches for Jennifer's.

"I have no words," Beverley says, the only true thing she can manage. It would have been insincere to apologize for so many years of blaming them when blaming them had been her only option. "I don't understand how Nora could let us suffer for all these years. That's been the hardest part. The not knowing."

The not knowing had been the wound that wouldn't heal. No matter how many years passed, it festered and rotted away more and more of Beverley's insides.

"We're hopeful you find some measure of peace now," Dehlia says. "Hopeful that your sweet girl can finally rest."

Tia stands behind the others, her head lowered as if trying to give them privacy. Beverley reaches for her.

"I'm sorry for your loss, Tia," she says. "I'm sorry Nora hurt your sister, and I'm so grateful she found the courage to share what happened."

Tia nods but shrinks away from coming closer. Beverley knows the look. Tia is still blaming herself for Mandy's death. She's blaming herself for not being good enough.

"We wanted a different ending for you, for Francie," Jennifer says, wrapping an arm around Tia.

She's a good friend, kind, caring, protective. Beverley is happy to see that, proud even. Proud like she would be of a daughter.

"But this isn't the end, is it?" Beverley touches Jennifer's face in the same way she used to touch Francie's. "Now we have to wait for Nora to be found. How many more years will that be? Or maybe she'll never be found. Maybe we'll go on waiting for the rest of our lives and this nightmare will never end."

Jennifer steps forward, away from Tia and Dehlia, as if to say something to Beverley. Tia stops her with a hand to her arm. Jennifer turns toward her. Something passes between them in the silent look they share, and Tia nods for Jennifer to go ahead.

"I'm going to ask you to trust me," Jennifer says to Beverley. "And I'm going to ask you not to question me or ask how I know what I know."

Beverley lifts tall, a habit left over from the early days of the search for Francie. She's older now. It takes more effort to hold a strong posture, but she does it to signal she's ready for whatever is coming and because, yes, she promises not to ask.

"Nora is dead," Jennifer says.

Beverley can't help that she inhales sharply. She stares, wondering if she heard correctly.

"How do you know that?"

"I just do," Jennifer says.

"But when? How? How can you be sure?"

Beverley wants to know if it was an accident or an illness or someone serving justice. Because it matters. An illness or an accident aren't punishment, and she wants to know that Nora was punished. As awful as that is and as much as she hopes she doesn't always feel that way, Beverley wants to know Nora's death was delivered with a blow.

"Please don't ask me how I know," Jennifer says, her eyes soft but her voice firm. "Just trust me. I wouldn't say it if I didn't know it for certain. Dr. Farrow, your days of waiting are over. Nora Banks will never be seen again."

By the time Beverley walks back to Robert, Jennifer's words have sunk in. This really is the perfect way to say goodbye. Not only to Francie, but to all of it.

"Let's go," she says, wrapping a hand around Robert's arm.

Before heading for home, she takes one last look at the setting sun. It's gone and has left behind only an orange glow that lifts out of the horizon. She rests her head on Robert's shoulder. One day soon, she'll tell him what Jennifer said. She'll tell him that Nora Banks is dead.

But not today. Today is just for Francie.

CHAPTER 26

I wonder if you know Francie Farrow's body was found. Everything Mandy shared and everything the final episode unearthed has proven true. We're hopeful that means good things for you, and now we wait. We'll wait as long as we have to, and we'll keep pushing. I talk to Henry Baskin every day. We have an attorney, though you surely know that.

A few days ago, Dehlia, Tia, and I went to see the spot where Francie died. Her mother invited us to share that moment with the family. After twenty years of never being able to tell Mrs. Farrow what she wanted to hear, I was finally able to tell her something that could ease her pain. I told her Nora was gone. I told her Nora would never come back. I told her just enough so she'd know I was telling her the truth and so she'd trust me. She spent years waiting to learn the truth of what happened to Francie. I didn't want her to spend one more day waiting to learn the truth about Nora.

She didn't need to know how it happened. She only needed to know Nora was dead.

The night the final episode aired and we found the key under the brick pavers, Arlen and I fell asleep on the sofa after watching videos. I slept like I never had before, deep and peaceful. I was free to remember you as the man you had always been to me, and Nora Banks was dead. Even though Arlen hadn't been ready to tell me the truth, I knew, and I slept well because of it.

My phone vibrating in my pocket woke me. It was still dark outside, and the house was quiet. The phone vibrated again. It was a notification from the camera I'd set up to keep an eye on the front door. I'd paused it for a few hours when Henry Baskin came earlier that evening, and it had turned on again. Henry Baskin had said he might be back, so it could be him. And that worried me.

Slipping out from under Arlen's arm, I walked into the kitchen where I wouldn't wake him and pulled up the saved clip that would show what set off the camera. If it was Henry, that could only mean bad news. He'd have waited until morning if it was good news.

When the saved clip opened, I saw a view of the patio and entrance. The lighting was poor, but it looked like someone was crouched just outside the door. Maybe Henry or one of the deputies had forgotten something. A tool maybe. Some piece of equipment.

I closed the saved clip and opened the live view.

The person was still there, now kneeling on all fours, and had snapped on a phone's flashlight. It threw a soft glow over the torn-up pavers. It looked like a woman. Pushing to her feet, she tipped her head toward the sky, reached her arms overhead, and stretched her back. The phone in her raised hand sent a stream of light straight down her body. Yes, definitely a woman.

She held the position for only a moment, just long enough to ease something that ached, but that was all it took. The sight was familiar, that arched pose. I'd seen it before.

In the front room, where Arlen slept on the sofa, the image of us four girls was still frozen on the screen. Nora had been the tallest back then, so Mrs. Norwood had asked her to stand behind the rest of us. While Tia, Mandy, and I made our silly poses, Nora had arched her back, stretched both arms overhead, tipped her face toward the sky, and turned herself into a crescent-shaped piece of art.

It was distinct. It was purposeful. The shape was the same. The arc was the same. The tension in the arms and the drama of the head thrown fully back were the same. It was no coincidence.

Nora Banks was right outside the house.

By the time I reached the door and threw it open, the woman was already walking away. She stopped and turned. I took a step outside to get a better look. Under the light of a full moon, I could see enough. Her hair was what I noticed first. It shimmered like red silk in the soft lighting.

Confused, I grabbed the doorframe and held tight, thinking I'd been wrong about Nora being right outside. Because it wasn't Nora. It was Eva Oakley.

As I clung to the door, staring, thinking, running through all the reasons that might bring Eva to my home, I realized I'd seen the pose from the video somewhere else. That distinct, deliberate, dramatic pose. I'd seen it in the black-and-white picture that hung in Eva's office. I'd complimented it even, trying to get off on a good note with her, hoping she'd hire me to replace Tanya.

So many times, I saw something coming before it came, but not this time. The pieces didn't snap easily into place. They didn't settle at my feet, one perfect picture of what was to come. Instead, I squinted at the scene outside my house, straining to make sense of just one thought. And then the first piece fell into place and the next. *Click. Click. Click.*

Arlen didn't kill Nora Banks. He couldn't have because I'd been living right alongside her, cleaning her closets and pantries, for five years. I'd liked her, respected her even. I'd been that close and never once felt danger lingering nearby.

Being so wrong doesn't go down easy. Being fooled doesn't go down easy. It was a blow I didn't have time to feel in the moment, but that's the part that'll haunt me. The shame sits like a rock in my gut even now, and trusting myself will be a high hurdle to clear from here on out.

Eva Oakley was Nora Banks.

"Aren't you going to ask?" I said to her as she walked away.

"Oh, you surprised me," Eva said, taking a step in my direction as if she weren't running away. "My apologies. Thought you'd still be up, what with the show and all. I'm sorry if I woke you."

"We found it already," I said.

I'd not once seen the similarity, but now that I knew Eva was Nora Banks, I couldn't stop seeing it.

I stepped outside and didn't turn when I heard footsteps in the entry. It was Tia and Arlen. They'd heard me throw open the door.

"What's happening?" Tia asked as the outside light popped on.

Arlen didn't ask, because he already knew. He was right about Nora's mannerisms having followed her from childhood to adulthood. Other things had changed, but not the way she moved. A sigh, as if she were indifferent. A glance off to the side, like she couldn't be bothered with us.

"That's why you're here, isn't it?" I said. "The key?"

"What are you talking about?" Tia said, but I could hear in the tone of her voice that some part of her knew.

Just like with the Old Man. As children, even if we couldn't see him, we could feel him. We could feel him hiding in the tall grass or floating just below the surface of Halfway Creek. Somehow, for all Dehlia's talk about me having the second sight, I'd lost those sharp senses, but not Tia. Or maybe Nora was just that good. All these years, she'd been better at hiding than I'd been at seeing. But back at the swamp, knowing she'd been outed, she no longer bothered to hide. She slithered out into the open, making it easy for us to see her because she thought that we had nowhere to run, and that she had nothing to lose.

"Let me call the police." Arlen stepped up next to me and took me by the arm.

"Such a stupid mistake," Eva said, her eyes lowering as she looked at something behind me. She gathered her long red hair and pulled it over one shoulder. "In a hurry, I suppose. All I had to do was put the key back."

I looked where Eva was looking. Tia had followed Arlen from the house, and dangling at her side was the gun she'd been carrying every day since she arrived.

"But it was too late when you realized that," I said. "Couldn't open the cabinet's doors from the inside, could you? I know. We checked."

Keeping her eyes on Tia, Eva took a step away. Tia held the gun with both hands now. Her arms were fully extended, and her head was tilted slightly off to one side. She was aiming at Eva.

"Tia, don't," I whispered.

"How did you figure it out?" Tia said, glancing at me and taking a sideways step that put distance between her and me. Between the gun and me.

"It was that last video your mom shot," I said, wishing she'd lower the gun but afraid to touch her. "All of us were mugging for the camera. And Nora, she struck that pose, turned herself into a piece of art. Eva Oakley here has a picture of herself in her office, striking the same pose."

"I don't really care what you think, you know," Eva said, shaking her head in that same way she did when we were kids. Dismissive with a hint of pity. "Nora Banks has been gone for ten years, and Eva Oakley is already as good as gone. You won't see me again."

"Why did you come here?" I said. "Why me?"

Eva was puzzled to hear me ask that. She paused as she thought it over.

"Why did you stay?" she said, instead of giving me an answer.

Or maybe the answer was in her question. I stayed because this was home. This was the only place I could be close to you, or rather, the memory of you. For twenty years, that was all I had. My memories.

There must have been some memory that drew Eva, Nora, back. Maybe a memory of her family before it fell apart. Maybe a memory of the way she once felt and hadn't felt since . . . loved. Because Lily Banks was a good mother, and I knew she loved Nora. Or maybe a homing instinct drew Nora back. Like a gator, she'd been drawn home where she knew the hunting was good.

"And you," Eva said, laughing at the story of me. "Someone recommended you. Didn't even recognize you the first time we met.

But the name, when I saw the whole name, I knew. Jenny had become Jennifer, but it was still the same old you."

"And I didn't recognize you, either," I said.

"Not like I had to see much of you, but my closets were always clean."

Next to me, Tia's arms quivered under the weight of the gun. She was shaking her head, not wanting to listen to Eva anymore. I was reminded of the day Mandy held the palm frond, trying her best to be brave by poking the Old Man. Her arms quivered the same way. Tia was trying her best to be brave, too, for Mandy, I think.

"Mandy is dead because of you," Tia said.

"Maybe she is," Eva said. "Never did have much staying power."

As if Nora landed a glancing blow, Tia flinched. But just barely.

"She bested you," Tia said, lowering the gun and exhaling like she was relieved. Like she finally understood. "That day in the hospital, she pieced together what no one else did. You hated that, didn't you? Her getting the better of you."

We saw it all unfold in the final episode, the moment Mandy outsmarted Nora and wrenched the truth of what happened to Francie Farrow out of her.

"Whole lot of good it did her," Eva said.

"That's why you moved back here," Tia said, her face breaking into a smile. "I'm betting you showed up in Naples around the time the show started asking questions about Francie's story. About that summer. That sound right to you, Jenn?"

I nodded, because yes, that sounded right.

"For years, you called Mandy, but then you lost track of her," Tia said. "I did too. I always assumed she was running from us, her family. But she was running from you."

"Tia." It was Arlen again. "Let's call the police. Let them handle this."

"That's why you came back to Naples," Tia said, pulling away from Arlen. "You were looking for Mandy, still wanting to keep a tight rein on her. Did you stake out our mother's house? Was that your plan? Bet it never occurred to you that Mandy lied about the key? Until you saw it on the show. Until you realized she bested you again."

I was right. A homing instinct brought Nora back. She didn't come to Naples for revenge or to wheedle her way into my life. She came looking for Mandy.

She came home to hunt.

"Like I already told you," Eva said, exhaling a laugh as she turned to me. "Eva Oakley is already gone. And thankfully, so is Mandy Norwood. Police can't get testimony from a dead woman, can they, Jenny?"

"Right," I said, the sound of that laugh the loudest echo yet from our last summer at the swamp. It reminded me of that same day, the day Mandy broke her arm. As she was screaming and crying and Tia and I were straining to help her to her feet, in the background, Nora laughed.

The laughing, that's the stickiest memory. It's at the root of what is broken in a person like Nora. Every ugly trait stems from that laugh.

Eva was broken, and there was no fixing her.

Next to me, Tia whispered, "Cover your ears."

I think Nora's laugh reminded Tia of that day too. She knew there was no fixing Nora either.

One shot was all Tia needed. The single crack sent me stumbling backward. Arlen wrapped me in his arms and covered my head. When I looked up, Tia stood firm, the gun pointed at the spot where Eva had stood.

If Tia had needed a second shot, she was ready. But one was enough.

CHAPTER 27

I've made this trip to the prison before but always alone. I'd sit in this same parking lot, and knowing the guards would turn me away because I wasn't on your list, I wouldn't bother going inside. Instead, I'd stay in my car as long as the heat would allow and wonder what kept drawing me back.

Eventually, I'd drive home and try again to get on with my life. I'd be disgusted with myself and feel ashamed, as if I were siding with the wrong person—you instead of the victims. But then, I'd make the drive again and sit alone in this prison parking lot, because as much as I wanted to let you go, I couldn't.

And now I know I was right to never quite give up on you.

Today, I'm not alone. Dehlia is with me. Tia too. And Arlen. I've told you about him. You'll like him, I'm sure.

We've brought pictures to show you. Dehlia insisted. Organizing them by year and putting them into albums, it's how we kept busy as we waited. For the first time in a long time, looking at old pictures of you made us happy. After you went away, Dehlia did her best to capture our milestones. Many of the smiles were manufactured, particularly mine. I think Dehlia insisted on the pictures, sometimes having to strong-arm me into playing along, because she knew that one day, this day would come.

To put your mind at ease, I'll tell you that no one will ever know what became of Nora Banks. Tia knew how to clean up the blood. I knew what part of the swamp would swallow her car. And when the heat of the day reached its peak, we pushed Nora into Halfway Creek. Arlen waded into the water, grabbed her by one hand, and guided her downstream to where mangroves lined the banks. Tia and I followed along on shore, keeping watch for the dark, armored back of a gator.

When Arlen reached the woody mangroves growing in the spongy creek bed, he wove Nora's arms in and out of the tangled roots. He did the same with her legs. She was bait snagged on a hook.

It was a rainy summer, as you know, and a wet fall. The creek will be high for another month. Until at least December. When the water level does begin to drop, the gators and the swamp will have done their job. Nora Banks will be gone for good.

No one has come looking for Eva. Before she came to Dehlia's house, hoping to find the key, she'd already put in motion her own disappearance. She told us so herself. Eva Oakley is already gone, she said to us that night when she still thought she'd walk away.

And Nora Banks has been missing for ten years. That's nothing new. No one's come looking for her either.

I wish I felt something about Nora's death. Sadness. Regret. But I don't.

Nora got what she gave.

I don't mean to sound callous about what we did. In the days after, I found myself worrying that you would be ashamed of me. Even though I didn't pull the trigger, I would have. But agonizing over what you thought of me quickly turned to joy. I had a father again with an opinion that mattered. That was a luxury I hadn't had since I turned eleven years old.

I hope you'll forgive me for what I did, and I hope you'll understand. I hope you'll forgive me all the times I hated you, too, and all the times I said . . . I'm not that Jennifer Jones. But I don't agonize over any of it. It all brings me joy. I'll go so far as to say I crave a scolding from you, a life lesson, words of wisdom because I have a father again.

The Final Episode

Over the next several days, we settled into a routine as we began to wait for your future to unfold. Arlen went back to work and came home to Dehlia's every night. Tia and I tackled projects around our two houses. And Dehlia started cooking, filling the freezer with all your favorites. Crackling bread. Stuffed peppers. Sweet potato pone.

I thought all the surprises were behind us.

A week after the final episode aired, I was up early to walk Belle. Stepping outside, Belle leading the way, I coughed as the soggy heat and the rot coming off the swamp hit me. When we reached the end of the driveway, I stopped. Down the road, at the house where Nora once lived, a single light had popped on.

She appeared at the front door as if she'd been waiting for me. Standing just outside the house, her hands clasped in front of her, she didn't move. At first, I wondered if she was real. I hadn't seen Lily Banks in over twenty years, though I'd thought of her often. I went through stretches of hating her and stretches of wishing I could see her one more time so she could tell me more about Mama.

I walked slowly down the road, the gravel crunching underfoot the only sound. As I got closer, Lily lifted her head. At the spot where her sidewalk met the road, I stopped.

"I didn't know," she said, loudly enough that I could hear. "I didn't know Nora lied about Francie, about seeing your father in her room."

Lily's hair was still short and tucked behind her ears, but it was speckled with gray. Still slight, she clung to herself like she did the day Mandy broke her arm. As she and I waited for you to carry Mandy back to the house, Lily held a wooden spoon, not even noticing that it dripped milky white ice cream down her arm. She looked lost that day. She looked the same when I saw her that morning, as if she were in shock. I think she must have looked that way for the last twenty years.

"He loved you," I told her. I thought you'd want me to say that.

"And I loved him."

Next, I wanted to tell her that she destroyed you by dragging you into her family. I wanted to scream at her that she should have known better, should have known how dangerous Nora was. The anger surprised me. It bubbled up, making my cheeks burn and my chest pound. The urge to hurt her left me breathless. But I didn't scream any of those things. You wouldn't have wanted me to attack her that way, and she'd only made the same mistake I made. Everyone made. We thought we knew what evil looked like. We were all fooled.

"I thought she might come here to find the key," Lily said, glancing up the road toward Dehlia's house. "In the show, Mandy's character said she never came back for it. Did she? Did Nora come here looking for the key?"

"Do you know what it means?" I asked. "Do you understand the key's significance?"

"I do now," Lily said. "It means Paul didn't hurt my daughter. Ever."

And then she paused as if bracing for me to say . . . yes, Nora came, and we killed her. But I didn't. Instead, I shrugged. I didn't even bother to answer her question. It was the callous type of thing Nora would have done. I could have told Lily we found the key and were working toward your freedom, but I kept it all from her. I felt badly even as I did it, because for a short time, I had thought Lily Banks would become like a mother to me. I had thought I loved her. And I guess part of me did. Or maybe loving Lily Banks was just the closest, widest path to loving Mama. Maybe it was a little of both.

"I'm selling the house," Lily said, nodding as if she knew I could tell her something about Nora if only I wanted to. "The last time I was happy, I was here, with your father. I hope Paul comes home soon. Please tell him, promise him, I didn't know it was Nora all along."

"Thank you for telling me stories about my mother," I said, mustering the only kind thing I could.

And then Belle and I continued our walk. By the time we returned, she was gone.

I know someday you'll want me to tell Lily that Nora is dead. You won't want Lily to suffer for years, waiting for the truth about Nora like Beverley Farrow suffered as she waited for the truth about Francie.

The Final Episode

And you'll be right. I don't want Lily to suffer either. I'll let you decide when and how we tell her.

Sitting next to me in the passenger seat, Dehlia is the first to see you. She gasps and that makes me look too. I scan the fence line, but I don't see you. A sob catches in my throat. I sit up in my seat, trying to see what Dehlia sees. My breath comes faster. My heart pounds in my chest. I stretch my eyes wider, trying to take it all in, but I still don't see you. I squeeze the steering wheel and pull myself forward to get a better view.

Throwing open her car door, Dehlia shouts at me to come on. Tia scrambles out, helping Dehlia to her feet. Arlen thinks he's going to stay behind and let the family have this moment. But he's family now. I know you'll trust me on that.

Dehlia once told me most people can't see beyond their own noses and never once set eyes on the world beyond. Most will never even realize how much they're missing. She didn't know it, or maybe she did, but as she was telling me that, she was also telling me there is no second sight. There are only people brave enough and willing enough to see the world beyond. And people who aren't.

It's a better view, the view beyond, and I'm thankful to have it.

Gears are churning. It's a gate sliding open, and now I know where to look. Just like that, I see you. I recognize you. It's the way you move as you walk. It's the shape of your shoulders. It's the way your head lops off to the side when you're overflowing with being happy. And in that moment, twenty years' worth of missing you wash over me. The pain hits me like a wave. Knocking me back in my seat, the weight of it sits on my chest, clogs my throat, blurs my eyes. I struggle to breathe.

And then it's gone, all that pain, as the wave rolls on by. I right myself, suck in a deep breath, and I'm ten years old again. You and I are pulling up to the house at the swamp. The old place fared well, you say, and the whole summer is still ahead of us. Our whole lives are still ahead of us.

I asked Dehlia once what great thing she had done. It was during my teenage years, long after you'd gone away. I was tired of hearing about Margaret Scott and ghost orchids and the destiny of every Scott woman. I was tired of being Paul Jones's daughter and the girl with no mama.

"Why are you so sure I'll ever do anything with my life?" I likely cocked a hip and planted a fist on it. I was a handful back then. "You've never done your great thing. Mama didn't either. You're just ordinary. We're all just ordinary."

Dehlia shook her head and laughed at me. That made me angry.

"Don't you dare say your mama and I never did our great thing," Dehlia said, slipping from laughter to a harsh voice I'd never heard before and have never heard since. "Your mama brought you into this world, and I raised you up. I know of nothing greater than those two things."

And then Dehlia softened, in as much as Dehlia ever softens.

"And just like your mama did, you'll bend history too," she said to me. "In your own way. Your job is to figure out how, rise up when the time comes, and then damn well do it."

I'm only sorry it took me so long.

It'll be good to have you home, Daddy.

Love,

Jenny

The End

ACKNOWLEDGMENTS

Many thanks to everyone at Thomas & Mercer and Amazon Publishing for their dedication to my work. Thank you to Liz Pearsons for her enthusiasm and commitment and to Charlotte Herscher for her keen eye and for always making the story stronger. It's a team effort with many moving parts, and I'm grateful for the professionalism and passion I've found every step of the way. And, as always, my thanks to Jenny Bent and all the great folks at the Bent Agency for their support and guidance.

I'm usually surprised by the themes that emerge in my work. Often, a book is on the shelf before I truly understand what it's about. *The Final Episode* is no different. It's a thriller, rooted in our modern culture, that examines the influence of all types of media in our lives. But more importantly, it is a book about empathy. It's about the scarcity of empathy. It's about recognizing it, nurturing it, and valuing it for the far-reaching view of the world it affords those who have it. Given that, I owe great thanks to my many friends who demonstrate every day what it means to see the world beyond the tips of their own noses. And I owe a special thanks to my dear friend, Victoria. Your compassion, courage, and boundless commitment to the world beyond are inspirations. It's been through knowing you that I can boil it all down to one thing. Empathy.

And to my family—William, Andrew, and Sam—my thanks to you all for your support and for sharing in the celebrations and cheering me on during the tougher times. Thanks, too, for the long talks out on the lanai of the lake house, where we debated plot points and third-act twists. And thanks for playing along when I wanted to go stomping through yet another swamp.

ABOUT THE AUTHOR

Photo © 2019 VR Vision Photography

Lori Roy's debut novel, *Bent Road*, was awarded the Edgar Allan Poe Award for Best First Novel by an American Author. Her work has been twice named a *New York Times* Notable Crime Book and has been included on various "best of" and summer reading lists. *Until She Comes Home* was a *New York Times* Editors' Choice and a finalist for the Edgar Allan Poe Award for Best Novel.

Let Me Die in His Footsteps was included among the top fiction books of 2015 by Books-A-Million and named one of the best fifteen mystery novels of 2015 by Oline Cogdill. The novel also received the 2016 Edgar Allan Poe Award for Best Novel, making Roy the first woman to receive an Edgar Award for both Best First Novel and Best Novel—and only the third person ever to have done so.

Roy lives with her family in West Central Florida.